CALL NUMBERS

SYNTELL SMITH

ISBN: 0-578-44052-0

ISBN-13: 978-0-578-44052-1

Copyright © 2019 Syntell Smith Publishing

Published By Syntell Smith

To obtain permission to excerpt portions of the text, please contact the author at syntellsmith@gmail.com

Chapter graphic courtesy of the Boston Public Library, used with permission.

Library of Congress Cataloging-in-Publication Data is available.

For Opal, Irene, Tiffany, and Krista

ACKNOWLEDGMENTS

CHAPTER ONE

"I TELL YA, FRANK," ROBIN WALKER SAID, "THE WORLD'S GOING TO hell in a handbasket."

Frank's Pizza, located east of 23rd Street and Lexington, was the favorite place for the students attending Baruch College to spend a dollar twenty-five for a slice. The place was small and only occasionally crowded. It was the Tuesday after President's Day, and there was a clock overhead that said eleven in the morning. Robin was reading a copy of the *Daily News* while nibbling on a slice of plain cheese pizza.

He hated pizza toppings. *Why mess with perfection by putting something on top of something?* was his favorite explanation for his preference. He had finished his morning classes and was not due at the 58th Street Branch Library for another three hours. Frank noticed the student was feeling very opinionated this morning.

"I mean, it's 1994. We got 6 more years till the new millennium and God only knows if we're ready! We got terrorists trying to blow up the World Trade Center, shootings on the train out in Long Island, and the first and only Black mayor of New York City getting the boot after one term." Robin looked up and nodded toward the flour-faced Italian behind the register. "You voted for Giuliani, didn't you, Frank?" he asked.

"That's none of your business!" Frank grunted.

Robin took that as a confirmation that his observations had not been appreciated.

"Hey, man, you've been reading that paper more than eating your slice!"

Since Frank was done discussing politics, Robin ignored his remark and continued reading the day's "Jump Start" comic strip.

"This isn't a library, I hope you know!" Frank continued, trying to catch the young man's attention. Robin finished reading and chuckled at the joke from the last panel, or it could have been from the sense of irony. "I know!" he bellowed. "It ain't a library because I work for one, chump!" The obese, balding man blinked hard while scratching his head, unsure what to make of the response. Robin knew a cue to leave when he saw one.

The stocky eighteen-year-old sighed, then reached down and lifted his book bag over his shoulder as he stood up to leave. The newspaper he had been reading remained where he had been sitting as he made his way out to the sidewalk. Frank called out behind him "Hey! Hey! You left your paper!" Robin turned back at the door, a mischievous smirk growing across his face. "It's not mine," he replied. "Recycle it! Save the planet! We only got one Earth, Frank!"

At five-foot-ten, Robin's long strides on the Manhattan sidewalk maneuvered him through the vast crowd as he headed from Lexington to Park Avenue South and the subway station for the number 6-train. He wore a solid black wool parka over a gray pullover short-sleeved polo shirt along with blue acid-wash jeans.

The temperature was in the mid-thirties, yet the cold didn't bother him. He even wore his signature generic red baseball cap that exposed his ears, which were just as red. He also never wore winter gloves, but a conspicuous looking leather bicycle glove on his left hand was another of Robin's distinctive fashion choices.

Producing headphones from his lining pocket, Robin pressed play on his Walkman, which had his current favorite album *Midnight*

Marauders by A Tribe Called Quest in it, and rested the speakers to his ears as the track "Steve Biko" played. After arriving at 23rd and Park Avenue, he descended the steps underground, deposited a token in the turnstile and boarded the departing uptown train just as the doors were closing.

There were only a handful of stops from 23rd to 59th street. The song "Midnight" was playing while Robin scanned the train car for a moment between stops, bobbing his head to the beat. He made eye contact with a young Japanese girl who he caught glancing back at him. He flashed a flirtatious smile and she blushed while looking down.

A few minutes went by as subway riders got on and off. Robin waited another minute in the hopes of exchanging glances again. The shy young lady kept to herself for a minute, then looked up at him and waved, smiling back. They looked at each other for several more minutes. Robin waited, then decided it was time to make his move. He advanced deeper into the car, hoping to get a vacant seat near her when the door opened at the end of the train and a Chinese vendor emerged holding various trinkets in his hand—Double-A and Triple-A batteries, crazy glue, keychains, and whistles.

"Bataree, bataree, bataree. One dollah, one dollah!" the man exclaimed. He then showed a yo-yo that had lights on it when extended to the floor. "Yo-yo! Yo-yo! Yo-yo!" He made a straight line down the middle of the train, being ignored by everyone with no desire to purchase cheap, short-lasting batteries for their Walkmans or keychains that would break once they're tucked in a pocket.

Robin stepped aside as the man moved to the door leading to the next car and turned around just in time to see an empty seat where the girl was once sitting. She must have left at the previous stop during the distraction. Disappointed, he sat down and waited for his stop to get off. With eight million people in New York City, there was always the chance he'd see her again.

THE 58TH STREET Branch Library was a two-story facility embedded in the lobby of a ten-floor office tower. Opened in 1969, it serviced the midtown Manhattan area with patrons ranging from business-types stopping by during their lunch break to college students from neighboring universities.

Head librarian Augustus Chavez was having his daily briefing with information assistant Heywood Learner. For the pair, the meeting was as ritualistic as the ancient gladiator matches of Rome. Augustus wore tan slacks with a crisp white dress shirt, his matching tan suit jacket draped over the back of his office chair.

The dim office light bouncing off his shaved head, Augustus stroked his squared jaw while Heywood scanned a list of proposed films for an upcoming tribute festival. Heywood's lean frame sported an unshaven beard and long, brown unkempt hair. Wearing solid black jeans, brown work boots, and a blue cotton long-sleeved shirt, his sleeves were rolled up with grit and determination. He finished reading and extended the clipboard.

"Well, I see no problems with these selections for the Mel Brooks tribute in March."

A quiet sigh overcame Augustus as he accepted it back, relieved that there would be no arguments this morning.

"Except one,"

He rolled his eyes. *Why should this morning be any different?* the librarian thought.

"Please reconsider *Blazing Saddles*, it's just too offensive."

"It fits with all the others, Learner, as parody satire of 50s and 60s style westerns."

"Yes, complete with fart jokes and racism. It's unacceptable to show this to the public." Heywood replied tilting his head.

"It airs on cable TV every once in a while. Just the other night I saw it on HBO."

"People pay for HBO because they want filth. We should not be showing it for free here."

"Look, we need five films. We have *Young Frankenstein*, *Spaceballs*, which are horror and sci-fi parodies, plus we're lucky enough to have *Robin Hood: Men in Tights* on 35mm, a film that just came out last year."

"What about that film *Life Stinks*?" Heywood interjected. "Or even *The Producers*?"

Augustus slammed his fist on his dilapidated desk for emphasis as he barked, "Those aren't spoofs, dammit!"

Heywood turned and exited the office, slamming the door closed behind him. Augustus sighed and collapsed his shoulders at the meaningless argument. He rubbed his temples as he heard another familiar voice in the room. "He's so predictable, you know that, don't you?"

With her back facing his desk, minding her own business, Zelda Clein sat in front of the small wire desk in front of the right wall of the room, typing on her antique typewriter. At seventy-two, Zelda was well beyond the retirement age for New York Public Library standards but opted to remain as Augustus' assistant librarian. While offering sage advice from years and years of life experiences, she was also known for keeping the peace from time to time.

She wore tortoiseshell glasses with a navy blue knitted sweater over a gray blouse and matching palazzo pants. After finishing her memorandum, she pulled it out of the machine and looked it over.

"Yes, I know, I know, Zee. Tell me again why I let that pain in the ass irritate me?"

"He's just as passionate as you were when you arrived here 5 years ago."

A smile came across his face. Had it been five years? The controversial coup that resulted in the sudden retirement of his predecessor felt like a lifetime ago. Time had been swift. The silence between the pair made Zelda sense that her good friend was feeling nostalgic, so she changed the subject.

"So, I hear the new clerical hire transfers here today."

The head librarian snapped back to business, as a sneer of contempt replaced the smile. "A new piece of kindling for the *Dragon Lady* to torch. Their matters are no concern of mine. The only piece of

5

information I gathered was a name. Robin Walker. What have you heard about her?"

"For starters, how do you know it's a woman?" Zelda scoffed. "Robin is a common unisex name."

"The memo from HR read 'Ms. Robin Walker,' coming from Fort Washington," he said, producing a sheet of paper from his desk.

"Fort Washington, hmm…The Battle Axe is still in charge up there. I believe their senior clerk was named…Barnes? No. Burns, Theresa Burns. Why, she'd be just as old as I am by now, maybe even older, I remember when…"

"So," he interrupted. "What about Walker? Why down here? How did she get this position? Yi's been keeping it vacant for her page Simms to fill once she graduates."

"From what I gather, Walker declined various other openings due to the proximity to the school she's attending."

"Which is?" he asked.

After taking a moment to study the memo again, she replied, "Baruch College of the CUNY system. Down on 14th Street and Lexington."

Augustus furrowed his brow. "A business school? Where the stockbrokers and accountants come out of?"

"That, and Baruch has an advanced curriculum for computer operations. Perhaps she likes programming?"

The librarian reached for his blazer and stood up from his desk. "Interesting. Working part-time while attending school. She could be influenced to become a valuable asset to me." A lusty look grew across his face. He looked over and saw a surprised glance from his long-time confidant. He blushed and stammered, "Um, provided she's not corrupted by Yi, of course." He chuckled.

As he finished resting the jacket on his broad shoulders and dusted his sleeves, Zelda rose from her desk and moved to open the door. "Oh, I'm sure the young lady won't be able to resist your dashing good looks and irresistible charm!" She exclaimed while stepping out the office.

"Touché," he replied, thinking to himself that for someone in her early seventies, the gray fox may be sharper than she portrayed herself to be.

SONYAI YI, 58th Street's senior clerk, stood at a petite five-foot-two and weighed one hundred and sixty pounds. Despite her small frame, the woman commandeered respect from her fellow library clerical staff and pages.

Tommy Carmichael was Sonyai's latest apprentice in a line of protégés who had moved on, with her wisdom, to become senior clerks themselves in neighboring branches among the Midtown cluster.

A giant with an athletic build, the Irish behemoth towered over his mentor as they stood in the clerical office behind the circulation desk. Sonyai wore a white tunic with a high banded collar and black nylon slacks. Her short fiery auburn hair was tied back in a small bun.

"As I was saying, Thomas…" The supervisor was the only person Tommy allowed to call him *Thomas*. "Every library reflects the senior clerk who runs it. The librarian serves as a figurehead, the politician of the branch. They concern themselves with finances and their public image. A true senior clerk knows how to run an efficient staff and train others. We are always invested in the future of the branch, even when it comes to our pages. Encouraging their studies, monitoring their schoolwork, even recruiting them through direct contacts with teachers and counselors, we take care of our own here."

Tommy was wearing acid-wash blue jeans and a white long-sleeved turtleneck and had long brown shoulder-length hair folded behind the ears. His clean-shaven face registered undivided attention to Sonyai as his right index-finger traced around a paper-thin mustache. "But, ma'am, don't clerks become librarians themselves?"

The elder stopped cold in her tracks and turned to face her student with a strong look of disdain. "No! Those who attend colleges and receive their MLS Degree from accredited ALA schools become librarians. It falls to the clerks to serve the branch for the good of the branch no matter what! All those librarians are interested in is serving the public. Remember, Thomas, for the good of the branch."

Tommy nodded in silent agreement. Walking to the circulation area, they approached two computer terminals for the checkout and returns stations of the L-shaped clerical desk. The monochrome screens clicked on to life with a low hum and the limited telnet operating system started up the boot process.

"We have a new part-timer starting today, Thomas," Sonyai remarked.

"What? But I thought Nellie was supposed to—"

"Yes, I promised the next clerical position to Janelle," she interrupted. "But this Miss Walker has friends in high places. She specifically asked for this location for some reason."

"That could be a problem considering…" Tommy trailed off with a look of concern.

Sonyai glanced across the entire floor looking for eavesdroppers. Gerrald Coltraine and Ethel Jenkins were reading periodicals at the far right in the back while Heywood Learner sat alone muttering to himself at the information desk in the middle of the library floor. No one was in earshot, so she drew close to Tommy with a low whisper. "She'll be showing soon, and if Chavez finds out…"

"So what do we do?" he whispered back.

"I dug up some info on Walker. I believe with a certain amount of resistance, she shouldn't stay too long."

With a questionable glance, Tommy asked, "Are you saying what I think you're saying?"

Sonyai returned from hushed volumes to speaking out loud. "Now you are aware, Mr. Carmichael, that the NYPL does not condone acts of intimidation among staff members. We take care of our own in this branch, so extend a friendly and warm welcome to Miss Walker when she arrives," the supervisor said with a sly wink.

"They're scheming something again, Jenkins," Gerry Coltraine said under his breath.

Ethel Jenkins rolled her eyes as she read the latest issue of *Ebony Magazine* the library had available. The two resident African-

American clerks at 58th Street couldn't be more opposites if they were brother and sister, which they weren't.

Ethel kept to herself, barely conversing with anyone brave enough to annoy the stout, fierce forty-six-year-old. Her temper was known to all and her opinion unquestioned.

Meanwhile, the confrontational thirty-two-year-old Gerry Coltraine was tall with a thick full afro and handle-bar mustache. He had made his resentment toward Sonyai's leadership public several times and the two had a war of words on various occasions. Today would be no different.

"Coltraine, you think Yi's always scheming something when she's talking to Carmichael." Ethel sighed with exasperation. "You think she's scheming something when she's not talking to him, or when she's meeting with Chavez, or—"

"It has something to do with that new part-timer that's starting today," he interrupted her. He looked back at his newspaper he was pretending to read while observing Sonyai and Tommy at the circulation desk. "You know anything about that?"

"I still have my friends in human resources, and from what I've heard, the branch is about to be thrown for a loop."

"What's that supposed to mean?" Gerry turned to look at her when she didn't reply.

Ethel saw eye to eye with Sonyai, being five-foot-two while wearing two-inch heels. A solid two hundred and eighty-five pounds, she always wore various New York sports team headscarves on her head.

This morning she was wearing green cotton slacks with a matching green blouse. Her headscarf supported the New York Jets today. "For starters, Robin is a unisex name. *He's* identified as a woman on file, but he's actually a guy. Some sorta typo they can't fix."

"So," he mused, "She's expecting another woman. Makes sense, I guess, since every hire she's made has been a woman. Look at the pages. I guess she'd thought she'd tip the scales, outnumbering the men three-to-two on the clerical staff,"

"Coincidence," snapped Ethel. "I'm sure of it!"

"It'll sure be fun to see her reaction. Please tell me he's also a brother," he pleaded. "Walker could be a slave name."

Ethel grimaced, hoping Gerry wouldn't turn this incident into another of his infamous race conflicts. "He is," she said. "Our staff is very diverse. We are a melting pot, reflective of the city as a whole."

"Well, think about it," Gerry began and drew closer, maintaining a low whisper. Ethel tensed up at the violation of her personal space. "Three proud, intelligent black people, working together under one roof. We can manipulate the system to our advantage."

Ethel had enough of Gerry's ramblings. She lowered the magazine and stared at him. "Yi is in charge here, not you!"

Gerry sensed he struck a nerve, which he always seems to do. He smiled a wide, mischievous grin, "For now she is, Jenkins…for now." He raised his finger to magnify his thought. "But mark my words, *sister*. There's gonna be a time where you have to ask yourself, 'Which side am I on?'"

Gerry's eyes were wide as saucers. He looked crazed. "Don't forget where you came from." He rose to his lanky seven-foot-two frame, counting his afro, adjusted his blue suede sports jacket, and walked back to the circulation desk. Ethel questioned her co-worker's sanity often. She prayed whatever the instigator was planning wouldn't blow up in his face.

AT THE 59TH STREET & Lexington Subway station, the uptown 6-train arrived and screeched to a grinding stop. Passengers then exited and entered the train from the platform. An anxious Robin frantically checked his surroundings for the mysterious Japanese girl who caught his eye.

Canvassing everywhere, he didn't notice a hand grab his shoulder. "Hey!" Robin yelled, taking a defensive stance. He turned to see his classmate Walter.

"Robin, I've been hollering at you since I saw you get off. You zoning out, man?"

Robin sighed, "Dude, did you see an Asian girl around when you got off the train? We locked eyes and I could have sworn we had a connection thing going."

Walter looked at Robin as if he was delirious. "No, I didn't see anybody. It could have been Kim, Gillian Bascomb's friend. I hear she works at Alexander's around here on Third."

Robin shook his head. "No, no, no. Kim looks like a sumo wrestler. This one was...was..."

"Look, I'm glad I caught you. I need your notes from the 1929 Stock Market Crash for my paper in Basic Writing class. It's due tomorrow and I need some info."

"Look up *The Great Depression* by R. Conrad Stein, call number 973.916. We just got it on the shelves in our young adult section at Fort Washington. It's thirty-two pages, but there's at least ten about the crash. It'll give you all you need."

Robin walked toward the escalator leading upstairs, Walter following behind.

"Wha-what? What was that? R. Conrad who? 970-what? Hold on! Just give me your notes!"

"I'm not giving you my notes."

"Why not?"

"Why the hell didn't you take any notes in class?"

"I be asleep, man! It's an 8:40 in the morning class, Robin. I need this paper just to get a C. Please, man, I'm begging you!"

"Just find the book, Walt! It's not that hard," Robin yelled back to him from the escalator.

The two emerged out into the street. Robin took a turn around the corner and walked down Lexington toward 58th Street, Walter still following.

"Wait up, Robin! What if I can find this girl for you?"

Robin stopped short in the middle of the sidewalk as Walter caught up. "Okay. You got yourself a deal."

Walter smiled. "Whew! Thanks, you're a lifesaver,"

Robin turned his head, talking over his shoulder. "You find out who she is, you get my notes."

He resumed walking. "But…but…the paper's due," Walter called out. "Robin! Robin! C'mon, mannnn!"

Robin kept on walking but still couldn't get the mystery woman out of his head.

THE LIBRARY'S staff room was on the second floor with a small auditorium for video and film presentations. Two rooms separated by a single wall, solid concrete on all sides and special soundproofing, it was an ideal location for Sonyai and Augustus to hold their private meetings.

At one o'clock, the two sat on opposite sides of a six-foot-long dining table. The tension was thick, and neither made a sound. The low motor of the refrigerator in the kitchenette was all that could be heard between them.

Then, without hesitation, Augustus got the conversation started. "Human resources reports that a Miss Robin Walker starts part-time on the clerical staff today."

"Yes, I am expecting her within the hour," Sonyai replied sharply.

"Swing her by my office while doing the formal introductions. I'd like to meet her *as soon as possible.*"

The tone of his voice at the end of that sentence made her skin crawl. "I'll see to it."

That brought a smile to the otherwise stoic face of her adversary. *He's planning something,* she thought.

There was an uncomfortable moment of silence, so she tried to rattle him a little. "Any word on the schedule for next month's film tribute? I hear Mel Brooks is the honoree and there's a little *problem* with the movie selections."

Augustus nearly sneered in disgust at the implied jab at his leadership. How could she have known of the conversation between him and Heywood this morning? If he didn't know better, he'd almost suspect Zelda of betraying his trust, but he dismissed the notion and kept his poker face on.

"I'm still working out some of the details with Lerner, but the situation is well in hand."

"Ah, I see," Sonyai smirked to herself. "The situation is well in hand," was his favorite way of saying, "None of your Business, Yi."

"And how are the pages doing? Any problems to be addressed, hmm?"

Now it was Sonyai's turn to feel distressed as a flash of concern made her eyes widen and twitch for a moment. *"Could he know about Janelle?"* she asked herself. *"No! Impossible. He's fishing."*

The senior clerk stammered, "N...no, um, no...nothing, not at all!" Then she blurted out, "Everything's fine," as she cleared her throat.

The smile returned as Augustus acknowledged the small victory of getting under his opponent's skin.

"Well, that's nice. It's good to know everything's under control."

Sonyai took a moment to sip water from a glass and gather her composure. *Asshole,* she thought.

The librarian produced a red manila folder. "I received a memorandum," he began. "My petition to raise the limit of allowable checked video media here at 58th Street is under consideration. It has allowed us to conduct a 60-day preliminary trial for gauging circulation trends."

He pushed the folder across to Sonyai, who opened it to examine the single piece of laminated paper, her eyebrows scrunched together. "In the event of positive results, the policy will become permanent and they will reward the branch with three thousand dollars over the next two fiscal periods for more requisitions," he concluded.

An annoyed look came across her face. She lowered the document and continued to listen.

"As you know, such a drastic change to branch policy has to be approved by NYPL upper management and can only be implemented if both supervisors acknowledge the receipt of the memorandum—"

"Which cannot be reproduced or forged," Sonyai finished. "Yes, yes, I know the procedure. May I speak for a moment?"

The interruption annoyed him but he did not show it. "Go ahead."

She chose her words carefully. "We are lending out two videos at a time already. Increasing the limit may encourage theft."

"I see."

"And if we're the only branch allowed to change the limit, neighboring regional branches may see it as a tactic to draw circulation and file a grievance. To put the branch at risk for extra funding does not seem worth it."

Augustus knew Sonyai would object; the two of them could never agree on anything. "Those are all valid points," he began, "which I included in my proposal, and yet they approved it. We're not in competition with our fellow branches." He waved his hand in a fake chuckle. "They have only given us the chance to exercise a pending change first before its routine policy for the rest of the branches in the Bronx, Manhattan, and Staten Island."

"But—"

"We're the guinea pigs!" he exclaimed half-heartedly. Before she could protest further, he rose to leave. "They've authorized it, Yi. So sign off on it, make a copy, and circulate it to the clerical staff."

The librarian was around the table, making his way to the door. "The temporary change will go into effect next week," he continued. "I trust you'll instruct the clerks to keep this to themselves until then, and once it starts, not to mention anything when clustering to other branches on weekends."

And with that, he was gone, while Sonyai still sat at the table being dismissed like one of his subordinates. She crumbled the folder in anger and ground her teeth. The door opened again. "Oh and, Yi?" Augustus called back poking his shiny bald head back in the room.

She released the folder and gathered her composure. "Yes?" she replied.

"Return that original back to my office so it can be filed away, will you?"

She gritted her teeth again. "I'll give it back to you as soon as I'm done with it...*sir*."

The door clicked shut again, and she muttered to herself, "You sonovabitch!"

CENTERED in the middle of the branch on the main floor was the information desk. An executive in a three-piece business suit was waiting near the vacant chair when a young Native-American woman emerged from behind and approached the gentleman.

"May I help you, sir?" she asked.

Startled, the man took one look up and down at her. "Oh! Um, no thanks, just waiting for the librarian to return and help me find a book." He then turned away from her.

The young lady adjusted her gold wire glasses, then walked a lap around several bookshelves, and then took the seat behind the information desk. She looked up as the man registered a puzzled look.

"May I help you *now*, sir?" Angie Trueblood asked sarcastically with a smile.

"Yo...you...um, work here?" he asked flabbergasted.

"Yes, I'm an information assistant," she informed him. "I'm earning my masters so in two years I'll be a librarian, sir. We've come a long way from the reservation, you know!"

Angie was five-foot-five with long black hair and could easily pass for twenty but was in her early thirties. She wore a fringe waistcoat over a gray blouse and jeans. She had one beaded necklace around her neck and a beaded headband in the colors of the Oneida. The library had a business casual dress code and Augustus overlooked Angie applying cultural touches in her appearance.

He straightened up after being checked and cleared his throat. "I was wondering if you had a copy of *Time of War* by Michael Peterson."

Rather than antagonize the patron further, Angie typed the title in the digital catalog on the desk's computer terminal. She examined several titles while searching and the gentleman remarked, "In, um, my defense...you don't really look like a librarian."

Angie's fingers paused on the keyboard. "Were you expecting some old biddy with wire eyeglasses wearing a blue knitted sweater and her hair in a bun, hmm?"

The man blinked hard in surprise by the question. "Uh, yeah, I guess."

She then turned from the monitor stood up to look at him, face to face, studied him for a moment. "If I may ask, sir. What do you do for a living?"

"I'm a CEO for an advertising firm," he replied smugly.

A smile crept across Angie's face as she prepared to put the executive in his place. "Has anyone ever mistook you for a stockbroker, an FBI agent, or President of the United States, Mr. White-Man-in-a-Suit-and-Tie?"

"No! Of course not," he stammered.

"Well, why not? They all wear nice designer suits like the one you're wearing. You should get mistaken for one of those types of people all the time!"

The patron was beyond embarrassed and turned pale.

"But you know why that doesn't happen, sir?"

The man shook his head to answer her question.

"Because intelligent people don't make judgments based on appearances anymore. I may not look like the poster child for 'Reading is Fundamental,' but I can quote William Shakespeare and tell the difference between Richard North Patterson and James Patterson like the rest of them! I would think someone dressed like yourself would be *smart* enough to see beyond appearances, but I guess that would be my misjudgment."

She let the man take that profound statement all in for a moment, then sat down and returned her gaze back to the computer screen. "With that said, I'm afraid we do not have that book in stock at the moment. There are copies available in several other branches nearby. If you'd like, we can reserve the book and have it sent here…"

"Um," the man interrupted. "Tha-that's all right. I apologize for my disbelief, my presumptions, and other things I can't think of right now!" He took a handkerchief out of his pocket and dried the sweat from his brow. "I'll…find the book, elsewhere. Thank you very much for your help."

With a quick turn on his heels, the man made his way through the exit turnstile and left the branch.

Angie grinned to herself for a few moments feeling a sense of satisfaction, then rose to fix some of the periodicals in the reference corner. A tall woman wearing a winter coat over a gray blouse and matching skirt walked over to the vacant desk and Angie greeted her. "May I help you?"

The woman waved her away with a slight glance and replied, "No, just waiting for the librarian."

"HE'S FORGING THESE MEMOS, I know it!" Sonyai hissed as she paced back and forth at the circulation desk. Tommy checked in a few returns at his terminal while she furiously waved the laminated memorandum in the air as if swatting imaginary flies. *Flies with Augustus' face on them.*

"But how?" Tommy asked. "It's impossible to fake an NYPL memo."

The pair were working the tail end of the lunch hour rush as it was diminishing. Tommy approached Sonyai and pointed to the logo on the corner of the document. "He would need access to our letterhead paper."

"Which can be purchased from our office supplier," she remarked.

"But then it would need the seal of authenticity." He noted the gold sticker the document also had.

She began to reply again but he cut her off. "*And* it would have to be signed by President Dalton. That's something Chavez can't forge. It's the real deal, ma'am."

She knew it was a sign of respect, but she hated when Tommy called her ma'am, just as he wasn't fond of her using his full name. She snatched the memo from his hands as he recoiled with a quiet yelp.

"I *said* I know he's fabricating them. I didn't say I knew how!" Sonyai realized that her temper was getting the best of her. She sighed and put the troubling memo on the nearby file cabinet, then attended to some patrons checking out books.

"The other branches will have a field day if they discover we're letting patrons borrow more videos, Thomas."

He nodded in agreement. "I know. The limit is two at a time for a reason. I mean, we're not in competition with Blockbuster Video," he said with a chuckle.

Sonyai paced again. "Apparently he believes we are. That obnoxious, arrogant bastard always acquires all the box office favorites rather than educational or self-help videos." She clenched her fist in frustration. "We are supposed to be a learning resource for the public, dammit!" Her emotions were betraying her again. She took a breath and regained her composure.

"Maybe his little experiment will backfire, like the time he tried to do the same thing with the CD collection? All those thefts and claims of unreturned media really embarrassed him."

"Music has more constraints on acquisitions," she responded. "Unless you're one of the six influential branches like Donnell or Mid-Manhattan, you have to stay a year behind the curve."

"Well, just like with the CDs, we let the public borrow more videos, we won't be able to keep up with the supply and demand of things."

"Along with more thefts." They both nodded, knowing what to do.

"We have to make sure Chavez's little experiment produces mediocre results," she concluded.

"So upper-management can cancel the policy change," Tommy replied.

This was not the first time the clerical staff disagreed with the librarians regarding policy changes and it would not be the last.

"We'll let several of his favorable patrons borrow an extra movie here and there, but uphold the original rule and keep word of mouth to a minimum. Chavez will be too busy to advertise the change himself. He's got Learner getting on his nerves too, so he'll stay neutral in case it backfires."

"And it *will*," Tommy added with a grin. "This will be another failed attempt to get his way."

She smiled at the thought of thwarting her nemesis. "Yes," she agreed. "Let's hope Miss Walker doesn't fall head over heels for Chavez in the meantime!"

"Uh, I wouldn't worry too much about that, ma'am," an unknown voice said behind her.

Startled by the thought of someone overhearing and joining their private conversation, the senior clerk and her associate looked across the circulation desk to see a young man with a book bag slung over one shoulder smiling at them.

"He's really *not* my type." The newcomer took a moment as Sonyai and Tommy blinked with confused gazes. "Hi, I'm Robin Walker from Fort Washington," he introduced himself. "I'll be starting here today."

CHAPTER TWO

"I BELIEVE THERE MUST BE SOME MISTAKE," SONYAI SAID CALMLY.

Robin tilted his head and observed the two questionably. "Ouch, is that any way to greet a new employee?"

The short woman exhibited signs of a no-nonsense type. *Reminds me of The Battle Axe*, he thought. The giant behind her was all too familiar. He *appeared* to be trying to look menacing toward him. *Big, dumb and gullible. He's gonna be a problem…*

Sonyai reached over to a shelf above a huge three drawer file cabinet to her left. Robin took the opportunity to engage in a staring contest with Tommy. She finally produced a piece of paper and held it up for him to see. "This letter from Human Resources clearly says 'Ms. Robin Walker' from Fort Washington Library, not Mister."

Robin knew where this was going, but he played along. After leaning in to skim the letter, he smiled. "It's a typo. Happens all the time."

The senior clerk could not help to notice that the newcomer was still smiling, not taking the situation seriously, and it annoyed her. "Let me see some ID!" she commanded.

Robin slipped his hand into his pants pocket and produced a plastic card with his picture on it. The words Baruch College on the top.

"This is a college ID. I need something more official…like a birth certificate."

Robin's smile disappeared. "No offense, ma'am, but who goes around carrying their birth certificate on them in this day and age?"

Without a moment of hesitation, both Sonyai and Tommy produced their birth certificates out of their separate pockets in unison. This made Robin register a very astonished look.

Sonyai noticed the newcomer was staring in awe. "Okay, okay, just verify a few personal attributes and I will take your word for it." She tucked her birth certificate back in her pocket and looked at a second page in the folder that held his employee file.

"Your social security number, please…*Mr.* Walker."

He recited the number from memory as Sonyai checked the file, verifying that the number given was correct, but she still wasn't convinced.

"Your first day working for Fort Washington?" she asked.

"December 2nd, 1992, ma'am," he replied, a look of annoyance growing across his face. He made a mental note to contact Human Resources and speak to someone about correcting his title.

"My apologies, Mr. Walker," the senior clerk said in a lighthearted tone while closing the file, "but you were not what we were expecting here at 58th Street."

The young clerk straightened up his stance, doing his best to remove the impatience from his tone while addressing his new supervisor. "Well, I guess *I* must apologize myself then for my deceptive given name. Now that the unpleasantness is behind us, I've waited 8 months for the right position to come along, ma'am, and I'd hate to get things started on the wrong foot over a gender issue."

Surprised by his serious demeanor Sonyai nodded. "I understand where you're coming from, Walker. It won't happen again." She noticed two patrons approaching the desk. With a wave of her hand, she turned to Tommy. "This is Thomas Carmichael. He will show you to the back."

Robin walked around the circulation desk to a side opening as she picked up the phone and dialed the clerical office. "Coltraine, could you take the desk with me while Thomas shows the new arrival around?"

The pair exchanged glances as the door to the back office opened. Robin saw a tall black man with an afro and dated clothing emerge to stand at the returns side of the desk. He looked back at Robin with a surprised glance and then turned to Sonyai to read her reaction to this sudden turn of events.

Robin could tell from everyone's body language that his arrival was most unexpected, but he shrugged it off as he made his way inside. Once the door closed behind the pair, Sonyai turned and picked up the phone again, then dialed an outside number, clearly distressed over something…much to Gerry's delight.

"I'M NOT WRONG, AM I?" Heywood asked. "It's not *me* this time, is it? I mean if I'm going too far…"

"It's not you, Heywood," Zelda replied. "Your passionate manner has always been valuable. I've known Augustus for a long time. He's known for his tunnel vision."

The two were in the staff room upstairs, Heywood lying on the couch with his hands behind his head as if undergoing a therapy session. Zelda was finishing up her kosher meal at the table, her back to him as she continued listening.

"Then you agree with me on excluding the movie?" he asked.

With a light chuckle she replied, "Now, I didn't say all that!"

Zelda sensed Heywood's puzzlement when he let out a slight grunt and then sat up to look at the back of her head.

Before he could continue, Zelda asked, "Heywood, did you ever read *Fahrenheit 451* by Ray Bradbury?"

"The sci-fi novel? No, but I remember there was a film based on it."

"In the novel, structures become so resistant with the advances into the future they became fireproof, thus removing the need for firefighters."

"An illogical reality as if I ever heard of one."

"So, the totalitarian governments of the future assigned firefighters the task of actually starting fires."

"Bradbury always *was* a bit backward."

"They burned books, Heywood! 451 degrees Fahrenheit is the temperature at which books deteriorate."

"But why books?"

"They were all deemed offensive by the state. Books that would stir up repressed feelings among the public. Like *Mein Kampf, Uncle Tom's Cabin*, whatever would be inappropriate in the modern time."

Heywood stood and walked to face the elder at the kitchen table, learning the lesson she was giving him.

"But understand, when they burned those books, they erased their history. What kind of society would we be if we didn't acknowledge the bigotry and racism of the past?"

"I think I see where you're going with this," he said with a nod.

"When Steven Spielberg announced he was making a film addressing the atrocities of the Holocaust, the Jewish public thought the movie had no right to be made. Forcing us to relive such a horrible time. But in the end, *Schindler's List* has become one of the most important motion pictures in the 20th century."

"But where does it end, Zelda? If I relent on this issue, what's to stop Augustus from pushing further? Buckwheat and Farina from *The Little Rascals*? *Amos and Andy*? A tribute to blackface hosted by Ted Danson?"

"A frightening thought, I'm sure, but it hasn't come to that yet! We're only talking about *Blazing Saddles* for Pete's sake!" She took a breath for emphasis.

Heywood dropped his head and sighed. "So, you *do* think I'm wrong on this, right?"

She chuckled again, "No, I didn't say that either."

"Dammit Zelda, what *are* you trying to say then?"

Youth, she thought. *So impatient.* "What I'm trying to say is that Augustus knew you would object the way you did and that just made him push harder. If you had just read the list and only had a mild argument he might have removed the film with little or no hesitation. It wasn't until you revealed how much it angered you personally that he made his decision more final!"

She let her last statement sink in as the young man sat in silence for a moment.

"I…I don't understand."

"Think about it, Heywood. Just think about what I said."

Zelda got up from the table and left the staff room. Heywood went back to lie on the couch, staring up at the ceiling in deep thought.

Back downstairs inside the clerical office, Ethel was reading an issue of *Sports Illustrated* when the door opened and Tommy entered with a young man holding a book bag behind him. The newcomer surveyed the office as she lowered her magazine for a moment, then raised it again.

"Well, Walker, as you can see we have limited desk space in here so—"

"Wait a minute," Robin interrupted. "We haven't been properly introduced. Fort Washington was always reminding us of the procedures for representing yourself correctly."

Ethel lowered her magazine again. *This* was going to be interesting.

"Robin Walker, from the way of Fort Washington." He extended his hand toward Tommy, who returned a skeptical look.

"So you'll be sharing a desk here with Mr. Coltraine," he continued.

Robin narrowed his eyes at the insult. *Definitely going to be a problem,* he thought.

"Over here is Miss Ethel Jenkins." Tommy gestured to his co-worker.

Robin gave her a slight nod for a greeting and turned back to his new *friend.* "So, Carmichael…you've been in the system long?"

"What system is that?"

"The NYPL, the network of branch libraries we all work in. I'd assumed every clerk was once a page someplace else…and would have known of the procedures of conduct that are thrust upon us." *Like how to greet each other properly, goofball!* he thought.

"'Procedures of Conduct,' eh?" He chuckled. "That's pretty good there, Walker. Except I wasn't hired as a page."

"Oh?" Robin replied with a genuine look of surprise.

"Yeah, so you keep your little library lingo like 'the system' and 'Procedures of Conduct' to yourself till someone asks you what the names are of the 2 lion statues or what the fear of the number 13 is, okay, Mr. Holier-Than-Thou?"

He turned to leave. "Carmichael?" Robin called back at him.

"Yes?" he replied.

"Triskaidekaphobia. And the lions are named Patience and Fortitude," Robin said with a smirk.

Disgusted, Tommy walked out of the office and closed the door behind him. Robin then turned back to Ethel and gave her a wink. "I'm going against my better judgment and just going to greet you with a smile. Instinct tells me *you* are not one to be messed with."

She smiled back. "Stay on my good side Mr. Walker and you'll live longer. Welcome to 58th Street."

Tommy emerged from the clerical office back out to the circulation desk, only to find Gerry alone in the center sitting on a shelving cart.

"What happened to Yi?" he asked.

"She went out for a smoke…after having a very *intense* phone call with HR."

Tommy couldn't help noticing Gerry was smiling from ear to ear. He chose not to pry, plus he was still agitated from interacting with Robin.

"The new kid's a regular robot like from *Star Trek: The Next Generation*!"

"Hmm, the ol' 'Procedures of Conduct' type, eh? I'm not surprised. You put him in his place, didn't you?" Gerry asked.

"Is this going to be a problem with you? Me busting his balls?"

"Long as I don't hear you call him 'boy' or 'colored' or you know what else."

"What if he goes there with me?"

Gerry shook his head in a silent reply. He and Tommy shared a mutual respect for each other, but they both knew racial tensions could reduce the most civilized people into the deadliest of enemies.

"He's not supposed to be here, Gerry. Simms was next in line, you know that, right?"

"Best laid plans of mice and men often go awry."

Tommy tilted his head. "Malcolm X say that?"

"Burns, Scottish poet. I'm not *all* about Malcolm and Martin, Tommy."

"Sorry. You're definitely well read, but Yi's making a move to *persuade* Mr. Walker into transferring someplace else. He's not a good fit. I just want to know if it will come between us when I roll out the welcome wagon."

The two exchanged glances for a moment, each wondering what to say next. Gerry stepped forward to check out books for a patron. With his back to Tommy, he said, "I'll let you know when you step over the line. Until then, I'll be laying in the cut watching where the chips may fall."

A neutral response if I ever heard one, thought Tommy with a pout.

OUTSIDE THE LIBRARY, Sonyai stood near the entrance smoking a Newport cigarette. She had the misfortune of developing the habit back in Japan while in her mid-20s at college. At a pack a day now, she often lit up when highly stressed.

Someone approaching caught her eye and she flicked the cigarette out into the street while waving away the lingering smoke. "Janelle!" she called out. "How's everything going today?"

A young African-American girl wearing an oversized leather Yankee's jacket with a pink scarf and black jeans walked up toward her. Janelle Simms was the oldest of 58th Street's four pages. At seventeen, she was scheduled to graduate from Julia Richman High School in June but would have gained all forty credits by the end of the winter term. She greeted Sonyai with a spirited embrace.

"A bit queasy this morning, but nothing I can't handle."

"You get the results from your calculus final yet?"

She fished out a stapled pair of papers from her school bag "Got a 95%! Only missed one!"

"That's my girl!" Sonyai beamed with a seldom seen smile of approval.

Janelle sensed something was bothering her. "What's wrong, Miss Yi? You seem mad about something."

The elder sighed. It would best if she heard it from her. "We…have a new part-timer starting here today."

"What?" Janelle gasped.

"I tried my best to fight this, but we had no choice. Some hotshot who's been waiting for a clerical position downtown. He goes to college—"

"I finish school in two weeks!" Janelle interrupted. "I don't even have to take a spring term!"

"Shhhh…" Sonyai hushed her. Janelle was on the verge of tears and trembling in fear. "I know I promised you the next position. I'm sorry."

"What am I going to do?"

"Don't worry. I did my research. He *will not* last long. Thomas and I will see to it."

With a reassured sigh, she smiled. "Thank you, Miss Yi. I don't know what I'd do without you."

"We will get through this. Head on in. I need another minute to compose myself before introducing the newcomer to Chavez."

She turned and made her way inside. Sonyai produced another cigarette and with the flick of her lighter, resumed smoking nervously.

Back inside the library, Gerry was working the returns side, accepting back three borrowed books from a middle-aged Caucasian woman. She was wearing a mink stole fur jacket accessorized with expensive jewelry.

"Okay, ma'am, three books returned five days late at fifteen cents a day comes to a fine of $2.25, please."

The woman nodded. "Ah, well yes," she stammered. "I wish to waive the fine."

Gerry tilted his head, believing he misheard the woman despite her speaking clearly. "Excuse me, could you repeat that?"

"I wish the late fines to be waived," she replied calmly.

Being a public servant and an NYPL employee for a decade, Gerry had heard many unreasonable requests from people, but he played along. "And what would be the reason, might I ask, that you cannot pay these late fines at *this* particular time?"

"I have no money at the moment."

Gerry fought to restrain himself at the absurdity of the situation. *Remember your lessons at the last Public Relations Seminar,* he thought. "If that's the case," he began, "I could leave the fines unpaid on your record and you can pay them another time. You can even check out more books since the balance is less than 5 dollars."

In a perfect world, that would be the end of the conversation. She would smile, nod, then accept that she could still take out books and deal with the penalty at a later date. When dealing with wealthy individuals, Gerry noticed consequences are viewed in a different light than normal people and that it was best to stay non-confrontational.

"No, no, no, you don't understand. I have no money at all. I cannot pay this fine, so I wish to have it waived."

Apparently, it was not a perfect world.

There was an awkward moment of silence. Gerry's eyes darted in various directions as he tried to comprehend what he was hearing. Fortunately for him, there were no other returns at the moment, so he had time to make this exchange *uncomfortable.* Public Relations Seminar be damned.

"May I make an obvious observation, madam?" Gerry asked. "You are wearing a fur coat worth hundreds of dollars, you have on very extravagant jewelry, and you mean to tell me you have no money to pay the fine for these 3 books which you *deliberately* returned late now or anytime in the immediate future? Is that what you are telling me?"

"I don't know what you're getting at, but I am sure this is not an unreasonable request!" she exclaimed. "I demand it be honored!"

His patience had just run out. "Well I can't *honor* that request!" he barked. "If we waive fines left and right, we would have no money to buy more of those Danielle Steel and Mary Higgins Clark books you rich, upper-crust snobs like to read so much!"

Gerry noticed he was yelling now. From the corner of his eye, he noticed Sonyai coming back from outside at the entrance and Augustus emerging from his office in the far right corner at the back of the branch. He knew he was in trouble, but he continued his rant.

"And without money, we'll only be open for 5 days a week instead of 6, then only 4 days. Next thing you know, common day folks like me get laid off due to budget cuts followed by other lame excuses! *So*, Miss Waive-the-Fine, are you going to pay this $2.25 or am I going to lose my job?"

"Coltraine!"

Sonyai's voice echoed throughout the open floor as she stood at the check-outs side on the left. All eyes turned to the desk where the two clerks and patron stood. Embarrassed, the woman pulled out a crumpled ten-dollar bill from a purse. "Keep the change." She hurried past Sonyai on her way to the exit.

"Thank you very much for the charitable donation!" he called back to her. "Have a nice day!"

He turned back to see Augustus glaring back at him for a moment and then disappear back into his office. Sonyai walked around to stand right next to him, also glaring. "What the hell was that?" she hissed.

"A cheap-ass getting what she deserved," he replied.

She nodded. "I see, we'll discuss that *thoroughly* when I have a moment, but for now, why don't you step inside and introduce yourself to Mr. Walker before there are any more outbursts."

As if on cue, Ethel exited the clerical office to join Tommy and Sonyai while Gerry stepped past her to cool off from his encounter.

In the clerical office, Robin sensed tension from the heated exchange as he heard his new supervisor's booming exclamation outside. He thought against saying anything to the fourth and final full-time clerk working at 58th street when he saw him come in.

"Uh, hi," he whispered with a faint wave.

Gerry smiled. "Gerry Coltraine from Soundview Branch through

High Bridge and Woodlawn Heights before that." He then extended his hand in friendship.

Robin chuckled and shook Gerry's hand. "Robin Walker, from the way of Fort Washington! Nice to finally meet someone in the system!"

"10 years, 4 branches. You do the math!"

"Well, alright! What's the deal with that other guy?" Robin asked thumbing out past the closed door.

"Different upbringing. Long story. We'll go over it later."

"Oh, yeah? What are the names of the lion statues?" he challenged.

"Patience and Fortitude"

"And the fear of the number 13?"

"Triskaidekaphobia...rolls of the tip of my tongue I've said it so many times!"

"What's the Dewey decimal for sociology?"

"301.01"

"Nutrition and diets?"

"641.25"

"World history?"

"909.01"

"Math?"

"Too broad, be specific."

"Geometry."

"516.03"

"Algebra?"

"512.09"

"Shakespeare?"

"Shakespeare has his own entire call number, which is 822."

The rapid-fire tennis match between the two went on for three minutes. Robin shook his hand again with a wide grin. Gerry was the real McCoy. "That's what I'm talking about!"

Gerry nodded his head in a modest bow.

"I don't know about Jenkins, but Danny Boy out there probably doesn't know what the inside of a card catalog looks like!"

"Understand, man. Not everyone takes this job too seriously."

"Yeah, okay, but basic page training—"

"Tommy wasn't hired as a page like us."

"How is that possible?" Robin asked astonished.

"To paraphrase, he's one of the 5 Percenters."

"How surprisingly Muslim of him."

Gerry smiled at the joke. "He filled out an application outside the system and was on an extended waiting list before he started here directly as a clerk."

This was unheard of to Robin. "What'd he do? Call in a favor from his Uncle Mickey in Hell's Kitchen to pull that off?"

Gerry cringed at the youngster's prejudgment and was about to answer when the door opened and Sonyai stepped in. She looked at Robin questionably. "Why haven't you taken off your coat yet?" she asked and then quickly waved a dismissive hand. "It doesn't matter. It's time to meet our head librarian. Please follow me."

"Yes, ma'am," Robin replied. He gave Gerry a two-fingered military salute and smiled, then followed her out of the office. Finally alone, Gerry mused over the chances of Robin being accepted with indifference here. The odds of him not disrupting the amount of chaos and anarchy that already occurred at this once simple branch were not good.

Robin took a moment while following Sonyai to examine his surroundings. The main floor was open with no walls or columns divided into two sections. The right side where he was walking was the reference and media area. Waist high tables holding the card catalog were accompanied by a wide one-piece media counter that held CDs and packages of books on tape.

Behind the card catalog was a series of tables and chairs where patrons were reading or studying. On the left side furthest from Robin were eight metal shelves six feet tall and two feet wide stretching back from the glass windows up front to the back wall.

The walls themselves housed wooden shelves that were taller than the metal ones and wrapped around in an L-shape pattern covering the back and left sides. The wall on the right had three doors, one leading up to the second floor, one that was a public bathroom, and the door he was approaching to Mr. Chavez's office.

Robin noticed three teenage girls pretending not to stare from different vantage points among the shelves across the room. The branch pages if he had to guess. *I hope nothing's wrong with them*, he thought.

"Is that him?" Alex asked.

"I think so. Nellie didn't say what the new guy looked like," replied Tanya. "Only that it was a guy."

"Leelee, you're staring."

"Leelee?...Leelee?...Lakeshia!"

"What?" Lakeshia whispered with a squeak.

The trio of girls met in an area obscured to anyone across the room.

"Way to be conspicuous, small fry. I think he noticed us."

"What does conspicuous mean?" the youngest page asked.

"It means you were sticking out like my cousin Ezekiel's' sixth toe, cuz!" Tanya answered.

"Ewww, gross!"

"Okay, knock it off you two, this is serious," Alex ordered. "With this new guy here now, Janelle will have to transfer to Webster, if they even *have* a position."

"Oh no! What if they find out?"

"At least Andrew will take care of her."

Alex shook her head. "No, there's no guarantee they won't fire her once the cat's out the bag. If I know Miss Yi, she's got a plan to make this new guy regret he ever came here...and we got to see to it that he does."

CHAPTER THREE

"I DON'T KNOW WHY SHE HASN'T FIRED COLTRAINE YET AFTER ALL these years," Augustus said, shaking his head. With the outburst at the circulation desk fresh in his mind, he sat at his desk contemplating ways he could remove the troublesome clerk without undermining Sonyai's authority. A phone call to his direct line interrupted his musings.

"Yes?" he spoke into the receiver.

Zelda turned from her desk as he smiled.

"Ah, Charles, how are things at the Donelle video library?" He nodded and listened, an eyebrow raised as he exclaimed, "You're kidding! I don't believe it!" He then sighed. "All right, I'll see what else we can do. Goodbye." He hung up the phone in awe.

Augustus noticed Zelda looking back at him and was about to explain an interesting development when a knock on the door followed by it opening snapped the pair back to attention. Sonyai stepped halfway into the doorway.

"Mr. Chavez, sir?" she said, containing herself in anticipation.

"Yes, Miss Yi?" he answered and noticed the smirk on her face.

"Robin Walker has arrived."

He stepped around his desk with a flourish as a wide smile grew across his face. He had prepared some charming pleasantries to greet the young lady with. Sonyai motioned outside the threshold and then stepped inside, followed by Robin. A wave of emotions came over the librarian's face—shock, puzzlement, concern, and then anger while the young man approached and shook his half-extended hand.

"Nice to meet you, sir."

Augustus stammered "Ah, yes, welcome aboard, *Mr.* Walker." He noticed Sonyai still had a smirk on her face and stared daggers back at her over this twist of events. "This is Zelda Clein. Zelda, meet Robin Walker from Fort Washington." With a gesture, he turned the attention toward the elder and Robin turned to greet her.

"Soft! now to my mother. O heart, lose not thy nature; let not ever. The soul of Nero enter this firm bosom: Let me be cruel, not unnatural," Robin suddenly exclaimed. Sonyai and Augustus exchanged wild-eyed looks of surprise.

"I will speak daggers to her, but use none; My tongue and soul in this be hypocrites; How in my words soever she be shent, to give them seals never, my soul, consent!" Zelda finished the soliloquy.

"*Hamlet.* Act 3, Scene 2. I bring greetings and salutations from the word of The Battle Axe. She sends her warmest regards."

"How *is* Babs doing these days?" Zelda asked.

"Okay, what was that all about?" Sonyai interrupted.

"I was ordered to relay a message. Sorry for the dramatics. Miss Clein, anyone dares to call you-know-who 'Babs' is either brave or a fool, but rest assured she is doing well."

"Ah, I hope to hear from her soon enough. Welcome, young Mr. Walker, we've been expecting you."

"Yes, well, we better be going," Sonyai said with a nod to the door.

Robin smiled, then turned and left, the senior clerk lingering behind for a moment as if to mock Augustus about the encounter and then closed the door behind her.

When he was sure they were out of earshot outside his smile disappeared and he turned to Zelda, "Did you know he was a guy, dammit?"

Expecting his agitation, she said, "I didn't know for certain, but I suspected as much."

Robin and Sonyai walked back to the circulation desk. "Mr. Chavez seemed...distraught," he commented.

"Well, you were not what he was expecting. You really should have HR fix that whole 'Ms.' issue, or consider going by Rob or Bobby."

"I'll have you know my mother named me after Robin Williams. That or she had a thing for birds."

Sonyai didn't pry. "Chavez was definitely expecting a woman. He's what you'd call 'hands-on' with young female professionals.

Now it was Robin's turn not to pry. "Fancies himself as a ladies man, does he? Well, he does resemble the late Telly Savalas a little. Probably polishes his head on a weekly basis."

The two shared a chuckle at the joke. "Before we step back to the office, I would like to introduce our pages," Sonyai said when they arrived at the opposite side of the circulation desk.

Four teenage girls emerged from the shelves and lined up behind the senior clerk. "Mr. Walker, meet Janelle Simms, Alex Stevens, Tanya Brown, and Lakeshia Seabrooke."

Robin nodded at each page. "Ladies."

Fifteen-year-old Alexandra Stevens wore black business slacks and an olive green blouse as she stood an even five-foot-nine in white Adidas tennis shoes. A dark complexion that could be defined as onyx, Alex could easily be mistaken for a model the likes of Naomi Campbell or Grace Jones.

Sixteen-year-old Tanya Brown was wearing jean corduroy overalls with a gray sweatshirt underneath, her short brown hair matted down in a tomboy-like bowl cut. She had an athletic physique developed from hours of playing basketball both in gym class and in streetball on asphalt courts.

Lakeshia was the youngest page at fourteen. A petite five-foot-four, she was only ninety-five pounds and was often mistaken for anorexic. Her curly hair resting at shoulder length, she had a fair skin tone similar to Robin's. She wore black stockings with a plaid skirt and a cropped cardigan sweater.

Robin sensed a tense vibe from Janelle and Alex by their cold stares, matching the feelings Tommy had been projecting. *The smugness must be infectious around here,* he thought.

When the two returned, Robin looked around the office and asked, "Where are the lockers for coats and bags?"

"Here at 58th Street," Sonyai explained, "we leave our belongings at our desks. You may leave your coat on a chair and—"

"Whoa, hold up!" Robin interrupted. A wave of anxiety took over him. "No offense to your clerical staff, Miss Yi, but I need to make sure my things stay safe. When I was in elementary school someone stole my winter coat while I was in class. I nearly froze to death because they had the nerve to send me home just because I lived several blocks away. I'm not leaving anything in plain sight where it can just *disappear.*"

Sonyai sensed this was a sensitive subject to the young man. She sighed. "The pages lock their coats and school bags in mini-lockers upstairs. I believe there is one available, but you'll need a combination or key lock."

"Thank you for understanding, Sonya," Robin replied with a relieved smile.

"It's Son*yai*, Mr. Walker," she corrected. "Please pronounce it correctly or address me by my last name."

"Yes, Miss Yi." He looked behind her. "Since I have no lock, this being my first day, I wouldn't mind leaving my coat and book bag on one of these elevated shelves here where I can keep my eye on them from out at the desk."

Such a request was odd. The newcomer had no reason to fear that the staff would touch his belongings. "Very well," the supervisor said with a slight nod.

Robin removed his book bag off his shoulder and took off his parka.

Once settled, Sonyai pointed at the bike glove on Robin's left hand. "May I ask what is wrong with your hand, Walker?"

"Um, it's a slight disfigurement. I know there's a dress code, but Fort Washington…"

"This is *not* Fort Washington, Walker. I must insist you take it off."

He shrugged. "Okay."

Robin grabbed the glove at the wrist and quickly pulled it off.

Sonyai looked with a start as the flesh on the clerk's hand appeared to be eaten away, revealing exposed tendons and nerves. His fingers flexed as if someone held his hand under an x-ray with the first outer layers removed.

"How?" she gasped.

"Sodium hydroxide burn. Accident when I was 6," he explained. "I have 30% motor function in the nerves of this hand."

She became nauseated. "On second thought," she said with a gag, "I believe it would be best if you kept it on."

He slipped his hand back in the garment. "Thank you, Miss Yi," Robin said stoically.

"Now that all the pleasantries have concluded..." Sonyai led Robin back to the circulation desk where Tommy and Ethel were working their respective checkout and returns stations. She traded places with Ethel while Tommy allowed Robin to take his spot. The relieved pair took the door upstairs for a break in the staff room.

"Let me explain your work hours."

Robin focused as the supervisor began.

"As a part-time employee, you will work 17½ in a 5 day week. 3 days, you'll work 3½ , one day you will only work 3, and one day you will work 4 hours."

"Okay," Robin replied.

Sonyai continued, "Our branch is open Monday through Saturday from noon until 6 pm, with an early day on Thursday when we open at 10 am. We also have a late night on Wednesday where the branch stays open until 8 pm. You'll work 3 Saturdays a month and one late night Wednesday every 2 months on a rotation with the other clerical staff. Do you need to write any of this down?"

"No, I have a good memory. I'll write it down later, just in case."

"Okay, finally, on weeks when you come in on Saturday, you'll have a random day off during the week. While it rarely happens, there may be an instance we need you to come in on an early

Thursday, but that will only be if someone else is on vacation or calls out sick."

"There might be an issue with that," Robin began. "I have classes in the morning, and I also need evenings for my studies."

"I understand, but I do not believe this schedule is unreasonable, Walker."

"Okay, I have no issues at the moment so long as you're flexible."

"Be warned, there may be times where you'll be asked to serve beyond the call of duty."

He thought about responding to that remark but it was his first day, and he didn't want to make things tenser than they already were.

"Until you learn how to operate the cash register, you'll do checkouts when on duty," she instructed. "Let's see what Fort Washington has taught you."

"Gladly."

Robin picked up the lightpen used to read barcodes with a flourish and checked out several books for a line of patrons with ease. He zipped their library card and brought up their records. Zip the books and insert a date due card in the pocket on the book's first page beneath the cover. Afterward, he'd pass the checked-out items on the other side of the security threshold to be picked up by the patron leaving the building.

He was fast, accurate, and efficient. Sonyai was impressed. A patron handed him a plastic slip for a video checkout. "Um, what are these?" he asked. Sonyai stepped to the file cabinet holding the VHS tapes and pulled a drawer open. "What number?"

"362," he answered. She then pulled the item in question and Robin checked it out.

"We keep our movies in these cabinets," she explained. "They bring us the slip and we find them in here. Put the slips in this shoebox until they return."

Robin took a moment to scan all the drawers in the cabinet sizing up the movies available. "You have a copy of *E.T.*? These cost over $130."

"A donated copy from a patron," Sonyai replied with a chuckle.

He looked at the rest of the collection. "Well, you certainly have a vast selection of *adult* films as well. Heeeeey! *Angel Heart*! Lisa Bonet's topless in this! Wow, *9 ½ Weeks*!"

Sonyai grimaced at Robin's lusty display of excitement. "You pride yourself on knowledge of R-rated films for someone who can barely get in to see them at 18."

Robin scoffed. "Please! First R-rated movie I saw was *Robocop*, and I was *12*!"

"Be that as is it may, Fort Washington has taught you well."

The praise astonished Robin. "I'd like to think so." He stood back up and looked forward. "Such a small branch, but so busy."

He took a moment to observe the floor, a diverse mix of the upper class and average joes, executives and college students. Sophisticated women wearing extravagant wigs and brooches with high heel shoes and expensive purses. A homeless vagrant caught his eye, sitting alone at a small round table in an isolated corner. The beast of a man looked like he weighed over three hundred pounds and was wearing tattered layers of sweaters and a huge overcoat.

"It's easy to get caught up in the crowd of patrons who frequent our branch. You might even see a celebrity on occasion," Sonyai remarked, distracting his attention from the giant.

"Well, I don't get star struck."

Robin then noticed the pages working among the shelves. "You know, back at Fort Washington, we had a Russian page, an Asian page, Greek, Jewish and Hispanic pages. Washington Heights is a very diverse neighborhood."

The senior clerk nodded, wondering where he was going with his line of thought.

"The Greek page was the only female, but things still felt...*balanced*."

Sonyai's eyes narrowed. Out among the shelves, Alex felt an impulse to listen.

"But I've noticed the pages here all have something in common. It must be murder on them, sharing the same bathroom."

"You have a problem with me using an all-female page staff, Walker?" Sonyai asked with a challenging tone.

"No, not at all. But as a former male page myself, one feels compelled to ask."

Sonyai paced. Robin looked at her walking back and forth in such a small area quite puzzled.

"It has been my experience that teenage boys do not last long under my supervision. They lack discipline, get bored, and then slack off."

"Is that why there are only two male *clerks* here as well?" he asked folding his arms. "And why you were expecting another woman?"

"*I'm* not the one with 'Ms.' in front of my name on my HR record misleading everyone, Walker! Don't accuse me of being sexist on your first day!" *Especially when it could also be your last!* she thought.

"It's just an observation, Sonia, and I'll get my name fixed in HR soon enough."

"It's *Son-yai*, not Sonia, Walker. I will not warn you again! What's between their legs doesn't mean a damn thing. My pages are loyal, efficient, and above all reliable! They give me no problems!"

Tensions were escalating, so much for keeping cool on the first day, but Robin was not convinced by her rhetoric. "Being a page requires manual labor. The 4 of us shared 2 shelving carts, so we carried stacks of books to put back. And what about tying up and carrying boxes of discards? Except for one, the rest of your Charlie's Angels have got pipe cleaners for arms!"

Alex gritted her teeth and clenched her fist at the insult.

"That's when the male clerks come in handy," Sonyai replied with a smug grin.

"Is that so? Obviously, we have a difference of opinion over page and clerical duties. Well, my name's not Kunta Kinte and I won't do any task I once did as a page just because you're too—"

"My pages can do any task I require them to do!" she interrupted. "No matter how strenuous. And I need not be lectured by you on the duties of an NYPL employee! Is *that* clear!"

Once again, the branch was silent, all attention on them, whose conversation had evolved into a shouting match. Robin lowered his voice. "Yes...*Miss Yi*," he growled.

"PIPE CLEANERS? Where does he get off saying we have pipe cleaners for arms!"

The pages were upstairs in the staff room around four-thirty taking a break.

"Have you *seen* Lakeshia's arms, Alex? He wasn't that far off," Tanya replied.

"Hey! At least my arms don't look like Popeye's...Popeye!" Lakeshia taunted.

"Well if I'm Popeye you're Olive Oyl, Olive Oyl!"

"Popeye!"

"Olive Oyl!"

"Popeye!"

"*Olive Oyl!*"

"Will you two stop! Gosh, it's like you're actually sisters or something!" Janelle yelled from the couch.

Lakeshia and Tanya sat on opposite sides while Alex sat at the head of the table in the middle of the room. Janelle relaxed on the couch rubbing her temples.

"Alex was right, Walker talks to Miss Yi about his pages from Fort Washington like he's better than us!"

"He is, Nellie. He's a clerk," Lakeshia chimed in. Alex and Tanya gave her a look while she elaborated. "He may not be from around here, but I think he deserves the benefit of the doubt. Did you see how he checked out those books? Flipping the lightpen around his hand?"

"I was so damn close!" Janelle interrupted. "After Andy left to become senior clerk of Webster, Sonyai promised me the next position! I can't believe they brought this jerk in. It's not fair!" She sat up with an agitated scream.

"Easy, Nellie! Watch your blood pressure!" Alex warned.

Tanya and Lakeshia put their differences aside and moved to sit on each end of the couch with Janelle in the middle. Alex stayed at the table.

"Have you been to the doctor yet?" Tanya whispered.

"I'm waiting until the end of the month when I finish school early, then I'll tell my folks."

"You haven't told your parents?" Lakeshia gasped.

"What about the fa—" Alex began.

"I'm not discussing any more of this! I don't need to get worked up!" Janelle stood up and exited the room to return downstairs. With the trio alone, they all exchanged looks of worry and concern.

"Well, Alex has a point. With this new guy having a chip on his shoulder, he may be a real pain in the ass."

"I really don't think that'll be the case, Tee."

"What's with you defending him, Leelee?" Alex asked. "You're always too trusting!"

"You don't *like* this chunky light-brite boy, do ya', small fry?" Tanya asked with a smile.

"No!" Lakeshia yelled as she blushed with embarrassment. "I'm just a good judge of character, that's all!" She rolled her eyes.

"So is Miss Yi," Alex interjected. "She's always been there to take care of us." Once again a worried look came across the young page. "For Nellie's sake, I hope this new guy won't be a problem."

"So Jenkins, what'd ya think of the kid?" Gerry asked. Ethel and Gerry were back inside the clerical office before moving out to work the desk for the final hour of the shift. Robin, Sonyai, and Tommy were behind the closed door out of earshot.

"He's okay in my book, so long as he leaves me alone, unlike you!"

Ignoring the insult, he asked, "Do you know what a cabal is?"

Ethel sighed. "We got 10 minutes till we're back out there to close, so—"

"A small group, usually 3 to 5 members with a secret agenda to overthrow or undermine a corrupt authority figure. Dates back to King Charles II." Gerry interrupted.

"What are you talking about? King Charles II?"

"I've been doing research. With Yi tripping over this Walker newcomer, we can make a case citing that she is not mentally sound to be in charge."

"You really think anyone will believe—"

"You see how she mothers those pages like they're her own children. Chavez could help with his observations. He'd be on board with any plan that will see her out."

"Coltraine! Yi finds out you're doing this, she will fire you!" she hissed.

"You gonna tell her?" Gerry asked. "Because that's the only way she'll find out."

He let that statement hang in the air until she said, "You *are* playing with fire!" and stormed outside.

Augustus was putting on his jacket, ready to leave at the end of an exhausting day when Heywood knocked and entered the office. "You wanted to see me?" he asked, closing the door behind him. The head librarian cleared his throat while smoothing out the wrinkles of his sports jacket. "I was thinking, I…um. I overreacted this morning."

"I see," Heywood replied, wondering what he would say next.

"I believe the movie selection is fine the way it is, Learner. I…apologize."

The words nearly knocked Heywood off his feet. He contained his excitement with the small victory and continued to listen.

"There was a problem with the video archive department. Donelle Library called me a few hours ago to inform me that the only available copy we had of *Blazing Saddles* was chewed up beyond any splicing repair."

"Oh."

"So, it appears they stuck us with 4 spoofs," Augustus said with a nod.

"I guess we can add *The Producers* to the schedule. I'll call the printer so the flyers can be drawn up, sir," Heywood said as he turned to leave.

"Uh, Learner?" Augustus called back to him.

He paused in mid-stride and answered, "Yes?"

"Thank you for your professionalism in this matter…and not rubbing it in my face."

"Yes, sir," he said and exited the office.

Outside, the outcome astonished Heywood. A smile crept across his face and he chuckled to himself, then a puzzled glance registered in his eyes. Something didn't sit right with him about this unusual turn of events. He had some investigating to do.

"You have done well today, Walker. Since it is now 5 pm, you are relieved and can go home for the evening." Sonyai said to Robin.

He had just finished some checkouts while Tommy watched from the returns side. Ethel emerged from the office, followed by Gerry moments later to take their stations.

"If it's all right with you, ma'am, I'd like to stay to observe how things close here."

"Suit yourself. I have matters to attend to. Report back here tomorrow at 2 pm *sharp*."

"Yes, ma'am."

The senior clerk walked into the back office for a moment, came back out wearing her winter coat, and exited the premises. Tommy remained in the middle of the small area as Gerry stood beside him at the returns counter and Ethel stood in front of the terminal for checkouts.

Everyone stood at a corner of the tiny space.

"You got a problem, Lucky Charms?" Robin glared at Tommy. Ethel chuckled at the joke.

"How's about I knock that mouth of yours right off your fat ugly face?"

Gerry and Ethel each let out "oooohs,"

Robin grinned. "Yeah, right. I've dealt with jerks like you."

"You *know nothing* about guys like me! I'm smarter than you and better than you'll ever be!"

"Well, you just *stay* better than me then, jerkwad, 'cause this will be as far as you go! I'm just passing through! I'm going to breeze through school and graduate in 2 more years, then blow this popsicle stand and move on to bigger and better things! I'm going to Seattle and develop software for Microsoft! Work my way up the corporate ladder and buy out the company from Bill Gates himself! By the time I'm 30, I'll be the richest man on this planet! And you'll still be *here*, being the best you can be!"

The three clerks were stunned speechless by the youngster's powerful tirade.

"Whatever," Tommy said flatly and then left to retrieve his coat, walked around the desk, and exited the branch. He found Sonyai outside waiting for him, smoking a cigarette. The pair walked together toward Lexington Avenue, leaving 58th Street behind them.

"He's a piece of work. This could be a serious problem," Tommy began.

"Indeed," Sonyai answered.

"His arrogance makes me more eager to take him out, the obnoxious punk!"

"Don't take this personally, Thomas. Your anger can betray you, make you lose focus."

"Yes, ma'am. I don't intend to."

"I have a personal errand." She lit a cigarette and took a draw. "Give Sarah my best."

He nodded and walked across Lexington Avenue to the Queens-bound N and R subway entrance.

Gerry, Ethel, and Robin stood at their separate corners behind the circulation desk, still quiet from the earlier outburst. It was fifteen minutes till closing.

"Zoology?" Robin quickly asked.

"591.03" Gerry answered.

"Damn! You're good for someone who hasn't put away a book in eight years!" Robin exclaimed. The pair shared a laugh.

"She as good as you?" Robin nodded to Ethel.

"Naw," Ethel replied. "In my day we didn't say call numbers. They were Dewey decimals. And I've long since forgotten them by now."

"So, Microsoft, huh? You reaching for the stars there, computer genius."

"Windows 95 will change the world, Gerry. Bill Gates is an innovator."

"Uh-huh. What about Steve Jobs?"

"Who the hell is Steve Jobs?" Robin asked.

Gerry rolled his eyes. "Okaaaay. Next question then, computer whiz. Why the library?"

Robin shrugged. "Why not? When I was 9, my grandfather brought me to Fort Washington for the first time and I saw all those books. I was amazed by the place. I developed my reading skills early. It was my favorite subject. Schools were the only place I thought you could get books, so I told him when we left I wanted to go to the library to learn, as my new school.

"He laughed and explained it wasn't a school. It was a special place where anybody could borrow books to read for a little while as long as they promised to bring them back. I didn't believe in such a place until we were walking home. When we got back, I looked up and asked him, 'What do they call the people that work in that place?' He said, 'They're called librarians.' So I said, 'That's what I wanna be when I grow up, a librarian.'"

Gerry and Ethel reflected on the touching story for a moment in silence.

"That's…just a load of crap, right?" Gerry asked.

Robin smiled. "Yeeeaaah, when I was 9 I wanted to be an astronaut, but that's what I said at the job interview so, here I am."

That brought a gasp of laughter from Ethel while Gerry shook his head and smiled. "You know what, man? You all right." He stepped forward and held his hand out. Robin slapped him five with his left hand.

He noticed and pointed. "About that now, how'd you get Sonyai to let you keep that glove on?"

"We really going to have a conversation about fashion while you standing there looking like you from a junkyard in Watts living with your father?"

Gerry blinked hard while Ethel laughed again. It was her turn to slap Robin five at the quip.

Angie Trueblood walked to the center of the room and announced, "The library will be closing in 10 minutes. If you have any materials you wish to check out, please do so now."

Gerry and Ethel snapped back to attention as the patrons lined up in front of Ethel while she processed their items for borrowing.

"C'mon, funny guy! Lemme show you how to work the cash register," Gerry called to Robin.

"Architecture?" he asked when next to him.

"You know, it was cool at first, till you dissed my clothes."

"Aww, c'mon! Just one more…"

"720.02," he answered with a sigh.

"Damn!" Robin exclaimed.

THE UPPER EAST SIDE WOMAN'S Center was located at 63rd Street between 3rd and 2nd Avenue. Sonyai ignored the closed sign and entered the clinic. There was no receptionist, so she locked the door behind her. The lights were off except for one lit examination room where she found Janelle sitting on the medical table and an elderly European woman possibly of Russian descent.

Janelle was quiet, looking down at her bare feet, wearing a white hospital gown.

"How are we doing here?" Sonyai asked with a smile.

"She's 7 weeks. Conception dates back to about mid-January." the gynecologist said.

"Oh God," Janelle whispered.

"We do ultrasound end of April to determine sex of child," the gynecologist explained in broken English and a rough accent.

"Don't worry, Janelle. We will get through this."

"She can get dressed in next room now."

Janelle stood up and left the room. Once the two adults were alone, the doctor asked, "You sure you wish to charge *your* insurance for her care? If employer finds out, they will charge you for fraud."

Sonyai nodded. "I understand the risks. Put all her medications in my name and file the claims."

"She will show soon. She cannot hide this forever," the doctor warned.

Sonyai turned to Janelle as she returned holding her backpack in front of her. She sighed heavily and said, "I will deal with it."

Tommy entered his one-bedroom apartment at 93rd Street off Rockaway Boulevard in the middle of Ozone Park. He sighed at the thought of today's events. The stress evaporated once he gazed upon his wife, Sarah. At an even seven feet tall, Sarah Gonzales-Carmichael was teased in school over her height. The other students called her Big Bird because she also had brown curly locks that resembled the fabled character's fluffy hairstyle.

She was wearing a white apron on top of a blue New York Mets T-shirt and gray sweatpants in front of a busy four-burner range preparing dinner. At four and a half months pregnant, his wife looked radiant to Tommy as he wrapped his arms around her from behind and gave her a small peck on the cheek.

"Dinner will be ready in 10. Wash your hands, mister," Sarah ordered.

He gave her a lingering bear hug and went down the hallway to the bathroom. Ten minutes later, the two were sitting at the kitchen table.

"How was work today?" she asked.

"This penne a la vodka is incredible, hon'."

Sarah frowned. Tommy always talked about the food when he didn't want to discuss work.

"Thank you. Anything going on at the library I should maybe know about?"

"What kinda vodka did you use to thin the sauce? Is it Stoli?"

"Smirnoff, and if you don't tell me what's bothering you, I'm gonna break the bottle over your head!"

Tommy knew she actually would. "We got a new part-timer, some college student with a chip on his shoulder the size of Shea Stadium. He took Nelly's spot before she could finish school and get the promotion, so now Sonyai and I are making it our mission to make the kid transfer someplace else."

"Wow," was all Sarah could say.

"Yeah, I know," he replied.

"Y'know, it's really not fair treating him like that because he's new. Everybody has to adjust to new situations all the time."

"He's not one of us."

"But he could be in time. What if they did that to you when you started there?"

"This time it's different."

"How?"

"It just *is*! Look, we have a nice tight-knit staff, and he's a loose thread sticking out. We're not trying to get him fired, just to move along."

"But—"

"End of discussion, Sarah."

They continued to eat in silence after that, but Tommy knew the discussion was far from over.

TWENTY-ONE WAS at 21 West 52nd Street in the heart of midtown Manhattan. In the days of prohibition, it served as a speakeasy known for its celebrity clientele. Inside the restaurant, a mysterious female benefactor was sitting at her favorite table opposite Augustus, who was finishing his steak tartare.

"I can't remember the last time we had dinner together, Gussie."

He cringed at the sound of his pet name. "Well, my dear, I have so little time."

"Oh, I understand. But it seems you only woo me when my charitable donations make the newspapers."

"I'm hurt you'd think that!" he said in mock disappointment.

"I'm just kidding! You know I'd do almost anything for you!" the woman said with a chuckle.

He took a moment to sip on his glass of water.

"Tell me, though. If my family donates thousands to the library already, what difference does it make if I contribute alone to one particular branch?"

Augustus knew this was coming and had prepared his speech. "The percentage our branch receives on general contributions is very minimal. There are 82 libraries spread among the 3 boroughs we serve. Some needier than others. There are branches located so remote they see only 30 patrons a day."

She nodded while sipping on her daiquiri as he continued.

"Ours is sophisticated, equipped to serve the public to the fullest extent possible…provided we continue to receive occasional acts of goodwill. As an influential institution in today's society, it would honor us to reciprocate any help called upon whenever such a benefactor would require us to in *any* way, shape, or form."

Augustus could sell ice in Alaska.

"In layman's terms, if I scratch your back, *you'll* scratch mine." A coy, seductive smile grew across her glossed and bright red lips.

"Exactly," he replied soothingly.

"And would such…*back scratching* be required of me tonight, perhaps?" Her hand caressed Augustus' right hand to emphasize the innuendo.

The librarian wiped his brow with a napkin and smiled. "Ahem, well, let's see where the night takes us, shall we?"

ZELDA LIVED in a co-op on the corner of 21st Street and 3rd Avenue a few blocks away from Gramercy Park. She unlocked the door and entered her living room, then took off her coat and locked the door behind her.

With a flick of a wall switch, two lamps filled the interior with some much-needed luminescence to reveal a uniquely decorated apartment. Zelda opened a closet, hung her coat on a hanger, and tucked it inside. After walking to the kitchen to pour a glass of wine, she sat on a lazy chair in the middle of the living room. She took a long sip and let out a relaxing sigh of relief, then reached for her cordless phone and dialed a number.

"Hello, Charles? Zelda Clein here. Thank you for arranging that *accident* in the video library. I owe you one."

There was a pause as the caller asked her a question.

"Why? I guess to teach those two a lesson. Augustus has terrible taste in movies, and Heywood will learn how to beat him at his own game if he ever learns to check his temper. And besides, I found none of his movies funny. He may be one of us Jews, but Mel Brooks's sense of humor is warped. Thanks again, Charles."

She hung up the phone and took another sip. "*Blazing Saddles...* hah, puah!" she said with a pretended spit on the floor in disgust.

The Pig 'N' Whistle was an Irish Bar not too far from 58th Street and a frequent after-hours spot for Heywood to drown his sorrows while chewing the fat with the friendly bartenders, always ready to lend a helpful ear.

"...and turns out, the only copy of the damn movie gets torn up somehow in the video library!"

Heywood and the bartender shared a long and loud bellyaching laugh. As he finished a beer, the bartender replenished his glass.

"That's a helluva story."

"Yeaaah, it is, izzn't?" Heywood said, his speech very slurred from the libations. "But there's one...one thing that's been buggin' me."

"What's that?"

"This morning, I...ca-called the video library...to double check that all possible selections were available before we picked 5...and they said they were present and counted for."

"So?" The bartender replied.

"So...don't ya think it's kinda weird, the exact tape in question gets sabotaged at the last minute?"

The two share a moment of silence to reflect.

"Ah! You're thinking too much into things!" the bartender dismissed, stepping away to tend to another customer.

"Maybe!" he yelled to his back. "Or maybe I got me a guardian angel…" he murmured to himself and took another swig of his beer.

At 111 Wadsworth Avenue was a thirty-two-story high rise apartment complex, one of the four iconic "Bridge Apartments" that stood mere blocks away from the George Washington Bus Terminal and the infamous suspension bridge itself.

Robin entered apartment 16D at seven in the evening. He lowered his book bag next to the door. The living room was dark and lit only by a television playing the local Fox 5 news moments before *A Current Affair* would come on.

To the left of Robin was the kitchen and on his right was a writing desk, followed by the hallway leading to one of the two bedrooms in the apartment. At the opposite side of the living room, in front of the windows tending to a series of house plants of different sizes, an elderly gentleman wearing a house robe stood with his back to Robin. He reached over to the light switch and flicked the lights on and off twice in order to gain attention without startling his deaf grandfather and announce his arrival.

At the age of seventy-seven, Jon Walker had seen it all but had been a while since he heard any of it. A retired track worker for the MTA, Jon worked the underground tunnels of New York City's subway system for over twenty-five years. He began losing his sense of hearing when he was forty-seven but continued working for ten more years until he retired despite becoming completely deaf at fifty-five.

When Robin was six, his mother left him to be raised by Jon in hopes a male influence would change his developing destructive behavior. She was right. The two overcame a communications gap in which Robin learned sign language, and by the time he was thirteen, he had become a disciplined teenager exhibiting multiple talents and creative hobbies.

"You are late, young man!" Jon signed to him.

"I'm sorry, I stayed an extra hour at the new job. Today was my first day," Robin signed back.

"There're some french fries in the oven. Heat them up for 10 minutes. You have any homework?"

"Just my paper for Basic Writing. I have a draft already done."

"Good. I want to proofread the final copy when it's finished before you hand it in."

"Yes, sir."

Robin walked into the kitchen and turned the oven to 425 degrees, then returned to the living room where Jon was sitting in a recliner under a tall floor lamp reading the latest copy of *Reader's Digest.* As he approached the TV's cable box to change the channel, Jon protested with a grunt.

"Leave it."

"But you're reading…"

"I *said* leave it!"

Robin rolled his eyes and took a seat on the couch. A moment passed, and Jon closed the book.

"How's this new library you're at now? The staff friendly? Like up here?"

With a shrug, Robin replied, "You could say that." But to himself he thought, *I wouldn't, though.*

There was no point having his grandfather worry about him not fitting in.

"Can I please change the channel now?"

"Oh, go ahead!" Jon signed with a wave of annoyance.

Robin stood up and changed the channel, then returned to the kitchen and poured a plateful of fries from a pan in the oven. He opened a cupboard for the salt and sat back on the couch. Jon noticed Robin failed to get a fork and was eating with his hands but let him be.

"Don't let this job distract you from your studies. You think you can pull this off? Going to school while working part-time?"

"I think so. I have a feeling I'm going be there for a while," Robin signed to his grandfather and smiled as he raised a fry to him in a friendly salute.

CHAPTER FOUR

TANYA BROWN WAS IN RARE FORM TODAY. THE TEENAGER HAD A reputation for disrupting class at Park West High School. As she sat in her classroom for Social Studies, tuning out the teacher's lesson about the Civil War, a plastic straw she appeared to be chewing protruded out of her mouth.

"Well, Miss Brown, since I appear to be boring you with my lesson today, perhaps you can tell me who Robert E. Lee was?"

A smile grew across her face as she stood up to address the class. "In Kansas, Robert E. Lee formed the Lee Mercantile Company... around 1889. They started with jackets and dungarees until 1920 when he developed a remarkable invention called the zipper fly..."

She stuck out her waist and gestured to her zipper on her pants for effect, then continued, "...thus coming up with the overalls, then moving on to the jeans we wear today! We remember Lee now with the distinct commemoration of..." She reached behind and tugged, with an astounding rip she presented a leather patch associated with the brand of clothing, "His very own patch. Thank you! You've been a great audience!"

The class erupted with applause and the teacher stared open-mouthed at the inaccuracies of her speech.

After eating lunch in the middle of fifth period, Tanya arrived at her locker and found a note inside. A puzzled look crept across her face as she opened the folder paper and read.

I heard in second-period math class from Tenshia's friend who overheard that Vickie Florence is out to get you because Johnny Jones said he likes you and Vickie likes Johnny.

The run-on paragraph of a sentence wasn't signed by anyone. Tanya didn't know a Tenshia, Vickie Florence, or a Johnny Jones. She crumbled the note with a dismissive shrug, chalking it up to mistaken identity, someone putting it in the wrong locker. She couldn't imagine a boy being interested in her, or a girl jumping her out of jealousy.

Across town at LaGuardia High School, Lakeshia was in music class during seventh period. It was her turn to play a music piece on the piano. An overweight dark-skinned woman with an oversized larynx, Ms. Louis, called Lakeshia up to the stage of the auditorium where the class was being held.

"And what is it you plan to perform for us today, Miss Seabrooke?"

Without answering, she took her seat in front of the instrument and played in the key of B-major. While playing what sounded like a random jazz selection, Lakeshia sang Madonna's "Sooner or Later," a song the class was all too familiar with.

"Okay! Okay! Stop right there, young lady!" the teacher interrupted after the second line of the last verse. The class erupted in laughter as Lakeshia blushed bright red. "I'm not finished!" she protested.

"What is a 14-year-old girl doing listening to Madonna? Such dirty filth!"

"It's from the movie *Dick Tracy*…"

"Lakeshia just said dick!" a classmate yelled and more laughter ensued.

The teacher waved her hands to get order restored. "It's obvious a crush you have, Miss Seabrooke, that inspired this performance, but a child your age knows nothing about 'love' or what you plan to do when you're 'all alone' with someone! I'll give you 85% for creativity, but next time stick to something more classroom appropriate."

The teacher gestured for Lakeshia to step down from the stage. Rolling her eyes, the teen pushed back from the piano and descended the stairs on the left. The rest of the class made fun with catcalls and blowing fake kisses in the air as she passed them.

"GOOD MORNING, everyone. It's Monday, so here are your schedules for the rest of the week."

Sonyai handed out a sheet of paper to each of the clerical staff assembled in the office. "Now, I'm compelled yet again to remind you all that Chavez has implemented a temporary change in the limit of borrowed videos from 2 to 3. Any of his usual 'pet patrons' come to check out an extra VHS tape, override the computer terminal alarm with the password BRAVO-dash-seven."

From his desk, Gerry lowered his copy of the schedule after a quick scan. "With that in mind, are we allowed to *encourage* other patrons to take out an extra video with an off-hand remark?"

Sonyai narrowed her eyes, giving Gerry an icy cold stare. "It would be...*advised* to use discretion when exercising this policy... experiment." She couldn't help but notice his arrogant grin. "They do not expect it to produce any drastic circulation results."

Gerry continued to pry. "Meaning?"

"Meaning the public is on a need-to-know basis, and certain people within the public do not need to *know*!" she exploded.

Gerry stood up with a start. "But wouldn't denying the public knowledge of an experimental change in the circulation rules curb the results in an unfavorable manner and defeat the purpose of said experiment in the first place?" he said in a taunting, singsong voice.

Sonyai was preparing to answer, but Gerry continued.

"Unless...these precautions you are asking of us intend to sabotage said experiment from within because its implementation came from above your head and without your support even through a circulation experiment such as this requires confirmations from *both* branch supervisors?"

"Wow," Sonyai began. "That was a mouthful, Gerry. And just what are you trying to imply?"

"I guess I'm trying to imply that any actions taken by us clerks to counteract said experiment would make it a moot point and make the supervisory staff seem somewhat *obtuse*."

"Well, Mr. Coltraine, if that's your opinion, feel free to reveal the temporary limit on videos to whoever you want." She was tired of playing into his psychological games.

He bowed mockingly. "Thank you. It's so nice to see a senior clerk view a proposed change in policy with such an open mind."

Sonyai gritted her teeth. "I believe there are some new books to process at the checkout terminal on the circulation desk." She chucked her thumb behind her pointing to the door for effect.

Taking the hint, the lanky clerk turned and made his way out of the office. "I'll get right on those, oh exalted one!" he called back behind him. Sonyai turned to Tommy as Gerry left and gave him a slight nod, which he returned with a certain understanding. He waited for Ethel to leave and then approached his mentor.

"If we weren't working to get rid of Walker I'd devise a plan to eliminate *that* upstart off the face of the earth!" she snarled.

"Gerry's just being Gerry…" Tommy scoffed. "He'll keep his mouth shut."

"Yes, well, there are other matters at hand. Mr. Walker has been here for 2 weeks now. He has learned the desk duties and handles himself pretty well."

Tommy gave an unimpressed snort of contempt. "He's okay. I've seen better."

Sonyai scolded. "Don't be jealous, Thomas. You must respect your adversary in order to defeat him." Tommy stood silent and regarded her advice as she continued. "It is time we move to the next step of our plan. Take a look at the schedule."

The clerk pulled out his schedule and scanned it. "He and I are closing every day this week? What gives?" he exclaimed.

With a cold scowl, she whispered three words. "Little. Big. Horn." Tommy raised his eyebrows remembering a painful memory. "Ahh, the rite of passage. I remember when you and Gerry did it to test my will."

"And you learned a valuable lesson in humility and the importance of your fellow co-workers back then," Sonyai replied.

"Gerry and you only did it a day. You expect him to endure the whole week without saying something?" he asked.

"Leave that to me. And, Thomas? No matter how much he pleads, no matter how much he begs, even if the patrons say something…" She let the sentence hang as they both nodded in unison.

"Congratulations on fixing that Mel Brooks festival situation between Chavez and Learner, Clein."

"Why, I don't know what you're talking about, Ethel," Zelda replied, containing her composure.

The pair were upstairs in the staff room drinking tea, sitting on opposite sides of the kitchen table.

"Play innocent all you want, but if you ask me, you did the right thing. *Blazing Saddles* would have been a whole lot funnier if Cleavon Little hadn't replaced Richard Pryor."

Zelda changed the subject. "What is Sonyai doing about the clerical situation?"

Ethel decided not to press Zelda to admit her actions and moved on. "She sees the boy as a threat…"

"Is it because of the page?" Zelda asked deadpanned.

"Uh, which page would that be?" Ethel asked after an awkward silence.

"Oh, come now. Who's playing innocent this time? As women, we can sense these things amongst ourselves like canines hearing a dog whistle."

The two shared another couple of moments, sipping tea in silence until Zelda asked, "Ethel?"

"If you know, how come Chavez doesn't know?" Ethel asked sharply.

"What good would come out of that? Augustus would pull rank and have the girl fired, Sonyai would be more resentful toward him, and the war between the two would only get worse."

Ethel nodded. "Yes…yes it would." A wave of worry flashed across her face.

"He won't be in the dark for long. Eventually, the secret will be out. What is Sonyai going to do then?"

"She has a plan," Ethel began. "When word got out he was coming, she read his profile and did some research. There are no signs of him making a career here. She believes with the right resistance, he'll move elsewhere."

"Just in time for the page's early graduation from high school. Sounds like a good plan."

Zelda was impressed and said, "But I take it there are problems?"

"Sonyai's Plan B was to use her connections in the Bronx to play on the new hire's sympathies, then ask her to transfer. But Walker turned out to be a man."

"She had it all thought out, accounting for almost every scenario," Zelda said, but thought, *Sonyai's extensive thinking would value the branch more if she played on our side.*

"Soon she will come to me for help in her campaign to get rid of this boy—who's done nothing to deserve my wrath—just to save this girl who's thrown her life away by getting pregnant." Ethel slammed her cup in frustration, which startled Zelda.

She blinked rapidly for a moment and then took a sip. "It's a difficult choice. I wish I could help."

Ethel sighed. "Our private conversations are a help, Clein. You're the only one I can relate to. You know when to do the right thing and whether to get noticed doing it." She was referencing back to their earlier conversation.

Ethel stood up and took her dishes to the sink to clean. "I gotta get downstairs. I'm due on the desk at the top of the hour." Ethel left the room, leaving Zelda to continue sipping her tea, wondering how she found out about helping Heywood.

The branch was just opening to the public at noon and Sonyai and Ethel were working the circulation desk. After attending to a few patrons, Sonyai called out to get Ethel's attention.

"Jenkins."

She turned to the supervisor as she continued.

"We've never seen eye-to-eye on issues in the past."

Ethel replied with noncommittal, "Um-hm."

"But I have never regarded you as a threat...just an outsider." The pair stared at each other as Sonyai chose her words carefully.

"I...also have the utmost respect..."

With an exasperated sigh, Ethel exclaimed, "Spit it out, Yi. I'm growing old here!"

Sonyai flinched over the disrespect, but held herself and stepped in close and whispered, "I need your help. There is a sensitive situation with one of the pages."

"Janelle Simms is pregnant," Ethel replied, much to Sonyai's astonishment.

"How did you know?"

"C'mon, Yi!" she scoffed. "People talk and whisper secrets to one another. Nothing gets by me. I'm not blind, I just don't give a damn! You're lucky the bookworms haven't figured things out."

"Which is why we need to act quickly!"

"Whadda mean 'We?'"

"What are your observations on our new hire?"

A smile grew on Ethel's face. "The kid? he hasn't said 2 words to me. He leaves me alone, I'll leave him alone."

"He is the only thing stopping Simms from working a part-time position here!"

"Hey, there was a vacancy, and he was next in line. Why should he pay the price for little missy's mishap?"

Sonyai cringed at the clerk's cold demeanor. "We take care of our *own* here at 58th Street, Jenkins. Her shame is *our* shame!"

The two women exchanged menacing scowls to intimidate each other. Jenkins was armed with experience while Yi countered with determination.

"So you want me to join you and Tommy on your crusade to run this boy outta town for no good reason?"

A wave of concern overcame Sonyai as Ethel asked the question.

Seconds felt like hours until the clerk's scowl turned into a devious grin. "What's in it for me?"

Julia Richmond High School was located on 67th street and 2nd Avenue. Once an all-girls school when it opened in 1923, time had not been kind to the vocational high school, even when it went co-ed in 1967. Vandalism and low test scores took its toll on the institution and morale was at an all-time low.

Janelle sat on a bench in the hallway outside the principal's office. She wore a gray hooded sweater and black sweatpants. As students walked by, she couldn't help noticing a few of them whispering and staring. The principal's secretary opened the door to the office and called Janelle inside.

"Good morning, Miss Simms. So glad you could make it here today," the tall gentleman greeted her. The student took a seat in front of the desk and waited.

"Let's get to it. You have accomplished a rare academic achievement for this school, completing 40 credits worth of coursework an entire semester early!"

"Yes, thank you. I'm very excited," she said with a half-hearted smile.

"Have you made any plans to attend college? You scored 1530 on your SAT."

"I'm exploring my options. I may take the summer off and start in the fall."

"Okay." The principal narrowed his eyes into a piercing stare. "There have been whispers and rumors among the students saying you are...you are" he cleared his throat "—uh, with child."

"Huh?"

"Are you pregnant, Miss Simms?" he asked bluntly.

Janelle's lower lip wavered as her eyes watered. "Yes," she whispered.

The principal closed his eyes and rubbed his forehead with his right hand. "You understand how this changes your life, young lady, forever. A child is a big responsibility, huge even."

"And I will deal with it. I have help, friends, family, a support system—"

"Do your parents know?" the principal interrupted.

Janelle sat silent and looked down in shame.

"I didn't think so." He shook his head. "Well, before we can process you graduating from Julia Richmond, you, your guidance counselor, your parents, and I will all have to convene and discuss this."

She sighed. "Okay."

"Please see the school nurse and be back here by the end of the week. You're dismissed." Janelle stood up and made her way out of the office and back out to the students' leery glances in the hallway.

"Why do you insist on pissing off Yi so much, man?" Tommy asked. The two clerks were working the desk together at one o'clock, handling the normal busy lunch crowd rush.

"I'm just keeping her on her toes. It comes with being the boss," Gerry replied.

They worked in silence for a few minutes, then Tommy said, "So, you and the kid have been closing his first couple of weeks, huh?"

"Yeah," Gerry replied nonchalantly.

"Well, how you'd think he's doing?"

Gerry tensed up at Tommy's question, worrying where was he going with this. "He's doing okay. Checks out the books fast."

"How fast?" Tommy asked quickly.

Gerry nodded and smiled with impressed approval. "He can flow. He's got skills." He then turned to Tommy who was also grinning.

"You think he's fast enough for…"

Gerry gave a puzzled glance at the trailed off question, which was replaced by horror when he remembered the weekly schedule. "Aww, wait! You don't mean?" he groaned.

"Yep," Tommy confirmed with a chuckle.

"C'mon man, he's not ready to go through that yet. And I know you 2 haven't gotten off on the right foot, but—"

"Sorry, man—"

"That tradition is intended to teach trust in your fellow clerk and would only happen if it was ordered by the senior clerk!"

Tommy stared back at Gerry, not saying a word.

Gerry's entire body shook in anger. "Why is Yi doing this?" he hissed.

"I guess she's keeping *him* on his toes," Tommy joked. "It comes with being the boss."

Gerry didn't appreciate the irony of his words used against him and continued to look at his co-worker with shock and disgust.

"Don't worry," Tommy said. "I'll give you all the gory details tomorrow morning." He turned to attend to a patron as Gerry glared at the back of his head.

At two thirty, upstairs in the staff room, the four pages gathered before starting their shift at three. Janelle sat on the sofa while Tanya laid on the other couch, staring up at the ceiling chewing on her straw from class.

Lakeshia sat at the head of the kitchen table in the middle of the room, occasionally glancing at the clock, and Alex was pacing back and forth in front of the counter and refrigerator. Alex stopped and addressed the trio.

"Okay, we all know why we're here. It's time for the shelf reassignments. Miss Yi has elected again to let us come to terms to determine who does what ourselves, so long as we can agree on them."

"Ugh," Tanya grunted from the couch. "Has it been 3 months already?"

"Yessss," Lakeshia chimed. "Remember when we switched in December?"

"Not really, but if y'all say so…"

"Okay then," Alex began. "At this moment, Janelle's doing the paperbacks, children's books, biographies and science fiction. Tanya's doing the 400's through 600's, mysteries, and new books. I'm doing the 000's through 300's, along with the first half of general fiction. And Lakeshia, you're doing general fiction L through Z, the foreign books, and the 700's through 900's."

The girls waited while Alex took a breath and then she continued. "Now, I think we can all agree, with Nellie's situation, it would be right to give her the light load."

The three girls nodded in unison while Janelle glanced down and whispered, "Thanks…"

"So, I think it would be fair to just give her all of general fiction, A through Z. Cool?"

"S'fine," Tanya said with a shrug.

"No problem here," Lakeshia agreed.

Alex sighed in relief. "That's great, y'all. I really appreciate you being cool with that."

Lakeshia looked up at the clock again as Alex continued. "Now, as for the 3 of us, I thought I'd take paperbacks, sci-fi, and mysteries, Leelee can do the new books and children's books, while Tanya takes foreign books and bios."

"What about the numbers?" Lakeshia asked.

"Well, I'd figure we'd split them up again between the 3 of us," Alex replied.

Tanya sprang up from the couch. "I call 000's through 300's!"

Lakeshia turned around to face Tanya. "Hey! I want those!"

"Yeah, Tee. I was kinda thinking about giving those to Leelee," Alex said compassionately.

Tanya scowled and took the straw out of her mouth. "Then what were you gonna give me?"

"Um…The 700's through 900's?"

"What?" Tanya stood up. "Screw that. I *want* them 000's!"

Alex gave her a confused look. "Why?"

"I got all them foreign books. That's fiction and nonfiction in Greek, Russian, Spanish, and Chinese plus I'm doing bios? I deserve those 000's!"

"You were doing them when I first started here back in June, Tanya!" Lakeshia whined.

"Yeah, then they went to Nellie, then me, Leelee's next in line, it's only fair."

"And I got new books!" Lakeshia added. "That's also fiction and nonfiction. That's a lot to do!"

Tanya scoffed. "Leelee, please! We all know Mr. Chavez be working on keeping the new books presentable for the public eye to see. Any page assigned to them is getting a break!"

"Break? Break my ass! If Chavez is making the new books easy for you, why are the mysteries so out of order?" Lakeshia was also standing now. "Y'know, Tanya, sometimes I think you only like to work the numbers because your country-hick ass don't know your ABCs that well!"

Alex moved to get between the two as Tanya gasped at the outburst. "Why, you skinny ass, pencil-necked, matchstick of a toothpick!" Alex outstretched an arm to brace Tanya, who was about to charge at Lakeshia, who was getting into a defensive stance when a moan echoed in the room.

All eyes turned to Janelle, who had been quiet during the whole debacle, a look of disorientation on her face. With a sudden gasp of air, she bowed forward and grabbed a nearby trash bin, placing her head over it. The sound of violent retching nearly made the other three lose their lunches.

Janelle lifted her head and wiped her mouth with her sleeve. She moaned, "That's been wanting to come back up since late this morning."

"Damn, girl…" Alex said. "Check and see if a lung landed in there too!"

"Alex!" Lakeshia snapped.

"Yeah, cuz. That was somethin' fierce!" Tanya agreed.

"Okay, look, it's time to get on the clock. We'll discuss this again later."

Once hearing Alex's dismissal, Lakeshia looked at the clock again and quickly left the room to go downstairs. Alex and Tanya exchanged puzzled glances, then Alex tended to Janelle while Tanya ran out to follow Lakeshia.

Lakeshia walked the floor and stopped at a vantage point among a line of rotating shelves holding paperbacks near the branch entrance where she could secretly watch anyone coming in. She pretended to arrange books and froze when something caught her eye.

Robin arrived, making his way through the entrance turnstile. Lakeshia stared at the young man as he walked his way around to the circulation desk and inside to the clerical office. She let out a breathless sigh when a shadow caught her eye.

"Ohh, I see now!"

Lakeshia yelped in surprise as she turned to see Tanya approaching her. "The checking of the clock, the rushing downstairs, the hiding among the paperbacks. You do got yaself a little crush on that new guy!"

Lakeshia blushed and waved her hands in a panic. "No!...Tha-that's...Nuh...nu...not!"

"Oh, save it! It's all over you like mud on a pig, Leelee!"

Lakeshia grabbed Tanya's shoulder and gritted her teeth. "Tanya, you *cannot* tell anyone!"

Tanya's eyes went wide and she grabbed Lakeshia's left arm and squeezed. "This *country hick* can do whatever the hell she wants to do!"

Lakeshia squeaked in pain as her anger evaporated from her body, then her head sunk into her chest in a sign of defeat. "Please..." she pleaded. Tanya rolled her eyes and released her arm. She blew air from her nose, then sighed. "Okay, okay. Don't go wimping out on me, dang girl!"

A moment passed between them. "Look, just let me have the 000's through 300's and this stays between us."

Lakeshia fought back tears as her eyes watered. "That's really not fair, Tanya," she said still looking down.

Tanya lifted the youngest page' chin up to face her. "*Life* is not fair, Lakeshia," she said with a wink.

Sonyai and Ethel were sitting at their separate desks in the clerical office when Robin walked in. He took off his coat and book bag and put them on the usual shelf.

"Mr. Walker!" Sonyai called out. "It has been two weeks since you started. I believe we agreed you would put up your belongings in a locker upstairs."

"I'm sorry, Miss Yi. I haven't found a combination lock yet."

"If you insist on using a locker, please do so in the next few days." She looked at the clock. "You're quite early today."

Robin rolled his eyes. "Just eager to serve, I guess," he sarcastically replied. The senior clerk didn't appreciate the flippant reply and stood up from her desk to scold the young man.

"Oh, Walker?" Ethel called out, freezing Sonyai in her tracks.

Robin turned with a hesitant glance at Ethel. In the fourteen days he'd been working at 58th Street, she'd barely said anything to him. "Um, yes, Jenkins?"

"Could you run back out and get me a Diet Pepsi? I finished a salad and I'm very thirsty."

Out at the circulation desk, Gerry did a side glance, eavesdropping on the conversation. A sinister grin grew across Sonyai's face.

Robin was lost for words. "Umm, you want me to do *what*?"

"Go back outside, cross the street, and get me a soda from the newsstand," Ethel instructed.

Robin turned to look back at Sonyai, who stared blankly back at him. There was a moment of total silence in the room. Ethel still had her back toward Robin and the middle of the room. He stared at the back of her head, dumbfounded and shocked so stiff he was unable to move.

Ethel turned around and faced the clerk. "You're still standing there, sugah," she said with a coddling tone.

Robin took a moment to think about the proper response to the request. He stammered uncontrollably. "Um, Uh…I can't get you a…soda…"

At that moment, he wasn't standing in the clerical office of the 58th Street Branch Library. He was in a small one bedroom apartment at 1535 University Avenue in the Bronx. He was five years old, wearing tattered clothes standing in the middle of the living room. "The fuck is my can of Miller Lite, boy?" a woman's voice echoed in his head.

Robin looked down to see a white beer can on the floor in a pool of brown liquid seeping in the carpet. "You better not have dropped it, boy!" the voice bellowed. He heard heavy footsteps approaching and fear overcame him.

"I...I, um, don't know the neighborhood that well..." Robin said, bringing himself back to the present from the childhood memory.

"Oh, so you mean to tell me you don't wanna get me a soda because you don't know this area that well? Is that what you're telling me?" Ethel asked.

Robin continued to stammer as Ethel stood up to make her way out of the office. "Okay, Mr. Walker, you don't have to get me a soda. I don't want you getting lost in the neighborhood because you've only been here, oh what, 3 weeks? And still don't know your way around... Don't trouble yourself another second, Mr. Walker. I'll go outside and get me one myself..."

"It's just that...I...no! I can't get you..." Robin blurted out.

She was walking past him and through the doorway, still talking. "Gee, I hope I don't get lost while I'm out getting my soda. It's a big a scary world out there, Walker, you know!"

Robin could only stand there despondent, his face red from embarrassment. That terrifying childhood memory that could only have been triggered by the unusual request left him jaded. He left the clerical office to go upstairs and rest his nerves in the staff room before his shift started, leaving Sonyai smiling to herself in his wake.

"Now, Mr. Coltraine, I trust you understand how important positive relationships are with the public?"

"Yes, sir, I do."

Gerry was sitting in Chavez' personal chair inside the librarian's office. Chavez was wearing a charcoal gray suit with a tan dress shirt as he paced around the clerk. Each step of his suede Italian loafers echoed in the small room as the pair continued their discussion.

"So little incidents like that one you had with that young lady several weeks ago where you raised your voice and humiliated a patron over a fine dispute…are *not* to happen again, right?"

"Mr. Chavez, sir," Gerry began. "It wasn't my…"

"*They will NOT* happen again, correct?" Augustus bellowed.

Gerry bit his tongue. "No, sir," he replied.

"This is not the first time you and I have had this conversation. Your antics with the public over the years here have made you *quite* the nuisance in this branch." Augustus stopped pacing to face Gerry, looking down at him as he sat. "And I have tolerated you only because of your experience."

He took a pause as Gerry let the remark set in.

"You are the only one I could trust to supervise the clerks in the event that something should *happen* to Sonyai."

This caught Gerry's attention as he looked up at Augustus with a surprised and flattered glance. "Sir, I had no idea you saw me with such regard. I believe we can help each other. I am planning—"

The librarian slammed his fists on his desk. "Don't let it go to your head, Coltraine! Any more incidents with the public and I'm recommending you to repeat the PR seminar. You understand me?"

Gerry cringed in fear. The thought of enduring the public relations seminar a second time shook him to his core. Augustus stepped back and gathered his composure. "That is all." The clerk took a moment to catch his breath, then left the office, hoping not to return for another discussion.

Alex, Tanya, and Lakeshia gathered in an isolated corner among the shelves on the library floor. The trio decided to make another attempt without Janelle present, hoping to come to an agreement.

Lakeshia gave a sheepish look toward Tanya, then turned to Alex. "Alex, look, I was thinking. I don't want the 000's if it's gonna be that much of an issue."

"Why the change of heart, Leelee?" Alex asked with a confused look.

"Who cares!" Tanya interrupted. "Leelee gets the 400's through 600's and I get the 000's. Problem solved!"

"Whoa! *I'm* not doing the 700's through 900's! There's no way!"

Lakeshia sucked her teeth, "Oh, c'mon!"

"Yeah, what gives?" Tanya added.

"Hey! I don't have to explain anything—"

The girls got agitated once again when a new voice entered the conversation.

"Ah, the things I miss as a page."

All heads turned as Robin walked toward the group. Lakeshia smiled nervously for a moment before she noticed Tanya glancing at her with a smirk. Alex stared coldly at the new arrival.

"Or *don't* miss," he said with a smile.

"This is *none* of your concern, Walker," Alex began. "We can handle our own problems."

Robin ignored the page's tone. "I couldn't help overhearing. For someone trying to be discreet, you 3 talk very loudly. This is a library after all," he added with a chuckle. He took a moment to read each of their faces. Alex was cold as ice while Tanya was nonchalant. He couldn't help noticing Lakeshia unable to hold a glance at him.

"This was a predicament I had to go through myself, so I figured I'd offer my help. Oh, and please, call me Robin. Using my last name is expected from clerks and librarians, but pages are left to their own devices." *Were they even aware of the P.O.C.?* he wondered.

"Sorry, *Walker*. We don't need your help!" Alex said.

"Yeah, no offense, cuz, but we don't know you from a can of paint!" Tanya added.

Robin looked at Lakeshia for her two cents, but she remained silent. Robin's smile disappeared. Their reactions truly hurt him, but he was persistent. "I'm giving you a chance to get to know me now," he pleaded.

The girls thought about his offer as he continued. "When I was a page back at Fort Washington, we saw the clerks as bullies. They would push us around and pick on us like we were in high school because they could get away with it!" The speech seemed to hit the mark with the girls.

"I don't want y'all to see me like that, like one of *them*." He backed away and lowered his eyes with a defeated sigh. "But I guess if you want nothing to do with me," he said over his shoulder while turning away, "I'll understand." The girls exchanged looks as he took a few steps. Sympathy got the best of them and Lakeshia reached out to call Robin back.

"We're having problems agreeing on new shelf assignments," Alex said before Lakeshia could say anything. "Any insight you can give us...we'd appreciate."

Robin's face brightened as he celebrated his small victory. He turned and approached the young ladies as they explained with further details of their predicament.

CHAPTER FIVE

GERRY STARED COLDLY AT THE BACK OF ETHEL'S HEAD AS SHE performed a few checkouts as they approached the end of the hour. Once they had a moment to themselves Ethel said, "You can be pissed all you want, Coltraine. The kid's on my shit list and that's final."

She didn't even turn her head to face him. He was about to reply when the door to the clerical office opened. Sonyai walked around the circulation desk and headed toward the exit turnstile where Janelle was waiting for her while Tommy walked over to relieve Gerry.

Robin emerged from the bookshelves on the main floor and walked around to the checkout side to face Ethel.

"You are relieved, *Miss Jenkins*," Robin said sharply.

She regarded the youth with a hard look that lingered as he stared back emotionless. She then made her way past him and left the branch. In the final hour before closing, the tension was thick enough to be cut with a chainsaw. The two adversaries would tend to their clerical duties and then resume engaging in a stare-down contest. Neither of them said a word.

After a half hour, Tommy broke the silence. "I know what you're doing, just so you know. It won't work."

"What won't work?" Robin asked.

He looked out and nodded toward the shelves. "Helping out the pages, tryin' to get on their good side? Looking for acceptance? They'll see right through you for the phony you are!"

Within the shelves, not too far from the circulation desk, Lakeshia peeked out from around a corner. Being called a phony hurt, but Robin refused to give Tommy the satisfaction of getting underneath his skin. The argument was broken up by an incoming phone call to the main line. Robin noticed that the information desk was vacant, with one of the information assistants helping someone on the floor, so he reached behind and answered the phone next to the checkout terminal.

"58th Street Branch Library," he answered into the receiver. After he listened for a moment, a puzzled look came across his face. "May I ask who's calling?" he asked. He then gave Tommy a smirk and held out the phone. "It's for you," he taunted.

Tommy approached and snatched the phone out of Robin's hand. The young clerk smiled and put up his hands playfully, then walked away to give some privacy, checking in some books on the other side. A few moments later, Tommy hung up the phone and the two changed places to their original stations. A huge grin was on Robin's face.

"What's so funny?"

"That was your *wife*?" Robin asked with a chuckle.

"Yeah. So?" he replied defensively.

"Hey man, it's cool, just surprised is all. I think it's nice, you being a family man and all. You seem so young, I was kinda ready to make that commitment myself at a very early age. Everyone said I was crazy."

"At a very early age? What? When you were 12?"

Robin squinted at the insult, then smiled again. "Plus, all this time I thought you were gay. The hair and attitude were strong signs of, you know, sugar in the veins."

"What?" Tommy exclaimed.

Zelda shushed Tommy from the information desk as patrons looked up at the break in silence. Out on the library floor, Lakeshia and Tanya giggled to themselves while Alex rolled her eyes.

Embarrassed, Tommy fired back a glance at Robin, his face was crimson red. Robin returned with a non-apologetic look as he shrugged his shoulders. The two kept to themselves for the rest of the shift.

At ten before six, Zelda approached the middle of the branch and announced, "The library will be closing in 10 minutes. If you have any materials you wish to check out, please do so now."

Robin prepared for the outgoing rush while a sneer grew across Tommy's face. He handled the checkouts at a remarkable speed, but the line of patrons on his side grew. Five minutes went by and the line was halfway to the middle of the branch while he worked furiously to keep up.

Tommy stood at his terminal, watching the frenzy. Robin turned and called out, "Uh, I could use a hand here since you're not doing nothing but watching me!" Tommy folded his arms and held his post. Robin got the message. He was on his own. He nodded to himself and continued to work the checkouts as fast as he could.

The clock went past the hour. Zelda had to man the front door, allowing people to leave but blocking others from coming in since the branch was technically closed. The pages stood way behind the line with their coats on, impatiently waiting as Robin worked every checkout as the line grew shorter.

He weakly whispered to Tommy, "C'mon man! Help me…please." Tommy had already deposited the branch funds and printed out the day end receipts from the cash register, still refusing to help.

By six fifteen, he completed the last patron's transaction, and Zelda locked the door. Robin's shirt was rumpled and unkempt. He was exhausted as if he was in the middle of finals week. He put away the lightpen and turned off the computer terminal. The pages made their way to the exit as Zelda let them out.

Tommy put his coat on and walked around the circulation desk, leaving without saying a word. Robin slammed his fists on the desk then ran to grab his coat and book bag from inside the office. After putting them on, he stormed out behind him.

Tommy was walking away from the branch when the door flew open and Robin ran out on to the sidewalk calling back to him, "Hey! What was *that* all about, man?" Tommy stopped and turned to face the angry young adult as he continued. "Look, despite all the shit between us so far, in front of the public we're supposed to help each other. It's a professional courtesy!"

"Maybe at the Candyland branch where you're from, but you're in the big leagues now!" Tommy barked back.

Robin was furious. He had had enough. "You fuckin' asshole! It's time to teach your bitch ass how we roll uptown!" He dropped his book bag and took a fighter's stance.

Behind him at the library entrance, Zelda closed the window curtains, locked the door, and ran inside with a worried look.

Tommy chuckled to himself. "Whoa, you kiss ya mama with that filthy mouth?"

"No, but I kissed your wife with it last night, motherfucker!" Robin yelled back.

That got his attention. Stunned at first, Tommy clinched his fist, roared, and charged.

Robin continued, bracing himself for the telegraphed blow. "But I only kissed the bitch on her cheek 'cause she was too busy sucking my—"

Tommy socked Robin square in the jaw, leading in with his right. Robin expected the punch and turned just in the nick of time. The punch felt like a light slap instead of a thunderous hit.

Robin leaned back with the expected attack and countered with a fast right hook to Tommy's breadbasket. He howled as all the air exhaled out of his lungs and his knees buckled. Robin then let gravity do its work as Tommy collapsed in a crumpled heap, hitting the concrete hard.

He then unloaded a series of kicks at his back and solar plexus, followed by a perfectly placed heel to his shoulder blades. Tommy did his best to block the barrage but to no avail. Something about his attack, it was too thought out and calculated, as if Robin had self-defense training.

The pain almost got the best of Tommy, but he found his opening and caught the foot of one of Robin's kicks and twisted with all his might. With a yelp of pain, Robin jumped back and tried to assess his ankle.

Tommy got up with barely the strength to stand and put all his energy into embracing Robin in a massive bear hug. He locked his hand around his wrist and squeezed into the small of his back, then lifted him up in the air and slammed him down with a satisfying thud.

Robin had felt as if he was just tackled by Lawrence Taylor. His ribs ached and his breathing was becoming difficult, Tommy was now pounding fierce blows on top of him, but they were landing on his forearms as he blocked to protect his face. His mind was racing, thinking of an escape plan. He got desperate and brought his knee up hard with a low blow to his scrotum.

The two broke away putting space between them when a siren sounded and flashing lights filled the dark street. Tommy was in no condition to run, but Robin feared what an altercation with the police would lead to. So against his better judgment, he did what came naturally to him. He ran.

As the two police cruisers arrived from opposite ends of the street, they found only Tommy collapsed on the sidewalk. Robin had already turned the corner at 58th and Park Avenue, running north when several officers exited their vehicles. Two were in pursuit behind him but he had a decent head start. He couldn't go that far, his body was already breaking down. After darting around another corner, he circled back to Lexington and turned past 59th Street approaching 60th.

The street was filled with pedestrians who were startled as the youngster sped past them. Not looking back, knowing the police were still after him, Robin had one shot at escape—the subway. There was an entrance on the side of Bloomingdale's and he bolted for it.

"Stop! Police!" he heard a voice cry out.

Robin vaulted down the flight of steps. He bent his knees as he landed and rolled his shoulder into the tile wall. Pain shot down his arm like lightning as he continued down the second set of steps. Pushing his way through a group of people, he ran through an electric gate someone buzzed open out to the train platform.

"Hey! Pay your fare!" a token clerk yelled from the booth as a police officer still giving chase came down the steps. Without checking, Robin leaped on a departing train just as the doors were closing and took a seat in a corner away from any windows. The last thing he heard as the train moved was someone pounding and kicking the metal doors and glass, screaming at the top of their lungs.

Once a moment went by to catch his breath, Robin noticed the train was in the tunnel in between stops for a while. He looked around puzzled. He was unfamiliar with this subway line.

"Hey," he asked a gentleman sitting across from him. "What train is this?"

"This is the R-train. The next stop is Queens Plaza," the man answered.

Robin's eyes went wide. *Queens? Oh shit!* he thought. He had never traveled to Queens before. Only once to attend a Mets game when he was twelve. He checked his watch—it was almost seven in the evening—then fished into his pocket for some change.

"Just hope he's driving tonight," he whispered to himself. His breath was getting shallow, certain he had at least two cracked ribs and a dislocated shoulder. With the adrenaline wearing off, it was only a matter of time before going into shock. Hopefully, it wouldn't be too late. That Cervantes would be on duty tonight.

"Sir, can you tell me your name? Do you require medical attention?" The officer spoke slowly and clearly in order to be understood. Tommy was sitting up on the sidewalk as a trio of police officers canvassed the area. Two were out of breath and frustrated after coming up empty.

Tommy looked up at the fourth cop, still dizzy and humiliated after getting his ass kicked. "My…my name is Thomas Carmichael. It's March 8th, 1994. The president is Bill Clinton." He had been through the process of being questioned for head injuries in the past.

"Do you know the kid you were fighting against? Do you wish to press charges?"

"We had a mutual disagreement, officer. A debate on sports teams.

I didn't even know him. He just followed me from the bar up the street," Tommy lied.

He knew what to say to police in order to de-escalate a violent situation. "Well, all right, then," the officer began. "We're still gonna have to file an incident report. Can you walk? You need a ride to the hospital?"

Tommy attempted to stand on one bended knee and it gave under pressure. "I...uh, might need a ride home, sir, that's all. My wife can patch me up."

The cop waved his hand for help from the other officers. "Why do I think this ain't the first time you've been in a fight, son?"

Tommy just smiled as the three men gingerly helped him to his feet and walked him to the back of one of the cars. In the back, he tried to assess how severe his injuries were. He couldn't help be impressed by how Robin handled himself. *He's definitely going to be a problem,* he thought, before passing out.

At eight thirty, Augustus was startled awake by the ringing of his telephone. He already knew who it was before he answered because only a select few had his home phone number. "Damn it, Zee!" he barked into the receiver. "I have a 6 am meeting with the 84th District Assemblywoman in the Bronx. This better be important."

"Gus, there was a fight in front of the branch between Robin and Tommy." Zelda was deadpan with her tone and she called him 'Gus,' something she only did when it was serious.

He sat up in bed. "What?"

"It happened after closing. The kid couldn't handle the final rush of patrons checking out. Tommy didn't provide any assistance. It's their hazing ritual again."

"That goddamn fire-breathing bitch!" he spat.

"I called the cops and got the hell outta there! They didn't even see me as I locked the door and left. They were wailing on each other like those tight-wearing kooks on the WWF!"

"Damn them if they got arrested! What it'll do to our image! All right, I'll make a call to the 18th Precinct. Did any of the pages see the fight?"

"No. Only the two of them, you, and me know. I doubt they'll tell anyone about it tomorrow."

"Good, keep this under wraps. I'll see you when I come in." He then hung up the phone, picked up the receiver again, and dialed.

After a moment of the phone ringing, a voice answered. "Midtown North Precinct."

"I need to speak to the desk sergeant. Tell him it's Gussy. I'll hold."

Robin walked off the R-train at Queens Plaza and looked around. His breathing was improving but it was still shallow, his legs were buckling as if made of rubber. He walked up a flight of steps to the upper level, which was still underground but gave the rider an opportunity to walk to the other side of the platform to take the train back to Manhattan.

Rather than take that chance, he exited upstairs to the street. Luckily there was an elevator for wheelchair passengers. Once outside, Robin found a pay phone and deposited two quarters, then dialed.

"Liverty Cab Service. Where you need a pickup?" a voice answered.

"I need medallion number 2Y68 for a preferred customer pickup," Robin gasped, he was getting dizzy, shaking his head to focus.

"What's ya ID Number?" the dispatcher asked.

"338. Is he driving? This is an emergency!"

"Hey, he ain't no ambulance. If you've been shot and you're bleeding, take a fuckin' bus!"

"Just send him to the Queens Plaza R-train station, and hurry!"

"Alright, alright! 2Y68 pickup at Queens Plaza Train Station, Preferred Customer 338, on the way." He heard a click and a dial tone before he could thank the jerk.

Robin hung up the receiver and leaned against the wall. *This would be a lousy time to get mugged,* he thought. His head was pounding, and his vision was getting cloudy. "If I don't die tonight, Granddaddy's gonna kill me," he whispered to no one.

His knees were giving away again, and the pain from his shoulder was intensifying. He saw black and white specks in front of his eyes.

Just before blacking out, Robin heard a screech of car brakes and a familiar voice calling out his name.

THERE WAS nothing more dangerous in the world than a five month pregnant woman in a bathrobe standing in front of an apartment building with an eighteen inch frying pan in her hand. Tommy was over an hour late from work without even a phone call.

Sarah Gonzales-Carmichael clenched her fingers on the handle of the frying pan, imagining what dumb excuse she would hear on why Tommy didn't come straight home after work. In five years of marriage, she had put up with a lot, especially those first years when they were still in college.

In the last two, however, Tommy had come around and there were rules established, by both parties, in order for respect to be paid. Rule number one: no coming home late without a phone call and a good explanation. Still looking up the street, Sarah didn't notice a police car pulling up to the building until the door had opened and Tommy emerged from the back seat.

"Oh my *dear God*!" she screamed and dropped the frying pan.

"Hi, honey…" Tommy called out as the police escorted him up to the entrance.

"Um, ma'am, is this your husband?" an officer asked.

"Of course he is, *la hada*! Just because he's white he can't be married to a Puerto Rican? Geez, baby, look at you! You look like Stallone at the end of Rocky! What the hell happened?"

The two officers gave her a stern look as Tommy waved them off. "I'll tell you upstairs. Go inside. Watch how you talk to these guys, huh? What the hell were you doing with that frying pan? Were you gonna klunk me?" He turned toward the cops as she headed toward the entrance. "Thank you, gentlemen. Sorry for all this. I'd like to forget the whole thing, really. No need to press charges or find the kid. Just a misunderstanding, y'know?"

The two exchanged glances. "Well, we have your contact

information and we'll be in touch if anything comes up. Possibly the same guy fighting someone else in that neighborhood..."

Tommy chuckled. "I seriously doubt that, officer. You have a good night."

"YOU DROPPED THAT CAN, boy! Can't you do anything right? No, worthless little bitch! You clean that mess up right now! I'm going to beat your ass bloody with the belt, you hear me? Give me your arm! I'm going to spank your little fat legs right now!"

"No!" he cried out. "No, mommy! Don't hit me anymore. I won't do it again, I promise! Mommy, no! No! Not my hand, mommy! No! NO! NOOO!"

Robin gasped and opened his eyes. He felt the vibrations of a moving car beneath him as he lay in the backseat of a vehicle. In front of him was a glass divider with a small flip door for cash payments. The driver was a dark man wearing a brown tweed peacoat and a matching brown beret with a plaid pattern.

"Cervantes?" he called out hoarsely.

"Welcome back to the world of the living, young traveler! God smiles upon you as you have returned from the great abyss."

"Ugh, not the God talk tonight, please," Robin begged. "It's been a rough night as it is."

The cab was just crossing the 59th Street Bridge back into Manhattan. For the last eighteen months, the man Robin only knew as Cervantes had been driving for Liverty Cab Service twelve hours a day, six days a week. He arrived in New York City from Ghana, then became a citizen and had been sending whatever money he could to his family in hopes of one day bringing them over to the United States.

Robin and the immigrant met when two carjackers attempted to rob the driver and Robin alerted some nearby police officers. The cabbie expressed his gratitude by offering a lifetime of his services for free. Robin always used public transportation to maneuver throughout the city but occasionally he would take him up for a ride when it was available.

Al Green was playing on the radio. Robin moved to sit up but thought against it when the pain from his shoulder shocked him back to reality.

"Don't take the FDR uptown!" he yelled. "Take the West Side Highway, I wanna see the bridge as we come in."

"You're the boss," the cabbie replied. "I believe you have a separated shoulder, my dear boy."

Robin stared up at the ceiling as the streetlights streaked by the window. "Granddaddy'll fix it. How long have I been out? What time is it?"

"A little after nine," Cervantes replied. "Still want me to head to Riverside?"

Robin knew his grandfather went to bed at ten, but wouldn't dare go to sleep without knowing where he was in the city. He felt light-headed again. He didn't remember when, but before passing out, as he was looking out the night sky, he sighed "Yeah."

"YOU HAVE a small fracture on your collarbone, massive spinal trauma, your left kneecap is shattered, and you have a bruised diaphragm. If I didn't know better, I'd say you've been kicked by a mule and trampled on by a bull."

Father Carmine "Steely Eye" Steele was a medic in the army during the Vietnam War. Due to the atrocities he had seen, he heeded the call from God and became a priest at Saint Mary Gate of Heaven. Tommy instructed Sarah to call Father Steele, and he arrived within the hour. The priest wrapped his shoulder and bandaged his knee, but his resources were limited.

"He needs rest and something for the pain. If I had a prescription pad I would suggest some methadone and buprenorphine, but I'm out of practice."

"Don't worry, Father," Tommy said lying in bed. "I got somebody for meds too from my college days."

Sarah shook Carmine's hand. "Oh thank you, thank you for coming, Father! I'll take good care of him from here. Expect an extra pie for the next bake sale at St. Mary Gate of Heaven."

"Bless you, my child," said the priest with a smile and a nod as he turned to leave.

Once the couple was alone, Sarah turned to Tommy...and she was no longer smiling.

"S-Sarah, before you get started, let me explain..." Tommy begged.

Sarah screamed a tirade of frenzied Spanish profanities that Tommy did not understand. He just rolled his eyes and let her vent.

"So? Don't you have anything to say?" she asked.

"I had a *minor* disagreement...with the new guy at work."

"*What*? You had a fight with that, that, that kid? He sounded so polite and respectful on the phone! 'May I ask who's calling?' I mean, who talks like that? What did you do, Tommy?"

"Why I gotta be doing something? Don't you think *he* coulda had something to do with the start of the fight?"

Sarah leaned down and applied pressure on Tommy's shoulder. He howled in pain and squirmed in agony. "Thomas. Connelly. Carmichael," she hissed under her breath. "You tell me right now what happened or Father Carmine will be back here to perform your Last Rites."

"Alright! We're testing the kid. It's an initiation! He got mad because I didn't help him out when he had a long line of people at closing time! It was Sonyai's idea! Sonyaaai!"

She stood up and folded her arms as he sighed in relief. "Initiation? You know who has initiations? Gangs! These days, kids gotta run up on someone in the street and slash them in the face with boxcutters to get in. Is that the behavior to act in a goddamn library?"

"Look, we'll discuss this tomorrow. I need to get some sleep so I can go back..."

"No way, José! You are taking tomorrow off to recover!"

"Sarah! I can't call in sick! I'm already off Wednesday! They have a schedule to…"

"I don't wanna hear it! You are staying home the next two days and that's final, *cabrón*!" She turned to leave the bedroom.

"Hey, I know what that means, I'm *not* an asshole!" Tommy called back. "Where you goin'?"

She stopped at the doorway. "I'm sleeping on the couch tonight!" She then slammed the door behind her. "And *cabrón* means dumbass, you…dumbass!" she yelled from the hallway.

ROBIN COULD BARELY TURN the key in the lock when he staggered into his apartment. To his disbelief, the lights and television were turned off as the living room was pitch black and silent.

He dropped his book bag near the door. *Unbelievable! It's after ten!* he thought. He limped to the hallway on the right leading to the two bedrooms and found his grandfather sleeping with his bedroom door wide open. Robin staggered to the foot of the king size bed and sat on the corner.

Jon felt the shift in weight on the bed and woke with a startle. He reached for the small lamp on his nightstand and when the light came on he gasped, "Robin! What the hell happened to you?"

"Had some fun after work," Robin signed.

Jon pulled his blanket off and came around to inspect Robin's injuries. "Shoulder is separated. Lie back and hold still…"

Jon straightened Robin's arm as he lay flat on the bed, then bent his arm up at the elbow.

"*Relax!*" he ordered.

He grabbed Robin's wrist and pulled the humerus back under the shoulder blade with a slow muffled pop. The youngster grunted in pain as his eye shed a tear.

"Don't you fucking *think* of crying on me, boy!"

Robin gritted his teeth and shook his head in a stifled affirmation.

"There, try to move your arm."

Robin did as he was instructed and tested the arm's movements.

"Good. Take off your shirt. I'm calling cousin Esme, see if she can send Pepsi down here to look you over. If either one of them ain't home, we're going down to Presbyterian at 168th and Broadway."

"It's 10 at night! Can't I sleep it off?"

"No, your eyes are dilated, your face is swelled up, and you have bruises on your chest and back. It's a miracle you're still standing."

"Okay, but let me call. It'll take you a while to type everything on the titty."

"Don't call it that! It is a TTY machine that allows me to communicate with people on the telephone! It is *not* to be mocked!"

Jon reached over for the telephone and threw it on Robin's lap. He picked up the receiver and dialed.

After looking sheepish, he signed to Jon, "I'm sorry."

"Hello?" a voice answered.

"Hi, Esmerelda? It's Robin, downstairs."

"Boy, have you lost your mind? It's 10:15 at night!"

"I'm sorry, cousin, but is Pepsi there? There's been an...emergency."

"Robin Walker, you are 18-years-old and *still* getting in fights in the street? What is wrong with you?"

He thought about responding but sat silent.

A sigh of exasperation echoed on the line. "I'll send him down. His shift doesn't start 'till midnight. He woke up and ate breakfast 30 minutes ago. Tell Jon he owes me one. Soon, I'm going to take payments for his visits outta your ass!"

"You're best, cuz!" Robin said and hung up the phone.

"Pepsi'll be down here in a bit," Robin signed back to Jon.

"Good."

"Why didn't you wait up for me? For all you know I coulda been dead."

"You grown now, and besides, I was tired...and I still am! Let Pepsi in and make yourself a peanut butter and jelly sandwich. Close my door behind you!"

"Yes, sir."

Robin grabbed his shirt as Jon got back under the covers. He closed the bedroom door behind him and went back to the living room. *Nice to know you care*, he thought.

At a quarter to eleven, the apartment doorbell rang. Robin opened the door and a short gentleman wearing blue hospital scrubs under a brown three-fourth leather coat walked in.

"Rockin' Robin! What'cha got yourself into *this* time?"

"It's a long, long story," Robin said with a sigh.

Matching the family's fair-skinned complexion, cousin Pepsi sometimes passed for white with his pointed, chiseled nose and straight black hair. Some believed his descendants trace back to the French, who came to the states and settled in Louisiana before the purchase.

The nurse lived with his mother, Esme, a few floors higher than Jon and Robin and had been tending to either one since finishing medical school in 1991. He worked the second shift at the Allen Hospital ER that just opened at the northern tip of Manhattan on 220th Street and Broadway.

"What is that on your face? You've been eating peanut butter? Sit down here and let me look at ya…" After a few minutes of examining Robin, Pepsi asked, "So, the other guy got his licks as well?"

"Mmm-hmm. Bolo would be proud," Robin answered, wiping his face with a paper towel.

"Still with that kung-fu shit, eh?"

"Hands are registered lethal weapons," he joked.

"Riiiiight. Well, okay. I feel two cracked ribs, and you likely have a concussion, severe head trauma. Without an X-ray, I can't be sure, but I'm guessing there's some swelling of the brain. Any dizzy spells, loss of balance?"

"Yeah."

"Then you should take your ass to the emergency room—"

"Not happening."

"Of course! Why should you do the right and logical thing? Fine, I got some painkillers and I'll fix you a compress to get the swelling down. But promise me *one* thing—do not lie down. Sleep sitting up tonight. If the blood pools in the back of your head, you'll have a hematoma and fucking die. When the swelling goes down, your sensory functions should come back and the vertigo will go away. I'll patch up the ribs, make sure not to aggravate them again or they'll never heal. I'd go to school, but skip the job if I were you."

Robin remained silent.

"That quiet response tells me you're still going to go to work and act like nothing happened. Well, I did my best. I gotta go, the 1-train is running shitty tonight. Some track work being done. Check back with me in a few days…if you live." Ten minutes later, the nurse was gone.

Robin turned out the lights and walked to his bedroom. The door leading outside to the terrace opened with a metal scraping groan. Sixteen stories up, Robin could see the western part of Washington Heights. He stared at the George Washington Bridge. He had been passed out when Cervantes drove north approaching his neighborhood and missed watching all the lights outlining the giant gray structure.

As a child, one of his favorite books was *The Little Red Lighthouse and the Great Gray Bridge* by Hildegarde H. Swift, which taught him the importance of even the smallest of individuals. There was a small foldable lawn chair on the wall near the entrance. Further down were the two windows of Jon's bedroom.

The sounds of city traffic echoed beneath him, lulling him to sleep like an urban lullaby. He unfolded the lawn chair and propped himself up with a few pillows behind his back, then closed his eyes. *Bolo would've been proud*, he thought again.

THE BAKERS WERE JUST PULLING out a fresh batch of bagels from the oven at Dunkin' Donuts on 56th and 7th avenue. NYPD Desk Sergeant Carl Weller was meeting with Augustus in a small booth at four in the morning. The streets were deserted as the librarian sipped his coffee trying to wake up.

"Kind of living into the stereotype, aren't we? Cops in a doughnuts shop and all that."

"You prefer we do this in my precinct, with all those surrounding officers asking questions?"

"I see your point," Augustus replied.

"I can put a lid on this, but we lose face over the kid getting away. They're gonna do a sweep around the area and ask questions of your staff. Make sure he's nowhere to be seen when they arrive or I can't help with what happens next."

"Understood."

"Shouldn't warrant too much attention after that, I'll see to it. We're done here?"

"It appears so." Then the two men stood up and shook hands. "I'll see to it you get your copy of *Debt of Honor* when it's available."

Weller smiled. "Have a good day, Gus. Keep your nose out of trouble." As he left, a baker behind the counter handed him a box of fresh doughnuts with a friendly salute.

ZELDA WALKED into the Famous Famiglia Pizzeria on 169th and Broadway at ten thirty in the morning. The place was tiny, but there were a series of tables for dining in. A stout elderly woman with short gray hair wearing a purple sweater and black slacks was eating a bacon, egg, and cheese breakfast stromboli. Zelda approached the table and took a seat.

"Heavy breakfast there, Babs. I can practically hear your arteries clogging."

"We all can't eat like a bird, Zee. You just make it seem easy."

Zelda ignored the smart remark and gave Barbara Schemanske a hard look.

"What kind of hot-tempered individual did you send to my branch, Barbara? Walker just had a fight outside our door with another clerk last night!"

"The boy has rough edges, but I trained him right!" Barbara replied. "From what I hear, your senior clerk, to put it lightly, is acting like a cunt. She's going about her little page problem all wrong."

"You know?"

"*I know everything!*" the elder bellowed. "And I demand respect for doing so."

Zelda gulped over the admonition.

"Walker is but a pawn in the elaborate scheme of things. It's no coincidence he was sent there at that precise moment in time."

"You saying what I think you're saying?"

"I'm saying that if I know Chavez by now, the investigation into what happened last night is quietly being dismissed. You have nothing to worry about, Zelda, and you should be thankful I agreed to this meeting. But know this, Sonyai Yi is treading on *very* thin ice. Her favoritism and secrets will soon see the light. She may keep Augustus at bay, but she won't have a snowball's chance in hell against me. So the next time Robin Walker acts out in *your* branch, take your grievance with her and not me."

Zelda stood up and made her way toward the exit.

"And, Zelda?"

The woman turned to face her adversary.

"*Don't* call me Babs."

ROBIN WOKE up out on the terrace in the lawn chair at the sound of a car horn's long beep. There was a city bus blocking the box in the middle of the crosswalk at 179th and Wadsworth.

Routine traffic jams in the city, he thought.

He stood up and walked around, testing his footing. His sense of gravity had returned and the headaches were gone. Once inside and washing up in the bathroom, however, the blemishes on his face were still grotesque and noticeable. The left side of his face was still puffy and he had a black eye, a swollen lip, and a gash down one of his eyebrows.

After painfully washing his face, brushing his teeth, and taking a hot shower, he emerged from his bedroom in a fresh set of jeans and a polo shirt. He walked into the kitchen to see Jon eating breakfast in the dining room. After slipping on his glove, he poured a bowl of cereal and reached in the refrigerator for the milk.

"I finished the milk," Jon said instead of signing.

Robin closed the refrigerator door with an annoyed grunt and brought his bowl of dry cereal to the table and sat opposite Jon. They looked at each other so Jon could read Robin's lips rather than signing while eating.

"You still look like hell."

"Thanks."

There was a moment of uneasy silence.

"So, you don't wanna know what happened?" Robin asked.

"You told me. Work."

Robin slammed both palms on the table. Jon flinched, startled by the outburst.

"First, you go to bed before knowing I'm home and now this! Don't you care anymore?"

"I was tired! I haven't been feeling well lately…"

"Why haven't you said anything? I'm still concerned about you, despite the contrary."

"It's nothing to worry about! I'm just getting old. And so are *you*. I don't care what they did to you, there's no reason to be starting fights! I raised you to defend yourself, but you're acting like you're still in elementary school!"

That struck a nerve with Robin. He looked down and sighed. After another moment of uneasy silence went by, he looked back up. "Granddaddy?"

"Yes?"

"Why doesn't she love me anymore?"

Jon sighed. "Robin we've been over this. Your mother is busy managing your sister. Ver—"

"*Don't say her name!*" he interrupted.

"Sorry! What brought this on?"

Robin shook his head. "There's a co-worker…She reminds me of her," he said, thinking of Ethel.

"She wasn't the one…" Jon began.

"What? No! You think a woman did all this?" he said pointing to his face. "I just wish she'd call or something. I haven't heard from her since my high school graduation. I really think she wants nothing to do with me."

"Son, your mother loves you. She put you in the best hands. Now go on, you gon' be late for class."

Robin finished eating, stood up, and put his spoon and bowl in the sink. He put his coat on and grabbed his book bag, then left the apartment. At the table, Jon began to wheeze violently under shortness of breath. His hands shook as he closed his eyes and concentrated. A minute passed and he began breathing normally. The tightness in his chest subsided. He wiped a tear from his eye. He hated keeping secrets from Robin. He reminded himself to make an appointment with his doctor.

CHAPTER SIX

TANYA WAS ON HER WAY TO SCHOOL, RIDING THE 2-TRAIN SHE boarded from her stop at 149th Street and Grand Concourse. She was lucky to get a seat, considering it was ten minutes after seven in the middle of morning rush hour.

After crossing into Manhattan and arriving at 125th Street, Tanya looked back at the previous car and noticed someone pushing their way toward the door leading to her car. She stood up and moved away, pushing past several riders. The door to her car opened and Vickie Florence stepped in. She had two other girls behind her.

A short stump of a teen, at five-foot-three and two hundred and seventy-five pounds, she was wearing a red North Face mountain guide jacket with black shoulder pads. Her two taller friends were both skinny and wearing matching gold and green puffy supreme jackets. The trio scanned the car. "I know I saw her on here," Vickie whispered.

Up ahead, Tanya glanced at the subway map. She had at least five more stops until she could transfer to the 1-train at 72nd Street. She thought about getting off the next stop and waiting for the next train, but that would make her late for first period. The door opened and the three girls entered, Tanya stood between two boys on the far left side as the train filled up with many standing riders.

She faced the train doors with her back to the center, fished out a ski cap and put it on her head. Vickie passed by without as much as a glance toward her as the girls moved on to the next car.

Tanya sighed in relief and one guy who had provided her cover turned his head and asked, "They lookin' for you?" She blushed and nodded. "You better be careful," he said. "She had a piece in her left pocket."

Sonyai walked inside the clerical office to find Gerry and Ethel sitting on opposite sides. Gerry was writing notes in his small notebook and Ethel reading the sports section of the *Daily News.*

"Where's Carmichael?" she asked.

"Not here yet," Gerry replied.

Did he get his days off confused? she thought. The phone rang and she walked out to the circulation desk to answer it. She looked up at the clock and noticed it was nine fifteen.

"58th Street Branch Library," she answered into the receiver.

"This is Sarah, Tommy's wife. Is this Miss Yi?"

"Yes," Sonyai replied with a concerned look on her face.

"Tommy won't be coming in this morning. He's…sick. I apologize on his behalf for the inconvenience, ma'am."

"Uh, it's no problem. We'll make due. Is he all right? May I speak—"

"Thank you so much for understanding," Sarah interrupted. "You have a nice day."

The phone clicked, followed by a dial tone. Sonyai hung up the phone stunned.

Gerry walked out and asked, "Everything all right?"

The senior clerk stammered, "Y…yes, um, Carmichael will not be in today. He's out sick. The three of us will have to manage…I will close tonight with Walker." She walked to the desk schedule on the wall to make changes, then made a mental note to talk to Zelda. *What the hell happened last night?* she thought.

"I called you two in here for a quick pat-on-the-back at the great job you're doing. Everything's going smoothly." Augustus was all smiles this morning, this latest crisis behind him. Angie and Heywood were standing in the librarian's office exchanging pleasantries at the rare show of praise from the supervisor. *Something is amiss,* they both thought.

"Now then, on to business. Angie, I'd like to you to teach Heywood how to do the patron reserves."

The pair exchanged worried glances. "O...kay, umm, does this mean you're reassigning?" Angie asked.

Augustus scoffed, "No, no, no. Even though you never take time off, Angie, I feel Heywood needs to learn how to process the reserves so when he moves on to another branch, he'll be able to handle all tasks required of him."

"Does this mean a position has opened somewhere?" Heywood gasped with excitement. "Or eventually will?" he added.

Angie gave Heywood a weird look.

"Hmm...Not that I'm aware of," Augustus said dismissively.

Crestfallen, Heywood began to ask a follow-up question.

"That will be all. Thank you very much," the librarian announced, concluding the meeting.

Angie and Heywood walked out of the office toward the information desk. "Any idea what that was all about?" she asked.

"None whatsoever," he replied. He sat in front of the terminal while she took the seat on the right that faced him.

"Do you have a problem showing me how?" he asked.

"No, not at all. It's just that I've grown accustomed to doing them since I've been here. You've been here three years and they never showed you?"

"Nope."

"Well, I never needed a backup. I scatter my vacation time over the entire year. I'm never gone more than two days at a time."

Heywood shrugged. "Okay, long as we're both cool with it." She shrugged and nodded in agreement.

ROBIN WALKED out of his writing class a few minutes before ten and headed toward the study hall. Despite getting a few stares from his classmates, he heard the teacher for his algebra class was out today, so he laid low to not draw any more attention to himself.

He approached the threshold and froze. Sitting inside was the Japanese girl from the train. She was a student at Baruch! Studying and writing notes, she was wearing a teal blouse and a white skirt with stockings. Her hair was tied up into two short pigtails that edged her shoulders. Robin hid back against the wall before she noticed him. *She can't see me looking like Quasimodo!* he thought. He backpedaled, praying that no one yelled his name. And as if on cue, he heard someone scream "Robin! Is that you?"

Gillian Bascomb ran down the hallway waving at Robin. She caught up and gasped when she looked at his face. "Whoa! What on earth happened to you?" At five-foot-nine and two hundred pounds, the Guyanese student wore amber glasses over a pair of emerald green eyes.

Robin grabbed the woman's arm and pulled her over to the nearest staircase. "What is it, Jilly? My dream girl is in the study hall and I'm all tore up. She can't see me like this, and here you are yelling my name in the hallway—"

"It's Walter. He wasn't in class this morning. Didn't you notice?"

"No. So what? He probably slept in."

"I think he could be in trouble. He seemed upset last night, getting plastered at McSwiggan's. I think it's another breakup."

"So? You and Kim go check on him. You know where he lives. Why you telling me?"

"His roommates would never let us in. You need to go!"

He rolled his eyes and sighed.

"He'd do it for you, Robin," she pleaded.

"Okay, fine. But do me one favor..." He nodded toward the study hall. "Ask the name of the girl sitting in the far back corner."

Gillian walked back out and looked inside for a second. She shrugged and turned back to him. "She's not there."

"What? No!" He looked for himself. The room was empty. "Dammit!" he hissed.

"YOU GONNA GIVE the boy a hard time again today, Jenkins?" Gerry asked Ethel. The two were working the circulation desk together as the branch opened its doors at noon.

"Don't you worry 'bout what I do, Coltraine. You just keep to yourself and mind your own damn business!" Ethel snapped.

He stepped to her, only an inch away, towering over her. "I'm not looking for a fight, but I will *make it* my business if you don't leave him be."

She looked up at him, her eyes defiant with fire. The unstoppable force versus the immovable object.

"You been down this road with me, Ethel. You know you won't win. I can make things uncomfortable for you when I put my mind to it."

"You don't scare me, Coltraine."

"That's because you haven't seen me at my *darkest,* Jenkins. I ain't the one to mess with."

"You told me before to know which side I'm on."

"That's right," he answered.

"Well, you know which one I'm on now."

The two remained quiet for the rest of the hour. It was clear now that the lines were drawn.

"Okay Heywood, this is the reserves index." Angie pulled out a small box full of postcards as Heywood sat next to her. The two were using the clerk's backup terminal in the corner of the clerical office for their lesson. Sonyai sat at her desk behind them, ignoring the pair. It was rare, but information assistants were welcome to use anything in the clerical office as long as they kept to themselves.

"As you know, when someone requests a book, as long as it's not on the New York Times Bestsellers List, they can pay 40 cents for a self-postage postcard that doubles as a request form." She pulled out a blank postcard with a flourish for emphasis.

Heywood interrupted, "The request gets logged in the system and they initiate a search routine. Yes, I know. You're telling me all this with a condescending tone, Angie."

"I'm not being condescending! Who's being condescending?" she asked.

"Look, if you feel too attached to…"

"I'm *not* being condescending! I have no problem showing you how to do this!" she shouted.

"*Ahem*!"

Heywood and Angie turned to see Sonyai giving them a scornful look. Heywood waved his hands. "Okay, okay. I'm sorry," he said to Angie. "Continue."

Angie nodded and typed a few keys on the terminal to bring up the library catalog search database, selected RESERVES and typed in a sample request for *The Chamber* by John Grisham.

"Once the search routine finds a checked-in copy of a title, it's sent here with a special flag to let us know it's for a reserve. We then…"

"See! There it is again!"

Angie slammed her hand on the desk, "What are you talkin' about?"

"You're annoyed! I can hear it in your voice!"

"You don't know what you're talking about!"

"I don't want to do this if it's going to piss you off!"

"It is *not* an *issue*!" Angie screamed.

"*Yes, it is*!"

"You're delusional!"

"*Enough*!" Sonyai yelled, startling the pair. "If you two cannot do this *quietly*, you must do it someplace else *at another time*!"

"My apologies on behalf of my colleagues, Miss Yi!" a voice replied.

Augustus was standing at the entrance to the clerical office with his arms folded giving his two IA's a look of disapproval. "I believe the reserves lesson can wait until cooler heads prevail." He stepped aside and held his arm out, gesturing for Heywood and Angie to leave. Sonyai narrowed her eyes at her adversary and then turned back to the work on her desk.

ROBIN APPROACHED the building on 2nd Avenue between 27th and 28th street. Baruch College had limited student housing resources, but most of its students were native New Yorkers and residents of the city's surroundings.

Walter was sharing a four bedroom apartment with three other students on the top floor of a two-story brownstone. He walked up to the separate entrance and knocked on the door.

"Please don't let it be Jacques. Anybody but Jacques..." he whispered.

The door opened and a six-foot-one tall slim individual with blond hair wearing black tights and a matching turtleneck stood in the doorway. Robin detected the stench of Limburger cheese and cigarette smoke as Walter's French roommate Jacques Sartre greeted him.

"Monsieur Robin, to what do we own the honor of your presence today?" he asked with a heavy French accent.

"Hello, Jacques. Coming in to check on Walter. He missed class this morning." He attempted to step inside, but the Frenchman impeded his way.

"I'm afraid he is indisposed at the moment. It would be best to return at a later time."

Robin was in no mood for these games. "Jacques, take a good look at me. I had a rough time last night. I nearly *killed* a man. Move aside or today becomes just as much fun as yesterday!"

Jacques shook his head. "Americans," he uttered underneath his breath and stepped aside to let him in.

Having visited Walter before, Robin headed to the second bedroom on the left side of the living room down the hallway. He knocked on the door. "Walt, it's me Robin. I'm coming in..." He waited for a minute, then said, "you fucking better not be naked in there," and waited some more. He then turned the knob and walked in.

The room was around six hundred square feet. It could serve as a modest studio apartment in New York City if it had a kitchenette along with a toilet and bathtub. The room was dark with the shade drawn on the sole window. There was a bed, a dresser, a writing desk, and a TV tray on wheels holding a twenty-one-inch television set.

A radio was playing "Nothing Compares to You" by Sinead O'Connor, and there were empty bottles of various liquors scattered on the floor. Robin found a slim floor lamp and turned the gold knob in the middle that activated a dim light to the ceiling. Sprawled out on the twin bed, lying on his stomach, Walter snored loudly as his head hung over the edge of the left side.

Robin walked around and sat next to his shoulder, scanned the floor, and picked up an empty bottle of Jack Daniels. Across the room was a metal garbage can with a picture of Garfield the cat on it. Approximately six feet away from the bed, the object was an intimidating target for amateurs.

He looked down at his classmate and flipped the bottle with his right hand. Spinning in the air, the bottle landed effortlessly in the can and shattered with a loud crash. Walter woke up with a startled gasp.

"Surprise! Avon calling!" Robin yelled.

"What the hell, man?"

"Yes, what the hell, indeed."

"Yo, not that I would mind, but how?"

"The mime let me in."

"That damn french fry." He pulled his head up and looked at Robin. "Whoa! What happened to you? Mike Tyson use you for a punching bag?"

"Long story. What happened to you? Jilly said you were getting drunk at Swiggy's. They didn't card you?"

"Bartender's my cousin…by marriage. She fuckin' left me, man."

Robin rolled his eyes and noticed Walter was slurring his words. "Walt, Walt, Walt." Robin had always been Walter's confidant after a breakup. He knew the drill.

"No, I mean it, maaaan…She was the one. She was it, man…And don't tell me it don't happen. Look what happened to you! What was her name? Delilah? Denise? Desiree?"

"Diedre," Robin replied somberly.

"Yeah, yeah, yeah. That was her name!"

"Look, Walt, you got to get your head back into your studies. We got finals coming up and you coasting as it is."

"Yeah, yeah, yeah, yeah…" was all Walter was saying until he giggled uncontrollably. "Y'know, you *look* how I *feel* right now," he said and then resumed laughing.

Robin stood up and grabbed him off the bed and stood him up. "Okay, it's time for you to sober up, then I gotta get to work." He escorted Walter out of the room.

The two entered the bathroom and Robin sat Walter on the edge of the bathtub, turned his legs and feet up on the rim, and then nudged him in.

"Hey!" Walter cried, moving the shower curtain.

"Sorry," Robin said with a deadpan tone as he switched the tap to shower. "I saw my mystery girl again when I was called away to come check on you. She was in the study hall. I thought you would get me a name. What happened?"

He turned a knob as he sat on the toilet seat cover and the shower started. Walter howled in agony as scalding hot water sprayed down on him. Robin winced and turned a second knob to add cold water to the shower. "Oops…" he said. Walter woke up and came to his senses. He reached up, turning off both faucets.

"Okay, you've made your point," he growled at Robin.

He looked back and smiled. "So glad we had this talk. Get me a name, get over whoever-the-hell, and get your shit together or you'll be retaking Basic Writing next term!"

Robin got up just in time to see Jacques approach the bathroom door in response to the scream. He pushed the French national back against the door hard as he walked past him to leave. Jacques responded with a tirade of French obscenities that Robin ignored.

"The principal said he has to meet my parents by Friday before I graduate early. He's heard rumors about…" Janelle trailed off and started sob.

Sonyai hugged the page as she cried on her shoulder, "There, there, shh…" she coddled. "You knew this day would come, child. It is time, and I will be there beside you."

The two were upstairs in the staff room sitting on the couch. She only had half an hour before she was due to relieve Ethel and Gerry when Robin arrived at two.

"I…I don't think I can do this," Janelle said. "My parents are real strict."

"It won't be that bad. They will understand."

"What if they don't? What if they kick me out of the house?"

"We will worry about that later. Think positive. Your parents love you, Janelle." A wave of comfort overcame the child as the elder's words echoed in the room.

"We will tell them tonight," she instructed.

"Together," Janelle replied.

"Together," Sonyai confirmed.

She stood up and smiled, then composed herself and walked out of the room. Once the door was closed, Sonyai's face turned to a look of regret and concern over what was to come from this revelation.

Robin walked into the library to a gasp from onlookers at his grotesque features. He smiled and strolled in proudly like a prizefighter who went the distance. Holding a brown paper bag tight in his fist, he went around the circulation desk, approaching Gerry and Ethel. Robin stopped in front of the female clerk who had intimidated him twenty-four hours ago. He pulled a small metal can out of the bag, then slammed it on the counter beside her with a start.

Sonyai emerged from upstairs through the staircase door and froze at the sight of Robin staring Ethel down.

"Here's your Diet Pepsi." He then looked into the clerical office, then out and around the entire room. "Where's Carmichael?" he asked mockingly.

Sonyai approached. "He called out sick today."

Robin gave a soft guttural chuckle that chilled the trio of clerks. "*Pussy,*" he hissed, then walked into the clerical office to hang up his coat and bookbag.

Ethel picked up the can of soda with a trembling hand and walked past Gerry and Sonyai. Gerry looked past and over her shoulder toward the entrance when a pair of uniformed police officers walked in. He tensed up as they approached the returns side of the desk to address the senior clerk.

"Excuse me, ma'am. I'm Officer Byron and this here's Officer Roven. We're doing a follow-up to an altercation that took place outside of here last night and a suspicious individual may have just come in. Have you seen someone who looks like he's been in a fight? He would have marks on his face or a broken nose."

The officer's eyed Gerry and Sonyai closely. Gerry snuck a glance to the threshold of the office to see Robin hiding behind the door in the sliver opening where the hinges were.

"No one matches that description, officer," Sonyai answered. The senior clerk had ice water in her veins. Not so much as a flinch betrayed her as she lied to the authorities. Gerry couldn't help but be impressed. She could stare down the reaper without batting an eye.

The two white cops looked him up and down, prepared to ask him, but then Augustus appeared, all calm and welcoming. "Gentlemen, may I ask to what sort of *altercation* are you investigating? Because I assure you, such an inquiry is unnecessary. Perhaps it would be wise to check with your precinct?"

Officer Roven put his hand on Byron's shoulder. "You're right. We're done here," he said with an authoritative nod.

"You all have a nice and pleasant day," Byron said with a salute as they both left.

"Yeah, right," Gerry uttered under his breath.

Augustus snapped his finger and gave him a scolding look. He then approached Yi. "I just saved your necks, dammit! Whatever happened between Walker and Carmichael, you better resolve it *quick*!" He turned on his heels and stormed back to his office.

"Guess that's my cue to come out now."

Robin stepped out from the office, but Sonyai pushed him back inside. She turned to Gerry and whispered, "Cover for us,"

"But I haven't had lunch yet!" he barked.

"Just for ten minutes!" She went inside, closing the door behind her.

"What happened between you and Tommy last night?" she roared.

"Why don't you ask *him*?" Robin replied. "Oops, his bitch ass ain't standing here!"

"Don't bullshit me! I'm not asking again, Walker!"

"I dunno what you're talkin' about! I was mugged on my way home last night. Happened on 181st Street and Saint Nicholas."

Sonyai folded her arms in front of her. "A likely story. I don't suppose you filed a police report to corroborate that what you're saying is true."

He stared back at her. "That's my story and I'm sticking to it!"

"I'm closing with you tonight. I'll sort this out soon enough. You're on checkouts for the next two hours. You so much as look at me the wrong way while I'm on returns, I'll make you wish I gave you up to those officers! Get your ass out there, *now*!"

Robin walked past her and opened the door fast enough to catch Gerry leaping back from eavesdropping and pretend to be working the checkout terminal.

"You're relieved," he said.

"'Bout time. I'm starving!" Gerry said walking out and around through the exit threshold. A moment later, Sonyai walked out to the returns terminal. The two clerks had their backs to each other, neither one giving the other the satisfaction of yielding.

"Whoa! Tommy's called out and Robin looks like a truck hit him. You think something happened after we left last night?" Lakeshia asked as she pushed her shelving cart among the fiction section. All four pages were working amongst the shelves at around three thirty.

"Bet'cha Robin don't look so handsome now, eh, Leelee?" Tanya joked.

The youngest page registered a pout as she stared daggers at her co-worker.

"Good for his ass," Janelle chimed. "He ain't so high and mighty now!"

"Yeah!" Alex agreed and slapped five with Janelle.

"If you'd excuse me!" Lakeshia said, bumping her way between Janelle and Alex, leaving them behind.

"Hey!" Janelle yelled.

"What's up her ass?" Alex asked.

"Forget it. Listen up, I got some crazy bitch coming after me, and she strapped! I didn't even do anything to her. I need ideas how to shake this nut off of me."

Lakeshia stopped her cart near a corner and looked over at the circulation desk. Robin's face looked like an old tattered pitcher's mitt, but underneath the bruises and the swelling, she was still enchanted by him. "Sooner or later, I always get my man," she whispered to herself.

HEYWOOD APPROACHED the center of the floor and announced that the branch would close in ten minutes. Robin prepared for the rush of patrons lining up and processed the checkouts as fast as he could.

This time around, he remained focused, driven even, knowing what he was up against. Sonyai was impressed at the display, but the line extended longer as the top of the hour was approaching.

She moved toward him to help, but Robin waved her away. "No!" he barked. "I can do this myself!"

She flinched but made another attempt.

"I said *back off*!"

She finally stayed at her post and tended to the cash register to tally the day's fines. Robin worked like a blur, and to his satisfaction, he finished the workload a few minutes after six. Heywood and the four pages gave him a round of applause, and even Sonyai nodded solemnly in approval.

He stared back, eyes colder than icicles. They stopped clapping as he walked inside the clerical office. He came back out with his coat on, carrying his book bag, then left the branch without saying a word.

Ten minutes later, Heywood, Sonyai, and the pages were all outside as Heywood locked the entrance door behind them. "Don't know what was wrong with Robin, but you ladies have a good evening." He put on his ski hat and walked toward Park Avenue.

Lakeshia said her goodbyes and ran to a beige 1987 Toyota Corolla that pulled up near the sidewalk. Alex walked to a nearby Lincoln Town Car and was greeted by a tall white man in his late forties dressed in a long gray trench coat. The elder closed the door to the back seat behind her, walked to the driver's side door, entered, and started the vehicle.

"You going to be all right, Miss Brown?" asked Sonyai as Janelle stood beside her.

"Yeah. I'm taking the 4-train home. No problem," Tanya replied with a nervous smile.

"We should go," Janelle whispered as she pulled Sonyai's coat sleeve.

"Okay," the elder replied, and the two walked their way to the corner on Lexington.

Tanya took a few steps after giving the two a head start for privacy when she heard a voice behind her.

"I couldn't wait till they left."

She froze as a short figure stepped out of the shadows.

"Well, well, well." Vickie Florence smiled as she advanced on Tanya. From the corner of her eye, she saw her two friends step forward from opposite directions, surrounding her in a deadly triangle.

"I ain't got no problems wit' you, Vickie. Let's not turn this into an ugly situation."

All three girls were moving closer to their prey. "I think it's too late for that," Vickie said.

Tanya heard three loud, distinct clicks. The stout bully pulled out an orange boxcutter with the blade protruding. The pointed edge caught Tanya's eye as the streetlights reflected off it. Fear took over, locking her feet in place.

"It's gonna get *real* ugly once I cut that face of yours!" Vickie was a foot away from striking distance when a loud and long whistle echoed in the wind, cracking the air like a bolt of lightning.

Officer Roven lowered his pinky fingers down from his lips as his partner stepped from behind him.

"Is there a problem here, ladies?" Officer Byron asked. "This here block certainly has a propensity for violence lately."

Vickie snarled in frustration and flipped her weapon beneath the wrist of her coat sleeve. Tanya took the opportunity to step closer to the officers, seeking protection while waving her hands mockingly.

"Nah, Nah, we cool here, officer. We cool." She let out a nervous laugh.

The trio came together and put some distance between the two cops.

"Yeah, everything's cool, officer." Despite catching sight of the boxcutter, the officers let the girls go their separate ways.

Tanya was halfway down the street when she turned to face them. "Thank you, officers! Um, see y'all at school tomorrow, girls!" she said with a wave and disappeared around the corner.

"Yeah!" Vickie called back. "See ya!" she said giving a wild-eyed look.

THE QUEENS COLLEGE of the City of New York was located in a remotely residential neighborhood of Flushing. Angie sat in an auditorium classroom among forty other students in a stadium seating arrangement. Up front, the professor had been addressing the class for the last hour as he took a sip from his glass of water and resumed his lecture.

"Aristotle stated that a play must have six major elements. They were…anyone?"

A murmur overcame the room as the students mused over the answer. Minutes ticked by as the professor waited. Angie rolled her eyes as everyone drew a blank. "Plot, thought, character," she began. "Diction, music, and spectacle."

"Ah, fantastic, Miss Trueblood. Very good," he praised. "Now then, your assignment till next class will be to compose a thesis on Aristotle's influence on the Greek playwrights of his time. As I always say, 'Be thorough, and as always…'"

"Be opinionated," the class replied in a monotone chorus.

"Yes! That will be all."

The class dispersed, but Angie stayed in her seat. Ten minutes later, the professor was still erasing his notes from the chalkboard and without even looking he sensed his best student alone in the auditorium. "And how may I help you this time, Miss Trueblood?"

"Sir, I'd think you would agree that I have exceeded your expectations in this class so far…"

"That would be an accurate observation," he replied.

She stood up. "Then I don't understand why you rejected my latest request to be skipped ahead to Advanced Literary History!"

The professor finished erasing and sighed. "I have no doubt in my mind you would do well in an advanced class, but you're forgetting one major detail, Miss Trueblood. This class is a required prerequisite for your curriculum."

"But—"

"You may know everything on my syllabus, young lady, but there is something else that's not on there that I'm teaching you." He turned to face her. "And that is patience."

Angie silently accepted her defeat as she picked up her books and sulked out the classroom.

"Mr. and Mrs. Simms, your daughter is pregnant," Sonyai said calmly.

There was a sound of a plate crashing to the floor, followed by a resounding bellow-type roar of a man asking *"What?"* and Janelle Simms was wishing she was not standing in her parent's living room with her world about to end.

She wished that this was all a dream and at any moment she would wake up in her bed and the events from the past six weeks never happen. There was no Robin Walker at 58th Street, she would get hired as the next in line part-time clerk, graduate early with no suspicions, and her parents would be oblivious to her medical condition.

Any time now, wake up! she thought.

As her father continued to scream and her mother continued to hyperventilate, it became obvious that this was *not* a dream. Sonyai continued to stand in the middle of the living room quietly, a pillar of strength in the eye of the hurricane, waiting for a moment to continue as Janelle stood hiding behind the senior clerk, using her as a shield.

"What happened to bracing them for a blow with a buildup about responsibility?" she asked Sonyai. "Like we discussed?"

"The best approach is the direct approach," was all she said in reply.

"How? How did this happen?" Luanne Simms cried. She was wearing a blue housedress with a daisy print pattern. She was in the midst of offering a plate of Pepperidge Farms Milano cookies to their guest when the declaration shocked her core.

"It doesn't matter how it happened. It's how are we gonna pay to get rid of it!" Chester Simms yelled. At six-foot-one and two hundred pounds, the construction worker was wearing blue acid wash jeans and a button down red and white checkered shirt tucked into his waist. "I don't even know if my insurance covers…"

"Janelle is keeping the baby, sir, and you need not worry about any medical costs," Sonyai interrupted.

"Is *that* right? Is *that right*? You gonna walk in here and *tell me* my little girl is having a baby?"

"That is correct, *sir*!" she answered, trying to contain her composure and not be disrespectful.

"And are you gonna tell me how she's expected to go to college while taking care of that child?"

"Mr. Simms, your daughter will have friends and co-workers who will do whatever it takes—"

"But she won't have any help from us!" the father interrupted. "Janelle, you think you're old enough to have a baby. You're old enough to get the hell outta my house!"

"Chester! What are you saying?" Luanne asked.

Janelle stepped forward. "Daddy!"

The man took a step toward Sonyai, intending to intimidate her with his size, pointing an accusing finger. "And *you*. My father didn't die at Pearl Harbor just to have a *twinkie* tell me…"

Sonyai grabbed Chester's wrist, stepped forward and twisted the man's arm clockwise as she tripped his ankle. He yelped and fell forward while she grabbed with both hands and pulled back, flipping the giant on his back.

She then bent the arm at the elbow and applied pressure to bend it back, pinning his arm underneath her knee. The Aikido wrist throw took five seconds to perform. Luanne and Janelle were frozen, mouths gaping open.

"Mr. Simms…" Sonyai began, straining her voice. "You and your wife have an obligation to provide a roof over her head until she is 18 years of age. You fail to do so and I *will* notify the authorities and they will force you to take care of your daughter or they will send you to jail. Now, you will visit her guidance counselor and principal at school and acknowledge that she is over two months pregnant. Despite her condition, you allow her to graduate and attend her ceremonies in June. You will not degrade her, you will not belittle, humiliate, or antagonize her in *any* way shape or form, sir! Do we understand each other?"

She applied further pressure for emphasis and he groaned in pain, panting in short breaths. "Yeah, yeah! Okay!" he relented.

She released her grip, stood up, and took a step back, holding a defensive stance.

"Miss Yi! I didn't know you could do that!" Janelle said with excitement.

The youngster's excitement turned to concern as she saw her father slowly get up, his eyes red from anger.

Sonyai turned to Janelle. "You call me if he does anything tonight." She then turned to face Chester, who was dusting off his clothes, still staring back at her.

"I'm sorry for your loss, sir, but none of my relatives fought for the Axis Powers." She nodded to Luanne, who quivered from shock, then turned and made her way out of the apartment.

CHAPTER SEVEN

HEYWOOD WALKED INTO THE VIDEO VAULT OF THE DONELLE LIBRARY Center Thursday morning at eight. He was wearing pressed slacks and a tucked in dress shirt with his hair tied back in a neat ponytail. A pair of Ray-Ban sunglasses over his eyes, he imagined his "disguise" would draw less attention so word would not get back to 58th Street about his visit. An elderly video librarian greeted him, his bifocal glasses two inches thick.

"May I help you, son?" the gentleman asked with a raspy cough.

"Learner, Heywood Learner. I called about a certain comedy film."

"Ah, yes. Comedies would be over here down the hall, follow me. I'm sure the selection is here. What was that name again?"

"Learner," he replied dryly.

"Hmm, any relation to William Learner from Kips Bay Branch?"

"I, er, seriously doubt it."

As the man rambled on, Heywood checked his watch in hopes this visit wouldn't be too long and he wouldn't have to explain being late for work. The two stopped, and after searching for a moment, the man pulled out a VHS tape.

"Ah, here we are!" the librarian exclaimed. *"Blazing Saddles* directed by the late Mel Brooks!"

"Um, Mel Brooks is still alive."

The librarian removed his glasses and looked at him puzzled. "He is?"

"Yeah."

"You sure?"

"Last I checked."

He shrugged. "Oh."

The two shared a moment of silence as the man took in that new information. He then looked down at the tape, undamaged and free from any tampering. "There, present and accounted for," he said lifting the object for Heywood to see. "So, what's the problem?"

"Was the tape recently returned to the library?"

"According to our records, the tape hasn't been checked out in the last 6 weeks."

"And it didn't require any tape splicing repair around February 22nd?"

"Nope. Don't know what could've given you that idea."

Learner thought about a response but then shook his head. "Um, never mind. You know what? Forget it. They must have made a mistake at my branch."

"Okay. Anything else I can help you with, son?"

"Actually, I was wondering if you could set aside 5 films for an upcoming theme—"

"Um, you do *know* film requests can only be issued by the branch's head librarian for events that only he or she has authorized in advance, right?"

Heywood stammered for a second, "Y-ye-yes, I'm aware of the procedures."

"Okay then. I can start the paperwork to have certain tapes held 'till the official request is sent."

"Um, okay. Hold *The Man Without a Face, Forever Young, Hamlet, Air America*, and *Bird on a Wire.*

After taking the list down on a pad, the old man looked up at him. "Hmm, all those starring that young Mel Gibson fellow." He raised an eyebrow. "You into him?"

"Huh?"

"Hey, I don't judge. Got a cousin who was attracted to Brando in his heyday. I can understand where you're coming from—"

"What? No!" he yelled and stammered. "Just make sure those are available when the request arrives! Sheesh!"

Heywood stormed off embarrassed as the librarian looked down at the list again. "Weirdo."

Tommy made his way inside 58th Street at nine o'clock. He was wearing loose-fitting sweatpants to hide his bandaged knee. Gerry and Ethel watched as he went inside the clerical office where Sonyai was waiting. She closed the door behind him and the two stood alone in the middle of the room.

"What happened Monday night?" her voice was cold as steel.

"He, uh, didn't appreciate the…initiation. An altercation ensued."

"In front of the branch?"

"It couldn't be helped. With all due respect, ma'am—"

"I don't want to hear about it!" she barked. "Chavez had to prevent the local authorities from turning this into a serious issue! Despite that, we were visited by 2 police officers asking questions and Walker was nearly discovered, looking like pounded hamburger!"

It astonished Tommy that Robin returned the following day while he took days to heal. "I don't know what else to say except I'm sorry,"

"When he comes back, no fighting! Continue as planned tonight, but I don't care if he spits in your face, you *walk away* tonight, understood?"

"Yes, ma'am." He turned and opened the door.

As he walked out, Ethel was waiting nearby and walked in. She stopped in front of the senior clerk. "Yi, I…I'm getting concerned over this soda thing with Walker. I think I went at him a little too hard. At *your* insistence, I might add."

Sonyai tilted her head. "Don't tell me that big, bad Ethel Jenkins is scared of a little boy?"

"I ain't scared of nothin'!" Ethel yelled. "But I ain't stupid, either. I know Tommy and Walker beat the shit outta each other and what you're doing to help—"

"Keep your voice down!" Sonyai ordered raising a finger. "You can leave him alone for now, but you're not out yet. I might still need you later on."

"That's good enough for me!"

At eleven o'clock, upstairs in the staff room, Heywood and Angie were busy eating lunch. There was an uneasy silence between the two as they tried not to notice each other.

"Do you think Chavez did this just to turn us against each other?" Heywood asked.

"I dunno."

"It...it wouldn't be the first time, you know?"

Angie nodded. "I'd like to think this was a test...for both of us."

After another moment of silence, Heywood asked. "Think we passed?"

"With Chavez, who knows? I think we both said things that were—"

"Yeah," Heywood interrupted.

"Hey, off topic, do you think it's wrong for a teacher to hold a student back if they show early signs of advanced skills just to appeal to the status quo?"

"Well, yeah, I guess. I take it this is about you at school?"

"God yes! It's not fair. I am dusting all the other students in this class and I should be moved ahead!"

"It's kinda hard to prove that in college, though."

Angie sighed. "I guess that's true."

"Can I ask *you* a rhetorical question now?" Heywood asked.

"Sure."

"Don't you think it was a weird coincidence that at the last minute the one movie I objected to adding to the film festival comes up spliced and unavailable?"

She thought about it for a moment. "You think it was purposely sabotaged?"

"I'm not sure," Heywood said. "But I'm going to find out!"

ROBIN WALKED into the branch at two thirty. He had just finished his finals in his Freshman Excel and Music in Civilization classes and was feeling emotionally drained. All that changed, however, at the sight of Tommy working the circulation desk. Augustus stood up slowly from the information desk.

Gerry looked inside the clerical office and signaled to Sonyai, who came out with a concerned look. Robin and Tommy exchanged hard glances, then both moved to rush each other in the middle of the floor.

"No, no, no, no..." Augustus whispered as he hurried to intervene.

"Thomas!" Sonyai called and rushed behind him. The patrons on the floor became startled by a possible confrontation and froze while others looked up from various locations. The men were inches away from each other when the supervisors broke them up at the last moment, Augustus tackling Tommy while Sonyai pushed against and braced Robin.

"Outside! Back outside now!" she yelled while Tommy and the librarian disappeared among the shelves.

"There will be *no* physical violence in my library, young man!" Augustus pressed all his weight on the strong clerk's shoulders.

"He was going to..." Tommy began.

"I don't want to hear about it!" he hissed as he pulled him close. It annoyed Tommy that this was the second time today someone had yelled that exact sentence at him.

"You calm down, you get *back* to that desk, and you act in a professional and courteous manner, got it?" Augustus let him go for emphasis.

Tommy stared back and sucked in a breath of air, then exhaled. "Yeah," he said. "I got it."

The two had a stare down for few seconds, then Augustus turned and walked back to the information desk.

"You weren't mugged. You and Thomas were in a fight!" Sonyai yelled at Robin, who was still tense at what almost occurred. He was seeing red and his heartbeat was pounding in his ears as he gritted his teeth.

"Alright! So what? He started it, and he hasn't learned his lesson!" Robin yelled back.

"We don't have fights, Walker! Not *outside* in front of the branch and especially not *inside* in front of the public!" Robin stood silently as she continued. "Whatever happened is behind us now. It doesn't matter who beat who, who won, who lost, and who walked away. We are your co-workers, and if you are trying to earn our respect, you're going at it all wrong."

Robin turned his face up. *I couldn't give a shit about earning respect!* he thought, but he dared not say it out loud. "Fine!" he barked at Sonyai. He turned to go back inside, her following right behind him.

Inside, Tommy was standing at the circulation desk again. Augustus watched closely as Sonyai walked in behind Robin. There were stares of confusion by the patrons over the heated tensions, but cool heads prevailed. Robin entered the clerical office and pulled out a soda from his book bag and placed it next to Ethel, who was reading the newspaper. She looked down at the can and then to Sonyai. The senior clerk gave her a dismissive hand gesture to let it go and Ethel went back to reading.

Sonyai approached Gerry at the desk. "Tomorrow night you close with Walker instead of Tommy."

"You brought this all on yourself, you know!" he replied. "With that Little Big Horn bullshit!"

"Not. Another. Word," she ordered.

At three o'clock, half an hour after the incident between Robin and Tommy, Augustus entered his office and picked up the receiver to his phone. He didn't even take a seat, still agitated over the confrontation. The phone on the other end rang and a voice answered.

"Yes, this is Augustus Chavez at 58th Street. That matter we discussed earlier? I believe we will go forward with that. When can I expect someone? Good. If I could ask, make sure it's someone *experienced.*" He hung up the phone. With an exasperated sigh, he whispered to himself, "I was hoping it wouldn't have to come to this."

"AND THEN MISS Yi just grabbed my dad's wrist and flipped him over!" Janelle explained. "Like a female Steven Seagal!"

The pages were all going upstairs before starting their shift. "After she left, they've been leaving me alone. Mom even lets me eat in my room now. I think it's because Dad's too mad to have us all eat at the kitchen table."

"Wow," Lakeshia said. "I didn't think she could kick anybody's ass." The others nodded.

"Proves she's a tough little package," Alex added.

"They agreed to see my counselor tomorrow and I'll officially graduate, then come back in June..." The four girls walked in to find Robin sitting at the kitchen table alone. He seemed tense about something and was trying to cool off.

"Hey," he greeted them halfheartedly.

Tanya glanced over to see Lakeshia's face brighten for a second, a quick smile flashing across her face. Scowls came over Janelle and Alex as they walked past him to the couch.

"Mr. Walker, you're looking better than you were yesterday," Alex taunted after looking him up and down.

Tanya took a seat on the second couch while Lakeshia pulled up a chair at the kitchen table. She wanted to sit right next to Robin but opted not to.

"Uh, yeah." He then opted to change the subject. "Hey! I um, figured out a way you guys can do your shelf assignments. Wanna hear?"

They all nodded in agreement as Robin captured their attention now.

"Wait up, cuz!" Tanya interrupted. Robin tilted his head and gave her a puzzled look. "If you want to start being cool wit' us, you start by calling us ladies, gals, or girls, got it?"

The others affirmed the statement.

"Yeah, Walker, take a good look around, okay?" Alex said.

Robin nodded and raised his open palms in an apologetic gesture. "Duly noted, *ladies*."

Hearing him correct himself brought a round of friendly smiles from everyone, even Janelle.

"As I said, I've thought of some shelf assignments for the 4 of you I believe everyone can agree on."

"This better be good," Alex chimed in. Robin ignored her and turned to Janelle. "First off, you all agreed to give Miss Simms the lightest of duties."

They all nodded in agreement.

"May I ask why?" he asked as he arched his eyebrow.

Janelle looked down as panic overcame the other three in a tense moment of silence.

"Um, seniority preference!" Tanya exclaimed. Alex and Lakeshia quickly agreed while Robin gave them all skeptic looks.

"Okaaaay. With that, I suggest she take the new books, the entire foreign books section, and the sci-fi hardcovers."

"I...I can handle that," Janelle whispered. Robin looks at the others. They also nodded. He sighed in relief.

"Next, instead of splitting the general fiction hardcovers in half with A through L and M through Z, divide it among the 3 of you."

"Huh? That's never been done before!" Alex gasped.

"26 letters don't divide into 3," Tanya added.

"I know, I know. Hear me out, okay?" he said waving his hands for patience. "Tanya, you can have A to L, Alex gets M to S, and Lakeshia gets T to Z."

"Hold up, *I* get 12 letters and these two only get 7?" Alex asked.

"Hey, you caught that quick. Math major?" he asked impressed.

"Alex is good with numbers," Janelle explained. "Comes from being a shopaholic."

The girls shared a collective laugh while Robin said, "I see you now with new respect."

"Don't try to flatter me!" she snapped as she got serious again.

"Okay, easy, easy! I made up for it with the rest of the assignments."

"Keep 'em comin', Flash!" Tanya said with a smile.

"Hey, hey! That mean I've won you over, too?" he asked turning to her.

"Don't count ya chickens yet, cuz!" she said with a pointing finger.

He then rolled his eyes. "Moving on. Alex, to make up for the 12 letters in fiction, I gave you all the paperback and hardcover mysteries. A light load and fair trade I might add."

The two stared at each other blankly for almost a minute before she said, "Thanks."

Robin cringed. "It's like pulling teeth with you!" he remarked. "Would it kill you to show some appreciation?"

She continued to stare at him. Robin sighed in defeat. "Fine, Lakeshia?"

"Yesss?" the young page purred.

"You got the biographies and the children's books."

She looked at him, completely infatuated. "Okay," she responded with a smile.

Tanya put her index finger in her mouth in a gagging gesture. "Things are looking good so far, but what about the call numbers?"

"Well, that's where things get tricky," Robin began. "Tanya, you would agree, next to Janelle, you've got some of the easy sections to manage, right?"

"True."

"That's why I'd think it'd be best if you took the 700's through 900's."

"I sure'a spit think not!" she yelled. Robin winced at the reaction while Alex and Lakeisha sucked their teeth.

Lakeshia stood up. "Alright! I'll take 'em. I'll take 'em!"

"Fine! Just to keep the peace here," Robin exclaimed, exasperated. *How the hell does Sonyai deal with these girls?* he thought. "Alex, take the 400's through 600's, and Tanya will have the 000's through 300's. We cool, ladies?"

The girls looked at each other around the room, then Alex stood up. "Thank you for your help...*Robin.*"

The clerk blinked in surprise at the sound of someone calling him by his first name for the first time. As the girls all stood up, filing out to leave, a huge smile grew on his face. Once he was alone in the room, he said to himself, "I'm finally making progress here."

The four girls opened the door and poured out from upstairs. They passed the circulation desk where Sonyai greeted them and called them all over for a quick briefing.

"Did you 4 settle on the new shelf assignments?" she asked.

They all nodded in unison. "We had a little help," Lakeshia chimed in.

"Really? Who?" the senior clerk asked.

"Walker broke it down for us," Tanya added. "He's coming along like the real deal."

Nearby, Tommy worked the returns and listened closely.

Sonyai looked over to Alex and Janelle for affirmatives and they agreed. "Well, then, start with the new duties on Monday. That is all." The girls dispersed and she noticed Robin emerging from the staircase. She approached him, and Tommy was still rubbernecking.

"Um, the girls just finished telling me how you helped with their new shelf assignments."

"Yeah, it was no problem," he replied.

She stammered, lost for words, then said, "Thank you."

His eyes got wide as saucers, and she immediately regretted the praise. "But," she began, bringing him back to earth, "you and Thomas need to patch things up."

Robin got back into defensive mode. "I didn't do anything wrong. *He* needs to apologize."

"Just think about it. Conflicts here leads to chaos, and chaos is not good for the branch. For the good of the branch, Walker...please." She turned and walked away from him as he looked ahead to see Tommy staring back at him from the returns terminal, angry as ever.

Robin was scheduled for ninety minutes on checkouts before coming back from lunch to close at five o'clock with Gerry. He just finished an hour of awkward silence with Ethel, and now Tommy was coming back at four.

It's only a half an hour, Robin told himself. *Don't get caught up in his bullshit!* He took a controlled breath and focused.

At four fifteen, Tommy taunted, "I said it before and I'll say it again, Walker. It ain't gonna work."

Robin remained silent and continued to ignore his adversary.

"If you think getting on the good side of the pages will get you nice with Sonyai, you're wasting your time."

He refused to take the bait.

That's when Tommy took a couple steps and Robin tensed up. "*Back. The fuck. Up!*" Robin hissed. Leaning in over his shoulder he continued, "I've known them longer than you…"

Robin closed his eyes and counted to ten…

"We're a tight-knit group here…"

"*1…2…3…*"

"…and you're just a loose thread…"

"*4…5…6…*"

"…waiting to be plucked."

"*7…8…*" Robin clenched his fist…

"You *don't* belong here…"

"*…9…*"

"Boy!"

Robin turned and nudged Tommy back. "Hey, man," he started. "I wanna be cool with everyone while I'm here. Back the fuck up off and leave me the hell alone!" he warned.

He kept his voice low but authoritative so as not to disrupt or draw attention to themselves. Sonyai came out from the clerical office to relieve Robin, who then stormed off and went back upstairs to the staff room.

"Stupid, long-haired, fake-ass John Travolta wannabe, sonavbitch!" Robin yelled as he entered the staff room. He looked for something to grab and throw, only to be startled at the sight of Lakeshia looking back at him, her eyes very wide.

"Oh!" he gasped full of embarrassment.

Lakeshia gathered her lunch and soda and stood to leave. "I'm sorry. I was just leaving."

He stepped forward to stop her. "No! Wait, I didn't mean to scare you off. I was just mad."

"It's okay. I'll leave—"

Robin pleaded, "Please stay."

She looked deep into his dark brown eyes and faltered for a moment, then straighten up and took her seat back at the table.

Robin sat next to her. "It's just...I...I don't understand," he started.

"What?" Lakeshia asked.

"I've been here almost 4 weeks and everybody's been against me. Without even trying to get to *know* me. I don't understand why they hate me."

Lakeshia shook her head. "Nobody hates you, Robin. You just came off so...full of yourself. You had a big chip on your shoulder."

"Okay, yeah, that's true. But I'm not really like that. It's just...this branch. It's so different than—"

"Well, that's the thing," she interrupted. "All branches have their distinct personalities."

He nodded, understanding the sentiment. "Okay, I feel you but..."

"But what?"

"It's almost as if no one wants me here for some *specific* reason. Like they actually want me to quit or...or transfer or something."

Lakeshia sat quietly, the guilt eating away at her. She couldn't hold it any longer.

"I wanna know why!" he continued. "Maybe I *should* put in for a transfer..."

She looked at how defeated Robin was with that last statement. This was what Sonyai, Janelle, and Alex would want so Janelle could stay, get the benefits to help her and the baby. Would that be so bad? Her mind was racing. She needed to decide. Her brain was telling her to say nothing. Her feelings for him made her heart think otherwise.

"No!" she gasped, startling Robin. "Don't...let them beat you so easily," she encouraged. *What the hell am I doing?* she thought.

"Why?" he asked. "Why should I stay where I'm not wanted?"

Lakeshia Seabrooke, fourteen years old, did the most compassionate thing she'd ever done in her life—she reached out and put her hand on his. "Give them time. I'm sure everybody will get used to you. Don't give up now."

Robin was nearly moved to tears as he looked at Lakeshia's face. Her spirit of determination empowered his. He looked down and noticed her hand was still lingering on his. She noticed as well and pulled back with a nervous smile.

"You know what? You're right!" he exclaimed and stood from his chair. "I'm not gonna let these people run me off!" He looked down at her still sitting and put his hand on her shoulder. "Thanks, Lakeshia. That was the pep talk I needed." He walked toward the exit to leave.

"Robin!" she called back. He stopped and turned. "You can call me Leelee. The girls at the branch always do," she said with a smile.

He smiled back and nodded. "I won't forget we had this talk, Leelee. I owe you one." He turned back and left.

After a few moments, Lakeshia jumped in place, then flopped on the couch, hugging a throw pillow and giggling. "He owes me one!" she squeaked.

"IT'S CALLED LITTLE BIG HORN," Gerry explained to Robin. Ethel, Sonyai, and Tommy had left for the day. Augustus was also there, working the information desk for the last hour. "Named after the infamous battle that took place—"

"When a cocky cavalry general named Custer fought a huge tribe of Sioux Indians," Robin finished.

Gerry nodded. Robin, comfortable working the cash register, was on the returns side while Gerry did checkouts. Sonyai scheduled them opposite sides on paper, but Gerry felt Robin needed a break and decided to only let him close on checkouts ten minutes before closing.

"As I recall," Robin began, "The general was outnumbered because three-quarters of his troops abandoned their post before the fight."

"Sound familiar? Sonyai started the tradition to teach a lesson in humility. She and Ethel did it when I got here, and the three of us did it to Tommy when he first arrived." A smile grew across Gerry's face at the memory. "Tommy, uh, reacted like you did at first."

"This is practically hazing. How long did this bullshit trial by fire last?" Robin asked.

"That's the thing I don't understand. Traditionally, we wait until the clerk was comfortable, then we'd do it only once to make the point." Gerry paced within the small confined area behind the circulation desk.

What is it about everyone here and pacing? Robin thought as he watched.

"For some strange reason, she stepped up her plans. But why?" Gerry stopped when a patron stepped forward carrying two VHS slips and a hardcover bookmarked with a red triangle on the spine. The man looked to be in his late twenties, wearing green slacks and a brown leather motorcycle jacket with a white buttoned-up cotton shirt underneath.

"Hi, I'd like to check out these videos and renew this book."

Robin stepped behind Gerry as he handed him the plastic slips. He then opened the video file cabinet and retrieved the VHS tapes. Gerry examined the book and announced, "I'm sorry sir, this book is non-renewable."

"What?" the patron whispered.

Gerry pointed to a sticker that read "One Week Loan" and explained, "All books marked with this red sticker are 7 day checkouts and there are no renewals. If you'd like, you can check if there's another copy on the shelf."

"And what if there isn't one?"

"Then keep the book, finish reading, and pay the late fine," Gerry replied with a shrug.

"This is insane! I'm less than a hundred pages from—"

"Sir, they mark books like these due to their popularity so they can be available to other waiting readers." Gerry interrupted. "Regular 3 week checkout books are used to fill the many reserves people have requested."

"I want to renew this book, and I want to renew it now!"

Robin looked between both individuals as the argument escalated. Gerry flinched in anger as he was about to reply when Augustus stepped up next to the patron.

"Is there a problem here, sir?" he asked in a soft, calming voice.

"This fella here won't let me renew my book!"

Gerry tilted his head at the thought of being called "fella," which was a stone's throw from being called "nigger" in his eyes.

"Well, understand, sir, we have rules about this," Augustus explained.

The patron pulled away from his staring match with Gerry and looked over to Augustus with a pleading look. "But I'm almost done," he whined.

The librarian looked over to Robin, still standing near the returns side. He then took the book from in front of Gerry and walked over in front of Robin. "Mr. Walker, please check this book in."

Robin looked at Augustus for a moment, then back to Gerry and the patron. The librarian waved the book in the air with a look of insistence. He took the book and used the lightpen to check it back in, the terminal chirped acknowledging the return and Robin pulled the book back, intending to place it on the shelving cart.

Augustus then cleared his throat as his hand was still out hanging in the air.

"Sir?" Robin asked with a questionable glance.

The librarian gestured for him to hand back the book. "Mr. Walker?"

"Sir, returned books *must* be reshelved in order to…"

"I won't ask again, Mr. Walker!"

Startled by the command, Robin handed back the book. The librarian smiled and walked back to the patron.

"Understand, sir, we here at 58th Street have rules to abide by." He handed the book over to the patron, who smiled. "But there are times we can be reasonable." He then turned back to Gerry with a hard look. "*Just* this once."

The patron held the book in front of Gerry with a smug look. He slammed it down on the desk with a loud thud, making Augustus and the patron jump.

"Your card, sir?" Gerry asked with a forced smile through his teeth.

With a shaky hand, the patron fished out his library card from his wallet. The clerk began the checkout process when his face lit up, struck with an idea. "You know, sir, you can check out 1 more video if you like."

A smile grew across the patron's face at the suggestion. "Really?" he asked.

"Yeah! We're exercising some new policy. Spread the word!" he said with feigned enthusiasm. Gerry noticed Augustus was still giving him a hard look.

"Well, that's good to know. Maybe next time I'll get an extra one." He passed through the security threshold, picked up the checked out items, and left. Gerry and Augustus continued their staring contest as Robin stepped forward.

"Sir, may I speak?" he asked.

The librarian broke his glare and turned to Robin.

"I have never seen such a blatant display! A…a total disregard for policy…"

"Mr. Walker, you have to use proper judgment when it comes to serving the public. Yes, we have rules to follow, but sometimes…we can *bend* the rules."

"But—" Robin protested.

"This matter can be discussed at a later time. I believe I have an announcement to make."

He turned and walked to the middle of the floor. With a flourish, he proclaimed, "Ladies and gentlemen, the library will be closing in 10 minutes. Any materials you wish to check out, please do so now. Thank you."

Still annoyed over the head librarian's actions, Robin waved for him and Gerry to switch places as he prepared for the swarm lining up on his side. "Don't try and help me," he told Gerry. "I'm getting better at this. I can handle it."

He processed the checkouts. Working the lightpen, applying the date due cards in each book's pocket. The line continued to grow as he worked as fast as he could. Suddenly, an extra pair of hands grabbed several date due cards and assisted by moving the books around to the opposite side.

Robin began to protest the help until he saw Lakeshia standing next to him. He looked concerned since the rest of the pages seemed to disapprove, but then smiled and finished working the line.

CHAPTER EIGHT

"VICKIE, I'M TIRED OF THIS WAITING. IT'S TOO COLD TO BE OUT HERE like this!"

Vickie Florence rolled her eyes as she sat inside her brother's 1990 blue four-door Acura Integra. She didn't have her driver's license yet, but that didn't stop her from "borrowing" the vehicle once in a while. She was determined to catch Tanya the moment she turned the corner of the block after stepping outside her building.

"At least turn the heater on!" pleaded the bully's other friend.

"It doesn't work! Look, that skank has to go to school. She'll be out any minute now."

The three girls were waiting for half an hour. It was almost six thirty in the morning. Vickie continued to watch the front of the building.

Tanya bent the fold of her third-story window curtains and peeked downstairs at the car lingering in front of the building. "This is getting annoying," Tanya sighed. She walked away from the window, picked up a cordless phone, and dialed a number.

"Leelee? It's me. Can your brother leave a 'lil early, swing by my place, and then drop me off midtown on your way to school today?"

"I dunno, Tee. You're all the way up in the Bronx."

"C'mon, pleeeeease? I got that crazy bitch stalking my building out front!"

"Then call the cops."

"If you don't, I'll tell Alex and Nellie you have a crush on Robinnnnn," Tanya teased.

"You promised to keep it a secret!" Lakeshia squeaked. A moment later, she sighed. "Oh, alright. We'll be there in 20 minutes. Be ready! This'll be cutting it close!" She hung up, and Tanya clicked off the phone with a devilish grin.

Vickie and her friends were still waiting outside when a beige Corolla pulled up in front of the building. One girl tapped Vickie's shoulder to bring her attention to the car. "Hey! Check that out." Tanya jogged out of the front door and entered the double-parked vehicle. Vickie quickly turned the key as the engine turned over.

Tanya and her mysterious ride took off down the street like a jackrabbit. Vickie pulled up with intent to pursue but was cut off by a *Daily News* newspaper delivery truck making a drop at the corner newsstand. She honked the horn and yelled "Yo! Move that shit!" She looked past just in time to see Tanya waving back from the car. Vickie hit the steering wheel in frustration and growled. "Damn you! Can't run from me forever!"

"So what do we do now?" her friend asked. Vickie waved her off as the truck moved, giving them the open path. "The 2 of y'all must be jinxes or something!" They both chimed in their protests as she gripped the wheel. "I'll settle this on my own before spring recess." She checked the street, then headed downtown to school.

"Whew! That was close! You should have seen the look on her face. Ha! Thanks, Leelee, and thank *you* too, Derrick," Tanya said with a wink to the rearview window.

"You're welcome," Lakeshia replied dryly.

"Leelee, you know I just be playin' girl. I needed a quick exit. I'd never tell—"

"Forget it!" she hissed.

"Whoa, whoa, whoa," Lakeshia's brother Derrick interrupted. "Tell what? Clue me in, clue me in!" Derrick was nineteen years old and worked as a street promoter/intern for local urban radio station HOT97. He hoped to break into public broadcasting as a DJ or radio personality.

He also was interested in getting a date with Tanya, so it was hard for him to keep his eyes on the street. Tanya changed the subject by reaching forward and turning on the radio. "Hey, Mr. DJ" by Zhane came on and the girls bobbed their heads as Lakeshia sang along. Tanya did the rap verse, and then the song trailed off to a station identification message and some radio banter.

"You 2 are good! Should come down to the station and drop a demo!" Derrick said with a smile.

"Yeah, yeah, yeah. You'd like that wouldn't you?" Lakeshia asked.

"What I would like is know is what dirt you got on my baby sister, Buster-Brown."

Lakeshia sucked her teeth while Tanya beamed at the pet name her brother made up for her. Derrick was pretty charming, and the only thing stopping Tanya from going out with him was that it would drive Lakeshia insane.

"Well..." Tanya began. Lakeshia pantomimed a shushing motion followed by a throat slashing motion with her fingers. "Lakeshia has a crush on the new guy on the job!" she exclaimed.

Derrick exploded in a fit of hysterical laughter.

"Snitch!" Lakeshia snapped at her.

"Hey, he's family. Family should always know first!" Tanya replied with a shrug.

Derrick wiped a tear from his eye and calmed down. "Whoo," he sighed. "Well, I hope you have better luck with this one than you did with...Carl Pierce!"

"Derrick!" Lakeshia screamed.

"Who?" Tanya asked.

"A little over a year ago—"

"Derrick Seabrooke, you say another word and I swear I will make you crash this car and kill us all!"

"Baby sis over here had a crush on this boy from junior high school. She knew him since the 6th grade..."

"Tanya don't need to hear this!"

"On the last day of school, she got the courage to ask Carl out. Got all gussied up and whatnot."

"Derrick, please!" Lakeshia pleaded.

"But she made a big mistake!"

"What? *What*?" Tanya asked as Lakeshia buried her face in her hands in embarrassment.

"She wanted to look sexy."

"Aww," Tanya cooed.

"So she stuffed her bra with Kleenex tissues!"

Tanya and Derrick erupted in laughter as the timid youngster's face blushed a bright crimson red.

"Oh, that is hilarious!"

"It gets worse," Lakeshia admitted.

"It does?"

"Tell you the rest later after school when we get to the branch. You're gonna have to talk to someone at school about this girl bothering you, Tee."

"I know, I know." She waved her hand.

Everyone in the car got quiet for a tense moment, then Tanya let out one last giggle as the two siblings broke out in smiles.

AT JULIA RICHMOND HIGH SCHOOL, Janelle and her parents were in the principal's office once again. The school's guidance counselor, a middle-aged African-American woman named Ms. Hoffert, joined them. The five individuals all sat on plastic chairs in a semi-circle as the principal started the meeting.

"Well, let's begin. Mr. and Mrs. Simms, congratulations on raising an extraordinary daughter. This accomplishment is very, very rare."

"Thank you," Chester Simms remarked. Luanne remained silent.

"Now to address the elephant in the room. Janelle, would you mind telling me how many months pregnant you are?"

"I'm 10 weeks," she said meekly.

"I don't have a calculator…"

"She conceived around the beginning of the year," Hoffert interrupted. "In January?"

Janelle nodded.

"Which means you're due late September or early October," the counselor concluded.

"Since your parents know of the situation, what are your plans, young lady?"

"I'm keeping the baby, and taking a year off to decide on college."

Chester exhaled sharply through his nose in a quiet gesture of protest.

"I take it you don't approve of this course of action?" the principal asked.

Luanne spoke up in Chester's silence. "We believe our daughter is responsible enough to make her own decisions and we support them no matter what."

"Very well, as long as we covered all the bases. We felt a need to inform you, in case you didn't know, and now she's cleared to unofficially graduate an entire term early. You may attend the senior trip, provided you paid your dues. Your yearbook will be available in May, along with your senior ring from Josten's…"

"Hold on," Hoffert said. "We're missing an important part of the puzzle."

Everyone turned to face her.

"The father."

"Well, I don't believe—" the principal began.

"Is he a student here? And if so, his parents will also need to be informed."

"Who's the father, baby?" Luanne asked.

"Um, it's Avery…Avery Boone."

"Boone? From the Varsity Boys Basketball team?"

She nodded.

The principal frowned with a concerned look. "He's only a junior."

"And only 16 might I add," Hoffert added. "Were you two aware of this?"

Chester and Luanne stared back at them. "What's the problem here?"

"Ahem, Mr. Boone is the star power-forward on the school's basketball team. He's on course to receive several athletic scholarships and is being scouted by over 6 competitive colleges."

"He could play for the Knicks one day," Hoffert added. "If he can keep something like an unexpected pregnancy quiet!"

Chester stood up. "Wait a minute...are you trying to say she did this on purpose intending to get money? How dare you!"

Janelle looked hurt. "It was just a one time—"

"Quiet, Janelle!" her father barked.

"She's older. She should have been more responsible!" Hoffert exclaimed.

"What!" Luanne yelled. "He's *just* as responsible as she is!"

"Calm down, everyone," the principal said with his arms stretched out.

"Boone and his parents need to be told. Have him paged, please." the counselor requested.

"No!" Janelle yelled as she stood up. "Don't humiliate him. The entire school will know about this within 3 periods if he's pulled from class!"

"Agreed. Miss Hoffert, it's best to use discretion," the principal said.

Chester put his hand on Janelle's shoulder. "We'll contact the boy and his parents and discuss this tonight. If we're done, I'd like to leave."

"Very well. As I was saying, you can pick up your cap and gown in June, then attend the commencement ceremony. 4 tickets will be provided for family."

Everyone stood up. The principal put his hand out for a handshake, which Chester ignored as he ushered Janelle and Luanne toward the door. He exchanged hard looks with Miss Hoffert, who glared back, then walked out.

"Keep me informed in this," the principal ordered as Hoffert nodded solemnly.

AT TEN O'CLOCK Robin walked into 58th Street and made a beeline for the clerical office behind the circulation desk, ignoring Tommy and Ethel at their stations. Sonyai turned from her chair and stood up to greet him. "Good morning, Walker. Here early for your first paycheck, I take it?"

"Yes, ma'am," he answered enthusiastically.

"Please, take a seat." She nodded and turned to the branch's ancient bank safe where the daily funds, checks, and financial records were held. The senior clerk worked the combination and pulled the door open. Sonyai withdrew an inter-office yellow envelope and produced a handful of checks. She identified Robin's and handed it to him.

"I can't help notice it still says Ms. Robin Walker on there. Do you plan to fix that gender issue with human resources?"

"I've made several calls," he replied. "They keep saying they'll fix it. Is there a check cashing place near here?"

"A block down Lexington, past the Sam Goody."

"Thanks." He folded the check and put it in his pocket. "Be back this afternoon!" he said, taking off. He rushed back out, still ignoring his favorite two clerks who watched him leave with matching smirks on their faces.

"I hear you got him bringing in a can of soda every day for you," Tommy said to Ethel.

"It was unsettling at first, but now I'm accepting it. I can get him to bring you one if you'd like."

"He wouldn't like that," Tommy said with a chuckle. "I'll consider it. Despite our *tussle* the other night, I think it's time for the next phase in our plan to get him outta here."

"Which is?"

"Physical humiliation. A series of pranks that will reduce him to nothing. You in?"

"Sonyai told us to back off for a while."

"This is bigger than her now. And we have to do this before Janelle—"

"You're making this personal," Ethel whispered.

"You damn right I—"

"Carmichael!" A voice snapped them both back to attention as Augustus appeared in front of the checkout side of the circulation desk.

"Yes, sir?" Tommy asked.

"May I have a word with you in private, please?" the librarian asked with a nod and then turned to walk back to his office. Tommy walked around the desk and reluctantly followed behind him.

Robin stood in line at the check cashing place as others were busy buying lottery tickets, money orders, and setting up wire transfers through Western Union. Three teller windows were cramped in a small space that made Frank's Pizza look like Grand Central Station. When a teller was free, Robin stepped forward to a female teller who was chewing gum and talked with a nasal tone.

"I'd like to cash this, please," he said, sliding the check to her through the open window slot.

She pushed it back to him. "Sign and date it on the back above the line, please."

Robin pulled his book bag in front of him and removed a pen, then endorsed the check with the required information. He slid it back to her then she pushed it back again. "Photo ID and social security card!"

He sighed. "I don't have my social security card!"

"You need at least 2 proofs of identification," she said pointing to a faded list of on the side of the wall. Robin scanned the list quickly.

"Next!" she yelled.

"Hold on! I got ID!" he objected. Someone on line behind him mumbled something unintelligible, but he ignored it while fishing out his college ID and his New York Public Library employee ID.

"That's a library check. This is their ID for employees. And here's my college ID complete with my social." He pushed the three items back to her with a frantic look on his face.

The woman examined them all, then simply said, "Okay."

Robin cheered in his victory and almost didn't hear the next question asked to him.

"Would you like to register for our regular cash checking services?

It's free and you'll be in our database so you won't need to show identification every time you come here. We'll give you a card."

"Umm, yeah, sure. Save me the time since I'll be coming here a lot."

"Okay," she replied again, then processed the check. After a few minutes of information gathering and then waiting for lamination, the teller slid over a plastic card followed by some money and loose change.

"Count your money on the left. Thank you and have a nice day."

"I counted along with you," he said as he picked up the money. "That check was for $287.15, you gave me $278.54!"

"There's a 3% service fee, sir. Please move aside. Next!"

Robin shoved the money in his wallet and put the card in his coat, leaving the dreary place. When he was under eighteen and working at Fort Washington, he depended on Jon to deposit his paychecks into the elder's checking account in which he would retrieve the cash amount for him.

That all changed nine months ago in August when Jon insisted Robin start a savings account at Apple Bank in their neighborhood. Like the typical procrastinator, he never got around to doing it and now he was paying the price. Today was the last day of classes before spring break and there was a house party where most of the students were attending, but he had a night class for sociology.

He did several calculations in his head. He needed to contribute toward the household bills. The Paragon Cable bill was thirty-two dollars, and then there was the Nynex telephone bill. He also promised to bring snacks after class to the gathering.

His watch read a little past eleven, Robin debated three options: to stay downtown until two and head back to the branch, to go to campus and socialize hoping to catch a glimpse of his elusive Asian girl, or go back home to the heights for a quick lunch only to turn around to head back down again. An idea popped into his head and he went with a fourth option. It was time to check in on an old friend.

"I'M glad we could talk and iron things out after our last confrontation, Carmichael." Augustus and Tommy were alone in the librarian's office while Zelda was outside at the information desk. Augustus was wearing a solid black suit with a grey tie while Tommy was wearing a white New York Knicks T-shirt and matching white sweatpants. He remained quiet as he sat, still unsettled at the thought of the librarian bracing him physically. Augustus sensed the tension and tried to break the ice.

"How are things at home?"

"All is well, sir," Tommy replied in a neutral tone.

"Good, good," Augustus said with a smile.

The two shared an awkward silence as Tommy shuffled his feet.

"Putting aside this latest situation with him, what are your honest observations on young Mr. Walker?"

"Sir?"

"Give me an unbiased opinion about him, if you can."

"He's, uh, a unique individual, sir."

"Well! Aren't we all, Mr. Carmichael?"

"Well, yes, I suppose we are."

"Then what would you suppose is your issue with him?"

Tommy could see where Augustus was going with this line of questioning, so he buttoned up again.

Augustus looked at him and rolled his eyes, then decided on a different approach. "Look, I know as long as you've been here you've seen me and your supervisor—"

"Miss Yi," he corrected.

"Yes, Yi and I have butted heads on various issues, but I want you to know that you and I don't need to be enemies."

Tommy continued saying nothing while he went on. "Like Yi, I too believe you will be a remarkable senior clerk one day, and I wouldn't want your judgments of fellow staff members like young Walker to be clouded by…outside influences."

"Uh, thank you, sir," Tommy replied, confused by the words of confidence and wisdom.

"Let me offer you some advice: be your own man."

"Yes, sir," he said with a nod.

The librarian continued to smile, hoping to get one back, but Tommy continued to look sheepishly at him. After another quiet moment, he gestured to the door. "Glad we had this talk. You are dismissed." Tommy nodded once again then stood up and left.

BOLTON'S WAS a woman's clothing store on 51st Street between 6th and 7th avenues, not too far from Radio City Music Hall. Robin made his way to the back and approached a metal door with no handle that could only be opened from the inside. He knocked the classic "Shave and a Haircut" pattern. A knock answered back "Two Bits" and then opened.

A white guy in his twenties with bad acne pushed the door out and stood behind the entrance, giving Robin a blank stare.

"Is he here?" Robin asked.

The greeter moved aside without saying a word and he walked in. The stockroom was littered with boxes, clothing racks, and mannequins. After walking around a few minutes, he came across two employees having a private conversation. He stayed out of sight but approached closer to eavesdrop.

"Hey, Frankie, you got any plans tonight? Why don't you take me out for a movie?" a woman asked. She was also in her late teens or early twenties, with blond hair, wearing teal jeans and a low cut tank top, with a very noticeable bust. Her companion, a skinny, white eighteen-year-old guy with curly blond hair cut in a distinguished flattop combed up at least three inches. He had flawless facial features that brought him a lot of attention from the female co-workers in the store.

"A movie? How about that new Paul Hogan movie, *Lightning Jack*? I love some Paul. He's so strong and muscular. Been a fan since *Crocodile Dundee*." His voice was slightly high to the point that it could be mistaken for feminine.

"Okay, okay. Forget the movie. Um, what about you and me just hang out somewhere? You're so antisocial. I…I really wanna get to know you." She drew in closer and stroked his shoulder. "I *really* wanna get to know you."

The two exchanged glances as Frankie laughed nervously. "Oh, Tabitha," the guy said playfully as he lightly slapped her arm. "You always playing! Go on out there to the registers. It's time to relieve Shannon."

Tabitha sighed, shaking her head as she walked past the stock boy out to the store's main floor. Once Frankie was alone, Robin stepped out from his hiding place. "You are playing a dangerous game, Franklin. Leading these co-workers on pretending to be gay." A smile grew on Franklin's face hearing his best friend's voice for the first time in months.

"Robin!" the employee said in a deeper more masculine voice. "You son of a bitch!" He stepped forward and greeted Robin with a slapping handshake that turned into an arm wrestling flex.

"Predator? Funny!" Robin said letting go as he caught the 80's movie reference.

"Remember when we snuck into the RKO at 181st Street to see it?"

"Twice," he replied.

When Robin and Jon moved into the Bridge Apartments, Robin met Franklin in the first grade of elementary school. Since then, the pair had been inseparable…until Robin started college. Franklin's father was the head superintendent of the high rise building complex and was hard on his son to maintain his work ethic.

"Good times. How's the new branch you working at? Been there what, three weeks now?"

"Nnnnggh. It's regular Addams Family of a bunch. Makes the hard cases from Fort Washington look like the Smurfs!"

"I find that hard to believe. Speaking of which, how's 'the family' been doing since you left?" Franklin was once a page at Fort Washington like Robin, but rather than move on and become a clerk, he quit to concentrate on finishing high school.

"Demetrius got promoted. He'll be taking the Senior Clerk Seminar in April," Robin began.

"Good for him. Alverez still around?"

"Yep, but he's eyeing retirement in about 3 years when he turns 60...so he says."

"How about the pages? Shinbaio, Ivan, and uh—"

"Shin graduated with me in June. Got called up to Inwood in the fall. Ivan's still there, but he's the top page now. Who'd a thunk it, eh? With his li'l shrimpy self."

Franklin shared the laugh at the thought. "And I know Mrs. Burns still there."

"Baking cookies!" they both said together, sharing another laugh. The two got quiet as Franklin got serious for a moment. "That asshole Trevor still there?"

"Yep. And he's still an asshole."

"Some things never change. What about...?" Franklin's voice trailed off, and he raised one eyebrow.

Robin knew who Franklin was talking about. He took a breath and sighed. "She, uh, left. I dunno when. Things got complicated when I..." he trailed off.

"The Game?" Franklin asked.

Robin simply nodded.

"The Truce?"

"Still on."

"And you say *I'm* playing dangerously, right? I take it Schemanske's still running shit?"

"Oh yeah. She's got all of New York safe and warm in her tight grip."

"They don't call her The Battle Axe for nothing," Franklin said. "Well, thanks for stopping by. I gotta get back to work."

"Hey, it's almost noon. I got time to kill. Take a break for lunch, man. That Blimpie's is still up the street."

"I dunno," Franklin balked.

"My treat."

In a high pitched voice, the stock boy yelled, "Giiirrrllls, tell Jenny I'm going to lunch! Be back in 30!" Then back in his deep voice, Franklin said, "Let's go!"

The two headed to the door leading to the alley in the rear of the store.

"How do you do that? Changing your voice?" Robin asked.

"I'm just copying Damon Wayans on *In Living Color*. Those "Men on Film" skits? 2 snaps…and kiss…"

"Can't touch this!" they both exclaimed.

LAKESHIA AND TANYA stepped out of a cab they took crosstown to arrive at 58th Street at two thirty in the afternoon. While walking across the sidewalk Tanya teased, "So, finish that story from the car this morning," a grin grew across her face.

With a pout, Lakeshia began, "When I stood next to him, to ask if he wanted to go out and catch a movie, someone splashed us with a whole bucket full of water!"

"Oh my god! Why?" Tanya asked.

"It was some sorta end of the year prank. They were aiming for him but got me too."

"Wow."

"Yeah, think about it. All that water and me stuffed with those tissues."

"Oh no!"

"Yep. I went from a D to an A-cup in seconds and the tissues oozed down my stomach out of my shirt in front of everyone! They laughed at me all summer. Couldn't show my face till I started at LaGuardia that September."

They stopped in front of the entrance for a moment.

"Wow, what a story. At least puberty came through for you later on," Tanya said.

Lakeshia looked down at her bust, "Yeah, my stuffin' days are done. But something like that scars you for life. Carl never looked at me the same way after that." She sighed and shook her head at the memory. Tanya put her hand on her shoulder.

"There, there, small fry. As usual, your secrets are safe with me."

"Are they?" she snapped. "If anyone hears about…"

"Easy, Leelee!" She made a zipper motion across her lips.

The two walked in to see Robin and Sonyai working the circulation desk, Lakeshia froze at the sight of Robin. He looked up and saw her staring and gave a friendly wave with a smile. She swooned and continued walking toward the staircase leading upstairs while Sonyai watched with a concerned raised eyebrow. Once the girls were out of sight, Robin continued his attention on the mysterious homeless vagrant who sat at the far left end corner.

He had ashy brown skin, with a face covered by a salt and pepper, unshaven beard. His most unique and outstanding feature was his eerie looking eyes. They were a weird mix of gray or green, depending on the angle of light refracting on them.

Robin turned and asked Sonyai, "Um, what's his story?" hitching his thumb.

"He's to be left alone, Walker. Just a crazy old man that comes here all the time. That's all."

"I can't help but notice how no one sits around him…like he has his own personal force field or something,"

"It's called B.O."

Robin gave a half-smile at the dismissive remark and dropped the subject, but made a mental note to investigate further.

"On an unrelated subject, I'd like to thank you for resolving the shelf reassignment issue among the pages. They bicker among themselves when switching them around. I've given up trying to figure out new ones."

"Not bad for a *male* page, huh?" Robin asked with a smug grin.

"No, not bad at all." Sonyai scowled back.

A patron came up to check out a book, and Robin attended to the task. Afterward, the two clerks shared a moment of awkward silence.

"Why did you do it?" Sonyai asked.

"Huh?"

"The pages, why exactly did you help them?"

Robin scoffed. "What difference does it make?"

"Exactly. What business was it of yours?"

Robin rolled his eyes. "Look, no one likes me here, okay? I did it to get some appreciation, okay? Happy?"

"That's true," she agreed. "You've won over Lakeshia I've noticed. But that wasn't the only reason you did it."

The clerk gave his supervisor a questioning glance as she paced.

"You know, when you first arrived, you didn't meet my expectations."

"Gee, that's encouraging!"

"You did what you were told, followed the rules. But when you helped the pages, I sensed...something."

"You're reading into this too much."

"Maybe, or maybe you are more dedicated to the job than you think."

"You wanted to see me, sir?" Heywood asked as he stepped inside Augustus's office. He looked up from the paperwork on his desk to see the information assistant enter his office.

"Yes, sit down, Learner. Take a load off. Have you and Trueblood settled that issue with the reserve duties?"

"We have," he said taking a seat.

"Good, good. Now then, I couldn't help noticing you took some comp time this morning,"

Heywood swallowed hard and chuckled nervously. "Ju-just a personal errand, sir."

Augustus nodded. "Nothing wrong with that. I'm sure you didn't feel a need to investigate the mysterious and convenient unavailability of a particular *media object?*"

Heywood straightened up and put on his best poker face. "No, sir. Whatever would you mean, sir?"

"Normally I wouldn't pay any attention to your overzealous dedication regarding our public events. If the two of us weren't colleagues, I'd *wonder* why there would be a need to look into strange coincidences...right?"

"Of course." A smile grew across Heywood's face.

"The idea that someone with a hidden agenda was manipulating the two of us intervening with events from the past would be preposterous…wouldn't it?"

The two engaged in a staring contest as the last remark hung in the air, each expecting the other to add anything else or reply.

"Yes," Heywood replied, deadpan. "Yes, it would."

"Good, I thought so. Glad we had this talk."

As Heywood stood up, Augustus watched him leave…confident he got his point across.

AFTER RETURNING from his break upstairs, Robin entered the clerical office to see Sonyai and Gerry at their separate desks. The direct line at Sonyai's telephone rang and she answered it. With the receiver on her ear, she turned to him, a look of concern on her face.

"Yes, he is right here." She covered the mouthpiece. "Walker!"

Robin flinched and turned to look at his supervisor.

"It's for you." The look on her face worried him as he stepped to the phone. She walked out to the circulation desk to give him some privacy.

"Uh, hello?" he said to the unknown caller.

"You have been making quite a reputation for yourself down there, young man," Barbara Schemanske said in her low, guttural voice. Fear grabbed Robin by the throat and electrified his spine as she addressed him over the phone.

"Hello?" she barked. He was so shocked he couldn't speak.

"M-M-Miss Schemanske, to what do I have the honor…"

"Save the pleasantries, Walker. It's just you and me. What is going on down there?" The woman had the bedside manner of a drill sergeant, direct and to the point. He gathered his nerves and spoke as if he was right in front of her.

"What have you heard, and from who?" he asked.

"Whom," she corrected. "Don't concern yourself over that. Just pretend that I *don't* know and you tell me."

"You expect me to recall more than twenty days of hell while still in earshot of everyone?"

"Don't feed me Alpo and tell me it's meatloaf! I know you engaged in an altercation with a staff member in front of the branch and that is *not* how a representative from *my* branch carries himself!" Robin was convinced that Schemanske and his mother would have been the best friends back in the day.

"I'm sorry, ma'am. It won't happen again," he said, humbled. Anger coursed through Robin's veins from the humiliation.

"See that it doesn't. Remember, Walker, you represent Fort Washington wherever you go. You represent *me*."

"Yes, Schemanske," Robin barked.

"We will speak again." The malevolent woman ended the call.

Robin hung up the phone...only for him to yelp in surprise as it rang once again. He looked around for Sonyai, but she was still out of the room, so he picked up the receiver. "Hello?"

A cackle echoed in his ear as another chill came over him. "You've been a baaaad boy, Walker. Tsk, tsk, tsk."

"Trevor," Robin growled. His hand nearly crushed the phone as he gritted his teeth.

"The one and only, fun stuff. Hear you been getting into some deep doo-doo, *pendejo*. Whatsamatter? Can't handle it out there in the real world? You need Burns to bring you some cookies?"

He heard the cackle again and nearly lost it. "Why don't you come down here and say that shit to my face, bitch! You and I got some settling to do."

"Ooh, you got me shaking in my British Knights, *bacano*. But remember, we got to play nicccce! Don't wanna break the truce now, right?"

"Don't worry, garbage man. You'll slip up eventually." He lowered his voice to a whisper. "She's gonna find out the truth about me, and when she does, she'll never forgive you for lying to her. Think about that for a while and lose some sleep, pretty boy!"

He heard Trevor say something else but quickly hung up the phone. Robin was livid. Someone had ratted him out, and it could only be one person.

CHAPTER NINE

ZELDA RETURNED TO THE INFORMATION DESK TO FIND ROBIN SITTING IN the main chair. He turned and gave her an icy stare. "Caesar, beware of Brutus. Take heed of Cassius. Come not near Casca. Have an eye to Cinna. Trust not Trebonius…"

"Artemidorus's letter, *Julius Caesar*, Act 2, Scene 3," Zelda finished.

"The Battle Axe told me you're a fan of Shakespeare. Taught 9th grade English. Having your students learn almost every play?"

"A lifetime ago, yes."

"I just had a recent phone conversation. It turns out someone took the time to bother her with a personal matter that didn't need her attention."

"Hmmm."

"We both know she values her time just as much as she values the image she maintains of herself. With that said, I only have 2 words for you, Miss Clein…" He stood up and leaned forward, whispering in her right ear, "Yosef Lifsh."

Robin then pulled back to see Zelda's expression change drastically. Her eyes wide, body trembling in shock and fear.

"There is blood on your hands," Robin continued to whisper. "It's a wonder you can sleep at night."

The clerk took pleasure in making the elder uncomfortable with this haunting secret. His eyes narrowed. "So the next time you feel the urge to go chatting with 'Babs' about something I did, think about this. I make two phone calls and the Reverend Al Sharpton along with his congregation will be so far up your Jewish ass…"

Zelda snapped and turned her head looking directly at him, her face crimson with anger.

"You'll be shitting sweat suits, gold chains, and hair grease for the next six months." His eyes locked with hers. "Do *we* understand each other?"

After a moment, she calmed down and in a low, hoarse whisper said, "Yes."

"Good." He turned and walked back to the circulation desk where Gerry was waiting for him.

"What was that about?" he asked.

"Just making sure she minds her damn business next time," Robin answered.

Twenty minutes went by and Zelda was still sitting at the information desk shaken up. Gerry, Robin, Lakeshia, and Tanya were working the last hour. Angie was off the clock, staying to prepare for her class that evening. Tanya and Lakeshia were busy working the shelves. The branch was actually quiet and serene for once, with very few patrons around.

"If only it were like this every hour," Robin said, breathing a relaxing sigh.

"Like what?" Gerry asked with a smile.

"No Tommy, no Sonyai, no Ethel, and no Alex." He turned with a grin. "I could get used to this!"

"I see you on half of that, kid."

"Yeah?"

"But you shouldn't be so hard on Alex or Ethel," Gerry said waving his forefinger. "We have to stick together and respect our sisters in order to survive in this world, my brother."

Robin snorted. "What bullshit! Those 2 have gone down the path of almost every modern day black woman since the 90's began."

"Which is?"

"To trample the spirit of the nearest black man around them!" Robin exclaimed.

"What?"

"It's been my experience, that black women—"

"Lemme stop you right there, not all black women are alike." Gerry interjected.

"Right, it's around…97% of them! Everything I've been through so far lets me know I'm not black enough to be accepted by my own sisters, so they can just hang for all I care!"

Robin was agitated by this current line of the conversation. Gerry had hit a nerve. He wondered where this hatred came from? The animosity couldn't have been only due to Ethel. After opening his mouth to say something, he waved it off. "You know what? Sorry I brought it up. I'll drop some knowledge on you when I have the time, but you? That mentality? That shit is wrong, man. It's wrong."

Robin shrugged, he was always down for a good debate when he had the ammo, but relaxed and noticed Lakeshia was eavesdropping nearby. The look on her face made him regret the outburst. He had to make amends.

"Leelee?" he called out to her, then waved her over to approach the desk.

She hesitated at first but stepped forward.

"You've been working here for…8 months, is that right?"

"Yeah."

He flashed his best smile. If she was anything like the pages back in Fort Washington, there was one sure fire way to smooth things over. "You ever done a checkout at the desk before?"

A look of concern came across Gerry's face, and out on the floor, Tanya poked her head out among the shelves. Lakeshia giggled nervously as the smile made her waver like jelly.

"No," she shyly replied.

He nodded for her to come around. "C'mon over. See how it feels."

Gerry stepped forward. "Uh, I don't think that's a good idea. Sonyai—"

"Is not here," Robin interrupted. "No one's around, it's a light crowd, the perfect time."

He winked at Gerry and the clerk relented. Within seconds, Lakeshia was standing next to Robin, barely able to contain her excitement.

"Okay, so when someone comes with some books—" he began.

"You ask for their card!" she interrupted. "I know, I know! How do you use the wand?" she asked enthusiastically.

He chuckled at her eagerness, remembering when he first stepped in front of a terminal, the thought of being a clerk far from his mind. He had come a long way, thanks to Schemanske.

"The *pen* is used by scanning the barcode on the card, like a supermarket scanner." He pulled out his wallet and found his library card. Flipping it around to the back where the barcode was, he swiped it with the lightpen. The terminal chirped and his record flashed on the screen, his name in the top left corner.

"Walker, Robin S." Lakeshia read. "What's the s stand for?"

"Sincere," he answered with a smooth tone.

"Reaaaaally?" she purred back, nearly melting into herself.

Tanya rolled her eyes from her vantage point.

Robin grabbed a random book, *Along Came a Spider* by James Patterson and continued his lesson. "Once the patron's record is up, just swipe at the barcode inside."

"Your middle name's really Sincere?" she asked, not paying attention.

"No, it's Salamander," he joked.

Gerry laughed as the young page pouted at the light remark. A patron came to the returns side with a book and Gerry walked over. With the pair having a moment alone, Robin drew closer and lowered his voice. "Now I know you heard what Gerry and I were talking about earlier and I wanna clear some things up." She nodded as he went on. "A lot of the sisters out here don't give me any play because they think

I'm too light. They call me Lite-Brite and White Chocolate. So as a defense mechanism, I lash out. But that doesn't apply to you, know why?"

She shook her head.

"Cause you're in-between. You're mixed, right?"

She registered a look of surprise, then nodded slowly.

"I thought so."

"What about you? Are you...?" she asked.

"No, no, no, I'm just light-skinned. I get it from my mother's side."

"I didn't mean to offend..."

"The only way to offend me is *not* thinking I'm black at all. Mistaking me for mixed is fine, get it all the time."

"How did you know I was by the way? I've never mentioned my parents to anyone."

"Your features are perfect. You remind me of Lisa Bonet. She's mixed too, you know. Black father, Jewish mother."

"Denise from *The Cosby Show*? I don't look like her!" she said with a giggle.

"Okay, if you say so," he said canceling the transaction. A female college student arrived to check out a book. Robin stepped back and let the page attempt the process.

The patron handed her card to Lakeshia, who picked up the lightpen and took a swipe at the barcode. Nothing happened. She tried a few more times nervously, but the terminal remained silent. She made one last try and the computer chirped with the record flashing on the screen.

Robin picked up a date due card and placed it in the pocket. Lakeshia then swiped the barcode on the book. After several awkward attempts, the item was passed to the other side waiting to be picked up. When they were alone, Robin stepped forward with a grin on his face.

"You need more practice."

She waved the pen, obviously embarrassed. "It's this darn thing! It doesn't work!"

He laughed. "You'll get used it."

"Yeah, I guess," she said and looked up to see Tanya watching them. An idea popped into her head. "Um, Robin?" she whispered.

"Yeah?"

"Um, I wanna tell you something, but you need to keep it a secret."

Robin looked around. Gerry was still working some returns and helping someone fill out an application for a library card. "Umm, sure. What's wrong, Leelee?"

"It's not me, it's Tanya. She's got someone out to get her from school. She's been chased on the train. They've waited outside her house. All she's been able to do is outrun them, but this is starting to get serious."

"Why doesn't she tell a teacher or somethin'?"

"She's scared. Tanya puts on a front like she's a tomboy but this other girl has pulled boxcutters on her. She has two other friends helping to jump her."

Robin saw the urgency in her eyes. Something bad would eventually happen. "Alright, tell me what you know so far, starting with what school she goes to."

THE LAST TEN minutes before closing went smoothly this time. Everyone parted ways after locking up. Gerry took the 4-train to the Bronx, arriving at 161st Street and Yankee Stadium around six twenty-five in the evening. He walked down the steps from the elevated tracks, then heading up to Gerard Street.

The Newsroom was an adults-only nightclub for the thirty-and-older crowd. Gerry walked in and shuffled his way to the bar. He took out his paycheck and slapped it down. "My mojito in La Bodeguita, My daiquiri in El Floridita," he said quoting Hemingway. The bartender took the check and handed him four stacks of multicolored plastic chips.

Gerry pocketed the chips and headed to the back near the bathrooms. There were two doors marked "Ladies" and "Gents", but in between the pair was a hallway leading to another door where a man stood guard. He straightened up as Gerry approached. Raising his left hand halfway Gerry said, "Sit biblioclasts occidetur."

The guard nodded and pulled the door open to let him enter. Inside was a room that had a round table with six surrounding chairs. Gerry took a seat and pulled out his chips. Three others sat at the table as the secretive poker game began.

"Evening. This all we working with tonight?" Gerry asked.

"We got 2 coming in later," a woman answered.

The ritual game had held in several locations over the last twenty years. Clerks and librarians under false names from various branches in the three boroughs. Playing their wages and drinking the night away. They knew Gerry as "Jazz" and he was playing with "Poker Alice," "Tin Man," and "The Captain."

A few hours went by when another woman known as "Jack Frost" came in and took a seat. After ten thirty, "Tin Man" and "Jack Frost" were gone and Gerry was ahead three hundred dollars on a hot streak. "Poker Alice" was holding her own, but "The Captain" was hanging by a thread. As they played, everyone discussed the current situations going on at their branches.

Throughout the night, other players came and went. At times, the card game could go on till the next morning. Players would take a break, stretch their legs, go to the bar or bathroom. At one in the morning, Gerry and "Poker Alice" were in a dead heat when a newcomer came in. The man seemed familiar to Gerry, as if they knew each other several years ago.

"We're almost done. Adding a third would keep us till the sun comes up," Gerry said.

"I'll only be in for a few hands. I have $100 worth of chips," the stranger said as he sat down.

"You don't look like any of the faces we've seen here before. What name you go by?" "Poker Alice" asked.

"Serpico," he replied. "They call me "Serpico"."

That made the other players freeze.

"What?" the newcomer asked.

"Nobody working the branches would go by that name. You S.I.U?"

"Not that it matters, but I am."

Gerry threw in his cards. "You know what? I'm cashing out "

"Yeah, me too," "Poker Alice" said, also throwing in her hand.

"Hey! C'mon!" "Serpico" protested.

"How the fuck you heard of this game, man?" the woman asked. She grabbed her purse and stormed off. "They letting anyone in these days!" she said, slamming the door behind her.

"Sorry, copper. We're used to doing things outside your jurisdiction."

"It's okay. It's you I was looking for, *Coltraine.*"

Gerry was shaken by the sound of his name. "You got me at a disadvantage, jack! You know my name, but I don't know you from Adam!"

"Last time you saw me, I had more hair and no goatee, and was probably a lot skinnier."

Gerry took a moment. "Still ain't registering,"

"Alright, I have one of those faces. Name's Eugene Iscaro, but everyone calls me Gene. My friends call me "G.I."." He offered his hand to shake, but Gerry just looked down at it.

"Iscarooooo, yeah, I remember you! You worked security at 58th street around...'89 was it?"

"Around that, yeah. I was with a third-party security agency but then got offered an investigator position in the unit."

"Okay, so what'cha looking for me for?"

"I've been asked by your Mr. Chavez to work security again in light of...recent incidences."

Gerry grimaced at the remark. "We've been doing all right. Just because of a few..."

"Save it, the paperwork's been done. But I'm here because the special investigations unit has reason to believe your senior clerk is doing something funny with her branch's earnings."

"Bullshit. Sonyai wouldn't steal money."

"We hear otherwise. The audits from the last 3 fiscal years have

58th Street reporting no overages or shortages every…single…day. That's impossible. Someone always says 'keep the change' once in a while or mistakes a dime for a nickel. If she's reporting false receipts, she's going down, with or without your help."

"Even if I believed that fairy tale, which I don't, why would you think I'd help?" Gerry asked.

Eugene smiled a wide grin, "Because I know you want Sonyai Yi gone. I know you think you'd do a better job running things at 58th Street."

Gerry remained silent.

The visitor went into his jacket pocket and produced a business card. "All we need is proof. Those accounting books would be a start."

Gerry looked at the card, then back up at Iscaro. "She guards those like Fort Knox, locked in a vault safe."

He waved the card in front of him.

Gerry took the card. "I'll see what I can do," he said, sticking the card in his pocket.

Eugene nodded. "Good. I don't start back down there for another week. I'll keep in touch. Once I'm there, you don't know me and I don't know you, *capisce*?"

"Yeah, I got you."

"I know that look. We ain't asking you to rat on your supervisor. If we're lucky, she'll put her own neck in the noose. We're the good guys, here."

"Riiiiight."

As Eugene turned to leave, Gerry called back at him. "How'd you know about this setup, man? How'd you know I'd be here?"

Without turning around he said, "We're special investigations, Gerry, we know everything. Have a nice morning. Get some sleep— you could use it." He disappeared in a shroud of darkness down the long hallway, his footsteps echoing in the room. Gerry stood alone, feeling the card in his pocket, a worried look over his face.

ANGIE EDGED her way through the row of seats in the auditorium classroom and found a spot in the middle, waiting for the lecture to start. When all the students were seated, the door opened and the professor walked in. He walked to the podium and pulled out a stack of notes from his briefcase.

"Tonight, class, we're doing something a little different." There was a low murmur among the students registering their surprise. "My voice is a little hoarse tonight, so without further ado…Miss Trueblood?"

Angie's eyes darted left and right, checking for the exits as the entire class drew their attention to her. She stood up slowly, waiting for further instructions.

"Could you step up to the podium here, please?" asked the professor. She nearly began to protest, but shuffled her way to the aisle and walked up to the front of the classroom. Still facing the professor, she took a side glance at everyone looking up front. All their eyes focusing on her, she became extremely nervous.

"Um, yes?" she asked in a frightened tone.

"I'd like *you* to read tonight's lecture this evening."

She let out a light chuckle with full belief that the professor was joking, but after seeing his face, cold and unfazed, she realized he was serious.

"Huh?" she grunted in disbelief.

"You heard me," he said gesturing to the podium. "The notes are all there. All you need to do is read. You can read, can't you?"

Swallowing hard she began to sweat. Accepting her fate, she stepped to the podium, looking out at the vast audience before her. She looked at the notes. There was a line on top of the first page that said "Start of Lecture."

She began to read the paragraph underneath in a low mumble. A shout from the room said "Louder!" followed by scattered laughter as she blushed crimson from embarrassment. She then continued in a cracked, louder voice.

Twenty-eight minutes later, the class was done. Angie stood behind the podium, frazzled and disheveled. The students dispersed and the professor put back his notes when she angrily turned to him.

"Was that really necessary?" she snapped.

"Well, I figured you might as well be teaching the class since you think you're wasting your time being a student of it."

Angie balled up her fist. "If your intention was to humiliate me just to prove a point, it will only make me more adamant about leaving!"

"Which is why I've decided to let you," the professor replied.

Angie gasped. "What?"

"I've reconsidered your request and decided that you can move ahead to the advanced class next semester. The paperwork is all in order," he said as he handed her a sheet of paper detailing the advancement.

She looked it over, mouth gaping open in shock. "I...don't believe it."

"That look on your face is thank you enough...along with you doing that lecture for me, of course."

She lowered the page and looked at him at the mention of the lecture, a half-hearted smile grew across her face. "Thanks," she whispered.

The professor walked past her toward the exit. "Don't thank me yet," he said over his shoulder. "I've spoken to the advanced class professor and she's assured me you will be extremely challenged with her."

Angie's face changed from jubilation to horror. "Hey! That's not fair!" she scoffed.

The professor chuckled. "Whoever said college was fair?" He waved and pointed to the wall switch next to the doorway. "Turn out the lights and lock the door on your way out, Miss Trueblood. Good night!"

She stood alone in the auditorium, hoping she hadn't bitten off more than she could chew.

"I DON'T SEE why they couldn't come to our place," Chester Simms complained. Sonyai, Janelle, and her parents were approaching 716 Saint Nicholas Street at eight thirty in the evening. They located the four-story brownstone between 145th and 146th street in Harlem. Walking up the stairs, they stopped at an intercom on the right side of the door. Sonyai pressed the button marked "Boone - Apt. #2" and a woman answered.

"Yes?"

"Mrs. Boone? I'm Sonyai Yi. I'm here with Janelle. We spoke over the phone."

Instead of a reply, the door buzzed open and she pushed it inside. The group made their way up more stairs to the second-floor apartment and knocked on the door. Several locks unlocked and the door opened. Evelyn Boone was a skinny, dark-skinned woman wearing a white housecoat with a floral print. Her hair was in curlers wrapped in a scarf and she wore flip-flops with white wool socks on her feet. She didn't look happy to see them but was cordial.

"So nice of you to meet us on such short notice this evening, ma'am," Sonyai said, putting on her best smile.

Evelyn looked everyone over as they stood in the hallway. "Uh-huh." She gestured for the group to enter.

In the living room, standing an even seven feet, wearing a black T-shirt and matching sweatpants, Avery Boone watched with nervous eyes as Janelle and her parents took a seat on a green leather couch. Evelyn closed the door and then took her place next to her son as Sonyai stood in the middle of the room.

"I apologize for the lack of chairs. The couch is all I have. I don't entertain much, it's just me and Avery here."

"It's okay. We won't be too long," Sonyai said.

"Oh, I know you won't," Evelyn said sharply. "I know my Avery and I know there's no way—"

"No way *what*?" Chester interrupted.

"Calm down, everyone," Sonyai said. "There is no need to get loud. Mrs. Boone, let's hear from Avery himself since he's been so quiet." She walked over to the giant of a child. "Young man, do you have something to tell your mother?"

He looked down and mumbled something underneath his breath.

"You'll have to speak up," Sonyai pleaded.

The boy lifted his head up and looked over to his mother and said, "I…I had sex with Janelle."

The mother struck the child on his forearm with an open-hand slap. "Avery! Goddammit! How could you do this?"

The child winced and stepped back. "I'm sorry, mama!" he cried.

Sonyai stepped between the two. "Mrs. Boone, please."

"I'd listen to her!" Chester said from the couch with a smirk. Luanne nudged him.

The mother snapped her head to her visitors and pointed a bony finger to Janelle. "*You* did this to my boy! You seduced him! He's only 16!"

Luanne stood up. It was her turn to be angry. "Excuse me?"

"Mom!" yelled Avery, his voice deeper and more adamant now.

Evelyn turned to look at her son. "Boy, who the hell you think you talking to like that?"

"Okay, everyone, calm down," Sonyai ordered. "Thank you for being brave and speaking up, Avery. I know you're scared, but we're going to talk this out and reach an understanding." *Why is it the children are more mature than the adults in this situation?* she asked herself.

"Mrs. Boone, we know that Avery is being scouted for basketball, and something like this could blow his chances at a scholarship."

"You damn right!" she barked.

"Which is why Janelle and her parents have agreed to keep this situation quiet."

"Uh-huh, for how much?"

"What?" Janelle squeaked.

"I ain't stupid. You all want money to keep this quiet, right? You did this on purpose!"

"Mom! It wasn't like—" Avery started.

"Hush up, boy!"

"How the hell you think we want money when you ain't got none yet, you little—" Chester began.

"Enough!" Sonyai yelled. She turned to Evelyn. "We aren't asking for money, but the boy *will* be involved in the baby's life, one way or the other. That's all we ask."

"When the baby is born," Janelle said stepping forward, "he or she will bear *my* last name."

"We will not name you the father, so the scouts won't learn about this. But you will provide support when you can," Sonyai instructed. "Diapers, food, clothing. It's not only about money it's also about *emotional* support."

Evelyn nodded. "Alright, we'll help. And when he makes it to the NBA, he'll claim the baby then."

Janelle and Avery both sighed in relief.

"And we demand the baby be tested to make sure it's his!" Evelyn added.

Luanne and Chester both stood up at the insinuation, but Sonyai waved them down.

"Your doubts are yours to have, Mrs. Boone, and the doctors can fulfill that request. I think we're done here."

The two teenage soon-to-be-parents exchanged worried glances, and then Janelle joined her parents as they made their way to the door. Sonyai was close behind them. Chester worked the locks and opened the door. As Evelyn approached to see them off, Sonyai turned to the mother. "Thank you for your hospitality," she said respectfully, then turned and left.

ROBIN APPROACHED the door to the apartment at ten o'clock. He had just finished his class and swung by a Duane Reade to buy a huge garbage bag and over eighty dollars' worth of snacks as his contribution to the end of the term party happening inside. Robin had no clue whose place this was, but considering he was in Tribeca, the owner was either rich or a squatter. He knocked three times and waited.

"Password?" a voice asked from behind the door.

"Mouse, it's me. Open up."

"Ah, um, password?" came from behind the door again.

"Open the damn door, Mouse. I'm not playing!" Robin was growing impatient.

Silence followed. Robin rolled his eyes and said, "Up, up, down, down, left, right, left, right, B, A, start."

The door unlocked and opened. Standing there was Carlos Rivera, who everyone called "Mouse." He and Robin attended George Washington High School back in Washington Heights between 1989 and 1993. Olive skinned and a meek four-foot-ten, the Dominican got the nickname because he was always the last one standing when playing dodgeball in gym class. Even with his pencil-thin mustache and protruding front teeth, Mouse came to terms with the nickname and has always been the mascot of the cliques he hung out with. Robin stepped inside as the meek individual locked the door behind him.

"S-s-sorry, Robin. They told me...EEEEK!"

Robin grabbed Mouse by the collar and pressed him against the wall.

"Mouse, we go way back, right?"

"Y-y-yeah, yeah! Gee-Dubs! Class of '93!" Mouse replied, terrified.

"And you notice the password is actually a cheat code for Konami video games, like *Contra*, *Gradius*, and *Teenage Mutant Ninja Turtles*?"

"Uh, yeah?"

"Well, it's also a cheat code for *me!* Whenever I knock and identify myself, I don't need to say it. You just let me in, got it?"

"But—"

Robin lifted Mouse several inches off the floor. He squeaked as his legs dangled in the air.

"Got it?"

"Okay, okay! Yeah, I got it. You the cheat code, Robin. I'll just open the door for ya!"

Robin lowered him back to the floor. "Good." He reached into the garbage bag and pulled out a couple bags of Cheese Doodles. "Here."

Mouse snatched them out of his hand and had one open in a matter of seconds. "Hey, thanks! How'ya know?" he asked.

"Lucky guess," he said and walked upstairs to the main floor.

The living room was a vast cornucopia of festive activities. From dancing to drinking to smoking, even playing video games. There had to be at least forty students in one huge setting, with some even going upstairs to another floor of what appeared to be a multi-level loft.

He passed a few people in the crowd as he maneuvered to the kitchen. He unloaded half the contents of his bag, pulling out bags of chips, pretzels, and popcorn and grabbing a few bowls to pour them in.

Jarvis Brody approached Robin and greeted him with a hearty slap on the shoulder. "Robin! My man! How's it hanging?"

"Fine, Jarvis, fine. What's the setup here? I'm looking for a certain someone."

"Well, everyone's got their separate little corners and rooms all around! Seniors are in the basement, Juniors are in the back, everywhere else is us undergrads. You got the jocks over there in the left, the popular kids on the right—"

"Okay, okay, I get it. Segregation at its finest. Where the Asians?"

"They all upstairs. But they ain't letting anyone other than their own in. You're wasting your—"

Robin didn't let Jarvis finish his sentence and made a bee-line to the staircase leading to the second floor. He climbed the steps upstairs, where at the top waiting for him was a male Japanese student Robin had seen around campus.

At five-foot-seven, Kondo Yuudai was stoic as a caricature on a Ming vase. He had an athletic build with short spiky hair shaped in a low flat-top. Wearing black sweatpants and a collarless banded buttoned up long-sleeved shirt, the student tilted his head when Robin approached.

He put on his friendliest smile. "Hey, Kondo, how's it goin'?"

"You lost? Party's downstairs."

"But I gots the goods! I'm in charge of bringing the food and music!" he said as he went into his garbage bag.

"I got some…Rice cakes! Fortune Cookies. Ooh, I got that Wu-Tang album! 36 Chambers! Mysteries of Chessboxing, y'know, 'Wu-Tang Clan ain't nothing to fuck with!'"

That brought a smile to Kondo's face, "Oh yeah, yeah! Dollah, Dollah, Bill, yaaahhh!"

The two shared a light laugh until Robin tried to move past.

"Ah-ah! Party's downstairs," he repeated.

"C'mon, I just wanna take a peek. I'm looking…"

"I *said*, party's downstairs, sandpaper boy!"

"Sandpaper? Oh, you got jokes, huh? Okay, I gotta joke for *you*, my new friend." He put down the bag. "Why'd the asshole fall down the stairs?"

"Why?" Kondo asked.

Robin grabbed the student's arm by his wrist and twisted it behind his back in an awkward angle. Then he turned him around and repeated the move on his other arm followed by a push down the staircase. His body bounced a couple of times as he landed at the bottom of the stairwell in a tangled pile of limbs. "Because they broke his arms and he couldn't stop himself!" he called out, finishing the joke and then turned around going upstairs to the second floor.

As Robin walked through the open area, he surveyed his surroundings, looking for his mysterious girl.

Six guys suddenly approached him from all directions, encasing him in a circle. They spoke to him angrily in Japanese, pointing back to the staircase leading downstairs. Each of them tensed up, preparing for a fight. Robin looked around sizing the circle. They outmatched him.

If all the kung-fu movies he watched growing up taught him anything, they would each engage with him one at a time to see how tough he was. *What would Bolo Yeung do in a situation like this?* he thought. Robin lowered his bag and pumped up his chest. "Alright! Who's first?" he yelled. The entire circle attacked him at once.

Combinations of kicks and punches to every part of his body plummeted him. "Hey, what happened to fighting fair? Oww!" he cried. Two guys opened a nearby window and kicked the window guard out, exposing a one-story drop. The other four each grabbed a limb, lifting him off the floor as Robin struggled. "No!" he protested. "C'mon! Let's talk about this!"

He screamed as the group pulled him toward the window and threw him through it. Robin flailed his arms and braced for the worst. "Ohshitohshitohshitohshiiiiiit!" He landed in a huge blue recycling container full of plastic soda bottles. He sighed, thanking the man upstairs he didn't land on the sidewalk.

He looked up and gasped as his garbage bag landed on his lap in front of him. After a moment to gather himself, Robin jumped out of the container with his bag and circled around the corner to the front of the building again. He hid back against the wall as he noticed the door opening and two guys carrying out Kondo to a nearby cab, screaming at the top of his lungs in agony. He waited ten minutes before stepping up to the door.

"Password?"

"Mouse! Let me in, *Goddammit!*"

The door flew right open.

"I thought you were upstairs! What happened?" Mouse asked.

"Never mind!" Robin yelled and went back up the stairs again.

He stepped back on the main floor and glanced to the top of the staircase where he once was. The two guys who opened the window were looking down at him. Robin knew when he was beaten, but he would still give them a piece of his mind. He pointed two fingers to his eyes and back at them, then bent his arms in an L-shape with his fist pointed up, the universal gesture for "fuck you!"

The pair almost came down at the sign of disrespect, but instead, they stood their ground. Back inside on the second floor, a Japanese girl and her friends came out of the second room to see what the commotion was. She was wearing her signature pigtails with a pink dress and white stockings again. Her friends convinced her that everything was fine and the group of ladies went back in their room for some drinks.

Robin walked through several rooms on the main floor, handing out more snacks and cassette tapes of music. He noticed one room was playing dance music. The music video for "Big Time Sensuality" by Bjork was being shown on a television tuned to MTV. Another room was for the R&B crowd as TLC's "Baby, Baby, Baby" played on the radio.

Someone caught his attention, asking for a cassette tape. He threw the guy his copy of *The Inner Mind's Eye* by Leaders of the New School and went into another room. After passing through several rooms, he came across a hallway with more doors that led to other smaller, intimate rooms. *Man! This place is humongous! Who the hell lives here, John F. Kennedy, Jr.?* Robin thought.

He opened one door and found the room full of men—Black, White, Hispanic, and Asian. They all were wearing make-up, glitter, and flamboyant clothing. "100% Pure Love" by Crystal Waters was playing from a radio. As all eyes moved to the entrance. Robin waved and slowly closed the door. A few more steps down he found sanctuary and familiar faces.

Walter, Gillian, and Kim were among a group of ten students sharing drinks as they sat around on couches discussing their grades for the past term.

"Thank God I passed Elementary Algebra II!" Kim was saying.

The trio spotted Robin as he approached. He tossed over the last contents of his bag, some Doritos, Cracker Jacks, and Wise Potato Chips.

"Ooooh, lemme get those Wise! I love reading the riddles in the bag!" Gillian asked.

Robin took a seat as he sighed from exhaustion. "Damn, I've been through hell just to get here."

"I know. This place is huge!" Kim said while eating some Cracker Jacks.

"Kim? How come you ain't upstairs? You could have vouched for me. I got my ass kicked and tossed out the window!"

"What were you doing up there?" she asked.

"Looking…for someone."

Gillian and Kim looked at each other and both grinned.

"Never mind! Did you pass Basic Writing, Walt?"

"By the skin of my teeth! A C-minus! That damn teacher's a Nazi!"

Everyone shared a laugh. "Yeah, right!" Kim yelled.

Embarrassed, Walter stormed off. "I'm going to the stoners' corner and taking a hit."

"Right! That's the last thing you need!" Robin called out.

"So, Robin, tell us about this girl you've been looking for," Gillian asked.

"I keep seeing her for brief moments and then she disappears. It's so hard to describe her. She's just…beautiful," he said as a goofy smile grew across his face. He then noticed the two were staring back at him. He snapped back to normal and said, "So um, if either of you sees her…"

"We'll let you know," Kim said sharply. The two then sat up and left the room. Robin wondered if he offended them somehow. He shrugged and reached behind the couch into a cooler and pulled out a can of Budweiser, popped the top, and downed the beer in a single chug.

A few hours later, the numbers in the room thinned and then grew. Everyone was getting more rambunctious as students got drunk or high and conversations got loose. Robin looked around and noticed all the girls were gone, so he felt more opinionated.

"Gentlemen," he bellowed, "I would like to talk to your all about the complicated subject…that is women!"

Walter sighed. "Oh no. He's doing the Jack Nicholson speech from *Witches of Eastwick* again." The student stood up to stop him, but a hand held him back down.

"Nah, man let 'em rant. He needs to get this off his chest," Jarvis said.

Another student came over and whispered, "What's his deal with God and women?"

"It's a long story," was all Walter said as he looked on.

Robin performed the monologue verbatim, as the film left a lasting impression on him. He punctuated his performance by throwing a bottle to the back of the room for effect. It shattered into a million pieces. His face contorted into a twisted ghoul-like expression, with his eyebrows arched, eyes wide, and a crazed grin across his face.

"So who's with me? Who wants to find that cure?"

No one raised their hand. Some in the room were shaking their heads, not finding the spectacle funny anymore.

"Aw, c'mon! Like the man said, '20 push-ups a day, and you never have to be afflicted with women!' Could you imagine how fucking happy we would be if...if..." He sobbed uncontrollably. "Ohh! Why man? Why didn't she trust me, maaan. I wasn't doing nuthin'!" Robin dropped to his knees, which was all that Walter could stand.

"Okay, and on that note, we're done for the night," Walter said, glancing around the emptying room— it was almost four in the morning. He attended to his friend and helped him up. Other students were mumbling as they dispersed from the room.

"Way to bring the night down," someone said, and others agreed with the sentiment. A gentleman made his way into the room looking around.

Robin recognized him and called out, "Heeey! My ride's here! Over here, Cervantes!"

Drunk and disoriented, he waved his free arm, making calling sounds as the cabbie found his passenger. Expecting a night of drinking and debauchery, Robin pre-arranged for himself to be picked up and taken home. "Hey, Cervantes!" he called out, greeting the driver.

The African immigrant stepped forward and said, "I'll take it from here." Walter transferred Robin's arm to the newcomer's.

"He's all yours."

"Hey, Cervantes, tell 'em about the women in Ghana. How African women differ from these chicks..." Robin couldn't finish his sentence as the last bit of energy finally left his body.

His head dropped into his chest as his body went limp. Cervantes' knees buckled. "Uh, my cab's right outside. Can you take the other side of him?"

Walter nodded and the two dragged the exhausted young man out of the building to the sidewalk and into the cab. The driver sat in the front seat and checked his rearview mirror to see if Robin was breathing. His eyes were closed and there was drool coming out the corner of his mouth. Robin was muttering to himself when Cervantes started the car.

"Take the West Side!" he exclaimed.

"Yes, yes, I know."

"Just…20…push-ups…a day, dammit."

CHAPTER TEN

"Do you know what the average blood sugar level for a woman your age and weight, Miss Jenkins?" Doctor Chan asked. The city was cooling off after warm temperatures at the start of the week Thursday morning on Saint Patrick's Day. There were hints of an early spring, which the groundhog had predicted. Ethel was sitting in an examination room of the Morris Heights Health Center clinic in the Bronx. Doctor Herman Chan looked so young she thought he was fresh out of medical school, which made it difficult to take him seriously.

"If you fasted for the last 12 hours and drank nothing but water this morning, it should be in the range between 77 and 99 milligrams," the doctor said.

"Okay," she said.

"You tested 137. Which tells me you didn't completely fast."

"I'm telling you, the last thing I ate was a cheese danish at 5:30 pm yesterday!"

"If that's the case, your current levels are dangerously in the range for type-2 diabetes."

"They've told me I could have that once before, but then I get tested again and my levels go down."

"Since you're taking this lightly, I'd like to recall the long-term consequences of diabetes if it goes untreated." He flipped over a page on his clipboard. "Kidney failure—you'll have to endure manual dialysis sessions to clean your blood, which would take at least 6 hours a day 4 times a week. Heart disease—you'll need an oxygen tank to help your heart pump enough blood in order to breathe. Possibility of a stroke—if not enough blood gets to your brain—"

"Okay! I get it! I wanna reschedule and do another test, with *another* doctor, I might add." She sat up and grabbed her coat.

"You think someone else will tell you something different from what I'm saying?"

"Not doubting you personally Doctor Chan, but even the weatherman can't get the forecast right all the time. I'll see myself out."

"Very well, Miss Jenkins," Chan called out behind her as she left. "Diabetes is only the 3rd highest killer of African-Americans over 35, next to high blood pressure and AIDS. You have a nice day."

"I'm dying, Esme. This is it."

Jon was in the living room of his sister's apartment several stories above his own inside the high-rise of 111 Wadsworth Avenue. She never learned how to sign, so he read her lips as he sat in front of her at the kitchen table as they both sipped tea. Esmeralda Hodge was the oldest of the three Walker siblings at eighty-two. She had been married twice and worked most of her life in the banking industry.

She worked for the federal reserve when she was thirty-five, then Chemical Bank, and retired after working for Chase at 55 Water Street for fifteen years. Her four children, Avery, Bianca, Calvin, and Deborah were spread out across the United States, with Calvin—whom everyone called "Pepsi"—still in New York.

The matriarch had lived her retirement years as a socialite, participating in various acts of philanthropy for causes she felt needed support. Her relationship with her brothers was estranged at best, so it must have been really serious for Jon to see her.

"David," Esme began—she always called her younger brother by his middle name—"we've been here before. You have nine lives like a cat. How many times has death stared you in the face and blinked?"

"This is different. I know I've had my near misses, but my time is almost up. I'm not afraid to go, I just want to make sure someone looks after Robin."

"He's a grown man now, he can take care of himself. And he'll do just fine when your time comes *further down* the line. You're not going anywhere."

Jon shook his head. "Why is it when I tell you I'm dying you refuse to believe it? You think I'll say 'told you so' when I'm 6 feet deep in the ground? I'm telling you now so you don't be shocked!" He stood up. "Don't believe me if you want. I know we don't see eye-to-eye. We never did, but Robin...don't take out any grudges against me on him. He's innocent, he'll need you after I'm gone. He has no one. Not his mother, and his father doesn't even know he exists. I've been all he's got most of his life. He's not ready to fend for himself, not yet. I've done all I can, but it's not enough."

He walked to the door. If she said anything back to him, he didn't hear her...and didn't want to. Jon knew now that the relationship with his younger brother and older sister was as dead as he would soon be. And he was just fine with that.

Augustus and Heywood were in the head librarian's office for their daily morning briefing as it was time once again to plan the next month's film schedule.

"I'd like to thank you again, Heywood. The Mel Brooks tribute has been doing well this month. We had a full auditorium yesterday."

"Um, yeah," he said nervously.

"So, any suggestions for April?"

"Well, I...I was thinking we'd do a series of Mel Gibson films, sir."

"Gibson, eh?"

"Yes, his latest film is an adaption of the famous TV western *Maverick*. It even has the star of the original in it, James Gardner." A trickle of sweat slid down the left side of his face down to his neck. If Augustus knew he already had a selection reserved for the branch without the librarian's authorization, he would be done for.

"Kinda funny, though, to go from Mel Brooks to Mel Gibson.

Perhaps in May we could do a musical tribute to Mel Torme as well?" That brought a fit of laughter, which Heywood joined along in sharing for a light moment. The two then contained their composure. "I'll put it into consideration. Good suggestion," Augustus said, closing his notepad and standing up to end the meeting.

"Thank you, sir!" Heywood said, then quickly got up and left. Once the information assistant was out of his office, Augustus knitted his eyebrows wondering why the young gentleman was so nervous.

For third period at Park West High School, Johnny Jones was in math class when someone passed him a note while the teacher was writing on the chalkboard. He opened the note and read it.

"Meet me in the third-floor girls' bathroom after 5th period —Tanya."

Johnny crumbled the paper in his hand and looked up, shocked.

Across the hall in social studies, Tanya was sitting in class chewing gum. Someone passed her a note, and she took a quick glance at it.

"We need to talk. I know Vickie is after you over me and I wanna squash this. Meet me in the third-floor girls' bathroom after 5th period —Johnny."

She pouted her lips and lowered her eyelids in a skeptical look. *Bullshit. This is a trap*, she thought. She decided to show up anyway but to be prepared to defend herself this time.

Vickie Florence snuck out of her fourth-period gym class fifteen minutes before the bell rang and went upstairs to the third floor. She was about to set up Tanya by tricking her and Johnny to meet in the bathroom. Johnny would confess his feelings, Tanya would reject him, and she would come in to beat her up. He would fall for her, finally, and they would go on a date to start their relationship.

It was the perfect plan. She entered the bathroom to clear it out, making sure no one was there using the stalls. After checking the first two stalls, she came upon the third, which suddenly opened on its own.

"What the—?" she yelped.

A chubby light-skinned guy wearing a red baseball cap with one black leather glove on his left hand sat on top of the toilet. His feet were up on the seat as he looked back at her deranged with a wide and evil smile.

"Hello, Clarice," the stranger whispered.

Vickie backed up and started to scream, but was grabbed and pulled into the stall. "Step inside my office for a moment!"

THE GEORGE WASHINGTON BUS TERMINAL was a transit hub where someone could transfer from the MTA Subway system to New Jersey Transit buses that ran to and from Northern New Jersey. Below the vast parking lot and bus gates, which all lead to the infamous suspension interstate bridge, was a promenade of vendors and storefronts.

Jon stepped off the escalator from the entrance on the first floor and walked to the off-track betting facility on the left side. The enclosure was a small room with four betting windows and a row of televisions suspended above from the ceiling. Inside, at least twenty people were placing bets and studying racing forms while watching horse races from various tracks in the tri-state area. The double door entrance was part of an entire wall of glass, boxed in a grid.

From the outside, the gamblers looked like caged mice on display in a laboratory, waiting to be studied and dissected. Once inside, Jon grabbed a racing form from a nearby writing table, then walked deeper inside the room and found a corner where he could stand alone.

Several minutes later, a short man wearing a wool peacoat and matching chocolate brown wool bowler hat with sunglasses stepped next to him. He was a white man who had mutton chops and wore brown penny loafers. Jon turned to look at him so he could read his lips.

"I never thought I'd see you again, Jon. What's it been? 10? 12 years?"

"Yeah, 1982. Niners beat the Bengals in the Super Bowl, out there in the Silverdome."

"I remember Cincy tried to comeback but fucked up the onside kick."

"Cost me a grand." Jon shook his head. "I told myself I'd never do it again after I gave you those 10 c-notes."

"And you never did. So why the social call? Thinking the Rangers are finally gonna get the Stanley Cup this time after 54 years?"

"I'm taking that walk. It won't be long now, so I'm making arrangements."

"I see."

"You'll have to be the contact for my executor. Tell my grandson, Robin, about everything after I'm gone."

The man stood quietly for a moment as Jon looked back at him.

"Well, say something, dammit," Jon said impatiently.

"I…I don't know *what* to say, man."

"You ain't getting soft in your old age? Because if you can't do this—"

"No! You're right. It's just that…I don't wish death on nobody. Not even you."

"You're a company man, Syn. You know it's just part of the job. The final punch-out. You'll be the first person they call. When you tell Robin, he won't know you. We have a secret phrase. You have to say it the moment he sees you or he might react a certain way."

"Okay," Syn said.

Jon turned to leave. He had made it a few steps when a tap on his shoulder stopped him in his tracks. He turned and looked at the man again. He appeared shaken by the news. "I just want to say…I'm sorry, Jon."

"Bit too late for sorry now, Syn. Bit too late," Jon said, then turned and left.

VICKIE OPENED her eyes to an open sky. A powder blue canvas with white scattered clouds moving to the east. Fear overcame her as she noticed she was bound and couldn't move. She tried to scream and noticed she was gagged as well. A shadow crept into her peripheral view and the stranger's face looked down at her.

"Hi there."

The girl struggled against her bonds, her eyes blinking rapidly with concern. She turned her head sideways and noticed she was on a ledge several stories up. Another muffled scream came out of her mouth.

"Careful. It's a long way down."

Robin was on the roof of the school. He had been observing Vickie since she arrived this morning. Lakeshia gave him a good description of her and the car she was driving when she was following Tanya around.

"I gotta tell ya, the security here is pitiful." He was standing on the ledge with his arms extended pretending to walk a tightrope. The platform was three feet wide, so there was nothing to fear, but Robin had a vivid imagination.

"I mean damn, back at George Washington up in the Heights, we had security guards, metal detectors, random searches. This is supposed to be one of the scariest schools in Manhattan. Ha!"

He jumped down and walked back to her. "I had a friend in junior high, crazy motherfucker named Benito. He came down here in September 1989. I caught up with him around the neighborhood. He told me he had to buy a bulletproof vest to survive down here!"

She continued to struggle while Robin went on. "Think about it. A guy can set up shop here on some Nino Brown or Scarface type of shit. Bribe the faculty to look the other way, get some students for runners and distribution. This place could be like The Carter in no time."

He nodded. "You see *New Jack City?*"

She didn't answer, and Robin rolled his eyes. "Gee, I hate one-sided conversations. Well, okay, enough talk. Let's see what we're working with." He checked her pockets. "What do we got here? A boxcutter, brass knuckles. Oh, hey, a switchblade! I heard something about a...ah! Here we are, .22 special, nice! Hmm, I don't think we're done yet. Don't wanna get too invasive, do we?" He danced his eyebrows.

Another pat-down and his hand stopped at her waist. "Oh, I felt that! What's this?" Robin pulled out three Japanese throwing stars.

"Wow! I am impressed! I remember these from the 80's." A smile came across his face. "You *are* all kinds of crazy!"

Putting all the confiscated weapons in a brown grocery bag, he looked up and winced. "Oh, I hope that .22 doesn't have a hair trigger. Gotta be careful." He let out a chuckle, then reached down and pulled Vickie off the ledge. Sitting her against the wall underneath, he took a seat next to her. Reaching back, he pulled out her switchblade and pressed the button. The blade swung out and extended four inches.

"Bet you thought I put *this* in the bag too, didn't ya?"

Her eyes stayed on the blade as he held it in front of her. It reflected the sun, nearly blinding her.

"We're gonna have a little talk," Robin began. "You scream, then we're gonna have some *fun*." He leaned in. "And trust me, you don't wanna have the fun I'm talking about. Are we clear?"

She nodded furiously.

"Good," Robin said. "Okay, let me check the scorecard and see if I can figure this out. You like this boy named Johnny, and he likes Tanya. But Tanya don't like him, right?"

She nodded again.

"So instead of pursuing Johnny and being straightforward with him, you go after Tanya, intending to do her harm. Why? What the hell does *that* accomplish? Really?"

She shrugged her shoulders.

"Think about it. You go to jail for murder, or assault because I don't think you got it in you to cap anybody. She becomes just another statistic, and Johnny's left wondering why because he didn't know nothing about you. Nobody wins."

She looked down, feeling ashamed for a moment.

"The way I see it, there are two kinds of bullies in the world. First, you have the real bullies—demented, unstable, irrational, no reasoning, no method to their madness. It's just 'fuck the world, I wanna see it burn!' Then you have the fake bullies—petty, driven, overcompensating, all about appearances." He pointed to her with the knife, then drew in close, his face inches from hers, his eyes dark and hypnotic as hers grew wide in paralyzing fear. Robin brought the knife right up to her left eye and waited. They held the gaze in a staring contest, breathing very shallow breaths. She trembled as he held the knife steady.

After two of the longest minutes of Vickie Florence's young life, a tear emerged from her right eye.

"Yes. That's it," he whispered. If he didn't know better he'd swear she just shit herself. "The fake bullies, deep down, are just part of an insignificant cycle. They go too far, and the victim becomes a bully too. They find another victim, who becomes another bully, and so on and so on. You get the idea."

He retrieved the bag, then turned back to her, eyes wide like a deer in headlights. "Here's what we're going to do. I'm letting you go and you're going to leave Tanya alone. *After* you apologize to her. Sounds fair, ninja girl?"

She let out a muffled, "Yes."

"Good." He cut the ropes.

Robin walked past her, heading toward the door leading downstairs. He held the knife up and said, "I'm keeping your toys…in case I have to come back." After opening the door, he turned back to her. "Oh, and hey!" he called out. She stopped shaking herself loose and looked up at him.

"Look me up in around 4 years when you get your shit together. Fix your attitude and you could be a nice sweetheart to take around the town on a weekend." A throwing star whizzed through the air and hit the wall next to her. He winked, then saluted. "Ciao, Francesco Rinaldi!"

ETHEL AND GERRY were both reading at their separate desks when Robin walked in and took off his coat. He put his hand in a brown paper bag and pulled out a can of Diet Pepsi. At that point, Ethel lowered her paper and sat up to address the young clerk.

"Mr. Walker, I know you've been bringing in a soda for me every day because of what I said to humiliate you, but a joke's a joke. You can stop that now."

"Afraid I can't do that, Miss Jenkins," Robin began.

"Well, I insist that you do!"

Across the office, Gerry snuck a glance to see how the exchange would turn out.

"You can insist all you want. You started this, and I'm gonna keep bringing you a soda every day. Throw it away, drink it, give it to someone else, do whatever you want." He winked at her for emphasis, and that only made her angrier.

Robin turned away when Gerry called out, "Where's my soda?"

"Huh?"

Gerry lowered his paper. "If you're getting her a soda every day to piss her off, you might as well get me one too!"

"You think it'll piss her off even more?" Robin exclaimed playfully.

"It'll drive her absolutely crazy!" Gerry replied with a laugh.

"Consider it done!"

The two shook hands on the deal, then Robin left the office in stride. Gerry looked over to Ethel with a grin on his face.

"Okay," she hissed to herself. "If *that's* the way we're gonna play it!"

The Saint Patrick's Day parade marched down 5th Avenue. Spectators packed the sidewalks held behind steel barricades. Cheers and libations flowed as about a hundred and fifty thousand people marched over forty blocks north. A few drunken stragglers dispersed once the parade passed 58th street, heading east passing Park Avenue.

At three o'clock, Robin and Tommy were working the circulation desk. Neither of them was speaking to each other outside simple pleasantries when required. Robin noticed rowdy drunks walking by the window. A bottle shattered against the glass, frightening a young woman reading at a table close by.

"What is this?" Robin asked. "What is going on?"

Angie emerged from the shelves. "Drunks from the parade. It happens every year. So annoying."

"They're disrupting the public! Where's the cops when you actually need them?"

Tommy responded from behind them. "They turn a blind eye. Nearly half the precinct for this area is Irish. Fucking embarrassing if you ask me."

"You embarrassed of your own people? There's a first," Robin said surprised by the admission.

"They may be Irish, but they're no kin of mine!"

"Anybody try doing something about it?" Robin asked.

"Like what?" Tommy replied.

"Like asking them to knock it off...*nicely,*" he said with a cocked eyebrow.

Tommy nodded. He understood the youngster's suggestion nice and clear. "I'm down, but who's gonna watch the desk?"

Sonyai was in the office while Gerry and Ethel were upstairs. "Well, I can watch the desk, guys," Angie volunteered.

The pair turned their heads to her and said in unison, "You?"

She folded her arms in the face of their doubt.

Another drunk staggered and fell against the window with a hard *thunk!* He slid to the ground as three of his friends laughed a few feet away. Robin was already walking around heading toward the exit; Tommy was just a few steps behind him.

The four drunks were singing a rendition of "Bonny Portmore," which sounded like a group of cats caterwauling. They stopped singing in between verses and laugh hysterically for no reason, then started the song over again.

"Excuse me, gentlemen!" a voice called out catching their attention. They turned to the double doors of the library entrance to see Robin and Tommy approaching.

"You are disturbing the patrons inside who are trying to read," Tommy began.

"On behalf of the 58th Street Branch Library, I'd have to ask you —" Robin tried to continue.

"Who the fuck iszzzis niggah?" one of them interrupted.

"Is he one of them darkies?" another asked. "Think he one of them Puerto Ricans or somethin'!" The four laughed.

"Okay, I got those 2," Robin said, and Tommy nodded.

"'Fraid we have to do this the hard way, gentlemen," Tommy called out to them.

The four took the challenge lightly and squared up for a fight. "Oh yeah?" the one who taunted Robin asked.

Robin punched his right fist into his open palm and flexed. "Yeah," he answered.

The men charged the two employees. Robin waited for the goons to throw their punches first in order to claim self-defense. Tommy was charged and ready, so he didn't hesitate in socking one of the drunks in the jaw. The second guy kicked Tommy in the ribs and they tussled. Robin danced around, ducking wild punches thrown at him with ease, tiring the aggressors out as they got agitated. He found his opening and grabbed the wrist of the one who called him a Puerto Rican, then flipped him over on his back, shouting a karate yell.

Tommy got the upper-hand, delivering a hard elbow to the nose and followed with a stiff-arm across the man's chest. The first guy, who didn't have a glass jaw, got up and grabbed Tommy from behind with a bear hug. Robin delivered a swift kick to his second opponent, and he crumbled like a bag of garbage. The man who received a stiff-arm from Tommy recovered and was about to double-team the clerk with his friend still holding on to him.

Robin ran over and tapped him on the shoulder, yelling, "Hey!" and then followed with a sucker punch across his face. Tommy broke free and signaled to Robin while delivering a few punches to the stomach and chest. Robin saw the signal, and the two clerks swung their opponents into each other, straight out of an exaggerated fight sequence from the sixties *Batman* TV show. The four drunks were all slumped over on their backs, laid out on the sidewalk.

"Happy Saint Patrick's Day, gentlemen," Tommy said.

"Yeah, top of the morning to ya!" Robin added.

The two jogged back inside the branch, hyped about dispatching the drunks. Angie was just finishing a checkout as they took their places with no one noticing.

"Thanks," Robin said to Angie.

"Yeah, thanks for covering. That was fun," Tommy added. He was actually smiling.

"You're welcome. You two looked good out there. Pretty much in sync."

The door to the clerical office opened and Sonyai stepped out. "What's going on out here? Your voices are carrying!" The two clerks looked away as the senior clerk gave Angie a look. "Miss Trueblood?"

Angie gasped and pretended to not know where she was. "I'm sorry. I was looking for a book on the shelving cart. I'll be on my way now." She exchanged glances with both clerks, then smiled and walked back to the information desk.

Sonyai closed the door and the two clerks loosened up. "You got some moves there." Robin nodded to Tommy.

"You're not so bad yourself, trying to do that kung-fu shit."

Robin held his finger up and whispered, "I know who you are," then winked.

Tommy's smile disappeared. "What are you talking about?"

"When I was busy kicking your ass—"

"Hey!" Tommy interrupted.

Robin waved his hand. "Okay, okay. We on good terms so I won't ruin the moment, but back then, I noticed you did a 3-point stance and it stayed with me. So I did some research."

Tommy remained quiet, but he became nervous about where this was going.

"You really got everyone fooled. Letting your hair grow, cutting your beard, but it's still you."

"You don't know what you're talking about."

"Number 38, University of Syracuse Orangemen?" Robin grinned.

"No!" Tommy exclaimed.

"Tom Connelly. Linebacker from 1988 to 1990." He finished with a smile.

Tommy stepped forward and brought his face inches from Robin's. "Don't you tell anybody, you hear me?"

"Easy, man! Your secret is safe with me." He let out a sinister chuckle. Tommy stepped back, but Robin was still smiling. "One day, you gotta tell me what happened."

The clock struck four as the door to the second floor opened. Ethel and Gerry made their way to relieve their counterparts. Tommy went inside the clerical office while Robin stepped out to the library floor and disappeared within the shelves.

Lakeshia was working on the tall five-shelf bookcase they dedicated for the children's books. The selection was quite small with only a hundred books.

"This is one of the best things about this branch," Robin said as he approached her.

She turned and blushed, taking the remark as a compliment.

"Fort Washington has an entire 2nd floor for children's books," he said, tracing his finger on the top shelf.

She registered a sour look at the misplaced sentiment.

"I *hated* working up there. They knew this and used it as a method of punishment. Tiny shelves, prepubescent children running rampant, full of energy, making a mess of things. It was terrible. Can you imagine?"

Lakeshia didn't feel like reminiscing. "Yeah, must have been terrible," she said dryly.

"Anyway, a little birdy told me somebody had a birthday this past weekend."

She brightened again. "Yes! I turned 15," she said with a smile.

"Nice. You know, I have a fun little game I do with friends on their birthday. Would you like to hear about it?"

Her pulse quickened and goosebumps tickled the back of her neck. "Okay," she replied in a throaty whisper.

He took a step closer to her. "Let's pretend today's your birthday, right?"

She nodded. "Mmhmm."

"You would walk up to me and say Happy Birthday, almost like you're saying it to me, but it's *your* birthday, got it?"

She looked puzzled, which Robin detected, so he continued, "Then I would say, 'That's *my* line!' Okay? And you would say, 'Beat'cha to it.' Then we both say, 'To save some time.' That's the game. Let's give it a try."

"Okay," she said.

Robin gestured with his hand for her to start.

"Ahem. Happy Birthday."

"That's *my* line!" Robin replied.

Lakeshia blanked on the next step, embarrassed and confused.

Robin chuckled. She joined in and giggled as well, then looked down for a moment. She asked to try again.

"Happy Birthday."

"That's *my* line!"

"Beat'cha to it."

"To save some time," they finished in unison.

They smiled at each other, sharing the moment. The two locked eyes for what felt like a lifetime. She felt like they were the only people in the entire world. Frozen in time and space.

"I...I like that game," she finally said.

"Good. Remember it for my birthday," he said, then walked up toward the back of the branch.

"Wait! When's your birthday?" she called out to him, but he was already gone.

Back at the circulation desk, Sonyai stood at the doorway to the clerical office. She didn't like what was developing between the page and the clerk. It was time to take preventative measures.

Angie was reading in the staff room when Robin walked in. She lowered her book and looked up at him.

"Um, sorry! I didn't mean to interrupt your reading."

"It's okay," she said.

He took a seat at the kitchen table, still facing her as she sat on the couch.

"Thanks again for covering us. I didn't think IA's could work the desk."

"It's technically not allowed, but I don't necessarily follow *all* the rules here."

They shared a light laugh.

"Is that why this is the first conversation we're having in the month I've been here?"

"There wasn't anything to prevent you from saying something sooner." she replied with a grin.

"You kinda keep to yourself. I mean, the lines are drawn between the staff, but you seem neutral as Switzerland in this…" Robin took a moment to think, "whatever you'd call this thing between Chavez and Yi."

"I guess you could say I'm the wildcard."

"I agree. So, what's your story? You're one of the few that even The Battle Axe has no dirt on, which means you're either squeaky clean or your indiscretions are known to no one."

"Like you, I'm attending school, only at night part-time, though."

"Yeah? Cool. Full-time student, part-time clerk." he said pointing to himself, "Full-time IA, part-time student." Robin finished pointing to her, "Opposites."

"I've been here a little over a year. It'll be 2 years in November."

He nodded again. "Um, what…uh…I…dunno how to ask without offending."

"We identify with Nations or Bands, along with Tribes if that's what you're asking."

"Ah," Robin smiled sheepishly.

"And it's also a question of whether I still preserve my tribal identity, which I do." Angie explained.

"Good to know. I love learning something new."

"I'm a member of the Oneida Indian Nation. Most of us can be found in upstate New York. Our nation has three clans. I'm from the Turtle Clan, but don't you even *think* of doing a ninja turtle joke!"

"No, absolutely not! Never crossed my mind,"

"Why the interest all of the sudden?" she asked tilting her head.

"To be honest, I've never met an Indian before." Robin instantly winced after saying the word. "I am *so* sorry! I didn't mean—"

"It's okay. It's a common, yet offensive, term that I'm used to. Well, this was fun, Mr. Walker."

"Please, call me Robin."

"We're not there yet," she replied coldly.

He blinked, feeling hurt by the dismissal. "Well, okay. Glad we talked!" he called back as the door closed behind her.

"THE WEIRDEST THING happened at school today," Tanya said.

Alex and Lakeshia were walking and listening behind her as the trio attended to the shelves of the fiction section after five o'clock. Robin and Sonyai were at the circulation desk while Augustus was working the floor, assisting patrons searching the card catalogs.

Tanya continued her story. "That crazy bitch who was messing with me walked up and squashed the beef like it was nothing!"

"Oh yeah?" Lakeshia asked, stealing a glance to the circulation desk.

"Yeah! She apologized and said she'll never bother me again. It was so weird."

At the desk, Robin was watching back, pretending not to hear their conversation. A thin smile across his face. Lakeshia looked back and mouthed the words *thank you* to him. He mouthed back *now we're even* and nodded.

"All this over some boy that I didn't even like!" Tanya said. "They hooked up on their own and forgot all about me. Weird!"

"Mr. Walker, a word please," Sonyai said, calling him over.

Robin snapped at attention, then walked over and stopped a few inches from his supervisor. "Yes?"

"Having been a page, I understand your need to befriend the girls. Your assistance with their shelf assignments was greatly appreciated."

"Okay," Robin replied.

"However, it has come to my attention that you and Miss Seabrooke are becoming *too* close."

He narrowed his gaze at the accusation. "I'm just being friendly, which is something you could teach the rest of your staff, by the way."

She shook her head and sighed. "I was lax about these situations in the past until Miss Brown developed a relationship with a clerk I was training before Thomas arrived. He had to transfer under extenuating circumstances. That will not happen again, Walker. Do you understand me?"

"I'll be 19 in August. She just turned 15. That's statutory right there. I'm not trying to go to jail."

Sonyai was about to reply when Robin continued, "I don't care what kinda pervert you had working for you before, but I know where to draw the line. We're just friends. That's it."

The two stared each other down for a minute, then Sonyai said, "Fine." and then turned to walk back to the returns side.

Heywood walked into the nightclub and found a seat at the bar. Happy Hour was extended due to the holiday, but since St. Patrick's Day was in the middle of the week and people had to go to work tomorrow, the libations only flowed so much. There was a small stage opposite of the bar with a lower level pit for standing spectators as a performer was being introduced.

"Coming to the stage, our very own siren of the city. Ladies and gentlemen, give it up for Storming Jackie Daze!"

The band on stage played an instrumental intro, and then a singer emerged from backstage in a quick trot, the spotlight shining on the center of the stage. Sporting a wild white-haired mohawk while wearing black leather pants and matching vest, the artist was energy personified as she started her first song.

Heywood froze in mid-sip at the sight of her. As he watched her perform, he was mesmerized. "Wow," he whispered to himself. She performed seven songs in a forty-five-minute set, ending it with a stage dive. The audience held her up as she crowd-surfed to the back of the pit and walked up to the bar.

"Lemme get my usual!" she called out at the bartender further down who was preparing a drink for someone else.

Back at the stage, another act was being introduced, but Heywood was still fixed on the singer who had enchanted him. He was apparently staring too long because she turned and caught his gaze and approached him. He darted his eyes in various directions, then looked down, convinced she would walk by him.

"Hey, stranger," the woman greeted as she stopped at his side.

"Hi," he muttered with a smile, still shocked that she was talking to him.

"You gotta speak up, hon, the crowd is a little loud in here!"

She was as black as the leather she was wearing. The Mohawk was neatly shaved with no trace of hair on the rest of her scalp. The white hair extended at least four inches up and was as wide as a soda can. Her eyes were a shade lighter than brown, possibly hazel. She had several piercings on her right ear but none on her left.

"I'm sorry, I didn't mean to stare," Heywood began. "I just really liked...your music!"

"Why thank you," she said.

"Uh, what exactly do you call it?" he asked. "I've never heard a sound like that before."

"It's starting to become popular here in the east. It's from back west where I'm from."

"Oh? Where's that?"

"Seattle," she answered.

The bartender handed her a bottle of Presidente. She twisted the cap with her bare hand, popped it off, and took a swig. Heywood was awestruck by the feat of strength.

"So you gonna ask me out or what, string bean?" she asked.

Heywood laughed at his new nickname. "Sure, once I eat a can of spinach and grow some muscles."

"Naw, I get hit on by beefcake jerks all the time. What I'm a sucker for are those skinny, quiet types!"

"Well, alright! When are you performing here again?

"I'm here every 2 weeks on Tuesdays and Thursdays."

"Great, on the 31st we'll go out after your performance."

"It's a date!" she said. She grabbed his hand and produced an eyeliner pencil from her pocket, then wrote her phone number on his palm. She then turned his hand over and kissed it, leaving a lipstick print.

"Gotta go. Call me later, string bean." She stepped away from the bar.

"Sure," he answered with a smile. He couldn't believe this was happening.

She started toward the exit, then stopped and turned around. "Hey!"

Heywood looked back to her.

"Grunge," she said.

"What?"

"The name of the music…it's called grunge."

CHAPTER ELEVEN

GERRY WALKED INTO THE CLERICAL OFFICE MONDAY MORNING AT TEN o'clock. Sonyai wasn't due in until noon, so he had a moment to snoop around the empty office. He was still unsure if there really was an investigation into Sonyai's management of the branch funds, but the accounting books would be the first clue.

He started by checking her desk. Searching all the drawers, then the folders and several binders, but coming up with nothing. There was only one other place that could have anything useful, the safe. Only Sonyai and Augustus knew the combination. He walked over, kneeled, and pulled the handle. The door didn't budge; it was still locked.

"What are you doing?"

Gerry shot up and backed away to see Ethel at the doorway looking at him.

"What the hell are you doing, Gerry?" she repeated.

"Nothing."

"Don't lie. Why were you trying to open the safe?"

"I can't...I can't tell you," he replied.

"Goddammit, Gerry!" she yelled.

"Look! Just pretend you saw nothing. I can't tell you what's going on, but things are at play here and I'm just looking out for the rest of us!"

He moved past her trying to leave, but she caught his arm. "That's not good enough."

He pulled his arm away. "It'll have to be," he said and walked out the doorway.

"I'll be out tomorrow and Wednesday for an endeavor of charity, but the deadline for media acquisitions is approaching." Augustus was in his office with Zelda. He adjusted himself and ironed out the wrinkles of his charcoal-grey suit jacket with his hands and checked his fingernails.

"Despite the deadline this week, you're absolutely sure you don't want me to submit any orders?" Zelda asked.

"That's correct. I have filed for an extension and they have agreed to wait another 2 weeks for the list of items I have personally selected."

"Are you ordering late based on the possibility of the branch winning that bonus?"

He turned to her and smiled.

"You're counting your chickens before they hatch, you know."

"I know what I'm doing, Zee. It's all according to plan."

"THANKS FOR COMING WITH ME, Alex. I really needed a break from it all," Janelle said.

Janelle and Alex were walking downhill on Fordham Road heading toward Webster Avenue in the Bronx. The area was a known promenade for anything from sneakers to household appliances. Mom and Pop stores lined up beside huge department outlets. There was an overhead sign that read Fordham Center in bright red letters as bargain hunters filled the sidewalks.

"I needed a good reason to skip school anyways. My attendance record was getting too perfect," Alex said with a giggle.

"Even though it's a little early for baby shopping, it eases my mind a little."

There was a silence between the two for a moment.

"Nellie?" Alex asked hesitantly, eyes darting sideways.

"Yeah?"

"Are you…are you scared?"

"Scared isn't the word. I'm petrified. I'm bringing a human being into the world that I'll be responsible for and I don't know if I can provide for it."

"Then why did you do it? What were you thinking?" Alex asked.

"It was a stupid thing I did because he said he loved me. I see that now."

The two stopped at a window and looked at a crib on display.

"This seems nice," Alex said.

"Yeah, for $300 the baby better do more than just sleep in it, jeez!" Janelle gasped.

"Babies cost money, Nellie. Don't you want the best for…are you having a boy or girl?"

"I don't know. I'm doing the sonogram next month. Yeah, I want the best, but where's the money gonna come from?"

"You have a point. I guess I'm going about this all wrong. If it were me, I would see this baby as a reflection of myself."

"Don't do what I did, Lex. We learned in sex education that girls are drawn into teen pregnancy due to peer pressure. One friend does it, and then they all do it."

Alex winced. "Pluh-leeze! I'm not trying to let a guy get all of this!" she said motioning to herself. "I'm just being supportive, girl."

"Good. I wanna be a warning to you, Leelee, and Tanya. See what I'm going through? It's no joke."

"Don't worry about me and Leelee, but Tee's been around the block with Drew at least once. She lucky she didn't get knocked up."

They continued walking down and approached the Sears Department Store.

"Wanna check in Sears?" Janelle asked.

Alex winced, "Eww. Their layaway clothes are so ghetto!"

Janelle pulled her toward the entrance. "C'mon, they're not bad."

ROBIN WAS BROWSING through the new books section shortly after one o'clock when Zelda approached the clerk and adjusted her glasses a moment before speaking. He was not due to start until two, but had been coming in early since he was off from school.

"Mr. Walker, I wanted to apologize for my actions several weeks ago. I had no right to contact Schemanske, I see that now. I hope we can move on from that transgression and maintain a professional courtesy."

"It's cool," Robin interrupted. "What's done is done. I also want to apologize for…you know…"

"Yes, yes, yes…" she said in a nervous shushing tone.

The pair was sauntering toward the far end of the room as the shelf with the most recently released books extended along.

"Your secret is safe with me." Robin began. "I was only given that information in strict confidence for the possibility that something would come between us. But I've moved on…and *you* got the message."

"Yes, ahem, I did."

"Aside from you-know-who, I believe you also had history with Fort Washington's senior clerk, Theresa Burns," Robin said changing the subject.

"Oh, yes. Theresa and I have known each other for over 15 years."

"Wow."

From the corner of his eye, Robin noticed behind him, at the end of the shelf the mysterious eccentric homeless patron was staring at them.

"She was working at the Riverside Library on Amsterdam at the time…" Zelda continued her ramblings. Robin was focusing on the stranger now. He noticed the man was mumbling incoherently to himself in a low whisper.

Robin nodded and gave a few audible "uh-huhs" as Zelda continued her story. She was unaware of her location and how they were footsteps away from the round table within the patron's personal space. He leaned in further, straining his ears to comprehend the mutterings of a potential madman.

"Wh-what?" he asked while confused.

"…whatschooldadja *go to*," the man whispered.

Robin took another step closer, and that's when Zelda snapped out of her reminiscing and realized how close they were.

"Wait! Don't!" she exclaimed.

"What was that, sir?" Robin asked.

But it was too late. The clerk turned to Zelda, wondering what was she panicking about, and that was the opening he needed.

Without warning, the man lunged at Robin and wrapped his gorilla-like arms around his neck underneath his chin. Locking his hand on the elbow of his other arm and bringing it up he squeezed Robin's head in a strangling sleeper hold. The clerk made a feeble attempt to pull the arms apart, freeing his windpipe to take in some air but it was no use.

The homeless man ranted out loud the same cryptic phrase repeatedly clamping down harder, "…whatschooldadja *go to*?", "…whatschooldadja *go to*?"

Zelda was screaming now as she pounded on the behemoth's arms like she was trying to bust down a door. "Let him go, Jones! Let him go! Gene! *Gene*! Help me!"

Robin's face was turning blue as he asphyxiated, feeling his arms going limp.

Seconds away from losing consciousness, the trio was broken up by someone slamming shoulder first into the homeless patron's back. The monster released his grip, falling back in his chair as Robin fell forward to his knees. The newcomer caught Zelda and straightened her up. He was wearing a security jacket and grey slacks.

"I warned you about attacking the staff, John!" the security guard bellowed.

"Iwasjustasking himwhatschool hewentto!" the man barked back.

"It doesn't matter where he went to school. No strangling! Or else I'll toss your crazy ass outside on the pavement!" He turned to check on Robin and Zelda.

"Thank you, Gene,"

Eugene Iscaro nodded then looked at Robin, who was gasping for air, still on his knees waiting to be helped up to his feet.

"Is he gonna be all right? Should we call someone?"

Robin coughed, waved his hands, and shook his head, dismissing the suggestion.

"That won't be necessary, Gene," Zelda assured him.

"Good. Next time someone should warn him about getting too close to John Paul Jones."

Robin looked up with a hurtful look as the security guard turned and walked away.

GERRY AND ROBIN were working the circulation desk at three o'clock. On the side of the turnstile entrance, a chair was placed where Eugene sat surveying the floor for any incidents that would require his services. Robin was working checkouts and observed the newcomer with a questionable look.

"Uh...Gene, is it?"

"Yeah."

"First off, thanks for the save. And, uh, two, did you *always* sit there?"

"I did when I was here before," he answered.

"You take a vacation or something?"

Eugene smiled. "I was asked to come back. Apparently, my services are needed again."

Robin looked him over then smiled himself. "They brought you in because of *me*. To keep the peace, just in case."

The two locked eyes, sizing each other up.

Robin chuckled and shook his head. "You're not gonna *be* enough."

He chuckled back. "You better *pray* we never find out. I'll remember this conversation the next time you're stupid enough to go near John Paul Jones."

"Uh-huh. You were snippy about it this time so there won't *be* a next time." He strained his neck, still sore from the choke hold. "Not that I'm not ungrateful."

"You should have known better."

"What's that's supposed to mean? The guy chokes me half to death and it's *my* fault?"

"You were told to stay away from him!"

"He tricked me! All that muttering and shit. I—"

Eugene stood up. "No one goes near John Paul Jones, got it?"

"John Paul Jones? What the hell kinda name is that?"

"He gave himself the name. We had nothing to do with it," Gerry said approaching Robin. "Got it from a navy captain who fought in the Revolutionary War. Chavez made a deal with him. We give him his private space and he leaves the public alone."

"That also includes the staff. Legally we can't turn him away if he doesn't make a disturbance," Gene chimed in.

"Y'all do what you want. I'm not letting Sasquatch over there scare me!" Robin stared down where the behemoth sat looking menacing. "I plan to figure out the mystery of John Paul Jones," he said narrowing his gaze.

Eugene sat back down while Gerry checked in a few books. Robin also checked out a few items, and when things slowed down again, the two faced each other. They had fifteen minutes until they were relieved.

"I wanted to revisit one of our last conversations," Gerry said.

"Yeah?"

"Putting the spotlight on your view of the cold-hearted, sister sellouts is usually the automatic response of a…white chocolate brother that's been rejected a few times."

Robin gave a wide-eyed glare at the white chocolate remark, but he let it slide. "Okay. Your opinion, but you couldn't be more wrong. I mean, yeah, that goes on, but it's not where my view comes from."

"Then your feelings toward black women most likely come from resentment of some sort. Possibly for your mother."

"Oh, look at Sigmund Freud over here," Robin snapped.

"Enlighten me. Your parents still together?"

"Well, like over 70% of African-American children these days, I know nothing about my father."

"That's a high number, inclining to the stereotype, but continue."

"My mother had me while having an affair with another man, so I have a half-sister. She gives her all the attention in the world and passed me along to be raised by my grandfather."

"Wow."

"Yeah. The 2 of them travel around the globe, mom playing manager, accountant and assistant. Mooching money off my sister as they live it up and forget I even exist."

"So, what does your sister do? She an actress or something?" Gerry asked.

"Something like that."

"And you go around hating your fellow sisters because of them?"

"You only have one piece of the puzzle. There's more to it than that."

The door to the clerical office opened and Ethel stepped out. Sonyai arrived from the staff room upstairs and made her way toward the desk.

"Oops, I guess our time is up," Robin joked.

The two waited for their replacements to arrive. Robin headed outside for a break while Gerry went to his desk in the clerical office.

Exactly one month to the day he started at 58th Street, Robin had only been around the neighborhood a few times on break. He knew about the McDonald's on 3rd Avenue and Alexander's on the other side of Lexington. Walking down toward 57th Street, he passed a Sam Goody music store and glanced inside. *That'll be a good place to get the latest albums when I'm not at Tower Records on 4th,* he thought. He needed a good spot to eat something and be back in fifteen minutes.

Passing 57th and then turning on the corner of 56th, he found a pizza joint nuzzled up between two office buildings. The place was as wide as a newsstand but ran deep. "Damn, this makes Frank's look like a parking lot!" he muttered to himself. There were a few chairs and tables with a counter taking up the right side of the shop. A skinny chef wearing a green Boston Celtics T-Shirt and apron greeted him.

"Welcome! How can I help you, today?" he asked.

Robin was skeptical. *Never trust a thin man making pizza,* was one of his mantras. "How much for a slice?" he asked.

"$1.75," the chef answered.

A bit pricey. This ain't Sbarro's. But it is midtown. He shrugged and pulled out a five-dollar bill. "Let me get two to go, not too hot," he ordered.

"Anything to drink?"

"You got anything that's under $1.50?"

"A can of soda's $1.25."

"I'll take a Sprite." *A .75 can of Sprite uptown selling for $1.25...is there a luxury tax down here or something? I'll have to brown-bag it from home three times out of the week at this rate!*

He waited two minutes and received his order in a white paper bag. He pocketed the quarter from his change and walked back out on the street. He knew right away he was never going back there. They put his slices on *paper plates* inside the bag. *Who does that?* he thought. As he walked, he ditched the plates in the nearest trash bin and pulled out a folded slice. Luckily, they gave him napkins in the bag, so he wrapped one around the corner of the slice, then took a bite at the tip.

The slice was still hotter than what he was used to. There was a lot of crust and the sauce was decent. However, the cheese wasn't as good as anything above 165th Street and Broadway. It was up to par with Frank's with the grease not collecting in the back dripping into the napkin. By the time he was on the second slice, it grew on him. *Maybe I'll head over there on a blue moon or when I feel like treating myself,* he thought.

ROBIN WAS BACK at the circulation desk. This time, Tommy was with him working the returns. Behind them, the door to the clerical office was open and Sonyai was working at her desk. The two clerks barely spoke to each other since Robin revealed that he knew Tommy's secret.

A tall gentleman wearing dress slacks and a turtleneck underneath a parka approached the desk in front of Robin. He had dark olive skin and his hair was slicked back.

"Good afternoon, young man, I'd like to renew these 3 books, please."

Robin detected an accent, but couldn't place it. Possibly somewhere in South America? He looked down and noticed each book was a one-week bookmarked with the red triangle on the spine.

"I'm sorry, sir, these are non-renewable due to their popularity. They're marked to be borrowed for only a week."

The patron chuckled. "You must be new here. I'm good friends with the head librarian. He lets me slide from time to time. I'll bring them right back. I just need another week."

Robin tilted his head. "I'm sorry, sir, but that's not going to happen. If you keep these books for another week, be prepared to pay at least .75 for each book in late fines."

"I don't have time for this," the man growled with an annoyed grunt. "Gus! Oh, Gus!" he called out and waved.

"Sir, I will have to ask you to keep your voice—" Robin began.

"Is there a problem here?" Augustus asked, approaching the desk. He made an extra effort to address the patron in a soft tone.

"This young upstart here refuses to renew my books! I only need a few more days with them."

"I see," Augustus said as he examined the books. He nodded to Thomas. "Mr. Carmichael?"

"Oh no! Not this time," Robin exclaimed. "Those are not our books. If he checks them in, he has to ship them back to the 96th Street Branch. They can't be handed back to him!"

Tommy looked inside each book. "He's right, sir. Nothing I can do."

The patron grew impatient as Robin stood his ground. "Gus! I will not be treated this way! After all the contributions I've given this branch, I deserve a little leeway!"

"You think you can *buy* favoritism within the New York Public Library? I don't think so!" Robin paused as he remembered something from his days at Fort Washington. "The library is a public resource…"

Sonyai poked her head out from the office, attentively listening in on the conversation as Robin continued.

"…where every man, woman and child of any race, class, or religion is treated fairly and equally."

The patron, Augustus, Tommy, and Sonyai were all silent from the message behind Robin's proclamation.

"Fine!" The patron reached over and pulled the books back. "I'll just keep them and pay later!"

He took a step through the security threshold and an alarm went off, locking the exit turnstile. The patron stopped in his tracks and nearly doubled over as his legs hit the exit.

"Oh, I'm sorry. If you take the books through, they lock the turnstile and will set off the alarm," Robin said with a smirk. He bent down underneath the counter and pressed the turnstile release button.

The humiliated patron stormed off. "I wouldn't expect any donations for a while after this, Gus!" he said, leaving the branch.

Sonyai stepped forward next to Robin. "Where did you learn that?" she asked quickly.

"What?"

"That phrase, what you just said."

"Fort Washington taught it to me. It was something to remember all the time as we worked there. It was known as—"

"The Clerk's Credo," she finished.

Sonyai turned to Tommy. The two exchanged glances and slowly nodded to each other.

"Okay…what just happened?" Robin asked confused.

"You said the magic words, Mr. Patience and Gratitude," Tommy mocked.

"That's *Fortitude!*" Robin corrected.

Augustus was still standing in front of the circulation desk, a scowl across his face. "Mr. Walker," he said dryly, "you disappoint me. Your actions will cost the branch dearly, young man."

Robin turned and gave him a defiant look. "Sorry to disappoint you, *Gus*."

The librarian glared at the thought of being mocked, then slowly walked back to the information desk.

When Robin turned back, Sonyai and Tommy were still standing behind him. Sonyai was *actually smiling.*

"I must apologize, Walker. I misjudged you," she said.

"I did what I felt is right. Fort Washington—"

She waved her hand. "No need to explain. I see now they taught you very well. What you just said has been passed down from generation to generation, dating back over 20 years."

"Okay," he replied with a skeptical tone.

"Consider yourself a part of our family now."

He almost flinched as she reached out and put her hand on his arm. She then went inside the office, got her jacket, and then left the branch.

Robin was awestruck. He looked at Tommy. "I'm here for a month, dealing with nothing but animosity, then I quote something and now everything's all good?"

"Yep," Tommy said, then he slapped his shoulder with a chuckle and walked back to the cash register.

The young clerk stood in place completely stunned. *My God, I'm working in a branch of lunatics,* he thought.

HEYWOOD AND ANGIE were having drinks at the Pig 'N' Whistle after work. He had a beer while she was nursing a cranberry rosemary cocktail.

"Angie?" Heywood asked.

"Hmm?"

"You were a roadie with a band before working for the library, right?"

"Yes, back in the 80's. For about 5 years."

"Ever been to Seattle and heard of grunge?"

She thought about it for a second. "Hmm, doesn't ring a bell. Why?"

He blushed for a moment. "I…I sorta met someone." A goofy smile came across his face.

She smiled. "Hey, that's great! Who is she?" she asked. In the year she'd know him, Angie had seen Heywood stumble through a few brief relationships, which shattered his confidence.

"A singer at a nightclub in the East Village. We've been talking over the phone since I saw her on Saint Patrick's Day."

"Well, well, well. A musician!" she giggled.

He joined in on the laugh, smiling from ear to ear.

"Be careful, though. I fell hard for someone doing music myself, and he broke my heart when…" She trailed off, still hurt from memories of the past.

"What?" he tried to pry.

"Just be careful, one day they're here and the next they hit the road. They live the life of 'the tour.' You either go with them or you get left behind."

Heywood saw the pain in her eyes. He dropped the subject but noted the advice. Too many times had he been hurt in the past himself and was very familiar with the pain of heartache.

CHAPTER TWELVE

"Exhale!" the instructor said.

The couples all let the air out of their lungs as a single conscious group. Tommy was off from work Wednesday in order to come in Saturday, so Sarah dragged him to the nearest YMCA in Queens for a free Lamaze class. There were ten couples arranged in two rows of five sitting on floor mats. Most were husband and wives. One mother was with a pregnant daughter and one very young teenage mother-to-be with her father attracted a lot of stares.

The instructor was an Indian woman named Eesha, with long black hair wearing thick glasses and a gray sweatsuit. The words "Queens Department of Health" in yellow letters were printed on her back.

"Remember, everyone, breath control is key during a successful labor. Push the air out from deep down in the diaphragm. Let's try it again. Inhale!" The class sucked in a gasp of air and held it. At the instructor's request, everyone released the breath and relaxed.

"Very good, everyone. Now we'll do a little Q & A. Ask me anything. I know you must have a lot of questions."

One woman raised her hand and asked, "Umm...is it gonna...hurt?"

"Labor is not about *pain*. It's best not to think of it in degrees of discomfort. The pain is all in your mind. Next question."

Another raised her hand. "On a scale of one to ten, how *painful* would you say—"

"Are there any *other* questions besides those about labor pains?" the instructor interrupted.

"How difficult is breastfeeding?" a woman asked. All the men groaned in disgust.

"Why don't we watch the tapes? They might answer your questions."

"Uh, tapes?" Tommy asked.

A man opened the door and pushed in a VCR and television set-up on a TV tray as the woman explained, "Yes. 4 30-minute video presentations showing the various stages of childbirth."

Tommy's eyes bulged at the thought of what he was about to watch. He squeezed Sarah's hand in fright.

"I'll inform Thomas tomorrow, but as of now, Mr. Walker is a welcomed addition to the branch, no longer to be antagonized," Sonyai announced.

Gerry and Ethel were stunned as they sat inside the clerical office. "What about Simms?" Ethel asked angrily.

"I have a backup plan I am putting into place. She will be relocated to another branch, but she will be fine."

"Just like that?" Gerry asked. "What happened?"

"I won't get into specifics. We're all on the same page now. The youngster stood up to Augustus in a perfect display of dedication. I just feel terrible we treated him so bad this far."

"Wow, the great Sonyai Yi showing remorse," Gerry mocked.

She narrowed her eyes. "That will be all."

Gerry stood up and left, but Ethel stayed behind. The two women looked at each other.

"This doesn't sit well with me," Ethel started. "We should still have the boy moved."

"He quoted the credo, Ethel." Sonyai said with a tone of reverence as she addressed the clerk by her first name. "The same one. You remember, don't you? The Man in White?"

Ethel sighed. "God rest his soul."

"That doesn't get taught everywhere. It's only from the older generation. Fort Washington must have people 50 and over working there. Dedicated types. You have to respect that."

Ethel shook her head. "Fine." *I'll just have to take care of him myself,* she thought.

Zelda was sitting at her small desk alone in Augustus's office. Despite him out for the day, she respected his personal space and would not dare sit in his chair. The phone rang for his personal line, and the elderly librarian was hesitant about answering it. While she pondered the decision, it rang three more times and then went silent. She sighed in relief and then gasped as the phone rang again, echoing in the room.

She stormed over to the desk and picked up the receiver. "Hello?"

"Augustus? It's Stanley here at Media Acquisitions. We need your order submitted."

"Stanley, this is Zelda Clein. Augustus isn't here today. He knew about the deadline and was going to put in a request for an extension."

"Good morning, Zelda. He may have wanted to put in for the extension, but he hasn't yet. We need an order by 6 pm today."

"Oh geez. What if I call him and he puts in for the extension today?"

"Well, you can try to get 'em, but to be on the safe side, I'd submit some titles ASAP. Take care." The phone clicked, followed by a dial tone.

"Oh dear!" she gasped.

ROBIN AND FRANKLIN walked into Apartment 3A back at 111

Wadsworth Avenue. The place was decorated with an assortment of Catholic deity motifs. Jesus candles on every corner, statues, and decorative rugs hung on the walls.

"I see the place hasn't changed since graduation. Is Supa home?" Robin asked.

"He should be downstairs at the office with the rest of the janitors by now."

"Lindy!" a booming voice echoed in the living room.

"Shit!" Franklin whispered.

Franklin's father, affectionately known to everyone as Supa—short for Superintendent—emerged from a hallway leading to the bedrooms. He stopped and turned his head. At six-foot-ten and all muscle, he was wearing a brown uniform and a cap covering a balding head of strawberry blond hair. He also wore leather gloves and a pair of size fifteen army boots.

"Did you take the garbage to the incinerator down the hall?" he barked.

"Uh," the teen stammered.

"No, you did not," the father answered. "Take care of that right now."

He walked by Robin to the kitchen. "Head to my room and play the Super Nintendo for a sec," he whispered.

Robin just froze, waiting to be acknowledged. *Maybe if I don't move he won't see me, like the T-rex from Jurassic Park,* he thought.

The large man turned and locked eyes with Robin. "I haven't seen Jon in the building lately. Is he doing well?" When he wasn't yelling, Supa's deep voice could easily have him mistaken for a soft-spoken Andre the Giant.

"He's doing fine, sir," Robin replied.

"Good."

The two were nodding in agreement at the same time for over a minute.

"You can go now," he ordered with a toothy smile.

"Yes, sir," Robin answered, and quickly zoomed to Franklin's bedroom.

Franklin always had the latest electronic toys among his friends in the building. Jon didn't believe in video games, but he bought Robin an Apple 2C personal computer for educational purposes. He fished around the floor and found the cartridge for Super Mario Kart, plugged it in, and turned the console on.

While playing, Robin overheard Supa and Franklin talking in the living room. Supa was giving a list of chores to do and a consequence involving Franklin's head and ass. A few moments later, the apartment door closed. Robin won his first Grand Prix in 100cc class as Franklin entered the room.

"What an asshole," he said.

"Guess the rest of the morning is a bust, huh?"

"Yeah. I got over 100 things to do before noon, then work, then another 100."

"Damn," Robin said shaking his head.

"God forbid I actually have a life."

"Speaking of which, what are you doing two weeks from Friday, April 8th? The Tunnel is doing Dollar Drinks and Funkmaster Flex is doing a set."

Franklin sucked his teeth. "I hate The Tunnel. Nothing but Club Kids, chickenheads and skeezers trying to get free drinks all night."

"C'mon, it'll be fun."

"Doesn't he usually do Mecca on Sunday nights?"

"This isn't Mecca. They're giving him a Friday set for the very first time.

"Fine. Knowing the bouncers, we probably won't get in anyway."

"Just dress to impress and leave getting in to me, okay? I wanna party in a club at least one time before going back to school. Registration is on the 11th."

"Alright. But under one condition."

Robin tensed up as Franklin turned to give him a serious glance. "Rick and the others—"

"Forget it!" he interrupted.

"We're getting together to play football, like the old days! Hiking all the way up to Inwood Hill and playing tackle, no two-hand touch."

"Man, I ain't doing that shit! You still thinking we're 16, 17 on some varsity high school kick? Thinking we gonna win the division at Kennedy against Fordham and move on to play for Saint John's?"

"We used to play all the time, and we were good! Remember when we beat those punks from 1365 Saint Nicholas. We were invincible! You, me, Rick, Clay, and the rest…"

"Franklin, I'm not hanging with them anymore. You remember what Ricky did on my 15th birthday party, right?"

"That was 3 years ago! How long you gonna hold a grudge? Just think about it, okay? We'll probably do it sometime next weekend, Saturday or Sunday. You do this for me, and I'll roll with you to The Tunnel. Cool?"

Robin said nothing, which Franklin took as confirmation. "Cool!" he exclaimed.

HEYWOOD WALKED into Augustus's office where he found Zelda frantically searching inside and around the head librarian's desk.

"Angie told me you called. What's wrong?"

"I have to get in contact with Gus. He didn't put in for an extension for the media orders and they're due. We either have to call him or put in the orders ourselves."

"He's out of town. There's no way to reach him. We should pick some movies ourselves."

"He would be furious, Heywood."

"What other choice do we have? If we do nothing, he won't be able to submit orders for another 3 months. Something's better than nothing."

Zelda looked at the desk, littered with catalogs. She picked a book and handed it to Heywood. "Thumb through these and pick 6 movies. I'll ask the rest of the staff for their opinions as well. What's the worst that can happen?"

Upstairs at two o'clock, all four pages were in the staff room sitting at the kitchen table playing Uno.

Tanya threw down a green seven and asked Janelle, "Do you know what you're having yet?"

"The sonogram is scheduled for April 22nd. I don't want to know until the delivery day."

Alex threw a green two, then Lakeshia changed the color by playing a red two. "I hope it's a girl!" Lakeshia added.

Tanya had no red cards, so she picked from the deck and passed her turn.

Janelle played a red skip card, which skipped Alex.

Lakeshia played a red nine and had only three cards left in her hand. "Have you thought about any names yet?" she asked.

Tanya still didn't have any reds so she picked from the deck again.

Janelle thought for a moment, then played a red draw two. "I'm leaning toward Melissa if it's a girl, after my cousin, and Michael if it's a boy." She noticed Alex was glaring at her. "Um, sorry, Alex."

Alex picked up two cards, and Lakeshia changed the color by playing a blue draw two card, leaving two in her hand. Tanya sighed and picked up two cards as well. Janelle put down a blue seven, which left three cards in her hand. Alex was relieved to have a turn and played a blue three. Lakeshia played a wild card and yelled "Uno! The color is yellow."

Tanya and Janelle exchanged looks, thinking of a way to prevent Lakeshia from winning.

The girls heard the door open and all looked over to see Robin walk in. "Hey, ladies. No school today?"

"We had a half-day. It's open school night," Lakeshia replied.

"Oh, hey, Uno! I used to play in junior high school. Cool!" Robin said approaching the table. He stopped and stood at the corner between Alex and Lakeshia.

"I'm about to win!" Lakeshia squeaked.

"We'll see," Alex said and nodded to Tanya to play her turn. She looked in her hand thinking of a card to play. "Uh, what's the color again? Green?" she asked.

"It's yellow. Don't try to cheat!" Lakeshia said.

Tanya sucked her teeth and threw down a yellow eight. Janelle rolled her eyes and played a yellow two with two cards left in her hand. Everything came down to Alex, who was grinning from ear-to-ear. She put down a wild draw four card. "The color is red. Pick up four, Leelee!"

"Hey! You can only play a wild if you have no yellows. You don't have any yellows with all those cards in your hand?"

"No, I don't. Draw four. The color is red!" Alex exclaimed.

"Ah, ah, ah! I see at least three yellow cards in your hand, Alex," Robin chimed in.

"Hey! You nosy little snitch!" Alex yelled as she folded her cards to her chest. "I call interference!"

"You tried to cheat playing a draw four when you had the color! I win!"

Alex slammed down her cards and Robin stepped back, holding his hands up smiling. "Sorry!" He moved to the couch and grabbed a magazine to read.

"We got another hour and we've played 3 games. Let's take a break," Janelle said.

Tanya collected all the cards and shuffled them a few times. As the girls all looked at each other quietly, Lakeshia broke the ice. "Um, hey, Robin, you said you played Uno in high school. Where was that?"

"It was *junior* high school, but I went to high school at Gee-Dubs."

"George Washington? Up in Washington Heights?" Tanya asked.

"Yeah, I live up there on 179th and Wadsworth."

"Lotta Dominicans up there, ain't they? You probably get mistaken for one all the time!" Alex taunted with a chuckle.

"Not! What about y'all? What schools are you going to?"

"I'm about to graduate from Julia Richman," Janelle began. "I've actually acquired my 40 credits early and don't need to attend my final term."

"Oh, super genius," Robin remarked.

"I'm attending LaGuardia. I'll be a sophomore come September." Lakeshia gave a beaming smile as Robin nodded.

"I know you're at Park West, Tanya," he said. "What about you, Alex?"

She hesitated for a moment, not interested in the conversation, but then she said, "I'll be starting my junior year at Norman Thomas in September."

Robin perked up. "The business school? With all those computer classes? Awesome! That was my first choice. I wanted to go there so badly! But my math scores weren't so good." He smiled. "It's great getting to know these little tidbits. What about family? Any brothers or sisters?"

Alex grunted in annoyance. "You first, Mr. One-Million-Questions!"

Robin clammed up. He had painted himself into a corner bringing up a subject he didn't wish to talk about himself. "I live with my grandfather, but I have an older sister who's *kinda* famous."

"Who?" the girls all asked in unison.

He sighed and stood up, tossed the magazine on the table, flipped the pages a few times and stopped at a woman's ad. He pointed. "That's my half-sister."

The girls looked in awe. "That's your sister? Do you know who that is?" Tanya gasped.

"That's Raven. She's a supermodel!" Alex said.

"Two-Time Star Search Spokesmodel of the Year, '83 and '87. Sports Illustrated swimsuit model. She appears in over 20 ads a month in various magazines around the world. Yes, that's my sister."

"Her full name is Raven St. Croix. Why isn't her last name Walker like yours?" Alex challenged. Lakeshia's jaw was still hanging open in shock.

"She was born Raven *Kincaid*. St. Croix is only a professional name she got from the place she had her first centerfold spread done. We have the same mother but different fathers."

"You're messing with us. She ain't your sister," Janelle said.

Robin shrugged sitting back down. "Why would I make it up? Or pick her specifically? It's not something I like to brag about. You asked and I'm telling you."

Lakeshia, Tanya, and Janelle all shrugged back and decided not to press on, but Alex joked, "Wait. Her name is Raven, and you're

Robin." She gave a little smirk. "You wouldn't happen to have a brother named Hawk, would ya? Lives down in DC, wearing a trench coat, shades? Sometimes in African gear?"

Robin grimaced as the rest of the girls shared a light laugh.

"Spens-suh!" she teased with a giggle.

"Very funny. Har, har, har," Robin said. "Okay, enough about me, your turn."

"Next time, Lite-Brite. We gotta hit the floor," Alex announced. The girls stood up from the table.

"Hey! Ease up on that, inkblot, or we gonna have to tussle!"

Alex froze and turned around. "Call me inkblot or anything in that nature and we *will* tussle!" Robin stood up as the three girls exchanged concerned looks.

Tanya then tilted her head, struck with a thought. "Waitaminute!" she exclaimed. "How did you know I went to Park West?" she asked with a squint.

Lakeshia started blinking rapidly as she let out a quiet nervous gasp.

Robin tried to keep a straight face and gave her a dumbfounded look. "Huh? What?"

"You said you already knew. I never mentioned it. How did you know?"

"Uh, that's an interesting question."

She opened her eyes wide, demanding an answer. "Well?"

Robin snuck a glance to Lakeshia, who shook her head and then looked back.

"Man, I don't have time for this, we all gotta go." He walked passed Alex and said under his breath, "Remember what I said, you don't want a piece of this," and left the room. Tanya looked at Lakeshia and Janelle. They both shrugged their shoulders.

DOWN THE STREET from the branch, on the corner of Lexington Avenue, New York and Company was a women's designer clothing store where a typical blouse cost eighty-five dollars. The store was way out of Sonyai's price range, but she was inside browsing around anyway a few minutes after three o'clock.

"I don't know why you insisted that we meet here," a man said behind her.

Twenty-three-year-old Andrew Friedman was a fair-skinned African-American gentleman who stood at an even six feet and weighed one hundred and seventy-five pounds. He wore gold-rimmed wire eyeglasses and his dark hair was cut in a hightop fade. He wore a thin brown leather jacket and black slacks with a matching black polo.

Sonyai greeted her former pupil with a heartwarming smile as she turned around. "I wanted to make sure we were alone."

"Well, here I am. Let's make this quick, ma'am. I'm due back at Webster at 4 pm, and it's a 45 minute hike back."

"Oh, you can take either the train or the bus back to 78th and York and be back in 15 minutes," Sonyai scoffed.

The pair shared a light laugh before they both went back to serious scowls.

"I need a full-time vacancy for one of the pages ASAP."

"Ah, sure. Why don't I go help the Knicks win the NBA championship while I'm performing miracles?"

"This is serious."

"I barely got a year under my belt as a senior clerk. How am I supposed to hire someone in a branch with 6 clerks already?"

"Someone takes the fall." Sonyai replied coldly.

Andrew shook his head, "I'm not pushing someone innocent off my boat to make room for someone with an inconvenient situation."

"I wouldn't ask you if it wasn't necessary. Sometimes we have—"

"To bend the rules for the greater good. Yes, I remember the lectures," the youth finished. He thought for a moment. "Give me time to call in some favors."

"I need an answer now," she pleaded.

"Then the answer is no. You're tossing me a hand grenade and my hands aren't steady enough to catch it and keep the pin in."

The two looked at each other intensely. The student has surpassed the teacher.

"Very well," Sonyai said with a dismissive nod.

Andrew turned and walked toward the exit.

"I'll tell Miss Brown you said hi," she called out to him.

He froze for a moment, but he didn't look back, and then resumed walking.

ANGIE WAS SITTING at the information desk when she noticed she was being watched by a trio of teenagers sitting at a nearby table. They looked straight out of a 1984 Members Only magazine ad.

"Hey, Sacajawea! Why don't you lead me to your pacific northwest!" one of them taunted.

"How droll. Didn't your mother teach you any respect?" she replied.

"No, she taught me how we came over here and civilized you savages."

"Yeah, without us you'd still be running around naked, smoking tobacco, and scalping people!"

The trio chuckled and exchanged high-fives as a sneer of contempt grew across her face over the insult.

A shadow approached the three upstarts and before they could react, Eugene pressed his massive hands at the back of two of the outspoken teens' heads and slammed both faces down on the desk. The loud thud startled nearby patrons. Angie even winced at the sudden interruption.

"Nothing to see here, folks," he announced. He bent down to address the teenagers. "I would be careful how you address the staff here, boys. You catch my drift?"

"Uh, yeah."

"Yes, sir!"

"Good. Now, apologize to the lady," he ordered.

"We're sorry," they both said in unison.

Eugene released them and stepped back. All three packed their books, stood up, and made their way to the exit without looking back.

The security guard turned to Angie, who was still scowling. "I don't need anybody protecting me. I can handle rude patrons myself!" she replied.

Eugene gave her a sadistic smile. "I know, but I *like* to re-establish my assertiveness from time to time."

Robin and Sonyai were working the desk, watching the incident between Angie and the teenagers from afar. As the trio left, Robin looked to Sonyai, who gave a harmless shrug.

"The new security guy's something else, huh?" he asked.

"He may look intimidating, but he has earned our trust over the years. It's unfortunate we require his services again. Chavez took pride in the fact that incidents at the branch were at an all-time low."

Robin thought about saying something implying that his return was based on him, but he stayed silent.

"I'd like to commend you again for holding your own against that patron of his. The credo is sacred, passed down from generation to generation."

"Fort Washington is the real deal. Old school," Robin said with a smile.

"Tell me about your previous supervisor, Miss Theresa Burns."

"She's probably the same age of Zelda, Strict—very strict—but fair. She can ramble on and on for hours. And she bakes a mean cookie."

"Did she tell you where she learned the credo from?"

Robin thought for a moment. "Hmm, no. Why?"

"The first time I heard it, I was a child growing up in Japan. My brother Benji and I came across a man dressed all in white. He left an impression on me, and as fate would have it, we met again when I was older, after coming to America. He helped me acquire my position here and taught me everything I know."

"What happened to him?" Robin asked.

Sonyai paused for a moment as if confronted with a painful memory. She turned to the clerk at a loss for words. "He…retired suddenly due to health reasons and then passed away 3 months later."

"I'm sorry."

There was an awkward silence. Robin was unsure of what else to say.

Lakeshia emerged from the shelves and approached Robin, who had his back turned at the desk. She had just finished reshelving all her books. "Robin? Can I practice checking out books again?" she asked with a smile.

Robin's eyes went wide with fright as he sucked in a breath. Sonyai clinched her jaw and squinted. "You let her check out books?" she growled.

He turned and glared at the young page, eyes still wide. She instantly regretted asking and covered her mouth timidly. "Oops," she squeaked.

"I was *just* starting to get on her *good side!*" he said through his teeth.

Lakeshia was about to apologize, but she looked over his shoulder at something. Robin noticed the look and turned around himself to see that Sonyai had disappeared into the clerical office. She came back out and approached them with a piece of paper in her hand.

"I warned you!" she hissed and slammed the document down on the desk. "I want you two to read this carefully, then sign and date it on the bottom!" she ordered, holding out a pen.

Robin and Lakeshia looked at each other, then he picked up and scanned the paper in question.

"Are you serious? I'm not signing this!" Robin scoffed.

"What's it say?" she asked.

"It's a non-fraternizing contract. She wants reassurance that we don't get too close…under penalty of termination."

"What?" she gasped.

"It's a standard requirement for individuals who exhibit signs of…"

"I told you, I don't care what happened here before," he interrupted. "But unlike your creepy little protégé, I have no intentions in having—"

"You will sign this now!" she commanded.

"Miss Yi! I didn't mean to get him in trouble!" Lakeshia pleaded. "It was just an innocent mistake. I never checked out any patron's books. I just practiced on my own card!"

Sonyai turned and looked at the page and saw the fear and urgency in her face. "Is this true?" she asked Robin, without looking at him.

"Yes," Robin said, confirming the lie. He then held his breath, hoping she would relent.

She reached out and crumpled the piece of paper. "The two of you stay at arm's length from each other. Understand? You so much as pass each other among the shelves, be seen whispering to each other, even locking eyes for more than 2 seconds, both of you are history."

Without looking at her, Robin put a hand up and waved Lakeshia off. She disappeared back into the shelves within a blink of an eye. Sonyai looked at him, her face full of disapproval, then turned away to stand at the returns side.

HEYWOOD STEPPED inside the librarian's office and closed the door behind him. Zelda was over in the clerical office asking for video suggestions, so he had to act quickly. He sat down at Augustus's desk, then picked up the phone. After dialing a number, the receiver rang for a few moments before he heard a click and an elderly male voice answer, "You've reached the Donelle video vault. How may I help you?"

Heywood cleared his throat and spoke carefully. "This is Augustus Chavez. I'm calling to confirm the selections for the 58th Street Branch Library's video presentations for the month of April."

A perfect impersonation—he had studied and practiced Augustus's voice over the past couple weeks since his trip to the vault earlier.

"You sound kinda funny, Mr. Chavez sir. A little under the weather, are we?"

"Uh, yes, yes. I have a sore throat, not feeling too well. I trust those Mel Gibson movies have been set aside, yes?"

"They have. Would you please verify the selections, sir? For record keeping purposes."

"Of course, that was *Hamlet, Bird on a Wire, The Man without a Face, Forever Young*, and *Air America*."

"Thank you, Mr. Chavez. They will be forwarded to the branch momentarily. You should receive them by Monday."

"Excellent. Goodbye." He hung up the phone, astonished that the deception worked. Heywood celebrated with a quick fist pump and then hurried out of the office.

"How about *Six Degrees of Separation*? I liked that Will Smith kid in it," Ethel asked.

"Sure, I'll add it to the list. Any other suggestions?" Zelda asked.

"You're sure Mr. Chavez is cool with us picking movies?" Gerry asked. "He's never asked us before."

Zelda was standing between the pair with a clipboard as they were looking through the catalogs. "We have no choice. An order needs to be submitted by 6 pm."

"Okay, then add *Posse, Bopha!*, and *Sarafina!* Those last two have exclamation points in their titles, Zelda. Make sure you add that on the end."

"Thank you very much. I believe that's everyone. We have a sufficient number of selections now." Zelda collected the books with a nod and left the clerical office. Ethel stood up and walked to the doorframe, looking out to where Robin and Sonyai were. She gave an icy stare to the back of Robin's head. Alex came behind to a corner of the desk and picked up some books from a shelving cart. She noticed Ethel staring daggers and leaned over to her.

"Pisses you off, doesn't it?" she whispered.

"What?" Ethel asked.

"That he's cool with Miss Yi now. That we gotta let him stay while Janelle goes someplace else."

"He's such a goodie two-shoes. All pleasant and shit. He has to have a weakness, something that gets under his skin!" she hissed back.

"He has been sensitive to *one* thing I've noticed," Alex said.

They watched as a patron stepped forward to Robin with a stack of books.

"Buenos dias, señor!" he greeted the clerk with extra effort.

"Huh?" Robin exclaimed.

"Oh, I'm sorry, I thought you were, um, Hispanic." The patron handed over his library card with an apologetic glance, and Robin accepted it without a word.

"I beg your pardon," the patron continued. "Are you Filipino, then?"

"No."

"Welsh?"

"No," Robin answered as his impatience grew.

"Guyanese?"

"No! Sir, your guesses are not flattering! So if you'd please—"

"I'm sorry, it's just that I see you and I see so many possibilities. Somewhere in the Caribbean perhaps?"

"No," he growled, sliding the books to the other side.

"Lebanese?"

"No! Now stop guessing!" he answered, his face turning red.

"Austrian? Welsh? No, I already said that..."

"Sir, if you'd please!" Robin handed back the library card.

Ethel and Alex looked at each other as Sonyai turned her head from a patron she was working on herself.

The patron took the card back and snapped his fingers. "I've got it, Egyptian!"

Robin slammed his hands on the desk with a loud boom that startled the man. "No, you goddamn idiot. Black! I'm a Black man. A negro. An African-American! Don't you know a black man when you see one? What's the matter with you, huh?"

The patron was frozen in shock, his mouth hanging open, eyes wide with horror. Robin looked around to see everyone else in the branch looking up at him, even Gerry, Angie, Heywood, and Zelda. The patron went through the threshold, collected his books, and left. Robin turned to his right to see Sonyai staring back at him.

"I'd think it would be *wise* if you sat the rest of this hour in the office!" she ordered.

Robin stormed past Ethel as she sidestepped from Alex and flinched when he slammed the door behind him. The senior clerk growled and went back to checking in the books her patron was returning. Alex whispered to Ethel, "I think we found that weakness."

CHAPTER THIRTEEN

LAKESHIA WAS WORKING IN THE FICTION SECTION PUTTING SEVERAL books back. There was no one nearby, the circulation desk was deserted, and nobody was sitting at the information desk. She turned and gasped when Robin appeared at the far end of the bookshelf.

"Sorry, I didn't mean to startle you!" he said.

"It's okay," she said taking a breath.

Robin was wearing his usual polo and jeans as he slowly walked down the aisle approaching her. A weird half-smile was on his face and there was a coy look in his eyes.

"I…I don't want you to feel bad about what happened with Sonyai. It's not that big a deal."

He stopped right in front of her and tilted his head down. She looked up and was lost in his eyes. She swallowed hard and noticed that she couldn't move.

"It's funny, the more she wants us to stay apart, it kind of draws me…" He leaned down and she took in a breath as his face stopped short at the nape of her neck. "To you," he finished.

"Robin," she gasped. "We can't."

"Isn't this what you want?" he asked.

She opened her mouth to answer, but no words came out. A gloved hand brushed against her ribcage and then pressed at the small of her back. "Yes," she whispered.

He pulled her over and gave a small peck on her neck. She moaned softly. His hand slowly moved down her stomach. She quivered as the hand kept going past her waist…sliding lower…lower…

She gasped as she sat up from the bed, her hair frazzled and her face extremely sweaty. Taking in a couple of breaths, still recovering from the dream, shaking from head to toe.

ZELDA WAS WAITING as Augustus entered the library at eight thirty Thursday morning. "Gus, before you go inside, there's something you should—"

"It can wait, Zee. I'm taking some comp time. I'll be back around 11 am. I just came in to check some paperwork."

He walked past her and made his way to his office.

Robin woke up and stepped out of his bedroom toward the bathroom. To his surprise, he noticed Jon's bedroom door was still half closed with a slight crack revealing him asleep in his bed.

He should be up by now, Robin thought. Jon rarely slept past seven in the morning. Tilting his head, he heard light snoring, then proceeded to the bathroom for a shower.

Leaving the high-rise building's lobby, he stopped in full stride before taking his routine jog throughout the neighborhood. Waiting for him double-parked on Wadsworth Avenue was Augustus and a four-door Lincoln Town Car Executive Limousine.

"Mr. Walker, may I have a word?" the librarian asked.

"Is…is *this* your car?" he asked dumbfounded as he approached.

Augustus opened the door. "Of course not! This is just a rental. We're in New York. Who in their right mind would own a car living in the city?" He gestured for the youngster to step inside, then stepped around and entered the car himself.

"Where are we going?" Robin asked.

"You'll see when we get there," Augustus answered. "I'd like to share with you some personal information about myself in the hopes of you understanding why I do what I do. I didn't appreciate that little show you did standing up for yourself."

"It wasn't a show. And I know everything I need to know."

"I was born and raised in Guadalajara, Mexico," he interrupted. "When I was your age, I began traveling the world. With an artistic eye, I transferred my hobby of photography into a prominent career. I took pictures all over for magazines and films. My work has even been displayed in galleries and museums. I even taught photography at several schools. Then I turned 30 and it all felt like none of it mattered."

"Why?"

"I guess you could say I was too good. There wasn't a challenge anymore, so I looked for my calling. Then, I thought I had found it."

"Working in a library?"

"No, archeology!"

Robin laughed out loud. "You wanted to be Indiana Jones, huh?"

Augustus clinched his jaw as his face darkened. "After 10 years, I found no worthy discoveries and suffered a midlife crisis."

"So what happened then?" Robin asked, suddenly interested in the story.

"Never mind. We're here."

The car came to a halt and both men stepped out. Robin looked around as he stood on the sidewalk, a pair of street signs at the corner indicated they were at West 181st Street and University Avenue.

"Hey, I grew up not too far from here."

"Really?" Augustus said after coming around to join him.

"Uh, yeah. This ain't the neighborhood to be riding around in a limo though."

"We'll be fine. This way, please."

They were at the base of a curved hill leading toward an oddly shaped building. As they advanced up and around the corner, Robin saw a tattered blue NYPL Banner that hung at the entrance to greet visitors. Like the dilapidated building itself, the banner had seen better days.

"This," Augustus began with a flourish, "is the Francis Martin Public Library." They stopped underneath the banner and noticed the branch's name embossed on the brick wall had several missing letters. The pair followed the wall to an accessible wheelchair ramp. The doors at the top of the ramp were dull copper with patches of green on them. As they walked inside, Augustus lowered his voice to a personal whisper while Robin looked around.

"This eyesore of a branch is frequented by college students from Bronx Community College, which is not too far from here."

The windows were opaque and dark, looking like they hadn't been cleaned in a while. Walls were cracked with chipped and peeling plaster while the furniture appeared older than both of them.

"This branch has the lowest circulation rates, the least amount of money set aside for its budget, and is last in line for renovations. This is why I bend the rules. To make sure 58th Street does not end up like this place. Please, take a good look around."

"I've seen enough," Robin said. "As bad as this place looks, it's not worth misrepresenting the library by giving privileges to those who contribute."

"Do you know how we got here? One word—charity. Libraries weren't built out of nowhere on a whim! It took the kindness of the wealthy to bring them to fruition. The government had nothing to do with it. Neither did the church. It was the dedicated bibliophiles and wealthy philanthropists that started an institution of a place free for the public to use for the purpose of reference. Where books could not circulate at first, but to just...be there."

He took a breath after his speech and Robin watched as he continued. "To this day, we still depend on acts of kindness and philanthropy to function, and to that we say thank you for such acts by bending the rules in their favor when it is called upon us to do so. Such is the way. And I wouldn't make it any different."

"Those men did what they did because they denied the poor and common people access to the private collections already established in the 19th century. 'Charity is its own reward. There's a pleasure in doing good which sufficiently pays itself.' Sir John Vanbrugh."

"It's *Virtue* that is its own reward. Nice try," Augustus corrected. "My point is that if branches aren't supported by charitable donations they decay and become this." He gestured around him. "And I will not allow that to happen. Is that clear, Mr. Walker?"

"Look, you can kiss the public's ass and get their wallets open all you want, sir, but favoritism is not the NYPL way and I will not stand for it. End of story."

The librarian narrowed his eyes. "I believe we're done here."

"Yeah, I believe you're right," Robin agreed as they headed for the exit.

Once outside, Augustus walked around to the middle of the street and opened the left side door. Robin reached out to the car handle on his side and noticed it was locked.

"Uh, the door is locked."

Augustus reached into his shirt pocket and slid across a subway token on the roof of the car. Robin slapped down and caught it before it went over the edge.

"You can find your way back, I'm sure."

"Hey!" he yelled as he heard the door slam shut. The car's engine turned over and pulled off.

"You Sonofabitch! Not funny, man!"

Robin kicked a rock out to the street, hoping it would hit the back window. His face was red with rage. "Photography and archaeology…" he mumbled to himself. "Scrooge McDuck got nothing on your punk ass!"

GERRY AND TOMMY were working the early morning after the branch opened at 10 am. Tommy was still frazzled by what he saw at the childbirth class the previous day. Gerry was once again writing in his small notebook muttering to himself.

"Did…did…did you know the vagina can stretch as wide as 15 inches during childbirth?" Tommy blurted out suddenly.

Gerry looked up from his notepad and dropped his pencil. "You okay, man?" he asked, turning to face him.

"I dunno if I can do it, man. We're still 3 months away, but…but…"

"C'mon, man, get a grip. It's gonna be all right."

"I've seen some gruesome things in my life. Limbs broken, car accidents. I even saw a man get his eyeball knocked out of his socket. But I tell you this, what I saw the other day would scare my father back to Korea."

"Geez, it's human nature, Tommy. Some would say it's a wonderful sight to witness, the beginning of life. To see your child grow, from an infant to toddler to an adolescent, then on to a teenager."

"Would you be in the delivery room if you were married?"

"Hell no!" Gerry exclaimed. "A man's place is in the waiting room!"

Tommy gave him a look.

"Besides," he continued. "Sarah will most likely be screaming for her mother to be in there with her, not you."

He thought about it for a moment. "Hmm, you're right, I got nothing to worry about."

"Yeah."

Gerry did a quick scan around the floor. Eugene was talking to Augustus at the doorway of the librarian's office. Sonyai was taking a cigarette break outside and Ethel was upstairs, possibly chatting with Zelda.

"Lemme tell you something real quick," he whispered.

Tommy took a step closer, his eyes darting sideways as he strained his ears to listen.

"This guy Iscaro is looking into Sonyai for fixing the books with S.I.U."

"Bullshit," Tommy hissed. "No fucking way."

"Hear me out. What if it's true? Before he started here, he approached me asking for help."

"What?"

Gerry shushed him, waving his hand up and down, signaling to keep it at a whisper. "I need to get a copy of the ledger. It'll prove her innocence. If the overages and short-changes are reported, then we don't need to worry. She's off the hook. But if every single day adds up perfectly, she's going down, whether we like it or not."

"You looking to help them take her out? So you can step up and finally be in charge?" Tommy asked.

"No man! No! This is all bullshit. I'm trying to prevent things before they get started!"

Tommy was silent in thought for a moment. Gerry looked at him puzzled.

"I can get you the ledger," he said.

"How?" Gerry asked.

"I learned the combination to the safe by watching Sonyai. She doesn't know I know, and I'd like to keep it that way."

"You have my word."

The two shook hands and went back to their terminals.

Robin stepped off the Bx3 bus at one o'clock and walked a few blocks down Wadsworth Avenue back home. In two hours, he had to be at the library. There was barely enough time to wash up and throw on some clothes. He noticed Jon's door was still ajar. Stepping inside, he found his grandfather still in bed sleeping. Robin walked to the bed and lightly tapped Jon's shoulder. He woke with a startle.

"What?" he gasped.

"It's 1 pm. You've slept all morning. Are you okay?" Robin signed.

"I'm fine, just tired."

"This is not like you. We're going to the doctor. I don't like this."

"Not for discussion, boy. I'm fine. Now leave me be. You need to be at work soon."

He then laid back down and pulled his blanket over his shoulders. Robin tapped him again and Jon turned to look at him.

"You're going back to sleep? You'll be up all night when you finally wake up!"

"Just another 2 hours! I'll have dinner waiting when you come home. Now, git!"

Robin stepped away from the bed, and Jon was already snoring again. He lingered with a concerned look. Jon was never this lethargic before. He left the bedroom and prepared to go to work.

AUGUSTUS RUBBED his temples for the sixth time in the last hour. "Let me get this straight," he said addressing Zelda as she stood in front of his desk. "Media acquisitions called in the morning. Who was the contact again?"

"Stanley," Zelda answered.

"No last name?"

"We spoke on previous occasions before. I never learned it. I believe he's related to—"

"He called in the morning," the librarian interrupted, "informing you that the deadline arrived and orders needed to be submitted."

"Yes."

"Despite instructions I explicitly left saying I had an extension already approved."

"Stanley said the request for the extension wasn't filed yet."

"Zelda, do you know who my direct contact for acquisitions is?"

She lowered her head. "I believe it's Julie—"

"Dryaton, Julie Dryaton. The head of acquisitions for the Manhattan branches. So naturally if she called, there would have been a cause for concern, but she didn't call, did she, Zelda?"

"No, she did not."

"No, she did not," he repeated and rubbed the sides of his head again.

Zelda fidgeted her hands as she braced herself for the bellowing.

"So you tell me. Why did this unknown simpleton convince you to submit orders with selections picked by the staff?"

"Gus, I tried to reach you, You answered none of my calls! What was I to do? Submit nothing and risk the possibility of us leaving funds unspent? How furious would you have been if that happened?"

"There was no chance of that! It was taken care of! I can't even leave for 2 days before the whole operation goes to hell!"

"I'm sorry! It won't happen again."

"I hope not. We better win this bonus or so help me *heads will roll!*"

Zelda stiffened. Something else was bothering him today. Any other time he would convey his frustrations but keep a cool head.

"Okay, that will be all. There better not have been any other mishaps I discover that went on while I was gone. I'm counting on you, Zee. I need you in my corner. Please don't let this happen again."

"It won't. Once again, I'm sorry."

She turned and left as he picked up the phone, dialing with one hand while rubbing his forehead with the other.

"Donelle video vault. How may I help you this morning?"

"This is Augustus Chavez. I'm calling to confirm the selections for the 58th Street Branch Library's video presentations for the month of April."

"Uh, Mr. Chavez, sir, you already called and the selections are already on their way."

Augustus tightened his grip on the phone receiver as his eyes bulged. "I did what?" he barked.

Robin made it in on time, arriving a few minutes before three. He walked inside the clerical office, placed a can of Diet Sprite on Ethel's desk, then put his jacket up on his usual shelf space. Sonyai and Gerry were attending their stations while Ethel sat at her desk reading the *New York Post*. The pages were reshelving books in various locations on the floor.

"I was starting to think you'd be late in relieving me, Walker," Sonyai said.

"Yeah, well, you can thank Chavez for my tardiness. He took me on a field trip to the Bronx and left me stranded out there."

"What?" she exclaimed.

"I'll explain later. What I really want to address is that outburst yesterday. That asshole hit a nerve that I tend to overreact to. I'm really sorry."

Alex emerged and walked near the circulation desk, pushing a reshelving cart. She shot icicles at Robin, which he returned with a stare of his own.

"It just bothers me…" he started. "And it doesn't help that *certain* individuals here make it their business to tease me about it as well."

Inside the office, Ethel lowered her newspaper and cocked an eyebrow.

"Believe it or not, Walker, I actually can relate," Sonyai said. "Which is why I didn't punish you…this time." She began to pace. "My brother and I received the same torment when we were younger. Our red hair and my freckles made us stand out. They called us Raggedy Ann and Andy, Ronald McDonald, and Carrot-Top. One name I particularly hated was Shoga."

Robin stared back blankly.

"It means ginger."

"Oh," Robin nodded.

"Luckily, his hair darkened and became black as he got older. I was not so lucky."

"Wow. How exactly…" Robin asked.

"My father was a journalist. When the Triple Partie Pact was signed between Germany, Italy, and Japan in September 1940, he published articles that were found unfavorable. In fear for his life, he left Tokyo and traveled to Scotland, where he met my mother. My own people mock me for my American look and the people here see 'just another Jap responsible for Pearl Harbor.' I'm just like you, Walker. Mocked by your so-called brothers and sisters…"

Gerry gave a questionable glance behind her at the remark.

"But everyone else sees just another wild, black boy waiting to attack another white jogger in Central Park."

There was a collective silence as she let the sentiment sink in. She then walked inside the clerical office and closed the door behind her. Gerry and Robin exchanged glances as the young clerk took his place at the checkout terminal. Ten minutes later, after handling several patrons, the pair were alone again.

"How do you self-identify?" Gerry asked.

"Huh?"

"After that little outburst yesterday, I'm curious. You said Black and African-American. You realize those are 2 different things. It's race versus ethnicity."

"Oh, I see," Robin said, narrowing his eyebrows. "You believe I can't associate myself with the Black race because I'm not dark enough, so I call myself African-American because our descendants from Africa were all shades and complexions." He tilted his head. "Right?"

"I didn't say that."

"You didn't have to!" Robin spat. "We've been having these reflective conversations, trying to get on the same page, but now I see. You're just as bad as Ethel and Alex! You don't think I fit in your circle of peers!"

The accusation hurt Gerry. "That's not true," he replied.

"Maybe, but why is it in the 5 weeks I've been here damn near all the clerks and pages except you and Lakeshia have been antagonizing me? What did I do to them?"

"Take them out of the equation for a moment. Let's get back to your preference. Do you even know your lineage?"

Robin snorted in contempt. "Believe it or not I do. My grandfather and his father were both born here. Before them, my roots trace back to the Virgin Islands, specifically Saint Thomas. The country changed hands between the Danish and the British several times while slaves were kept there. And you know they liked to mix things up with the help, hence the lighter broods were created."

"Yes, and you know what they called those of the fairer complexion? Who worked in the master's quarters as the rest of the slaves worked outside on the plantations?" Alex asked as she approached the desk and joined the conversation. Robin snapped back to her with a look.

"They called them *house niggers*," she hissed. "Is that what *you* are, Robin?"

Gerry cringed at the sound of the epithet.

Robin clenched his fist. "I've taken all I can take from you, you sorry excuse for a page! And like I told Tommy before I kicked his ass, I'm gonna show you how we roll uptown!"

Alex smiled at the challenge. "Bring it on, fat boy!"

Robin started to move, but Gerry put his arm out to stop him. "Don't! You're in enough hot water as it is." Then turned to the page. "Now ain't the time, Alex. Scram!"

"Fine! I said what I needed to say. He ain't got the balls to swing on me." She walked off.

"You're gonna find out soon enough, bitch," Robin said under his breath.

Five minutes before the hour, Tommy came down from the break room, and Ethel opened the door of the clerical office. A few minutes later, she approached Robin at the checkout terminal.

"You're relieved," she said with a nod of her head. "Niño," she added with a smirk.

Tommy and Gerry looked on, expecting Robin to lose his cool. The clerk just smiled to Ethel. "Hoped you enjoyed your soda. There's plenty more coming." He then walked past her into the office.

Sonyai noticed Robin keeping his anger in check and nodded in approval. "Very good, young man. Please have a seat for a moment."

He sat down with a concerned look as the supervisor closed the door.

"In light of that encouraging display, I've decided to have you start your first Saturday here at the branch this weekend. Since this is out of the blue, you'll have to take tomorrow off to compensate."

"Great, I get Friday off, but have to come in the following morning."

"I'd like you to report here by 10 am so you may observe us preparing in the morning before we open at noon."

"Okay."

"The door will be locked. Just ring the bell or wait outside and someone will let you in."

Sonyai opened the door again and then walked back to her desk. Robin grabbed Ethel's copy of the *Post* and turned to the comics to read the day's "Garfield."

At four forty-five Ethel met Alex in an isolated corner among the shelves.

"Make this quick. I need to get back to the desk," Ethel said to the page.

"I found out that Robin is working this weekend and he has tomorrow off, so I got a great idea! All I need you to do is to make sure he's the first to walk in Saturday morning, think you can do that?"

"Um, sure, why?"

"Just leave it to me. I'm going to set him up for the shock of a lifetime!"

Her smile worried Ethel, but she said nothing. Alex turned around and walked down a row of shelves toward the reference corner.

SATURDAY MORNING WAS cool and breezy. The temperature was forty-five degrees, but with the wind, it felt more like thirty-eight. Robin was listening to "Enter the Wu-Tang (36 Chambers)" on his walkman as he stepped out of the subway station onto the sidewalk. The streets looked drastically different compared to the weekday hustle-and-bustle traffic of pedestrians. "C.R.E.A.M." was playing through his headphones as he approached the library at nine thirty-seven.

While he waited, he noticed a small white doorbell embedded in the glass door frame that he had never noticed before. He looked inside for signs of lights or shadows. When nothing was visible, he tried the doorbell and waited a moment. "Hmm, guess I'm the first one here," he muttered to himself.

A figure caught his attention as Tommy approached. Robin turned and smiled, then hunched down pretending to be in a three-point stance. "Hut one! Hut two! Hike!"

"Very funny, har-har-har," Tommy said.

Robin chuckled. "I know, I know. Our little secret!" He made a shushing gesture, putting his finger on his lips. "You got the key so we can get in?"

"Nope. Only Yi or Chavez have keys to the branch. On the odd chance of either one being sick, Gerry has access to the emergency backup stashed around here somewhere."

"Great." Robin sighed.

A moment later, Heywood arrived, followed by Ethel, who was looking uneasy for some reason. Finally, at nine fifty, Sonyai greeted everyone and fished out the key from her purse.

"Now, Walker, once I open the door and we step inside, you'll hear an alarm sound. No need to be frightened. I'll walk to the security keypad and disarm it."

Robin nodded to Sonyai, then she bent down to the lock at the base of the door.

"Robin, why don't you step in front of me and follow Sonyai in? This being your first time here and all, you get the honor of going in first," said Ethel.

The youngster gave Ethel a skeptical look as he forward past her. Sonyai pulled the door open and walked in, followed by Robin and the rest of the staff. The lights were off and an ear-piercing klaxon alarm blared.

"Wait here," Sonyai instructed. She disappeared in the dim lit space, then appeared behind the circulation desk and opened a wall panel exposing a nine-digit keypad. After punching in the security code, the room fell silent, then she turned on the lights.

What was revealed would haunt Robin forever. Sonyai gasped while the rest of the staff looked in awe. The shelves, reading tables, the information desk, and the circulation desk were covered in brown cardboard sheets. Written on the sheets in large black letters were the following two words: HOUSE NIGGER.

Robin was appalled. A taunting laugh echoed within the library as Alex emerged and walked to the center of the room. Tommy, Ethel, Heywood, and Sonyai were petrified with their mouths wide open. Robin wasn't. He laid eyes on Alex's laughing face and saw nothing but red. Without hesitation, he took three long quick strides. Sonyai cried out "Robin!" marking the very first time she had called the young man by his first name.

Alex had little time to react. She only had to blink once before

Robin's massive right hand enveloped her throat and slammed her to the nearest bookshelf. Sonyai was halfway around the circulation desk desperate to break up the hostile confrontation. Behind the shocked trio still frozen in place, the entrance opened again and a streak of sunlight leaked inside.

"You think that's fucking funny, you crispy black bitch?" Robin yelled, his fingers squeezing tighter as he slammed her again. "You fucking oreo! I'll squeeze the life out of you till your last breath!" He felt a pair of small fist pounding on his arm, a voice screaming in his ears. Ignoring the blows, he raised his hand, elevating the child. Her legs twitching aimlessly, nearly going limp, the air gasping out of her mouth. Robin roared in anger as he was minutes away from administering a choking death when he was struck in the back and collapsed.

Alex was barely able to stay on her feet as she gasped for air while rubbing her neck, coughing and panting profusely. Augustus dropped the copy of John Grisham's *The Client* on the floor. The slam of the book echoed in the air, followed by the silence of everyone still floored by the series of events. The librarian looked around, unable to process, resorting to yelling the first thought that came to mind, "What the fuck happened in here?"

ROBIN OPENED his eyes and tried to focus. After minutes of straining his eyes, they focused on the ceiling light of the staff room. He found himself lying on the couch alone. Regaining his senses, he noticed his arms were behind his back. Sitting up, he struggled to bring his arms in front of him. There was tightness around his wrist. It was at that moment he realized he was handcuffed!

"I want his ass fired and arrested!" Alex yelled.

"You're in no position to make demands young lady!" Augustus replied.

The page and librarian were joined by Sonyai in Augustus's office. Alex was sitting in Zelda's office chair, still shaken up and furious.

"I can't believe you did this, Alex. What were you thinking?" Sonyai asked.

"I don't care about what you were thinking. I'm more concerned about the *how*," Augustus said. "Start explaining. How did you gain access after the branch closed last night?"

"I…I hid upstairs," Alex started. "Waited till the middle of the night and then covered everything."

"That's a lie," Augustus began. "We have custodians who clean the floors and empty the trash cans. They check everywhere. I want the truth *now!*"

"That's enough!" Sonyai yelled. "I won't have you interrogate her, Augustus!"

"Better me than the police! You committed at least 3 felonies. Do you really want to deal with them? Or Special Investigations? They will hear of this, so start talking!"

Alex whimpered in the chair. Sonyai, fearing the outcome of the situation, pulled Augustus aside.

"We can contain this," she whispered.

"I don't believe her story for a second. I want to know how she did this. I will find out, Yi."

"Fine. We have to make sure no one says anything. I think we can guarantee her silence by just suspending her without pay in exchange for not involving the police."

"We'll have to suspend Walker as well. That way she doesn't bring assault charges on him."

"Agreed. I'll talk to Alex and then we'll go upstairs and brief Walker," Sonyai finished.

"Give me a moment with her first," Augustus asked.

Sonyai gave him a concerned look, then reluctantly agreed with a nod.

Alex was a little calmer when the two approached her again. "I'll be right back," Sonyai told the page and walked out of the office. Augustus closed the door and turned to face Alex with a cold stare.

"I am so disappointed, Alexandra," he said calmly.

She stiffened at the sound of her full first name. No one ever used it except her parents.

"You and I both know how you got in here to do this. I know you didn't want to say anything in front of Miss Yi, but if you recall it was I who arranged for you to work here…on behalf of your father."

She remained quiet as he continued.

"Due to his charitable contributions in the past, I gave him confidential information and a unique gift, which I would wager I would find on your person if I had Miss Yi step back in here and strip search you."

Alex's eyes went wide as she resumed shivering in fear once again.

"But I'm not going to do that."

A sigh of relief came from the page as she exhaled.

"So here's what will happen. You will be suspended for 2 weeks. No police charges will be filed against you or Mr. Walker and he will be suspended as well."

"What?" she gasped.

"Both of you will leave immediately, and the rest of the staff will be sworn to secrecy. No one will know or speak of what occurred this morning, and it will stay that way. Is that clear, young lady?"

Alex was now shaking from anger rather than fear but whispered, "Yes."

Augustus nodded. "I will be speaking to your father tonight. Which means once you go home you return what you borrowed because I will retrieve it from him this evening."

She looked down, sinking her head into her chest as they both waited for Sonyai to return.

"Andrew, we have a situation here," Sonyai said over the phone.

She was in the clerical office as Ethel and Tommy sat nearby, occasionally exchanging glances. Outside, the cardboard sheets still covered most of the furniture, their message of hate still transfixed in their eyes.

"It's 10:25 am. What could have happened in twenty-five minutes?"

"I can't explain, but I need a part-time clerk to fill in here. Can you spare anyone?"

"No need. I'll come over myself. My second-in-command will cover for me."

"That's unnecessary—" she started, but the receiver clicked off, followed by a dial tone. She hung up the phone. "Damn it!" then picked it up again and dialed.

"Uh, hello?" Lakeshia moaned.

"Good morning, Lakeshia. I'm sorry to wake you. There's been an incident. Can you come in this morning for some overtime?"

"I...I would love to, Miss Yi, but I have singing lessons this morning from 11 am to 3 pm I can't make it. I'm sorry."

She sighed. "Okay, I understand." She hung up the phone. *I can't call Janelle, she needs her rest.* She gritted her teeth and picked up the phone for the third time.

Augustus waited for Sonyai to return and talk to Alex, then made his way to the clerical office where he found Tommy and Ethel sitting.

"Why haven't you taken those sheets down?" he asked them both.

"We thought the police would be called," Tommy started. "We didn't want to touch anything."

"We're not calling the police," the librarian announced. He then turned to face Ethel. "Ms. Jenkins, I heard you let Walker walk in first after Yi. Why is that?"

She blinked hard at the question. "Huh?"

"Did you know what Alex was doing? Did you have *anything* to do with this?"

"No!" she gasped.

"I don't believe that for a second! You and she conspired to make this happen. She's already been suspended. I ought to give you the same punishment!"

"What! I didn't do anything. You suspend me and I'll have the union on your ass so quick—"

Tommy stood up. "Okay, everyone, calm down. Sir, I don't think Ethel had anything to do—"

"Fine! I don't have any proof, so you're off the hook. Here's what we're going to do. Walker and Stevens are both going home today, suspended for 2 weeks. No one is to speak of this to anyone. We take everything down and clean this place up. No one gets called. Anybody asks you what happened this morning, you both say nothing. Got it?"

The two clerks looked at each other and replied, "Got it."

"Good." Augustus nodded. "Let's gets those damn things down. I'll be upstairs."

He turned to leave and noticed the clerks were still in their seats. "What are you waiting for?" he asked with an annoyed tone. The trio then exited the office.

ROBIN SAT PATIENTLY on the couch, thinking of numerous ways to extract his revenge on Augustus. He was contemplated pouring fire ants all over his body and watching them eat his flesh alive when Sonyai and Augustus walked in.

"Okay, 3 questions. First off, who the fuck hit me? Second, what kind of librarian owns a pair of handcuffs? And third, would you be interested in eating solid foods through a straw? Because that's exactly what's going to happen when I get loose."

"I wouldn't waste time with irrelevant questions and idle threats, young man," Augustus said.

"Come a little closer and say that, *Gus!*" Robin spat.

Sonyai stepped forward between them. "Enough with the macho bullshit pissing contest, you two! I understand you're upset, Walker."

"Oh, we're way past upset—"

"Be that as it may…" she interrupted. "We're willing to overlook what happened this morning in exchange for your silence."

"That bitch calls me the most despicable slur known to man and you just want me to keep my mouth shut? This is bullshit! I have a good mind to take this to court as a hate crime! My grandfather knows people that can get me in contact with William Kunstler and Ron Kuby! You want this place on the 5 o'clock news? Chuck Scarboro! Sue Simmons! Ernie Anastos!"

"You're not saying anything!" Augustus said. "I walk into this branch and find you choking a page nearly half to death. You think you're not accountable for that? What do you think the police would say?"

"That she was getting what she deserved!"

"Look!" Sonyai yelled. "This is getting out of hand. We open in 90 minutes and we have replacements en route. Let's wrap this up, shall we?"

"Replacements? The fuck is going on?" Robin asked.

"You and Stevens are being suspended for 2 weeks. In exchange, she doesn't press charges against you for assault, and you tell no one about what happened today," he explained.

"What? Are you shitting me? I reacted the same way any of you would have! What if she wrote up there on those sheets 'Kill the Zipperhead!' or 'Bang! Bang! Cap the Scap!'"

Sonyai flinched and nearly raised her fist to strike at Robin. It took all of her restraint to stay in check.

"Ah-ha! Admit it! You wanted to take a shot at me! You shouldn't have told me you were Japanese-Scottish mixed!" He then turned to Augustus. "What if it said, 'I always clean my pots and pans with good ol' *SPIC* and Span!'"

Augustus' eyes bulged as he growled under his breath. He refused to let Robin get under his skin as well. "If you didn't react the way you did, Alex would have been terminated instantly over a stunt like this."

Sonyai looked at the librarian, questioning the statement, but let him continue.

"But since you took it upon yourself to put your hands on her, you risk yourself into a world of hurt. So no, I'm not putting myself in your shoes, and if you wish to continue working here, you'll do as I say! You call your lawyers and news reporters, you'll be arrested once Alex's parents file charges with the police for assaulting a minor! Plus, I'll see to it they connect you with that fight you had in front of the branch!"

Robin locked eyes with Augustus as he dared the clerk to call his bluff. Sonyai looked back and forth between the two as over sixty seconds of silence ticked away. Robin faltered and sighed, yielding Augustus the victory.

"Alright. I won't say nothing," Robin promised.

There was a collective moment of relief as everyone calmed down finally.

"Wanna do something about these cuffs?" Robin asked frankly. "Let me guess. You toss the key and leave it to me to do it myself, right?" he joked bitterly, remembering his field trip the other day.

A chuckle came over the librarian as he fished in his back pocket and produced a small handcuff key. He handed the item to Sonyai. "You do it. He might try something foolish if I get too close."

"Smart man," Robin agreed.

Sonyai stepped to the couch. "Stand up and turn around," she instructed.

Robin allowed the senior clerk to unlock the handcuffs and stood in place as she took the restraints and the key back to Augustus without taking her eyes off the teenager. The clerk rubbed his wrists for a moment with a look on his face still registering anger.

"Okay, I think we're good now. I'd like to speak with Mr. Walker alone for a moment."

"You sure?" Sonyai asked.

"Yea, Gus, you don't have a book in your hand this time," Robin taunted.

He held out and dangled the cuffs in the air. "I think we'll be okay."

She shrugged and walked toward the door, opened it, gave one last look behind her, and left. Once the door was closed, Augustus said, "Sit down."

"I'll stand, thank you," Robin replied.

"I will not ask again."

Robin rolled his eyes and sat on the edge of the couch, leaning forward. Augustus took a chair from the kitchen table, turned it around, and sat on it backward. He folded his arms and rested them on the chair's back.

"I want to talk to you about your suspension," he started.

Robin stared blankly as he listened.

"It's not going on your personnel file."

That took him by surprise as he tilted his head in shock.

"I am completely disgusted by all of this and I plan to come down hard on Alex over it. I'm not condoning what you did, but I know where your anger is coming from."

Robin sat back from the edge of the sofa, his eyes softened as his emotions got the best of him. For all his chest-pumping and shit-talking, deep down this situation really struck a chord with him.

"You think you're the only one dealing with racism?" Augustus asked. "Out of 82 branches in the Bronx, Manhattan and Staten Island, fewer than 5% of head branch librarians are Hispanic. I am a pink flamingo standing in a flock of swans!"

Robin responded to the statement with a questioning look, which the librarian saw and sighed at the show of emotion. "Look, the theatrics were just for Sonyai's account. This will stay between you and me. You'll take some time to cool off, but the paperwork won't be filed. I can't falsify timesheets, though, so you won't get paid for this absence."

Robin's eyes went wide as he sucked his teeth and shook his head.

"But I'm willing to compensate you *myself*."

He perked back up and a smile grew across his face.

"$600.00. That's double your bi-weekly salary. Incentive for keeping this incident quiet—"

"$1000.00," Robin exclaimed.

Augustus hard blinked in shock over what he just heard. "Excuse me?"

"One thousand. Dollars. In cash. In an envelope, in my hand within the hour and this *never* happened. End of story."

The supervisor's face darkened in a flash of anger. "You drive a hard bargain, Walker. Agreed," he said with a nod and stood up. "You'll understand if I draw up a contract putting this all in writing… to make sure you keep your word." He slid the chair back in place under the kitchen table.

"Sure," Robin said with a grin. "Tick-tock, tick-tock, *Gus*."

As Augustus turned to leave, he stopped when he opened the door. "Oh, and one more thing,"

Robin turned his head to the entrance.

"You keep calling me Gus and the next time I hit you with a book, I'll take your head off."

He left the room and closed the door behind him.

Robin smiled at the threat and chuckled to himself, then winced and rubbed the back of his neck.

CHAPTER FOURTEEN

ALEX AND ROBIN LEFT THE BRANCH SEPARATELY AS THE STAFF WORKED to take down and dispose of all the cardboard sheets. At eleven fifteen, the doorbell rang and panic overtook Tommy, Ethel, and Heywood while Sonyai and Augustus looked at each other.

"That must be Friedman. He's early!" Sonyai said.

"Wha-what do we do? We still got to hide this crap somewhere!" Heywood exclaimed.

"Be calm," Augustus instructed. "Yi, you need to stall him for at least 10 minutes."

Sonyai resented taking orders from the librarian, but he was right. She hurried around and made her way to the door where she found her former pupil waiting outside. She waved and bent down to unlock the door. He pushed it opened and was surprised when she nudged him back outside.

"Hey, it's cold out here!" Andrew yelped.

"I need a smoke. It's been that kind of morning. Walk with me," she said, leading him away.

Fortunately, Andrew smoked as well. Sonyai shook two cigarettes out of her pack and handed one to him. She lit them both and the pair walked toward the edge of the curb.

"What the hell happened?" Andrew asked. "Any day of the week you can stare down a 747 coming at you on a runway without a blink of an eye. But you are actually shaking."

"I…I can't tell you," she stammered.

"That bad, huh? Okay. The less I know the better." He took a drag and blew a cloud of smoke. "This wouldn't have anything to do with Simms's situation, would it?"

"It might be a contributing factor, but never in a million years would I think she would be capable of doing this." Sonyai's cigarette trembled between her fingers. "Andrew, I wouldn't ask you again if it wasn't important. If you can't take her she's going to be lost in the system, alone, dealing with those who will shun her."

The visiting senior clerk said nothing. He hated saying no to her again. The sun bounced off his rimmed glasses as he stood there, wearing sweatpants and a white Howard University sweater under his leather jacket. Sonyai looked back at him. The silence was answer enough for her. From the corner of her eye, she saw Augustus slide away the window blinds and signal an all-clear with his hand.

She flicked the cigarette into the street. "C'mon, Let's go inside," she said with a nod. Andrew followed, still wondering what occurred this morning that shook his former mentor.

The branch opened without incident and no one was the wiser to the horrendous series of events that occurred earlier that morning. Tanya could detect the tension in the air, but paid no attention to everyone's uneasiness because she was focused on Andrew. She undressed the clerk with her eyes as he stood at the circulation desk alone. Inert, stoic, and absolutely delicious. She didn't see Sonyai slam a book on the shelf near her vantage point and gasped at the break in her fixation.

"You cannot be daydreaming here, Miss Brown," she scolded.

"I-I-I'm sorry, Miss Yi."

"Can you stay until closing? Would your mother have a problem with that?"

"I think she'll be okay with it."

She nodded, which Tanya took as also a sign to resume her duties.

After taking a few steps and turning a corner, she looked back out to the circulation desk and smiled.

Andrew could sense the page's lusty glances from afar, which made him nervous. The memories of their intimate relationship were still fresh in his head. They dated in secret for over three months, which they then consummated on Valentine's Day. An opening for senior clerk became available shortly after, and he accepted. They parted on sour terms, and now for the first time, a year later, he was back and she was waiting for him.

"Snap out of it, four-eyes!" Tommy said with a playful shove, surprising him.

"Heh-heh-heh, same ol' corny Carmichael. How's it goin', you so-and-so?"

"Doin' fine, man. How's it like being in charge up there at Webster?"

Andrew shrugged. "It's not too bad. You make the schedules, give out orders, maintain the peace. All that Sonyai taught me has been very useful."

Tommy nodded as Andrew changed the subject. "How's Gerry? Still pissing her off thinking he can do better? Does he still write in that tiny notebook?"

"Yep. Still haven't got a clue what he's writing."

"Maybe it's plans to take over the world or something."

The two chuckled lightly at the joke.

"So, um…what happened here this morning?" Andrew asked.

"I have no idea," Tommy quickly answered.

"Oh, c'mon, man. You can tell me."

"I got here little before 11 o'clock and everyone was shook, but no one said anything," he lied.

Andrew narrowed his eyes. "I don't know if you're a genius of a liar or incredibly dumb and oblivious!"

He shrugged. "Maybe a little bit of both," he said with a guffaw and slapped him on the shoulder again.

Andrew fixed his disheveled glasses and shook his head. *Same ol' corny Carmichael…* he thought.

Ethel was annoyed that Robin once again left a can of diet soda on her desk before departing the branch. Her role in Alex's terrible joke troubled her, but she couldn't let anyone know how she felt for fear of receiving punishment. She and Sonyai were sitting at their desks inside the clerical office waiting to relieve Andrew and Tommy at the top of the hour.

Sonyai broke the silence. "I still can't believe she did this. Even if we were still trying to push Walker out for Miss Simms, it would have *never* gone this far. This…this was personal. This was hatred, pure and simple. Jenkins, please tell me you had no part in this."

"I…I had no idea. She mentioned something after his outburst, but this took me completely by surprise."

She felt guilty lying, to the point it made her light-headed and queasy. Her stomach was tied in knots, which killed her appetite. Sonyai stood up and walked to the door.

"When she comes back, we have to get to the bottom of this." She then opened the door and made her way out.

Heywood took a seat next to the information desk where Augustus sat overseeing the floor. "All the sheets are in the maintenance closet upstairs. I guess the custodian can just dispose of them in any manner," he reported.

"Excellent." Augustus replied. "We dodged a bullet today. No one's the wiser. But the repercussions from today will have a ripple effect on how this branch is expected to function without any further disharmony. These events will not embarrass us in the eyes of the public!" *I only have myself to blame…* he thought. *My foolish generosity nearly got us compromised! I must speak to him tonight and take back that gift!*

"You have the floor, Learner. I have to make an important call in my office."

ANDREW ENTERED the staff room upstairs, pushing the door in and flopping on the couch. He stared up at the ceiling and blew out an audible breath in exhaustion. He finished a two-hour stint with Ethel, then Tommy, and now he had a forty-five-minute lunch break. All he wanted to do was catch forty winks with a quick nap.

He was moments from slumber when he heard a voice call out his name. "Hello, Andy."

The door closed, revealing Tanya standing in the corner. Andrew gasped and stood up as the page pushed the button on the doorknob, locking them in. "I've been waiting for you," she said with a seductive smile as she walked toward the couch.

"Ta-Ta-Tanya!" Andrew stammered.

"Ah, ah, ah. Don't you remember? You always called me Brownie."

She pressed up and eased him back down on the couch, then quickly straddled her legs around his waist. "You remember why you called me Brownie, don't you?" she asked. Andrew continued stammering as she playfully removed his glasses and traced her finger down the tip of his nose. She brought her face down to his and whispered softly in his left ear. "It's because I'm soft...*and moist.*"

"Please. You're s-s-sixteen. I know what we did, but we can't—"

"I'll be 17 in May. You'll have nothing to worry about." She turned her head sideways and laid it on his chest. "We can be together finally. I've waited so long. I knew you would come back." She sighed. "I can hear your heartbeat."

Andrew's mind raced. The moments came flooding back as he felt her skin on his. "I'm seeing someone else," he blurted out.

Tanya's eyes went wide and she shot up, staring down at him. "What?" she gasped.

There was a clicking at the door and Sonyai pushed it open after lowering the key she used to unlock it. The page jumped off and sidestepped a few inches toward the table looking down sheepishly.

"Ahem," she coughed. She stepped inside as Tanya walked quickly past her and out the door, her sneakers squeaking down the stairs.

"Do I have to spray the two of you with water like cats in heat?" she barked.

"She came onto me! What was I supposed to do?" he pleaded while sitting up and putting on his glasses.

"Resist! I knew it would be nothing but trouble keeping the two of you apart, which is why I tried to get one of the other girls, but Seabrooke wasn't available."

"As I was trying to tell her, I'm involved with someone else now."

"She wouldn't happen to be one of your own clerks at Webster, would she?"

"No!" he exclaimed, blushing from embarrassment. "She's an information assistant."

Sonyai sighed and shook her head. "Just keep your hands to yourself. Can you do that, please?"

He began to reply, but the senior clerk turned and left the room.

Two hours later, Andrew was saying his goodbyes as he exited the clerical office. He waved to Ethel, Tommy, and Sonyai, who were standing behind the circulation desk.

"It was nice seeing you again, Andrew," Ethel said.

"Stay crispy, apple polisher," Tommy added with a grin.

Andrew noticed that Tanya was nowhere around to see him off. Sonyai walked him through the threshold and they stopped at the exit for a few parting words. "Thank you for coming on such short notice," she said.

"Anytime. I'll always be here for you," he replied with an informal salute.

"Please rethink that other situation we talked about."

He tilted his head, brought his thumb and forefinger to his chin, "Tell you what. I'll guarantee a full-time clerical position for Janelle at Webster..."

Sonyai gasped in anticipation and relief, believing her problems were finally solved.

"If you tell me what happened here this morning," Andrew finished.

Her eyes narrowed as a scowl came across her face. *Sonofabitch!* she thought.

He rolled on the balls of his feet as he awaited her answer. Then he chuckled to himself. "Wow, that bad, huh?" He shrugged. "Okay, I tried. Have a good evening, ma'am."

Andrew turned and walked out of the branch. One of the first lessons she taught to him came to mind as he headed toward Lexington Avenue. *Learn everything you can. Knowledge is the most powerful weapon against your enemies.* She knew that whatever he found out about today would be used against her in the future—and she was right.

Tanya walked into her apartment at six o'clock on the verge of tears. The news that Andrew had another girlfriend crushed her heart. She was about to drown her sorrows by eating some ice cream when her mother called out her name.

"Tanya Clarabelle Brown! Is that you coming in 'ere this late in the evening?"

"Mama?" she replied.

Thirty-nine-year-old Cynthia Brown stormed out of the kitchen wearing sweatpants and a white apron tied around her waist. She folded her massive forearms on her huge bust and glared at her daughter.

"You didn't tell me you were working this morning. I woke up and you were nowhere to be seen!"

"Th-there was an emergency, someone called out. This was overtime for me. I'll get—"

"The next time you leave this house without telling me, you leave a note! You hear me?"

"Yes, mama."

"I wanted to talk to you about your grades and what one of your teachers told me this week. Your social studies teacher told me you disrupted the class, and the guidance counselor told me something about a rumor. Did you get someone to hang a student off the roof to leave you alone?"

"I passed all my classes, and that student threatened to kill me!"

"You are grounded! No going anywhere but to work this week off from school!"

"But I was going to the dance with Alex and her friends!"

"You better pass all your classes with at least an 85% average in June or you'll be going to summer school again! Now go to your room!"

"This is so unfair!" Tanya cried as she ran past her and closed the door to her bedroom.

"And I better not hear none of that rap music or I'm taking that radio of yours too!"

"I DESPISE THIS PLACE," the elderly gentleman said with a weary sigh. "I think my father frequented here back in the early 30's during prohibition. It had a sense of style for a while, but now it's just an overly decorated tourist trap. Hell, I think my wife has a favorite table somewhere that they set aside just for when she eats here."

"That's very interesting. Back to what we—" Augustus began.

"You ever been here?" the man asked, interrupting the librarian.

"Ahem, no...I haven't," he lied.

Augustus was once again at Twenty-One, sitting across one of his oldest, closest friends who was also a wealthy library contributor. The irony was not lost on him that his dear friend would mention his wife, whom he had dinner with on his previous visit.

"We have to talk about what Alex did," Augustus pressed.

Thin, wiry fingers held a silver fork as it played with a salad, then clanked on the porcelain plate in frustration. "Yes, I would like to hear how my delicate flower came home with bruises on her neck."

"What exactly did she tell you?" Augustus asked.

"She admitted to making a tasteless joke at a co-worker's expense and he overreacted...resulting in the both of them being suspended."

"Hmm, I see. Well, I took the liberty in documenting her little *tasteless joke* with some Polaroids." The librarian reached into his jacket's breast pocket and pulled out a yellow envelope. "Why don't you see for yourself," he said as he slid the envelope across the table.

The guest opened the package and pulled out six photographs, each showing the cardboard sheets and their message. A gasp of awe and disgust exited the elder.

"Sh-she did this? My God! I swear, we never taught her to…to… use that abhorrent word!"

"Well, she had to learn it somewhere. While repugnant the message is, I'm more concerned as to how she entered a locked facility in the middle of the night and set this up."

"She said she was sleeping over at one of her friends. How could we have possibly known?"

"We both know how she did this and I would like to retrieve what I gave you in the strictest of confidence that it would never be used without my presence accompanying you!"

"Augustus, my old friend, surely we can discuss this. How long have we known each other? Even before you worked for the library. All those expeditions I financed—"

"And I am grateful, but I must insist."

The man's wrinkled face looked like leather as he frowned. He reached into a pocket of his own and pulled out a unique, odd-shaped silver key.

Augustus reached over and picked it up. "I gave you this key as a symbol of gratitude, never to be used, just to have. You were to never let it out of your sight."

"All I can say is that I'm sorry. I had no idea she knew where it was."

"How did she know the security code?"

"I wrote it down and had it with the key. You know I would never trespass into the branch without—"

"What's done is done, and I have the key. I'm sure you will punish the child for this violation of our trust?"

"She's going to some dance tomorrow, but rest assured, she'll have a stern talking-to about this."

"Excuse me? Talking-to? Dance?" Augustus asked astonished.

"Look, she scored all perfect A's this semester. We reward good grades to keep her learning." His hand slapped the pictures. "Behavior like this is just a fluke." He finished with a dismissive tone.

He had heard enough. Augustus pocketed the key and stood. "It's going to be a long time before you earn this kind of trust again. Expect no more favors."

"I'll donate $10,000.00 to your library if you give it back to me on the promise I'll never let it out of my sight."

Augustus had a coughing fit, which caused him to grab his glass of water and take a huge swig to clear his throat. "Ten...thousand?" he stammered.

The man smiled. His teeth were a set of flawless dentures that glistened in the dimly lit restaurant. The librarian gathered his composure and shook his head. "I'm sorry, but no deal." He turned to leave. "Say hello to your wife for me," he said, smiling at the private joke and walked to the exit.

ALEX WAS ENJOYING HERSELF, dancing at a local hip-hop nightclub in Kips Bay. She needed to unwind after that disastrous practical joke on Robin yesterday. The party was a sixteen-and-older Sunday dance night celebrating spring recess. The teen was wearing a mock turtleneck top with thin black and white horizontal stripes and black cargo pants.

She arrived with a few friends from school at six, but some of them were not feeling the music and scene early on and left by seven thirty, but she stayed, not afraid of dancing alone. Sure enough, by eight a new DJ started a set and more people filled up the floor. Alex was attracting attention from every guy inside, even those who were dancing with their girlfriends.

By nine she had rejected at least six guys brave enough to engage her, but took a couple of phone numbers that were written on matchbooks. During a song transition where the DJ got on the microphone and did shout-outs, a girl tapped her shoulder and pointed toward the VIP corner in the back.

One of the three guys sitting at a round table was flagging her to come over with a waving hand. She was hesitant at first, but slowly made her way through the crowd. They were sharing a bottle of champagne on ice in a bucket.

"Hey there," one guy shouted over the music.

"Why don't you have a seat," another guy said, patting the chair on the left. "So we can talk privately."

Alex didn't move and called back. "I'll stand right here, thanks."

The three looked at each other exchanging "Oohs."

"She has spunk," the leader in the middle said with a grin. "I like that."

Alex stood there waiting, unimpressed by the trio.

The middle gentleman leaned forward. A short Hispanic with curly hair, he was wearing Karl Kani street clothes and Timberland boots. "You know who I am?" he asked.

The music had changed up to slow R&B as "Understanding" by Xscape started playing.

"Yeah," she replied.

The man smiled at being recognized.

"You're too old to be looking at girls in a sixteen-and-over party, creepo!"

The guys on the left and right exchanged worried looks at the diss, but Mr. Kani laughed out loud and clapped his hands. "You a trip, girl. You know that?" He laughed again. "Okay, I won't bullshit you or anything. I'm a scout for a lot of directors—TV, music videos, and even movies. You got a look, nice dance moves. You just need to check that attitude of yours."

He snapped his fingers and the guy on the right handed him a business card, which he extended. "Call me and set up an audition."

Alex just stood there. She put her hand on her hip, looking at the card.

Mr. Kani frowned. "You know, spunk can get old real quick! Take the card!"

She rolled her eyes and stepped forward, accepting the business card. Without looking, she slipped it into her pocket. The DJ played "Gin and Juice" by Snoop Doggy Dogg as the dancefloor got more lively. Alex moved back to the middle of the club to get a good spot to dance, the encounter with the three losers already behind her.

"HAVE your parents been treating you well?" Sonyai asked.

The senior clerk was in Janelle's room at her apartment Monday morning. Her father, Chester, was out working, so the tension was light. Outside in the kitchen, Luanne was washing the dishes and cleaning up from breakfast.

"Everything is fine, Miss Yi," Janelle replied.

"Okay." She let out a sigh. "There was an *incident* Saturday. Both Walker and Stevens have been suspended for 2 weeks."

"Oh my God, was there a fight? They've been snapping at each other lately but—"

"I can't go into details, but it's time to come to terms with the fact that despite this, Walker has to stay at 58th Street."

Janelle gasped.

"Which means you will have to take a position elsewhere," Sonyai concluded.

The news was too much to accept. Her emotions had finally broken her. She cupped her face in her hands and sobbed. "Not fair! This is so not fair!"

"I know this is going to be hard, child, but we will find a good branch for you."

The girl wiped away her tears. "It won't be the same," she whispered.

"You need to be strong, but I know you can do this. I'm starting the paperwork today. Depending on the vacancies, you should be able to acquire a full-time position in no time. Then you will receive medical insurance benefits yourself."

"Can it be at one of our neighborhood branches? So I can cluster and visit?"

"We will see. Andrew has already mentioned Webster is full.

Perhaps 67th Street or Yorkville. I will do everything in my power, child. Waiting is the hardest part."

"Okay."

Sonyai stood up to leave. "The sonogram has been scheduled for Friday the 22nd. Have you been feeling okay?"

"Yeah, I…I'm getting these…weird food cravings," she said with a light smile. "Sour cream and onion chips dipped in peanut butter!"

Sonyai's eyes grew wide in astonishment. "Oh my!"

The two shared a laugh, with Janelle feeling better.

"I better get going. I'm due at the branch by 10. See you at 3." She gave her another hug. "Be strong. It's all going to work out."

Gerry was stunned when Sonyai briefed him of Robin's suspension and puzzled by how tight-lipped Tommy and Ethel were. Whatever happened that Saturday morning must have been earth-shattering. Still, despite his efforts, no one was talking. Reluctantly, Gerry put this current series of events to figure out in the back of his mind. *One mystery at a time,* he thought as he ventured out during his lunch break around noon.

At a hotdog cart on the corner of 56th and 3rd Avenue, Gerry met a tall white woman wearing black jeans and a thin wool jacket with short cropped blond hair. She had just received two hot dogs from the vendor, stepped out of line, and smiled when she saw him approaching.

"Been a long time, Coltraine. I nearly jumped out of my skin when you called asking to meet."

She handed him a hot dog in greeting and the two walked north on 3rd Avenue.

"I don't have that much time, Betts. I only have a few questions about the S.I.U," Gerry started, then took a bite.

"Well a phone call would have sufficed, ya' know? Amazing invention that telephone is."

"I like my privacy. Pretty sure our internal calls are monitored. Special Investigations is not beyond wiretapping."

"When have I heard that before?" Betts replied. "I did some digging, and as far as I know, S.I.U has no open investigations on 58th Street."

"Are you sure?" he asked.

"As sure as the Bills losing the Super Bowl."

They stopped a moment as Gerry went into deep thought. "Makes no sense," he said, shaking his head. "Do you know a Eugene Iscaro?"

"Name doesn't ring a bell. Look, whoever's feeding you information is pissing on your head and calling it rain. You're chasing your tail here, slim."

"Hmm, okay. Sorry for wasting your time, then."

They exchanged pecks on the cheek. "It's never a waste of time when it comes to you. If trouble shows up, watch 'ya back, jack!" she said with a smile. As quickly as the pair met, they parted ways. "See you at the next poker game," she called out as Gerry headed back to the branch.

AUGUSTUS WAS ALONE in his office when he picked up the receiver on his phone and dialed an internal extension number.

"Thank you for calling the New York Public Library Human Resources Department located at the Mid-Manhattan Branch at 40 Fifth Avenue. How can I help you?" A female voice greeted.

"This is Augustus Chavez at 58th Street Branch located at 127 East 58th Street. I'd like to report an employee suspension."

"Name, rank, and employee number, please. Last name first."

"Stevens, Alexandra, part-time page, employee number 234964."

"Offense for suspension and duration?"

"Vandalism, 10 business days, 35 office hours. Effective Monday, March 28th."

"Estimated appraisal of vandalized property?"

"Uh, zero."

"It can't be zero. Vandalism is measured by the value of said property. If there is zero value of damage done, it cannot be considered vandalism."

Augustus lowered the receiver, rolled his eyes and sighed, then went back to the call. "Okay. $1,000.00," he replied. *At least I can possibly get my money back.*

"Since the amount is greater than $500.00, the authorities will have to be informed. A police report will—"

"Belay, belay, belay!" he gasped. "I was mistaken. Value of vandalized property is only $300.00."

After a slight pause, the woman replied, "Very well. Were any other employees assisted in or affected by the offense in question?"

Augustus swallowed hard and replied. "No."

"Okay. Any additional notes to add?"

He wiped his brow. "Umm, employee's first offense, leniency is applied. Will revisit case after 90 days from reinstatement for review and possible expungement from employee record."

"Paperwork has been filed. Suspension will be in effect as of today with the employee returning to duty Monday, April 12th. Copies of forms must be signed by both 58th Street representatives yourself and senior clerk…Sonyai Yi. Expect them via inter-office mail within the next 24 hours. Please send them back signed promptly and keep copies on file for yourself. Thank you for calling the New York Public Library Human Resources Department. Have a nice day."

The phone clicked off before Augustus could reply. *How that woman had time to breathe during all that was beyond me!* he thought.

"Man, I can't believe this suspension shit! With Alex gone I have to do her shelves along with mine now!" Tanya complained.

She, Lakeshia, and Janelle were reshelving books in the fiction section sharing a cart. The workload was substantial among the trio.

"We're all chipping in, Tee. It's not that bad," Janelle replied.

Lakeshia was unusually quiet. Hearing about Alex didn't surprise her, but she was more concerned about Robin and what he could have done to receive the punishment. Her dream the other night didn't help the situation and was still fresh in her thoughts.

Janelle finished her stack of books and moved on to non-fiction and work on the 300's. When they were alone, Tanya put her book down on the cart and turned to Lakeshia.

"My mother grounded me this weekend over what she heard during open school night, Leelee! How a certain strange looking, light-skinned fat guy wearing a red baseball cap scared the shit out of Vickie Florence by hanging her over the roof of the school!"

Lakeshia gulped and laughed nervously. "Gee uh, wonder how that happened?"

"I think you know, small fry. And the only reason you're still walking on 2 legs is because we're already short one page and I don't wanna be doing these shelves by myself with someone pregnant!"

"Tanya, I'm sorry! I was only trying to help!" Lakeshia gasped.

"Just because I had to repeat the 9th grade don't mean I'm dumb, Leelee! I knew Robin did it once he said he knew where I went to school! Believe me, when he gets back, he will have *to deal with me!*"

She turned to leave, but Lakeshia reached out to her. "Wait! I need your help with something!" she pleaded.

Tanya looked over her shoulder. "What? You got me grounded and now you want my help?"

Lakeshia sighed and looked down. "Nevermind."

Tanya's arms dropped to her sides as she blew out a breath. "Okay, what is it?"

"Not here," Lakeshia said, grabbing Tanya's arm and leading her toward the staircase upstairs.

AT THE INFORMATION DESK, Heywood dialed an outside number on the desk telephone. Personal calls were frowned upon but as long as they were kept brief people generally looked the other way.

"Hello?" a woman answered.

"Hey, it's, er, um, String bean. Are we on for Thursday?"

"Oh, sorry, baby. I meant to call you last weekend. I'm flying to Seattle this week. A friend of mine…is feeling real low, possibly sick."

"Oh…oh. Um, he's a boyfriend or something?"

"No, he's married, but we all grew up together. I'll make it up to you when I come back, I promise. My next show is Thursday, April 14th. Call me that Monday before, okay?"

"Uh, sure."

"Great, kisses!"

The phone clicked off and Heywood put the receiver back on the phone.

"She canceled the date, didn't she?"

Angie's question startled Heywood as he turned to find her standing behind him, "How

long have you been there listening?"

"Long enough to know you shouldn't be clogging the main line," she replied coming around and sitting next to him.

Heywood blushed. "Something came up. She's visiting a childhood friend that's going through something."

"Uh-huh," Angie replied.

"Doesn't mean she's leading me on. It's just bad timing."

"I didn't say anything."

"Right," he checked his watch. "It's almost five. Can you do me a favor? Ask Chavez for more reserve postcards. We're running low out here."

Angie looked toward the corner office just in time to see the head librarian step out on the floor. She nodded and stood. They met in the middle of the reference corner.

"Sir, Heywood needs more postcards."

"Ah, they're in the top shelf cabinet in my office with the rest of the office supplies."

"Okay," she replied and they passed each other heading to their respective destinations.

Back at the circulation desk, Tommy and Ethel were standing at their stations when a bike messenger walked in.

"Ethel Jenkins?" he called out looking around.

"You'll have to lower your voice, sir. I'm Ethel Jenkins," she warned.

The messenger pulled out a clipboard from his backpack and approached the clerk. "Sign here, please," he asked, handing her a pen.

She gave him a puzzled look and signed on the clipboard. The biker then pulled out two cans of soda and placed them in front of her. "Have a nice day, ma'am."

The messenger walked through the exit turnstile and left the branch.

Ethel slammed her fist down on the desk shaking the cans. "I can't believe him! He used a messenger?"

Tommy did his best not to laugh.

Tanya and Lakeshia walked inside the second-floor auditorium. Lakeshia flicked the light switch and closed the door.

"Why all the secrecy?" Tanya asked.

"Last week, Miss Yi said Robin and I were getting too close, so she instructed us to keep away from each other. Then one night...I had this...dream."

Tanya raised an eyebrow, "And?"

"And he was in it...and...and he...ki-kissed me..."

Tanya couldn't stop smiling. "Well, well. Lakeshia Olivia Seabrooke, you lusty little minx!"

Lakeshia looked down, ashamed and shaking.

"Oh, relax, Leelee. It's normal, girl! You just had your first wet dream."

"Wet dream?"

"Wow, your first wet dream! I was almost 16 when I had mine. It was about my gym teacher, Mr. Whaley. Oh! He had long rasta dreadlocks and this handlebar type mustache that he used to twirl, looking like Billy Dee Williams. I dreamed I was humping him on the pommel horse. Oooh, he was calling out my name. 'Tanya! Tanyaaa! *Tanyaaa!*'"

"Tanya!" Lakeshia yelled to snap her out of her train of thought.

"Yeah, like that."

Lakeshia gave her an annoyed look.

"Okay, small fry. I will help you handle this."

"Why?"

Tanya sighed. "As mad as I am, I guess I do owe you for getting Robin to take care of that business with Vickie."

"Okay, so now what?"

266

"Easy, meet me back here same time tomorrow. By the way…" She grinned. "How far did it go in your dream?"

"I…I'd rather not think about it. I've been putting it out of my mind all day," she replied blushing.

Tanya chuckled. "Oh, this is going to be fun!"

Angie entered the empty office and walked to a narrow black metal supply closet in the far corner. She turned the handle and pulled the door open, revealing four shelves of boxes. Augustus had labeled each box listing the various supplies inside. Pens, pencils, notepads. She recognized the box holding the postcards and reached up to grab a set of twenty-five wrapped in plastic.

As she pulled the batch down, she hit her elbow on the door and a bolt of pain shot up her arm to her fingertips. She cried out in a sharp gasp as an unlabeled box next to the postcards fell over and opened at her feet. Angie grabbed her elbow, not appreciating the jolt to her funny bone and examined the contents of the mysterious box before her. There was a collection of blank NYPL Letterhead pages, a sheet of gold seals, and a stamp and pad set. She narrowed her eyes and reached for the stamp. The indentation underneath was for a name in cursive. A signature.

Angie tested the stamp on a random piece of paper she dug out of the trash bin. She applied a few impressions, which resulted in a perfect-looking handwritten mark of President Peter Dalton. "Oh my God," she whispered, realizing what she stumbled upon. She packed the items in the box the way they were and placed it back where she found it. Then she grabbed the postcards and left the office, terrified of the disturbing secret she had accidentally discovered.

CHAPTER FIFTEEN

B<small>ENNETT</small> P<small>ARK</small>, <small>THE HIGHEST NATURAL POINT IN</small> M<small>ANHATTAN</small>, <small>WAS</small> located on Fort Washington Avenue and spans two blocks between 183rd Street and 185th. The sun was warm that April morning, and Robin was enjoying his time off with an uphill jog. His path took him up 181st Street to Fort Washington Avenue and continued further until he made it to the park.

Robin approached a group of stone rocks erected through the park a few minutes after eleven o'clock. A marker etched with a message indicated the legendary point listing the height at an official 26,505 feet above sea level. He had been to this same spot several times, which triggered a painful memory from the past.

"Okay, open your eyes," Robin said.

"Hey, what are we doing here?" Diedre asked.

"I told you I was taking you to the top of the world. Look down."

"Robin! That is so corny!"

"Nah, believe it or not, we're higher here than if we were on the observation deck at the World Trade Center! That's how hilly the northern part of the city is compared to downtown."

"You're so smart, Robin Walker."

"Why, thank you, Diedre Anderson."

"So, what are we doing here, at the top of the world?"

"What better place to ask you to marry me?"

"What?"

"Look, we've been through some rough moments lately, and they're mostly because I've been a jackass."

Diedre remained quiet.

"I just want you to know I'm sorry, and I would never intentionally hurt you. I'm here for you and I want to stay being there for you."

They shared a kiss.

"Well?" she asked.

"Well, what?" Robin replied.

"Why aren't you on one knee? Where's my ring?"

"We don't need such material objects and gestures to define our love! I still didn't hear an answer from you."

"And you won't without presenting me with a ring and proposing right!"

"Will you at least think about it?"

"I think you already know my answer. Now c'mon, it's chilly out here."

She kissed him again and they walked their way out of the park.

Robin brought himself back to reality and let out a long, deep sigh. He stepped away from the marker and walked toward a series of park benches. There was a familiar figure waiting for him sitting alone. Robin took a seat next to Barbara Schemanske, who was eating a slice of pizza she brought from George's Pizzeria located halfway up the hill on 181st Street.

"Kinda early for a slice, isn't it?" Robin began.

"Never too early for pizza, Walker. Now, what is it you got me coming out here on my day off to discuss?"

"This isn't working. I want out. Transfer me to another branch immediately or I'm quitting."

The librarian sighed and threw her pizza crust to a group of pigeons that attacked it feverously. "And how do you suppose I make that happen? Hmm? Wave a fucking magic wand like I'm your fairy godmother?"

"Normally I'd have the patience, but due to recent events, I must insist. Drastic actions must be taken. There was a... highly sensitive racial incident. I can't elaborate—"

"I'd rather not hear about it, then. But there's no way you can just up and leave. That's not the way things work. I told you when you took this position that it wouldn't be easy. I told you that!"

"Hey, I was up for consideration at Epiphany, which is mere blocks away from the Baruch campus. You torpedoed that and pulled rank."

"With your known reputation of loathing the children's floor, I knew you would hate it at Epiphany. I did you a favor, you ungrateful little—" She took a breath and sighed. "What do you think would have happened if Columbus had returned to Spain empty handed? What if Orville told his brother, Wilbur, 'This flying machine thing isn't going to work. Let's go back to fixing bicycles'? You're not walking away from this."

"I don't give a damn about Columbus. He was lost!" He stood up and turned to her. "Listen, you have a week. I register for my next term on the 12th. If I'm not transferred by the time I go back, I'm walking in there and submitting my letter of resignation."

He left the bench, walking toward the exit of the park. Barbara just shook her head, silently cursing the troubled youth.

TANYA AND LAKESHIA were in the 600's section around four o'clock, browsing the shelves. Behind them, Sonyai and Gerry were working the circulation desk.

"I heard Miss Yi put in the paperwork to find Janelle a full-time position," Lakeshia whispered. "How long do you think it'll take?"

"It depends. Might be a week, might be a month. Even a few months," Tanya answered.

"What are we looking for here, anyways?"

"We've been going over a few books to help you in the last week, but there's only one that's...Ah! Here it is. *The Joy of Sex* by Alex Comfort. Call number 613.96-C. C'mon! Back upstairs."

Moments later, the two girls were in the soundproof auditorium again. Lakeshia was sitting uneasily on a chair that was usually stacked in the closet. Tanya was thumbing through the pages and then stopped.

"Okay, Leelee. We've read some chapters and been through the mechanics of the birds and the bees, but it's time now…to see how it's done. First, some basics. Lakeshia, this is a man's penis!" She flipped over the book showing the young waif the graphic of a heavily endowed male.

Lakeshia gawked, eyes wide open, and gasped at the sight. She turned away and shut her eyes, her face crimson from embarrassment.

"Ah, ah, ah. Don't you turn away! Look at it, look at it, *look at it*!"

She slowly turned to look at the picture, her body trembling.

"That's what Robin has. That's what it looks like. Keep looking! You have to get used to it."

Once she was satisfied, Tanya turned the page to another picture. "Okay, now you see what he's doing? That is called *penetration.* It goes inside her vagina, and that is the act of having sex. It's not kissing, necking, groping. Those all lead to sex, but it's not sex. You can't get pregnant from a kiss, even if they put their tongue in your mouth, you understand?"

Lakeshia said nothing, just nodded.

Tanya turned another page. "Okay here, he is massaging her breasts—"

Lakeshia hugged her chest and cried out, "Okay, stop! Stop! Enough! I can't look anymore!" and closed her eyes hard while still shaking. "It's too much, it's too much," she whimpered.

Tanya lowered the book and rolled her eyes. "Alright, small fry, we'll call it day." She approached her in the chair. "But I want you to check out this book and take it home with you."

"What? Why?" Lakeshia squeeked.

"To learn what they should be teaching you at that preppy 'lil music school of yours."

"Hey!"

"C'mon, let's see if Mr. Coltraine can check it out for us discreetly."

When the two pages emerged from the staircase, Gerry had switched from checkouts to returns, replacing Sonyai, and Ethel was now standing where Gerry once was.

"This is it, the perfect opportunity. Jenkins won't give a damn what book we're borrowing," Tanya said as they walked to the exit turnstile in front of the clerk.

"Hi, Miss Jenkins," both pages said accidentally, then looked at each other.

Ethel looked up and cocked her eyebrow. "Well, if it ain't the Doublemint twins. What can I do for ya'?"

"This…is kinda embarrassing, Miss Jenkins, but could you check this book out for Leelee? She needs it for, um…biology class." Tanya presented the book while Lakeshia handed over her library card quickly. Gerry showed no sign of hearing the conversation. He was writing in his small book of secret thoughts.

"Sure, darling, no problem." Ethel grabbed the lightpen and swiped her card, then opened the book and swiped the barcode. A soft chime emitted from the terminal registering an error.

"Oh, your library card still has you down for borrowing YA books only. Your parents didn't change it to borrow adult books after you turned 14," Ethel explained.

"Oops," Lakeshia squeaked while Tanya slapped her forehead. "Well, I'll check it out for her," she said as taking out her own card. "You better return this book on time, girl!"

Ethel closed Lakeshia's record and swiped Tanya's card, then checked the book out, adding a date due card in the pocket. "Okay, here you go," Ethel said returning the book and their separate cards.

"Thanks," Tanya said, and the two quickly disappeared into the shelves.

Lakeshia walked by Janelle pushing a shelving cart and stopped to stare at her.

"What?" Janelle asked.

"I can't believe you *did* that!" she said shaking her head in disgust. She then continued walking while holding the book close to her chest.

Heywood and Angie were at the Pig 'N' Whistle, celebrating the end of the workday when he noticed she was unusually quiet.

"What's eating you today?" he asked.

"Nothing," she replied while stirring her Long Island iced tea.

"Nah, something's wrong. What's up? You can tell me."

"Do you think Chavez is a good man?"

"Huh? What do you mean?" he asked.

"Can you imagine him doing something…that breaks the rules? Something underhanded?"

Heywood thought about it. "I…I really don't know, he can be driven at times, bend the rules a little but—"

"I know, but it's just…never mind." She wanted to tell him what she had discovered but thought against it. She didn't know who could she trust. Anyone with this information could use it against Augustus with disastrous results.

FRIDAY MORNING AT NINE, Augustus arrived at the 96th Street Branch, located between Park Avenue and Lexington. The two-story building had just been renovated three years previously, bringing the ancient structure up to current building standards. Before he could ring the bell, the door opened and a stout middle-aged white man with slicked salt and pepper hair greeted Augustus with a hearty handshake.

Cleopheous Baker, 96th Street's head librarian, was born and raised in Goose Creek, South Carolina. For the last ten years, the colorful individual had mentored various employees with his wisdom and tact. His influence dominated the six-branch East Side cluster. Serving as the regional librarian, he ruled with an iron fist.

"Thank you for seeing me, Cleo," Augustus said, shaking his peer's meaty palm.

"My door is always open," the gentleman replied and gestured for the librarian to come in.

After securing the lock on the door, the pair walked through the vast open floor to the series of open offices that had no ceilings. The branch's loft-like interior exposed the staff from above to anyone climbing the wide staircase to the second floor. The two appeared to be the only individuals inside at the moment, which gave them all the privacy they needed.

"How are things with Jessica?" Augustus asked.

"The usual," Cleopheous answered. "She leaves me alone, I leave her alone. You should follow in our example, you'll live longer. Letting that Jap get over is gonna do you in from the stress."

"I should be so lucky."

"So, tell me what's bothering you these days?" Cleopheous asked, taking a seat at his desk.

Augustus took a seat as well. "It all started with this new part-timer we got, Robin Walker. A transfer from Fort Washington."

"Hmm. The Battle Axe."

"Right. He's all high-and-mighty, 'Procedures of Conduct,' chip on his shoulder, and naturally clashes trying to fit in."

"Okay. Why should that worry you? The clerks should handle clerical matters. Stay out of it."

"Look, he needs to learn who's running the show. My favorites are getting pissed off because some young upstart refuses to see the big picture. I won't have my operation fall like a house of cards!"

Cleopheous laughed so loud and boisterously that it echoed through the entire building. "We got a couple of those here ourselves. Bunch of robot sticks-in-the-mud. Just let them be, Augustus."

"Okay, fine. But when it's not him, it's others who usurp my authority. I have this IA who keeps undermining me with our movie festivals. And then my very own assistant, my right hand, she's getting up there—"

"You know what I'm dealing with on my plate?" the mentor interrupted. "Budget cuts. This renovation set us back thousands of dollars we're still paying for. I have a staff of 35 employees to manage, dealing with scheduling conflicts, personal grievances they might have among each other, and you think *you* have problems with this petty bullshit? You wanna switch places for a week and see if you still got it rough?"

Augustus narrowed his eyes. He didn't appreciate being slighted. "I guess that's why you're in charge of the region," he replied with a sneer.

"All sarcasm aside, the simplest solution for you is to crack the whip. Remind them who the fuck is in charge. This greaseball they elected wants to take money out of my pocket to clean up Times Square! I'd never thought I'd say it, but the *negro* before him treated the libraries a whole lot better. So you tell your staff what I intend to tell our new mayor: fall in line!"

"Valued advice if I ever heard any, Cleo. You're a regular Mahatma Gandhi." He stood up to leave.

"Heheheh. Smile when you say that!" the librarian called back.

ROBIN WAS SMOOTHING out the wrinkles on his new outfit. Jon was visiting Esmeralda upstairs, and Franklin would arrive any moment to pick him up on their night out to The Tunnel. He stepped in front of his full-length mirror. Using the thousand dollars from the library, he treated himself to some new clothes from Sterns.

The doorbell rang at six o'clock and Robin opened the door. Franklin stood out in the hallway, and Robin stared at his outfit.

"Uh, couldn't you find something a *little* less flamboyant? We're going to The Tunnel, not Studio 54!"

"You should talk, looking like you straight out of Wall Street meets New Jack City! Let's go, G-Money!" Franklin said with a nod.

They took the train and emerged from the 23rd Street station on 8th Avenue in the heart of Chelsea.

"Why couldn't we have taken the 1-train and gotten off at 28th and 7th?" Franklin asked.

"I like the walk from here. What do you have against it?"

"This neighborhood gives me the creeps. Fags everywhere."

Robin winced at his friend's homophobia. "Something happen to you down here one time, hmm?"

"No, and nothing will either," he replied ending the conversation.

The Tunnel was once a warehouse terminal on the edge of

Manhattan where the freight trains passed through in the early twentieth century. When it opened in the eighties, it was known for hosting parties among the gay community with dance, industrial, and disco music sets. Recently, the nightclub was transitioning to hip-hop, with DJs migrating from a crosstown rival nightclub known as the Sound Factory to make it big.

Robin and Franklin arrived at eight. There was already an extended line of clubgoers waiting, so the pair joined them.

"I meant to ask, how'd you get the threads?"

"I hit the number. Got five big ones and went down to Sterns," Robin answered.

"Classy."

At nine thirty, a bouncer opened the door and picked a select few from the front of the line and waved them inside. As time progressed, more entered and the line moved up. An hour went by and suddenly the line stopped moving.

"What the hell, man?" Franklin complained.

By eleven thirty, people became impatient and vented their frustrations. Some even left to find another scene. The bouncer came out again and started thinning the line by where they were trying to go. "All right, who here trying to see Flex in the basement? Step forward!" he called out. The line advanced enough for Robin and Franklin to pay their cover and go in.

They were ushered downstairs to the cellar, which was split into two sides. The main floor was like a cafe, where tables and chairs were laid out in front of a small stage with a separate DJ booth against the wall. There was music playing, but neither of them could determine what kind of music it was—it definitely wasn't hip-hop. Robin scanned the room, then tapped Franklin on the shoulder and pointed to a hallway that led to a small lounge. As the two approached, they heard familiar instrumentals and hip-hop breaks. They had arrived.

The lounge was a small intimate corner of the massive nightclub that was otherwise bustling with techno and house music. It was a reflection on the impact hip-hop was having on the world today. From house parties and back alley block parties in the Bronx to RUN DMC making it to Madison Square Garden in the eighties, the nightclub scene was slowly being engrossed in the culture of hip-hop and rap.

This Friday night set—no matter how minuscule the venue—was a landmark. They reserved Sundays for hip hop shows. DJs would draw smaller crowds due to people having to go to work or attend school the next day. On a Friday set, people would party until the wee hours of the morning.

"Okay, remember the plan. We stay in sight of each other while doing our own thing and give the signal if you leaving with a chick," Robin instructed.

"Ah-ight, man. I got'cha back," Franklin replied.

Robin smiled to himself hearing his friend talk street slang. He was basically a hip-hop street kid in a white boy's body. The pair went their separate ways and mingled into the crowd.

Franklin followed the ladies to the dance floor. He turned on the charm as he maneuvered around, flashing his boyish smile waiting for a response. *Bitches, bitches, bitches,* he thought. One girl caught his eye. They exchanged glances and she approached him. She had a short haircut that reminded him of the female rapper MC Lyte, wearing a blue and grey New York Mets baseball jersey and blue jeans.

"Hey!" she said over the music.

"Hey!" he replied.

She leaned into him. "Saw you come in with your friend over there. You and him like Light and Lighter? Y'all supposed to be Kid N' Play?"

"Nah, he's the DJ. I'm the rapper," he replied with a wink.

She nodded. "Ah…Fresh Prince. Very clever."

They sized each other up.

"Wanna see why girls ain't nothing but trouble?" she asked, taking his hand and leading him back to the dark hallway they came in.

"Do I!" he replied eagerly.

Robin squeezed his way to the bar and waved to get the bartender's attention. People were lined up elbow to elbow, some sitting on stools and others standing around.

"Ayyo, lemme get a Bacardi and Coke!" he called out.

The bartender, a tall black guy with dreadlocks, looked at Robin with a smirk. "ID, babyface?" he asked skeptically.

Robin stared back at him. "Club soda then!" he snarled.

"$2.50."

"What happened to dollar drinks?"

"$2.50, Muthafuckah!"

Robin slapped down a ten-dollar bill on the bar. "This is for the next 3 drinks of the night, asshole!"

"Whatever." The bartender shrugged, sliding the bill off the bar. He grabbed a fountain soda gun and a glass and placed a tissue in front of him with a straw, then lowered the drink on the tissue.

"Enjoy!"

By the time he picked up the drink, the bartender was gone. He took a sip, rolled his eyes and placed it back on the bar.

Franklin and his new friend were making out in a corner out of sight from everyone. "MC Lyte" was his kind of girl, ready for anything. He felt her chest a few times and even got a handful of her behind. She had soft lips and a lively tongue. Her hands were feeling his abs and moving around his waist.

"Wanna get outta here?" he asked. He didn't even know her name. He didn't want to.

"Why wait?" she whispered, then grabbed each side of his pants and pulled.

Robin finally got a stool at the bar, he was on his second club soda. It was an acquired taste he was getting used to. Nodding to the music, he scanned the floor trying to locate Franklin. *I hope his dumbass doesn't get into trouble,* he thought. There was a group of tables in a corner to his right.

One particular table got his attention. It had several empty seats with purses and handbags on them. They were being watched by a single occupant sitting alone. He only got a profile view for a moment, but then the girl at the table turned her head and Robin gasped. It was *her*! The girl from the train and the study hall. She was guarding the bags for her friends and couldn't move!

Franklin couldn't believe this was happening. He leaned back against the wall checking all directions for someone passing by. His pants were around his ankles with the girl down on her knees.

"Easy, easy, eassssssy does it! We about to get busted in here! Let's take it outside!" he hissed.

She was slipping her hand in and out the slit of his boxers, "You 'bout to bust yourself down here, baby. I want it, and I want it now!"

He made up his mind, thanking the good lord above for what he was about to receive...until he heard a snap that sounded like a switchblade.

Robin sprang off the stool as his heart fluttered. He eased his way through the dancers, apologizing for every bump and collision while shuffling his feet. He confirmed his doubts as he moved closer. It was indeed his mysterious dream girl. There was a moment of recognition on her face as they locked eyes again. He was a few feet away from the table when he heard a high pitched scream.

"Okay, whiteboy. Reach into your suit jacket and cough up your wallet! Do it or I'm cutting your shit off!"

Franklin dropped his head staring down a nightmare. There was a five-inch knife dangerously close to his crotch, and the girl holding it was no longer smiling.

"What the fuck is this?" he yelled.

"Run it, motherfucker, or I start slicing!"

"You fucking bitch! Help!" Franklin screamed.

Footsteps hit the floor as people panicked in the commotion. Security guards emerged from all directions. Robin followed the scream and found them.

"Hey!" he yelled.

In that split second, the girl turned her head, reacting to the yell as Franklin brought up his knee and connected hard to her chin. There was a muffled grunt as her knife hand swiped wildly. Franklin jumped in place with a gasp and the girl cupped her mouth with her free hand, blood dripping down her chin.

Security surrounded Robin, Franklin, and the girl in all directions. Hands and arms took hold of all three in moments as they were ushered upstairs and tossed outside from the side exit. Franklin pulled up his pants as the girl took off running up the street. Robin stood there, frozen and shocked from what transpired in a manner of three minutes.

"Well, way to go, Geronimo. Always jumping out the goddamn window! What the fuck, man?" Robin yelled.

Franklin was still holding himself, shuffling back and forth on his feet.

Robin turned and looked down the street for the assailant. "I think she bit her tongue off when you kneed her, fucking blood was everywhere—"

"Forget that bitch. I think she got me, man!" he yelled jumping up and down.

"We were only in there *20 fucking minutes!* After waiting 4 hours in line! And to top it off, I saw the girl again! She was sitting right there! She couldn't fucking go anywhere. I could have sat there and finally talked to her!"

"Did you hear what I said? She fucking cut me, man!" he squirmed. "I...I can feel it, man. She cut me on the bottom of my balls, man!" He stopped moving and looked at Robin. "I need you to take a look—"

"What?" he yelled.

"Please man! I think I'm fucking bleeding! You need to check and see how bad—"

"You want me to check your balls to see if their bleeding because some bitch got the drop on you! No way, not happening. We can take a cab to St. Vincent's. Let 'em check you at the ER."

"Don't be like this! This is my balls, man! I can't live my life if my boys are affected and I can't have kids!" Franklin sobbed hysterically.

Robin just stared at his childhood friend in awe. He thought back to their first meeting back at P.S. 132, then hanging out at I.S. 143. That time when Franklin let him watch while he popped April Santiago's cherry in the second-floor laundromat. When Franklin came to his 15th birthday party while no one else did. Robin owed him this.

"Alright, just...step over behind this dumpster where no one can see."

Franklin wiped his face and waddled over to a huge green trash bin, followed by Robin.

"Cup your thing, man. I'm only checking your sack. I can't believe I'm doing this shit."

Franklin slid his pants down, put his left hand in his boxers covering himself and then pulled the front of his boxers down exposing his scrotum. Robin closed his eyes shut for a moment, then knelt down. He opened his eyes and examined the area for a few seconds and then stood up.

"It's just a scratch. You're fine," he said quickly while turning away.

"Look for more than 30 seconds!" Franklin pleaded.

"Fuck!" Robin snapped. He turned back and took a longer look.

Out of nowhere, three guys up the street shouted "Faggots!" and laughed while walking by. Robin stood up and sighed. "There is a red line that is not bleeding. It's only a scratch. All you need is some mercurochrome on it and it'll heal. Let's go!"

"You sure?"

"I'm not looking again. There's no blood. Walk it off or I'm leaving you," Robin said as he headed toward Eighth Avenue.

Franklin pulled up his pants and shuffled behind him. "Wait up! Not so fast! Damn bitch tried to Lorena Bobbit me, man!"

"I SHOULD HAVE LET that ungrateful snot go ahead to Epiphany as planned," Barbara Schemanske said.

She was sharing a booth with Zelda in Tom's Restaurant, the famous diner that was the inspiration for the coffee shop frequented by the characters on the TV show *Seinfeld*. There was a steady downpour of rain outside that Monday morning as the clock on the wall read nine eighteen.

"He would have been miserable working in the children's room and none of this would have happened," she finished her thought.

"Oh, stop worrying. He won't resign," Zelda replied.

"When I first met that boy, he was nothing but a menace.

Intelligent, but headstrong, always getting into fights. He would always stand up for the underdog, risking his body to defend someone who was being picked on. I knew he had potential. I molded that child, instilled him with ethics and morale. And this is how he repays me?"

"Babs, you're going to give yourself a coronary!"

"Don't call me Babs!" The outburst attracted a few glances from the rest of the restaurant. The librarian's face was flushed with anger. She took a few deep breaths and calmed down. "Zelda, you have to make sure he stays. Don't let him throw his life away before it starts…"

Zelda lowered her tea on the table and looked across to her old friend. "Why do you care so much over this one? What makes him so special? You mentioned before that he's part of an elaborate scheme, that you placed him there for a reason. Why?"

Barbara looked down for a moment. Her silence revealed more than words could explain. The thin corner of her mouth quivered and her eyes went soft. "I've started a chain reaction of events that will reverberate ripples through a broken system. A domino effect of consequences I did not foresee. My eyes were blinded by vengeance and now, I must take steps to see this to the end."

Zelda saw a side of her she had never seen in over twenty years of knowing her. "Barbara, what have you done?" she whispered.

"He must stay there, Zelda. He is the key. Sonyai, Augustus, the conflict, the chaos that is your branch, he can put an end to it, but only if he's there. Don't let him slip away. I don't know if I can go through this again."

There was something in her eyes as Zelda listened, something The Battle Axe had never shown in the face of opposition throughout her entire career—fear.

What have you done, Barbara? she thought.

THE BARUCH COLLEGE registrar's office was in the heart of campus at 151 East 25th Street between Lexington and 3rd Avenue. Students lined up on the sidewalk leading inside the building to register for classes in the upcoming semester. There were two lines extending to opposite ends of the block in which students were sorted by the first letter of their last name. A through L approached from the corner of Lexington, while M through Z approached from 3rd.

Robin had been waiting for over an hour as the line shuffled along. He'd had his fill of waiting in lines since going to The Tunnel. Behind him, Kim, Jacques, Carlos, and Jarvis leaned against the wall of the building as well. Across the way, he spied Gillian and Walter among the second group of students. Everyone had a course catalog in their hand with dog-eared pages of their preferred classes. Best way to pass the time was through conversation.

"Hey, Jacques, what classes you signing up for?" Robin asked.

"Psychology 1001, English 2500 for Journalism, Music 1003...why?"

"Just checking if we had the same classes so I can sign up before you," he replied with a grin.

"You would do that?"

"Hell, yeah. It's anyone's game. First one there gets the chair! But don't worry, I took Music 1003 already. You're cool."

"You're a cold man, Robin Walker. A cold, cold man."

Several hours went by as Robin and his friends inched closer to the entrance. He checked his watch. It was only one thirty. It occurred to him that he wasn't going to make it to work by three. He needed to make a call.

"Hold my spot, I gotta make a phone call," he said to Jacques.

"You lose your place if you leave," the French student said with a smirk.

"Don't fuck with me, baguette boy. I'll break that glass jaw of yours!"

"Quit being a dick, Jacques. We got you covered, Robin. Go ahead." Kim said behind them.

"Thanks, Kim," Robin said and walked across the street to a trio of pay phones. After dialing the number to the branch, he waited for a few rings till someone answered.

"58th Street Branch Library. How can I help you?" Zelda answered.

"Afternoon, Miss Clein. It's Robin. Is Miss Yi there? I need to speak to her."

"She's with Augustus in his office. Can I take a message?"

"Ugh! Um, I'm registering for classes and it doesn't look like I can make it in today."

"Ooh, how unfortunate. I will convey the message. Perhaps you can make it up by working Saturday."

"Okay. I'll call again once I'm done. Thanks."

"Um, Walker, before you go! I...I know you've been frustrated lately with what's been going on. I don't even know what happened that Saturday, but please understand, the staff here are like a family, and families have disagreements. But in the end, it all works out. When you return, I hope you exercise patience...and do nothing rash."

"Uh, okay, ma'am, thanks for that. Um, goodbye." He hung up the phone.

When Robin returned, he saw Walter hanging with the others at the line. "You done already?" he asked.

"Yep, got Bus 1001, Cis 1357, couple other prerequisites. They moved through us pretty fast."

"Did Cis 1357 seem almost full? I'm shooting for that too," Robin asked.

"Really?" Carlos squeaked with a cheesy smile.

"Don't get any ideas, Mouse," he called back, then turned to Walter. "Which day for Cis did you get? Monday and Wednesday or Tuesday and Thursday?"

Before Walter could answer, Jarvis did a long wolf whistle that caught everyone's attention.

"Holy shit! Check out the hottie at 12 o'clock high!" Jarvis exclaimed.

All the guys turned around to see a woman approaching. She was something out of an eighties R-rated film. The one where all the high school or college students are trying to seduce the incredibly hot schoolteacher. She was wearing leather pants that were skin tight, a leather jacket over a tight white sweatshirt, with a matching white headband on her forehead. The jaws were hanging from nearly everyone as she stopped next to Walter.

"Hello, Walter," she said with a distinct British accent.

All the stunned faces turned to Walter, who was embarrassed. "Hi, mom," he whispered.

The dropped jaws and stunned faces turned to wild-eyed glances as everyone gasped "Mom?"

"My name is Maxie Shaw. I'm looking for Robin Walker."

"I'm Robin Walker!" Jarvis yelled raising his hand.

"No! *I'm* Robin Walker!" Carlos insisted.

Jacques stepped forward, took the woman's hand, and brought it up to his lips for a kiss. "Robin Walker at your service, mademoiselle. A pleasure to make your acquaintance."

Robin cleared his throat, then Walter pointed him out. The impostors all backed away with distraught looks and went back to waiting in line. Maxie stepped over and greeted the youngster with a heartwarming smile.

"Umm, hi!" he waved.

"Hello, young man. I'm Walter's mother."

Robin squinted and turned to Walter. "Hey? I thought your last name was Bar—"

"Walter's father and I divorced," she interrupted. "I went back to my maiden name. From what I hear, you've been an outstanding chum for my son, here. Keeping him out of trouble."

Walter rolled his eyes as Robin stared blankly, trying not to notice the woman's impressive bosom.

"We Brits have a concept you Yanks call a sponsor, being that person someone would call or turn to when vices arise and people are tempted to indulge in spirits."

"Huh?" Robin grunted.

"She wants you to keep me from drinking and stuff," Walter explained.

"You'd be a regular Jiminy Cricket, resting on his shoulder waving a finger like 'No, no, no…' We call them sober companions."

"That sounds more like a job, ma'am."

"Don't call me ma'am; it makes me feel old."

"And you are far from old!" he exclaimed. The guys behind them all grunted in agreement.

She turned and smiled, then faced Robin again. "If it's incentive you're looking for…" She reached into her jacket, and Robin flinched for a second until she pulled out an envelope and presented it to him.

"Sorry. Where I come from, when someone reaches in their jacket, it's usually bad news," Robin apologized, then took the gift and opened it. "Wow, four tickets to the Knicks-Bulls game at the end of the season!"

"I'm the executive vice-president of marketing at Madison Square Garden. I can get you into any event, concerts, plays, games. You name it!"

"Miss Shaw, you've got yourself a sober companion!" Robin announced.

"Excellent." She smiled. "I'll be checking in on you. Both of you," she said, nodding to Walter as well.

The woman turned and walked away, giving the guys a wonderful view of her behind.

"That is one fine girl!" Jarvis said.

"That there's no girl. That's a *woman*," Robin replied. He then turned to Walter. "How in the world can she *possibly* be your mother?"

"She had me when she was 15."

Robin did the math in his head. "You mean to tell me she's 33? She doesn't look a day over 26!"

"British woman age gracefully," Walter said with a shrug.

Robin looked at the tickets again, and then went back to his spot in line. They were almost inside the building as his stomach growled. He hadn't eaten all day.

"Hey, I'm starving. Anyone got any snacks? I can't leave the line again this close. We're almost in."

"I dunno about you, but I could eat Walter's mom for hours!" Jarvis said with a laugh.

"Hey! Watch that shit, Jarvis!" Walter warned.

A female student holding a clipboard in her hand suddenly appeared near the line. She was wearing a black T-shirt with an orange logo on it.

"Hello! Would you like to apply for a Discover Card?" she asked enthusiastically.

"Geez, what coffee did you drink this morning, little miss sunshine?" Walter joked.

The student ignored the remark and repeated the question to Robin. He looked at her from head to toe, questioning her sanity. "Why exactly would I wanna do that?" he asked.

"I'm glad you asked," she started and drew closer to him. "Discover is doing this limited promotion in an attempt to help students here at Baruch establish a line of credit that they can manage responsibly and help them maintain a certain lifestyle. Shop on credit with your Discover Card and pay over time with low payments over a 12-month period!"

Robin feigned fascination. "Wow, umm, what's your name?" he asked.

"Cindy."

"Wow, Cindy, that was a very persuasive speech you just gave, darling!"

The girl beamed and leaned her clipboard toward him.

"But I'm not interested in a credit card right now. Sorry!"

The smile on Cindy's face disappeared as she realized he was wasting her time. She turned away and repeated her pitch again looking for a potential signee. "Free king-sized Snickers bar with every submitted application…"

Robin's head tilted up as his stomach growled again. "Hold up, hold up, hold up! Cindy!" He waved her back over. "Why didn't you say anything 'bout them Snickers bars! Here, let me get an application, girl! Playing with me! Hahahaha!"

Cindy returned and handed Robin an application. While writing, he gave a non-verbal hand signal to Carlos and Jarvis who responded with a wink and a nod. The anxious girl reached into her bag and pulled out a huge candy bar as a show of good faith.

Once he was finished, he handed the application back and left his hand out for the candy. Cindy looked it over and gave the student a pout. "Are you kidding me right now? You expect me to believe all of this?"

"Is there a problem?" Robin asked with an innocent blink of his eyes.

"Your name is Elmer J. Fudd?" she asked skeptically.

"That's right," he replied with a straight face.

"You're fucking with me," she replied, deadpan.

"Wow, what happened to that cheerful enthusiasm?"

Jarvis suddenly walked past and called out, "Hey, Elmer! What's happening, man!"

He was followed by Carlos, walking a different direction. "Yo! Mr. Fudd, still on for the party this weekend?"

Robin waved as they went by and then looked back to Cindy with a fake smile, still holding out his hand. She rolled her eyes and muttered under her breath. "Whatever. They don't pay me enough to take this shit seriously." She then handed him the candy.

As she walked along to the rest of the students in line, Robin opened the Snickers and broke it into three pieces. Jarvis and Carlos returned to their places and received a piece each for their performances.

"Good one, *Elmer,*" Jarvis said.

"Yeah, thanks a lot, *Fudd,*" Carlos added.

"That's *Mr.* Fudd to you!" he replied and took a bite.

AUGUSTUS WALKED into the second-floor auditorium to find Alex standing in the middle of the room. He closed the door behind him and took a few steps forward to address her.

"Welcome back, young lady. Are you ready to return to duty and put this unpleasantness behind us?"

She nodded solemnly. "Yes, sir."

"Unfortunately, Mr. Walker is not here today. He had to take off to register for classes. He'll be back tomorrow. When he does, you, him, Miss Yi, and I will all sit down and resolve this matter. We are a family here, Miss Stevens. We don't have to like each other, but we *will* treat each other with respect. Am I clear?"

She nodded again. "Yes, sir."

"Good. I left an addendum in your suspension paperwork that states if the next 3 months go by without another incident, we will revisit this situation with the possibility of having it removed from your employee record. I didn't have to tell you this, but I chose to do so. Do *not* take advantage of my generosity."

Alex choked up at the revelation as she got teary-eyed. "Thank you, sir!" she gasped. "I won't let you down." She held back a sniffle and wiped away a tear.

Augustus held his emotions in check at the page's display. "Dismissed," he ordered, and Alex walked by him to exit the room. After the door slammed, he sighed as his shoulders relaxed. He hoped the worst of it was over.

"You wanted to see me, ma'am?" Tommy said as he walked into the clerical office.

Sonyai turned from her desk and stood up. "Yes, have a seat, please," she instructed.

Tommy sat and Sonyai folded her arms to address the clerk. "Robin can't make it in today so he's working this Saturday for the first time without incident...I hope."

"Okay."

"I wanted him to work here, but there's a family emergency for a clerk in Yorkville and they will be short-handed there this weekend."

"Uh-oh," Tommy uttered.

"Yes, I'm afraid Walker will cluster over there for the first time, and I want you there as well to keep an eye on him. He's ruffled feathers here. Can you imagine how he'll interact with the snobs at Yorkville?"

"He might just fit right in," Tommy replied with a chuckle.

"I seriously doubt it. I have enough headaches as it is trying to find a position for Janelle."

"How is that going?" Tommy asked.

"I put the paperwork in, but the only vacancies available so far are all in the Bronx."

"Well, she lives up there in the 'bridge around 238th Street."

"Everything's out west. Van Nest, Morris, Eastchester, Baychester, Allerton..." Sonyai rattled on.

"It won't be that bad. Just a bus ride away."

She looked up at him. "I want her close, Thomas. It has to be somewhere in Manhattan."

"We can't get what we want all the time. We have to face that reality."

"I still have some tricks up my sleeve. I just need things to go smoothly everywhere else." She pointed a finger at him. "Just make sure Walker behaves himself. With him and Alex back here, things will be tense enough as it is."

Alex was relaxing in the staff room around four twenty, slowly thumbing around the business card she got in the club. Tanya came inside, nodded at Alex, and went to the refrigerator to get a bottle of Poland Spring.

"Hey, welcome back. How was your suspension? With no work or school?"

"Fine, I guess. Still pissed off about that fat fuck *manhandling* me like he did."

Tanya waved her hands dismissively. "I don't wanna talk about that shit! The less I know, the better. Wha'cha playing with there?" she asked.

"I was at The Melting Pot on 29th Street Sunday night and this joker rolled up on me trying to impress. Saying he could put me on for music videos and shit. I thought he was fronting till I saw this."

She passed the card to Tanya. "Is he legit?" Tanya asked.

"Does it matter? I've been getting approached left and right about modeling since I was 12. I'm not about that life."

"But?" Tanya prodded.

Alex sighed. "But lately I've been kind of thinking about it... instead of going to college."

CHAPTER SIXTEEN

"SOMETHING'S BOTHERING YOU, GERRALD. YOU KNOW I CAN ALWAYS tell," Denise Coltraine said.

Gerry was having breakfast with his twin sister Tuesday morning. The siblings were fraternal twins, so they had separate identities, personalities, and mannerisms, but there was a strong bond between the two on a mental level. They could sense when the other was about to sneeze or feel each other's pain slightly when one of them got hurt. She was wearing a floral print dress while eating a piece of french toast.

"It's just something fishy at the job, Dee. That's all," Gerry replied.

"Gerry, sometimes I think your middle name should have been 'Conspiracy'. You think there's always one around the corner."

"Very funny. You check on mom and dad?" he asked.

"They're doing fine. Mom's been bothering me about getting married again."

Gerry chuckled and ate a sausage link.

"You know, she never bothers you about settling down. It's always 'Denise, you have to meet somebody and have a baby.' 'Denise, your biological clock is ticking.' 'Denise, I want to be a grandmother before I die!' God wouldn't be so merciful."

"She's only nagging you because we're over 30. Speaking of which, what's the plan for the big 3-2 next month?"

"It falls on a Saturday this year, so I figured we catch a show at Birdland or maybe The Blue Note."

"With our last name, the last thing I wanna do is jazz. Everyone will stare at us thinking about 'Cousin John,'" he said with air quotes. Gerry and Denise were not related to the famous musician they shared their surname with. They spelled it differently, but it didn't stop them from name-dropping occasionally.

"Well, it's an even year, so you have the honors of making the plans. I'll follow your lead," Denise announced. The twins had been alternating birthday celebrations since turning eighteen, with her getting the odd numbers.

Gerry finished his meal and took out a twenty from his wallet. "Well, this should cover breakfast plus the tip. I gotta get going." He stood up and walked over to give his sister a kiss. "I'll call tonight and we'll pitch some ideas back and forth. Take care."

"Don't draw any inside straights," she called out as he left.

ROBIN WALKED inside the branch for what he believed would be one of the last times in the following two weeks. He was up until eleven o'clock the previous night preparing his carefully written letter of resignation. Everything was just a formality with him from this point on. After picking classes Monday, he called Sonyai, who requested he come in a half-hour earlier than usual for a meeting between him, Alex, and the two branch supervisors.

After hanging up his jacket, he walked upstairs to the staff room where he found the trio looking back at him sitting at the kitchen table. He paused, taken back that he was last to arrive. "Sorry to keep y'all waiting," he said as he moved to take a seat opposite the page. Alex stared back with blank eyes showing no emotion. He didn't know what was told to her parents and how they reacted, but if she was punished for what she did, there was no indication of it.

"Let's begin," Sonyai announced. "No one is the wiser to the events that occurred 2 Saturdays ago, which is good. The hardest part now is where we go from here."

"Agreed," Augustus chimed in. Sonyai gave the librarian a side glance and continued, "Mr. Walker, you've suffered a terrible, personal racist attack and for that, on behalf of the New York Public Library and the 58th Street Branch, I wholeheartedly apologize."

Robin nodded, and there was a moment of silence.

Sonyai cleared her throat, "Miss Stevens?"

Alex clenched her jaw and mumbled, "I'm sorry."

"Speak up!" Augustus ordered as Sonyai flinched.

"I am sorry!" she growled audibly through her teeth.

"Without the attitude!"

"Chavez!" Sonyai protested.

"One more time, young lady...correctly," he ordered, ignoring the senior clerk.

Alex took a deep breath and stared defiantly at Robin. "I'm very, very sorry," she said with attempted sincerity.

Sonyai scowed as Augustus nodded with satisfaction. "Mr. Walker, we discussed nothing regarding apologizing, but if there is something you wish to say, it would greatly be appreciated."

Robin turned and looked at each person, he knew of these gestures from his days at Fort Washington. He cleared his throat and selected his words carefully.

"Miss Yi, I accept your apology, thank you very much." She nodded as he turned his attention to Alex. "Miss Stevens, what you did was a despicable act of hatred that I will probably never recover from. I will have to carry the memory of that morning with me for the rest of my life. My children will be told of it, and their children after them. It will be a sad reminder that no matter how far we come, we will never change in the eyes of others and ourselves."

"Mr. Walker—" Augustus interrupted.

"I am not done yet!" Robin hissed. The librarian remained quiet for him to continue. "My reaction, in which I caused you physical harm, I humbly apologize for. Were it not for Mr. Chavez's intervention, I would have throttled you to death, which would have been an unfortunate outcome, to say the least. I regret it in hindsight, but given the chance if the situation repeated itself...I *most* certainly would do it again."

That last statement physically shook Alex as she swallowed hard.

"We're required to put this behind us now, but know this. You may be a very beautiful young lady that will grow up to an alluring woman. Attracting the attention of men from all corners of the globe. But your soul is hollow. You are nothing more than a husk, a shell of a human being, beautiful on the outside, but *ugly* on the inside. I pity you."

The teenager backed her chair, stood up, and stormed out of the room. Sonyai and Augustus looked back to Robin. The three of them sat in silence until the clerk pulled out an envelope from his back pocket and dropped it in the middle of the table.

"I think we're done here." He got up to leave.

Robin walked back to the clerical office to find Ethel sitting at her desk. She looked up and asked, "No soda can today?"

"No, I'm trying to make peace. I'm not going to be here much longer and I'd rather keep my last days here pleasant."

"Oh? You're leaving?"

Robin opened his mouth to reply, but Sonyai interjected as she stepped into the office. "You're not going anywhere, Walker," she said. "Don't even think of trying to transfer either."

Ethel stood up. "I think I'll take that cue to leave."

"Please close the door behind you," Sonyai requested and turned to face Robin. "We have much to discuss."

Ten minutes before three, Lakeshia and Tanya entered the auditorium. "Have you been reading the book?" Tanya asked.

"Yes, yes, yes. I'm almost through with it," Lakeshia replied.

"Good, today's lesson will be—"

They both froze as a sound came from the closet. The pair looked at each other as they approached the corner. Tanya put her ear to the door and heard a moan. She grabbed the doorknob and pulled the closet open to see Alex sitting on the floor, knees to her chest and hugging herself. The page gasped as she saw the two girls looking back at her.

"What are you doing here?" Lakeshia asked. "Were you...crying?"

"No! *No!*" Alex yelled as she stood up wiping her face. "What the hell are you two doing here?"

"It's personal," Lakeshia answered, then turned to Tanya. "Maybe we should do this...later."

"No dice," Tanya dismissed shaking her head. "Alex, Leelee's been having wet dreams..."

"Oh my God! Tanya! One! Only one wet dream! How could you just tell like that?"

Alex smiled and broke out into a light-hearted laugh. "Oh, Leelee, it's okay. It's natural to fantasize a little bit. Who was in it?" she asked with a sly grin.

Tanya started to say but Lakeshia quickly covered her mouth with both hands and hissed inside her ear, *"Don't you dare tell her! I will rip your head off your shoulders!"* She shook her head hard for emphasis. Tanya's eyes went wide as she believed the threat.

"Fine, keep your little secret. Just let me see what you were planning to do in here. Please?" she pleaded.

"Okay," Lakeshia relented. She shook Tanya's head to get her attention. "Swear to me you'll keep your mouth shut about my dream!"

Tanya raised her left hand and mumbled, "I swear!"

Lakeshia gave her a stern look as she lowered her hand. Tanya looked at Lakeshia with new newfound respect. She rubbed her jaw and said, "Right, let's get to your final lesson."

Tanya walked to her book bag and produced another medical book. As she walked back to the center of the room, she explained to Alex, "For the last two weeks while you were gone, me and Leelee have been going over some books so she can get acquainted with 'doing the nasty.'"

Lakeshia gave her a look as she continued, "But now it's time to learn the consequences of unprotected sex."

"I know the consequences, Tee. A baby for one!" Lakeshia replied.

"Nah, that's not the only consequence. I'm talking about..." She opened the book and turned it to her. "Sexually transmitted diseases! Otherwise known as STDs!"

"I THINK it's best that I should leave, simple as that," Robin said to Sonyai.

The senior clerk paced back and forth for a few moments, then she simply replied, "Not happening," shaking her head.

"What?"

"Chavez and I discussed it thoroughly and for obvious reasons we cannot accept your letter of resignation at this time."

"Why?"

"He will explain it to you at the end of the day."

"Oh, I guess we know who's wearing the pants around here!" he taunted.

A tight thin smile came across the supervisor's face. "Make no mistake, Walker. I'd gladly see you walk right out of here today if it wouldn't jeopardize this branch. So, we will continue with the status quo, and if you feel this way a few months down the line, you may submit your letter again. Is that clear?"

Robin twisted his face in a mean scowl. "Yeah, it's clear."

"Good," she replied. "Now it's time to explain the clustering process to you."

Lakeshia was screaming at the top of her lungs.

"These are genital warts! They ooze pus when popped with a horrible smell!"

"Oh my God, oh my God!" the youngest page screamed.

"I think that's enough," Alex said.

"I haven't even got to herpes! Keep looking, Leelee! Blisters, sores, open festering wounds!"

"Tanya!" Alex protested.

"C'mon, Alex! I'm trying to turn a grasshopper into a butterfly!"

"What?" Lakeshia and Alex yelled.

Tanya closed the book finally. "Alright, alright! Keep having these dreams without my help, but eventually…*it* will happen." She turned to put the book back in her bag.

"It?" Lakeshia asked.

"Oh yes, *it*. And when it happens…" she rested the book bag on her shoulder and turned to Lakeshia. "You'll know it."

A worried look rested on the page's face as Tanya walked out of the auditorium.

AT FIVE, Tommy relieved Robin from duty and he walked directly from the circulation desk to Augustus's office. He didn't bother to knock, he just let himself in. After closing the door, he stared daggers at the head librarian as he sat in front of his desk.

"I hope you don't mind, but I decided to let myself in," he said with a snarl.

"Uh-huh," Augustus replied. He then opened a drawer in his desk and pulled out the envelope Robin left with him upstairs. Unopened with the letter still inside, he looked at the young clerk for a moment, then crumbled it in his hands.

Robin shook his head at the insult. "I spent 2 hours writing that letter with the intent of praising the branch and its staff!"

Augustus dropped the crumpled letter into his trash can. "Do you know what happens when an NYPL employee resigns? Human resources conducts an exit interview, in which they investigate why anyone would actually leave this prestigious establishment. So let's pretend for a moment I'm from human resources…"

He cleared his throat and spoke in a light-hearted voice. "So, Mr. Walker, what makes you want to leave the New York Public Library?"

"I just found out I have legionnaire's disease and I'm highly contagious," Robin replied deadpanned.

Augustus stared back at him not amused by the answer. "Not. Fucking. Funny. Not even the slightest." He sighed. "Your attempted departure would be right after a suspended employee has returned and Human Resources will put 2 and 2 together. They will then put this branch under a huge magnifying glass. I simply will not allow that to happen."

Robin rolled his eyes.

"So you will stay here, you will not request a transfer, and you will play nice with Alex and we'll all be the fucking Partridge family, you understand me? Come on, get happy!"

Robin snickered to himself and then shrugged. "Fine, if that's the way we're gonna play it." He got up and left the office.

A few minutes later, Robin exited the branch and froze. Standing several feet away, Alex was waiting for him in the middle of the sidewalk.

"I warn you," Robin called out, "the last person I confronted on this same spot, things didn't go too well for him."

"I'm not here to fight you. I'm delivering a message." Alex replied. "You put your hands on me again, I promise you, on everything I hold dear, I will kill you."

Robin grinned. *Everyone's on fire today with the one-liners and speeches,* he thought. Time for him to make a profound statement as well.

"Oh girl, you must be crazy if you think you could ever get the best of me. I will make you disappear in a heartbeat. You could just be walking down the street one day and never see me coming. Your parents will wonder why you never came home. After 48 hours, they'll file a missing person's report; then the FBI will be called in, your face will be all over the 6 o'clock news. Months will go by, and the case will go cold.

"A year goes by, there'll be a vigil for you, a whole bunch of candles surrounding your picture in a frame. People will see you with all the missing persons at the post office. Who knows, maybe, just maybe, you'll even get your own segment on *Unsolved Mysteries.*

"Whatever happened to Alex Stevens? they'll ask. And no one will ever know. Except for me. I will know, and I'll remember that last look on your face as you went off into that good night. They would never find your body, child. They will *never.* Find. Your body."

The chill went down Alex's back as his final words echoed in the wind. They stared each other down, daring for the other to make a move. A car pulled up and Alex slowly backed toward the curb, never letting Robin out of her sight. She opened the door and stepped into the car. Robin watched the vehicle take off, his eyes following as it drove toward Park Avenue, stopped at a light on the corner, then resumed heading east until it was out of sight.

HEYWOOD MADE it just in time to the club for Jackie's performance Thursday night. After a brief conversation over the phone, she confirmed their date for after the show. The opening act had just finished up and there was a hush throughout the crowd. With no introduction, Storming Jackie Daze walked out from behind the stage, followed by her band. There was a somber look on her face, her stage presence contrasted with the energy she radiated the first time he saw her.

"Good evening, ladies and gentlemen," she said into the microphone. "I will perform only one song tonight." There were sounds of confusion and moans of disappointment from the audience. "About a week ago, a friend of mine lost his life, and this rendition is for him." On that cue, the band played and she started to sing. The ballad was an emotional tribute. She held the final note for what felt like an eternity.

The raw emotion coming from her voice drove the crowd wild. There were tears in her eyes as the band finished. The microphone slipped from her fingers and hit the floor registering some loud feedback. She leaped from the stage and bolted for the back exit, leaving her audience stunned. The MC emerged from backstage and picked up the mic, drawing the crowd's focus toward the stage. Heywood elbowed his way through and followed her while the next act was being announced.

He found her on the floor in her dressing room, sobbing uncontrollably, muttering to herself.

"Hey, hey, hey. What's wrong? What's wrong?" he asked.

He kneeled down. She was shaking and wiping away the tears from her face. She looked up at him. Despite her distraught emotional state, he was enchanted by her. Her eyes pleaded with him. She reached up and caressed his face.

"Take me someplace quiet…and dark," she whispered.

He nodded and picked her up in his arms, pushing open the metal door leading to the back alley. A cab ride later, they arrived at Heywood's loft in Alphabet City. He made sure not to turn on the lights as he brought her in. She was still mumbling incoherently. Every moment or so he would hear a name that sounded like Kent or Curt.

The loft had a few furnishings and was decorated with a certain sense of style that reflected Heywood's conservative personality. He carried the singer to his couch and sat her down.

"Can I get you anything to settle your nerves? Tea? Coffee?"

"Bourbon. No ice. In a big glass," she requested.

He nodded and went to the kitchen, grabbing two glasses from the dishwasher and a bottle of Old Rip Van Winkle he saved for rare occasions. When he returned, she was sitting up on the couch a little calmer. He handed her a glass and opened the bottle.

She took a sip and sighed. "Ah, you must have had this bottle for awhile."

"Stole it from my father's stash when I first moved away from home. He paid $85 for it back in 1974."

"A rebel at an early age, huh? And I thought you were harmless."

"There's a lot you don't know about me," he replied with a chuckle.

"I think I would like to learn more," she said with a tear-streaked smile.

There was a slight pause as they looked at each other, then Heywood asked, "So, wanna talk about—" Before he finished she came across the couch and kissed him. He felt as if struck by a bolt of lightning. She was strong in her embrace. He practically melted in her arms.

After the kiss, he whispered, "My bedroom is just over—"

"You talk too much," she interrupted and kissed him again.

The sunrise slowly crept through the window of Heywood's bedroom around six o'clock Friday morning. He didn't even remember coming to bed. The night of passion he experienced was a blur to him. He turned over on the bed and noticed he was alone. After washing up and putting on a robe, he found the musician in the kitchen wearing his dress shirt from last night and a pair of black silk panties.

She was drinking some orange juice at his kitchen table. A glass was waiting for him in front of the other empty chair at the table. "Good morning," she said with a grin. "Do you know you talk in your sleep?"

"It's been a while since I've had company, so I wouldn't know," he replied taking a seat.

They shared a moment of silence as he sipped the beverage. Then she explained, "When I went to Seattle, I tried to help a friend of mine who was feeling low. Musicians live depressing lives sometimes. It's not all shows, tours, fans, glitz and glamour. There's a down period where you…just wanna get away from it all."

"Wow. I didn't know that."

"So I reached out to give him some comfort. I mean, he was doing so well in life. His music was selling, he's been on MTV. Anyone would think he'd be on top of the world. Little did they know, inside he was his own worst enemy. The success got to him, he just felt lost in the world. He told me himself in his final days."

"Final days?"

"After we talked, I headed back home Thursday afternoon last week. Then Friday, I heard the news. He…he killed himself."

"Wait a minute, last Friday? You mean your friend was…"

"Yes, Kurt Cobain. The lead singer of the group Nirvana."

"Whoa." Heywood had heard the news in passing about the artist's suicide. He had never heard of the band before, but he did notice the tribute song from last night sounded familiar. It was the group's hit single, "Smells like Teen Spirit."

"I'm sure they'll fire me at the club. That performance wasn't my best."

"The audience would disagree. You were terrific."

"Thanks."

Another moment of silence passed.

"I'm a little torn about what to do next," she began. "I'm not exactly a girlfriend/boyfriend-relationship type of person."

"I understand completely, I'm willing to take things as they are, one day at a time, no pressure."

She smiled. "God, you are so perfect. What did I ever do to deserve a guy like you?"

He smiled back. "Listen, I got to get to work. You can stay here if you like…"

"No, I'll leave with you. Got to check with the band, do rehearsals, and see if I can shake myself out of this funk I'm feeling."

Heywood stood up. "I think I helped with that last night."

She smiled and walked over to him and gave him a peck on the cheek. "Yes, yes, you did." She rubbed his beard and purred. "Those bristles made last night very memorable."

He chuckled. "Why, thank you. You wanna hit the bathroom first?"

She took off the dress shirt she was wearing, then walked toward the bathroom, leaving her panties on the floor behind her. "Or you could join me in a nice hot shower."

He followed right behind her, grinning from ear to ear.

GERRY MET Tommy in the clerical office at nine o'clock. Ethel was outside in the reference area reading the newspaper and Sonyai was using comp time to arrive at noon. The opportunity was set for them to execute their plan.

"All right, let's do this as quickly as possible while no one's around," Gerry whispered.

"Right," Tommy agreed. He bent down on one knee in front of the safe and started the combination. Gerry served as a lookout, checking the doorway every couple seconds, thinking this was almost too good to be true. Tommy took controlled breaths as he moved the dial to the last number and turned the handle. There was a satisfying thunk as he pulled the door open with a silent cheer. Gerry did a fist pump as Tommy handed him the ledger.

"Perfect," Gerry said after a quick scan of the pages. "Wait here while I make copies."

Gerry already had the key in his pocket that would let him use the copier machine without paying. He calmly walked to the machine, which was between two columns of shelves near the 900's and biographies were located.

He made copies of the records for daily returns going back six months. Twenty pages of penciled entries. While checking the copies he discovered a problem. Everything was color coded! Red pencil entries showed losses and expenses while the green showed receipts from fines and book sales.

"Shit!" he hissed. *It'll just have to do*, he said to himself.

After switching back to coin-operated mode and grabbing the key, Gerry walked back to the office. Tommy was waiting to place the ledger back where he found it. The safe slammed shut and locked again. Gerry put the copies in an interoffice envelope and tucked it in his desk. The deed was done. He would meet up with Eugene and prove Sonyai was innocent. She'd never know the lengths he went to protect her. Hopefully, he'd earn her trust and bide his time…before betraying her himself.

Heywood was walking on air as he arrived at the branch that morning. If he could dance he'd be waltzing in like Fred Astaire, twirling in the middle of the library floor. Angie noticed the pep in his step from the information desk.

"Good morning! You're in a good mood."

"Had a wonderful time last night on my date, learned some interesting information, and I must say…things couldn't be better between us." Heywood beamed.

"Well, hate to rain on your parade, but Augustus is looking for you."

"Isn't he always?"

"This is different. Zelda's been excused from the office. He wants to talk to you *alone*."

That wiped the smile right off his face. He turned and looked at her. She nodded, confirming the statement. The last time Heywood and Augustus squared off in his office alone he almost thought his hair would turn white from fear. This was not a good sign. It may be time to face the music.

Heywood entered the librarian's office and swallowed hard with an audible gulp. On any given day, Augustus would be wearing designer business suits, looking his best. Today he was wearing a shirt with no tie tucked in a pair of jeans. This would *not* end well.

"Um, good mor—"

"Sit down, Heywood," Augustus ordered quietly.

He knew things were serious when the supervisor used his first name. He took a seat in front of him and braced for the worst.

"I believe you need to be reminded who is in charge here."

"I…I know who—"

"You interrupt me again and we're going to have a serious problem, here," Augustus snarled.

"Yes, sir."

"As I was saying, clearly you don't know who is in charge of things here. I make the decisions here for the film festivals, I make the decisions for the media acquisitions, I call Donelle to set aside the selections. Not you impersonating me. Do we understand each other? Just nod."

He nodded saying nothing.

"I know you had good intentions undermining me. And your Mel Gibson theme is bringing in the numbers for our presentations. But get this through your thick skull, do not mess with me."

He took out a calculator from his desk and tossed it to Heywood, who barely caught it while flinching, not knowing what it was at first.

"How good is your math?" Augustus asked. "Calculate this for me," he ordered and took a deep breath. "80% of the NYPL annual budget comes from the City of New York. It used to be 85, but thanks to our new mayor, it's been slashed 5%. So the city has graciously awarded us 90 million dollars. That's 9 with seven zeros, Heywood, tap it in there!"

He tapped the number in the calculator.

"80% of that 90 million goes to our wages and salaries. So how much is that?"

After doing the calculations Heywood replied, "72 million."

"Alright, 72 million for the estimated 1200 employees among the 82 branches in the Bronx, Manhattan, and Staten Island. So that leaves what? 18 million for office supplies, building maintenance, and our media, books, and such. What's 18 million divided by 82?"

"Umm, $219,512.20."

"And that's *if* it was being divided equally, which it is not. Because not all branches are the same! There are 3 categories, based on their size, age, and location. They are small, moderate, and substantial, all fighting for a piece of the pie!"

Augustus stood up, and Heywood flinched again, but relaxed when he paced back and forth behind his desk. "So, that's the 80% from the city. Where does the other 20 come from? Fines, book sales, and charitable donations from the biggest philanthropists in the tri-state area. That's where I come in.

"Shaking hands, making connections, attending fundraisers and company outings, putting myself out there. Reaching the community leaders, scratching backs, secret arrangements, greasing the wheels and doing whatever it takes!" He slammed his fist on the desk for effect.

Heywood believed his hair was turning white again.

"I do all of this for the sustainability of this branch, to purchase the books and media the other branches don't have in their collection, nor would they dare. *Sex* by Madonna, *Lord Jim*, the collective works of Marquis de Sade, *Fear and Loathing in Las Vegas*.

"Everything from *The Claiming of Sleeping Beauty* to *Private Parts* by Howard Stern. Pushing the envelope! Giving the people what they want. And when they want it, they come to me, and if they want it before everybody else, they donate frequently. I run this show. I *fuck* these people for their money!"

Heywood cringed. Augustus was off the deep end with this rant. He contemplated how much more of this berating he could take.

"I am the madam. I am Heidi Fleiss," he continued, then pointed an accusing finger. "And *you* are the streetwalker at Hunts Point offering blowjobs in a back alley for $20. You're not even at front-seat johns yet!" He sat back down and wiped the sweat off his forehead. "So I suggest you know your boundaries and never step out of line again, or I'll make sure you're working at the most remote library Staten Island has to offer, do you understand me? Say yes!"

"Yes, sir!" Heywood barked, straightening up.

The head librarian nodded. "Now get the hell out of my face," he dismissed.

Heywood didn't reply, he just quickly sat up, left the calculator on the desk, and walked out of the office. Once back on the floor, his eyes went wide as he walked back to Angie at the information desk and took a seat facing her.

"Is my—"

"No, your hair is not white. He tore you a new one. You survived," she interrupted him.

"He…he…he called me a streetwalker from Hunts Point," he said astonished.

"Huh. I'll get you a nice flowery sundress. Maybe some red lipstick." She playfully patted his face twice and stood up, disappearing among the shelves.

Sonyai was working at her desk when the phone rang to her personal line. She picked up the receiver and held it to her ear. "This is Sonyai Yi."

"'Ello, Sonny, how's tricks?" a female with a cockney accent replied.

She sighed and tilted her head in frustration. "Doyle, how many times have I politely asked you not to call me Sonny?" Sonyai asked as she rubbed her brow.

"'Bout as many times as I'ave told you to call me Annabelle, luv. You know we Brits are colorful about names and all that, yeah."

"So how are things at Yorkville?"

"Squeaky as the wheel on her majesty's coach, doll. You and Gus the Goose being nice, nice?"

"As nice as you and the whiskey-toting Saint Bernard are over there."

"Quite," Doyle replied dryly.

"So, get to it then. I know this isn't a social call."

"Flip ya lid off if it was, I bet. I just called to be the first to send my congrats on the new amendment Gussy's been sticking up for all this time."

That got her attention as she sat straight up. "Yes, Augustus has worked very hard."

"And I guess hard work pays off then, yeah?"

Sonyai's eyes darted in various directions as she wondered what the senior clerk was saying.

"Anyone there, luv? You breathing?"

"Yeah!" she gasped and stammered.

"It's probably old news to you anyway," Doyle said with a light chuckle. "I had to hear it from one of my old friends down at Mid-Manhattan. That the limits on video loans will go up next month for 30 days is great news for all the branches, eh?"

Next month? Sonyai screamed in her head, her nostrils flaring with rage.

"I hear there's even a little incentive bonus to the branch that has the most video circulations by the end of the fiscal third-quarter on June 1st. An extra $3000.00 toward their VHS acquisitions!"

Sonyai was now grinding her teeth, the receiver shaking in her hand. "Wow," she said feigning excitement.

"Boy, what I wouldn't give to bend the rules and start lending 3 vids at a time now, huh?" Another round of laughs came about as Sonyai regained her composure.

"Yeah, bend." She did some mock laughing herself.

"Anyways, Sonny. Give my best to Gus and I guess I'll be seeing you at the next monthly meet up at 96th Street Regional."

"Yeah, take care of yourself, Doyle. Goodbye."

She hung up the receiver in complete shock.

Around seven thirty in the evening, Alex was in her room, watching a block of music videos on MTV. Unimpressed with the dance moves of the background dancers, she said to herself, "I can dance better than any of those chicks." She picked up the remote and clicked the TV off. After sitting up from her bed she grabbed her cordless phone. She pulled the card out of her pocket and dialed the number.

"Hello?" a voice answered.

"Hello," she replied.

"Who is this? How'd you get this number? You know who this is?"

"Ay! Chill out, man, *you* gave me this damn number! Why the fuck you freaking out over me calling you?"

"Who da f—…Oh! hahahahaaa! It's you! From the club, Miss Spunk! I didn't think you'd call. It's been a while."

"Yeah, well, here I am."

"So, you wanna come in and do that audition?"

"Well, I've been thinking about it. I'm gonna pass. Just wanted to tell you thanks."

"Hmm. Fair enough. Take care of yourself."

"Yeah, You—" The line clicked off before she could finish. "Too."

She walked over to a trash can, thinking of throwing away the card for a moment. At the last minute, she turned to her dresser and stuck it on her mirror instead.

Tommy made sure to arrive at Yorkville on time and let Robin in when he showed up at eleven o'clock. Annabelle Doyle, Yorkville's senior clerk, approached as he stood near the doorway looking outside.

"Mr. Carmichael, I'm sure young Robin Walker will ring the doorbell when she arrives. Any particular reason you are here waiting?" she asked. The English woman matched his height evenly at six-foot-one and carried herself at a solid two hundred and forty-five pounds. She was wearing a black button-up blouse over a low cut undershirt and matching skirt that stopped past her knees. Her chestnut brown hair was cut short with a fluff at the top and she had a pearl necklace wrapped around her neck three times.

"I'm sorry, it's just…It's his first time clustering," Tommy explained.

"Sorry, did you say *his*? The name listed in the employee directory is *Ms.* Robin Walker."

"It's a typo. They've been trying to fix it at human resources."

"I see. Good thing you told me—things would have been quite unsettling had I not known."

"Uh, yeah," Tommy replied.

The bell rang and they both turned to grab the doorknob. Doyle was a few seconds quicker and opened the door greeting Robin with a smile. "Good morning! You must be Robin Walker. I'm Annabelle Doyle, senior clerk of Yorkville. But you may call me Belle."

"Good morning, ma'am. Robin Walker of 58th Street, Fort Washington before that," Robin said, properly introducing himself with a respectful nod.

"Fort Washington, you say? Very crisp you are with the Procedures of Conduct. The Battle Axe has taught you well. Follow me, please." Doyle instructed then turned and led the way.

Tommy rolled his eyes and locked the door before following the two. Robin looked around as he walked through the branch. Yorkville was considered a hidden gem with a remarkable adaptation of Palladian-inspired architecture. The branch opened in 1902 and was given landmark status after an interior renovation back in 1987. The two-story building had a children's room on the second floor and a meeting room public space in the basement with a capacity for seventy.

"Is this a library or the set of *Are You Being Served*?" Robin asked.

Annabelle laughed. "Jolly good show, jolly good! Our classical decor is a tribute to the United Kingdom and the Victorian Age."

"It's very impressive."

"We like to think so. Let me show you where you can put your jacket. Please remove your cap and glove, then you can meet the rest of the staff."

"Um, I must insist on keeping my glove on, for medical reasons, Miss Doyle."

"Ah, ah, ah. I said you can call me Belle, and what medical reasons do you mean, sir?"

Robin turned to Tommy, who sighed and looked away for a moment. He then stood in front of Annabelle and slipped off his glove to reveal his scarred hand.

"Bollocks!" she gasped while clutching her pearls.

Robin put the glove back on.

"I…guess we can make an exception for your situation," she said while nodding rapidly.

"Thank you," he said.

The senior clerk tried to compose herself. "Yes, um…right this way."

An hour later, Robin and Tommy started their hour as the branch opened upstairs in the children's room. Robin was in a frenzied state with the visiting children on the floor. Most were calm and quiet, but when dealing with toddlers and adolescents, being quiet—even in a library—was not their strong suit. Voices carried, a few ran around excitedly, there was an occasional crying baby.

"What's with you, man?" Tommy asked.

"Kids, man. They kinda freak me out," he replied. "They don't know how to stay silent. It's very nerve-racking."

A young girl laughed at a book she was reading and it startled Robin half to death. "Whenever I was out of line at Fort Washington, they would send me to the children's room to fix the shelves. Here it's not that bad, but there…it…it…it was a zoo!"

"I'm starting to see why you were so persistent in transferring to 58th," Tommy said.

Robin looked halfway toward him with a light smile. "Time to change the subject. Since it's just us here, tell me. What went wrong with Syracuse?"

Tommy sucked his teeth, "C'mon, man."

"It'll make the time go by and calm me down a little bit," Robin pleaded.

Tommy leaned against the circulation desk and crossed his ankles. "I took money. It's the oldest tale in the book. It started off as an incentive for the fastest time doing drills. Next thing you know, they're giving whoever had the most tackles or pass rushes a car. Then your mother's living in a brand new house, free and clear."

"Damn. How'd you get caught?"

"Got too greedy." He shrugged. "Everything was supposed to be low-key, but then some dickhead got pulled over and arrested for speeding. He had a $75,000.00 watch that mysteriously didn't get checked-in with his belongings. Had he just let the shit go, everything would have been fine. But he got the media involved and they investigated the arrest.

"Then they asked what a 20-year-old full-time student with no job was doing with the watch in the first place? The school gets under fire, coaches are let go, and the athletic program itself gets a slap on the wrist with probation. But now the NFL wants nothing to do with me."

"You were that dickhead?"

"No, my roommate. We were all prospects. I could have been picked up in the second round of the draft. But the phone never rang and just like that, my life was over. With everything his fault, the guilt ate him up inside. They found him in the garage, the front seat of his car with the engine running. Carbon Monoxide poisoning. He was only 22 years old."

"Holy shit," Robin whispered.

A couple and their seven-year-old daughter approached the area of the circulation desk near Robin designated for library card registration. He walked to the couple and put a goofy smile on his face and greeted the family.

"Welcome to the Yorkville Library," he exclaimed in a pleasant voice, then bent down until he was face to face with the young girl. "Wanna sign up for a library card, little lady?" he asked.

The child was wearing corduroys and a pink T-shirt underneath. She had long brown hair and a smile missing baby teeth. She seemed too shy to answer the question, so she just nodded her head slightly.

"What do you have to do to get a library card?" the mother asked.

"With her parents present, all she has to do is write her name in print," Robin replied. He bent down to look at her again. "Can you write your name *all* by yourself?"

The child smiled and nodded again.

He reached behind the desk and produced a clipboard with a pencil on a string. "Fill out the top with your information, and have her write her name on the line at the bottom. You can't help, she needs to do it herself. You can fill it out here or take a copy of the application home."

The parents accepted the clipboard and walked to a nearby reading table to fill out the form. Five minutes later, after checking the database for any duplicate records, Robin presented the child with a shiny new plastic library card.

"Here you go!" he exclaimed.

The little girl held the card in her hand and hopped in place with excitement.

"You know what should be the first book you read?" he asked.

The girl looked up from the card with a daunting look on her face.

The clerk reached over to a shelving cart and held up a copy of Don Freedman's children's book *Corduroy.* She looked at the cover in awe as he handed it to her.

"I think you'll like it," he said with a wide smile.

The child hugged the book and looked up with huge doe-like eyes. "Thank you," she said quietly. Her parents looked at each other, surprised by the girl overcoming her shyness.

"You're welcome," he replied to her, then stood up and nodded to the adults. "Have a great day. Welcome to the New York Public Library."

They smiled and thanked him back, then walked around through the rest of the shelves to look for more books.

Tommy was genuinely impressed at the display of adoring customer service. Robin walked back to where he was during their conversation and his demeanor reverted in an instant. "So what did you do when you left school?" he asked in his normal voice.

Tommy did a double take. "What the hell was that? How'd you go from sweet to sour all of a sudden?"

"Huh? Oh, that? That's just a front they taught me at Fort Washington. I can turn it on and off like a light switch."

He shook his head. "Anyways, I married my wife in my junior year and we moved in together. I applied for the Queens Public Library first, then got a job working the docks at a warehouse in Red Hook. When I didn't hear anything, I tried the NYPL and waited another year, then got the call. Been at 58th Street ever since."

"Why the library, though? You could do damn near anything else out there using your muscles."

"That's a story for another time," Tommy replied, looking at his watch.

"See? I told you it made the hour go quicker."

AS THE DAY PROGRESSED, Robin familiarized himself with some of the staff at Yorkville. He met the rotund and stout head librarian Matthew Ballard, Nat Levine, a Jewish full-timer who was very talkative, and a beautiful full-time clerk from South Africa who captivated his attention. He knew he couldn't leave without approaching her, and found an excuse to say something to her. "Well, hello. My name is Robin Walker. What a lovely accent you have," he said at their introduction.

"Why, thank you, sir. You may call me Tiannah," she replied. Her dark skin and natural hairstyle made her radiant. She had a smile astronauts could see from space.

"Just Tiannah? Is that your first or last name?"

"It is my family name. There's no possible way you could pronounce my first name."

"Oh yeah? Try me. What's your first name?"

"Okay, it's Olorunfoyisayomi."

Robin blinked. "Tiannah it is!" he said with a smile.

At a quarter past two, Robin was working his last hour with a part-time clerk named Curtis. Things were slower downstairs on the main floor, and Yorkville was lax with clerks reading at the circulation desk.

Curtis was reading the latest issue of *Vibe* in a collapsible security periodical baton, or C.P.B. for short. Robin noticed a patron reading a newspaper that had been placed on a wooden stick at the spine.

"I see y'all still got the old school sticks here for the newspapers," Robin said striking up a conversation.

Curtis didn't bite. "Yeah, they refuse to throw them away," he said nonchalantly. After finishing an article, the clerk closed the magazine. "I like these batons better." He twisted the cap on the top and pulled the periodical out from the hollow slit within the stick. Putting the book down, Curtis held up the empty baton his right hand.

"So, Robin Walker by the way of Fort Washington, huh? You wouldn't happen to be one of The Infamous 6, would you?"

The clerk suddenly flipped the rod around his wrist, then through his fingers in a flourish.

Robin tensed up. "You in The Game?" he asked.

"They say it started up there, did it?" Curtis replied ignoring the question.

"Yeah...It did."

"Were you at Van Courtland Park?"

"Maybe. You know, you ask a lot of questions," he replied, his eyes darting back and forward.

The clerk twirled the baton once again. "I hear there's a peace treaty in place. Things got too...*exciting.*"

"You could say that," Robin replied, staring back at the show-off.

"It'd be a shame if someone...started things up again." The baton snapped back in his hand. "Wouldn't it?" He smiled as Robin looked on. There was a moment of uneasy tension.

The clerk then laughed and tossed the stick on top of the magazine. "Don't worry. We honor the peace treaty here at Yorkville. But it's only a matter of time, and when the treaty is broken, I'll be looking you up."

Curtis felt around the magazine, then turned to see the baton was missing. He turned back to find Robin standing next to him with the rod in his hand, the point a few centimeters from his neck. His body stiffened from shock at the move.

"I hope you're a whole lot quicker when you come against me,"

Robin whispered. "Or it will be a *very* swift result, not in your favor." He dropped the stick and it landed softly on Yorkville's thin carpeting. Robin walked back to his previous spot, leaving the clerk shaken.

Tommy was taking his break at three o'clock when Robin walked in. The breakroom in Yorkville also held the lockers for the staff to leave their belongings.

"Well, I'm done for the day," Robin said, retrieving his red baseball cap and jacket. "You here till 5?"

"Yep, 2 more hours to go."

"Well, okay. I'll see you Monday. Have a nice weekend." He waved, turning to leave.

"You too. Hey, Walker!" Tommy called back to him.

Robin stopped in his tracks and looked back, "Yeah?"

He nodded. "It...it was nice talking to you today."

Robin smiled back. "You're all right, Tommy...You all right." He then turned and left.

CHAPTER SEVENTEEN

"I REMEMBER HOW HESITANT YOU WERE WHEN WE FIRST MET HERE," Zelda said. She and Augustus were walking through the main hall at the American Museum of Natural History. There was a small group of people visiting, despite the downpour of rain hitting the city that Sunday on the 17th at ten thirty that morning.

"I hope I wasn't disrupting any plans you had today asking you to come with me," he began.

"No, my schedule was free," the elder replied with a chuckle.

"Good." He waited a moment, then said, "I'm sorry I accused you earlier. That damn Learner, he…"

"Forget it. Water under the bridge."

"As for that eventful day way back when, I wasn't hesitant as much as I was intimidated at the thought of meeting you. I had no idea what you had in store for me."

The two walked into the souvenir store where a woman waiting for them walked by and slipped Augustus an envelope, then walked out of the store undetected. Zelda purchased a keychain as Augustus opened and read the secretive message passed to him and grinned.

"Good news, I take it?" Zelda asked.

"Great news. The amendment to the media policy has been approved."

"Ah."

"Beginning next month, the number of video cassettes borrowed goes up to 3."

"And I take it since we've been letting the public borrow an extra video for the last month we're ahead of the circulation average?"

Augustus turned to Zelda, his grin now a huge toothy smile, like the cat that ate the canary.

"There was no experiment authorized for us to raise the limit ourselves, was there?"

Augustus stared back blankly. "Huh? Why, Miss Clein, whatever do you mean? What experiment?"

She shook her head as he registered a light chuckle to himself.

"Yi will be furious," Zelda warned.

"Let me worry about her. Just think about all those extra movies we can order once we receive that bonus! Let's go to the food court. Lunch is on me."

"BLESS ME, Father, for I have sinned," Heywood began. "It has been 6 days since my last confession." He kneeled in the confessional. There was the sound of a panel sliding and the priest spoke to him from an opening.

"Tell me your sins, my son."

"Well, I realize I am not my father's son. I have run away from home in an attempt to escape his legacy. I continue to be a disappointment in his eyes. But I still persevere in my endeavors."

"I see," the priest replied.

"Giving in to the temptations of the flesh. I have lain down with a woman before marriage. We are taking things slow in courting, but it was during an emotional moment of weakness."

"You seek absolution from this, my son?"

"Yes, yes, I do. I can't promise it won't happen again."

"It is a sin of weakness, but not of malice. Let us talk more about your father. How do you know he sees you as a disappointment? When was the last time the two of you spoke?"

"It's been over 6 years," Heywood answered. "He is highly regarded in his industry and I refused to follow in his footsteps."

"You must find peace in your relationship with your father. In time, he will come to respect what you do even if he does not agree with it."

"What you speak of will not be easy, but I will follow God's path that is laid out before me. I'm glad we had this talk, Father."

"A penance for you my son. May you show more restraint, and honor thy father for which it is written. Let us now recite the prayer of absolution."

They spoke in unison. "God the Father of mercies, through the death and resurrection of your son, you have reconciled the world to yourself and sent the Holy Spirit among us for the forgiveness of sin."

The priest finished the prayer himself. "Through the ministry, the Church, may God grant you pardon and peace. And I absolve you of your sins, in the name of the Father, and of the Son, and of the Holy Spirit. Amen."

"Amen," Heywood repeated.

"Go with God, my son," the priest said in parting.

"See you next week, Father." Heywood stood up and exited the confessional.

Elisse Jenkins lived at 610 West 145th Street, just before Riverside Drive. At four o'clock, there was a knock on the door of her third-floor apartment. She took off her apron and walked from the kitchen to answer it. With a smile and a hug, she greeted her sister at the door.

"Hey, sis, you the first one here for Sunday dinner."

Ethel walked in after the embrace and took off her jacket. "Ain't I always?"

Elisse may have been the youngest of the three Jenkins sisters, but she was also the tallest, standing a little over five-foot-eleven. She was wearing pink sweatpants and a Nike T-shirt while cooking. She wasn't skinny, but she wasn't fat either. Her figure was attributed to years of being a gym teacher at Philip A. Randolph High School. She took the jacket and put it on a hanger in the living room closet.

"Why'd you want me to come earlier than usual?" Ethel asked, taking a seat on the couch.

"Let me check on the chicken and I'll be right with you." She went back to the kitchen for a moment. Ethel blew some air through her nose and rolled her eyes. *Here we go...* she thought. *Another plea for money for some get-rich-quick scheme!*

Elisse came back with two glasses of tea and gave her one. She took a whiff of the cup and politely lowered it on the coffee table with a coaster.

"You know Ernie moved down to Savannah after turning 50, right?"

Their eldest sister, Ernabelle left New York City for early retirement after working eighteen years as a corrections officer on Riker's Island.

"Yeah," Ethel replied.

"Well, after 2 years of saving, she's putting down on a 5-bedroom, 4000 square-foot, 2-story house!" Elisse exclaimed with a chuckle!

"The hell is she going to do with all that by herself? Is she out of her mind?"

Elisse looked at her sister with a grin across her face. Ethel's eyes went wide when she realized where her sister was going, "Oh! Hell no!" she yelled standing up.

"I leave the boys my apartment—I can put them both on the lease when Mac turns 18—the 3 of us all go down there and live out our days."

"There's a reason we never tried living together, Lise. We're not exactly on good terms. We haven't been since Dad passed on."

"The place is so big we'll never see each other. Ernie is even thinking of asking Fran to come down."

"She can take my place because I ain't going nowhere."

"Sit down, please," Elisse pleaded.

Ethel sat back down and regained her composure.

Elisse sighed. "I know you went to the doctor—" Ethel opened her mouth to protest, but Elisse waved her hand and continued to talk over her, "You're sweating like a pig, you're not drinking your liquids, and I can tell your eyesight is failing. You're showing all the early stages like Dad. Do you wanna die the same way he did too?"

"That was a low blow," Ethel growled.

Elisse looked back with concerned eyes.

"Okay. So how much money does she need?"

That made Elisse narrow her eyes, her mouth curved into a twisted sneer. She stood up from the couch. "The house needs work. Electric overhaul, re-enforcement of the foundation, and a new furnace."

Ethel laughed. "Shit. What kind of Addams Family dump is she trying to save? Who's going to do all that work?"

"Ally."

"Aloysius? He couldn't unclog a toilet with a plunger!"

"Alright, so it's going to take time. They got 90 days until it has to pass inspection, and then we can put in an offer. Ernabelle says she can close on it as soon as October, but she's going to need help."

"And here we go! That's where we come in, right? How much?"

"She has most of it already—" Elisse started.

"How much?" Ethel asked impatiently.

"Ally has subcontractors who all owe him—"

"How much?"

"She's even offering to pay our moving expenses—"

"How much, Goddamn it!" Ethel yelled.

Elisse sighed. "$1,000.00. From each of us."

"Two grand." Ethel shook her head.

"Just think about it, okay? New York is so dangerous now."

"So dangerous you're leaving your sons behind? To be shot and killed by the trigger-happy police?"

She flinched at the thought. "They can take care of themselves, but we need to look out for each other. You need this. We'll be just like them white chicks on *Designing Women*! The 3 of us, like I said. Just think about it, okay?"

The building intercom buzzed.

"That must be Fran and the boys. Don't tell them yet. Ernabelle didn't want them to know till the homeowners accepted our offer." She pressed a button on the intercom. A few minutes later, the door opened and two young men were joined by an older woman in her thirties.

"Auntie Ethel! You made it!" one of her nephews greeted her.

"Hey, Deacon. Mac, how you doing, baby? Francoise! Give your auntie some sugar!"

Sunday dinner began and several conversations followed. Ethel couldn't imagine moving out of state and missing the ritual family gathering. New York was all she knew. She had a lot to think about.

TUESDAY MORNING, Augustus was sitting at his desk inside his office browsing several video catalogs for future selections. After the recent fiasco, he knew he couldn't rely on Zelda anymore with her taste of films. He heard rapidly scraping footsteps that could only be the high paced charges of a bull heading into a china shop. Sonyai stormed in and slammed the door behind her with a deafening boom. The senior clerk's face twisted in a furious scowl.

"You knew they would raise the limit, you sonofa—" she hollered.

"Sonyai," he calmly interrupted.

"Don't you *dare* 'Sonyai' me!" she barked.

Augustus stood up and raised his voice to match hers. "I *will not* be addressed in such a manner!" he bellowed.

Sonyai calmed down but held her defiant stare to his. "You fabricated that memorandum, forced this branch to break policy just to collect a few more dollars toward our massive video collection—"

"Jumping to conclusions like that can cause scandalous repercussions among—"

"Do you have any idea what would have happened if we got caught? To put the branch in jeopardy like this is so, so reckless." She took a breath. "It is *not* the way your predecessor would handle things if she were still here."

The head librarian sat back down. He rubbed his brow with a handkerchief and relaxed. "But she isn't here and hasn't been for quite a while, Miss Yi." He put the scarf back in his pocket. "And I for one am sick and tired of you making that comparison. As for that memo. I haven't the resources to fabricate anything! I'd appreciate it if you'd curb that vivid imagination of yours!"

The two continued their stare down for a moment, and then Augustus went back to his video literature. He waved dismissively with his right hand. "Now if you don't mind…"

"This is not over. You continue to endanger this branch, and I will see to it you never corrupt another library again!" She turned and left the office, slamming the door again behind her.

Angie witnessed the angry senior clerk storm back to her office and followed her. The senior clerk was mumbling to herself as she stepped inside. She grabbed the door and turned to slam it, then caught herself from swinging the door into the information assistant.

"Trueblood!" Sonyai gasped. "I nearly hit you. What are you doing here?"

She hurried past her and closed the door herself. The senior clerk took a step back, surprised as Angie leaned against the door.

"Is it true?" Angie asked.

"Is what true?"

"Chavez forging the memos—is it true?"

Sonyai took a deep breath as she tried to relax. "I got a call last week saying the amendment he campaigned for, the one he told all of us 2 months ago was passed, it actually goes in effect Monday, May 2nd! For the last 8 weeks, we have been allowing the public to borrow an extra VHS tape against regulations, and putting the circulation numbers in our favor ahead of everyone else!"

"Oh my God," Angie whispered.

Sonyai looked at her. "What do you know?"

"I…I can't. I don't want to get in the middle of this."

"You know something! I know you prefer to remain neutral, but—"

"I…I'll tell you what I found…but not here! I'll let you know where to meet me."

"Wait!" Sonyai called out, but she was already out the door. The senior clerk stuck her head out, watching her hurry back to the information desk. She sat down, refusing to look in her direction. Sonyai closed the door and pounded her fist in frustration.

AT ONE O'CLOCK, during the daily rush, Gerry was working the checkouts side while Ethel was on returns. Eugene was sitting at his chair, alert for any disruptions. There was a lull in activity. Gerry looked around and waved the security guard over with a quick gesture. He checked to see Ethel keeping to herself in deep thought about something.

"What is it?" Eugene whispered.

"I got the copies of the ledger. There's just one problem…"

"What?"

"It was written in color pencils, and the copier only does black and white."

Eugene rolled his eyes. "Oh great."

"You can still see that all the transactions add up and she's not pocketing any loose cash on the side."

"You know what? Forget it. You're a liability. If she is innocent, they won't find anything when the audit comes." Eugene turned his back and Gerry reached over to grab his arm.

"Wait, wait, wait!" he hissed. Eugene turned, his eyes wide with anger. He looked down at the hand on his arm and then back at Gerry, who immediately released him.

"Just look at what I got, okay?" he asked.

The security guard glared at him as if fire were coming out of his eyes. "Where?" he growled.

Gerry looked around again, checking on Ethel. "There's a McDonald's up the street on 3rd Avenue. Meet me there at 8 pm tonight."

"We close at 6 today. What'd you expect me to do for 2 hours?"

"I'm not taking any chances. I've been checking around. As far as I can tell, S.I.U isn't even investigating us!"

Eugene looked back at him.

"Just be there."

A patron came to the desk and Eugene took a step back while Gerry checked out the person's items.

Cynthia Brown arrived home at three o'clock from a ten-hour shift at the hospital. She was carrying several bags of groceries from the nearby Associated Supermarket. Before walking to the elevator in the building, she checked her mailbox embedded in the lobby wall. When she entered her apartment, she took the bags to the kitchen and dropped the mail on the counter. A piece of mail dropped and floated to the floor.

It was a sealed computer printed notice from the library with Tanya's name on it. She contemplated opening it but trusted and respected her daughter's privacy. *It's probably nothing,* she thought. Placing it back with the rest of the mail, she put the groceries away in the cupboards.

When finished, she looked at the pile on the counter again, fighting the temptation to snoop. What excuse could she give? *It's my house and I do what I want,* echoed in her thoughts. It was wrong, but before she could change her mind, she grabbed and opened the correspondence.

She quickly skimmed the contents. "Overdue reminder…please return the item in question…" She stopped and then shrieked. "*The Joy of Sex?*"

"SOMETHING ON YOUR MIND, TOMMY?" Ethel asked. The pair was closing during the last hour with Heywood at the information desk. She wasn't the type to start a conversation, but she could sense something was bothering him just as much as something was bothering her.

"Sarah and I are going to her parents' for dinner Sunday night. It's the first time since announcing the pregnancy."

"Ahh," she replied. "I'm sure everything will go well."

"Yeah, I hope so. You look a little distracted yourself."

She moved closer to him. "I still feel bad about that Saturday," she whispered.

Tommy looked over her shoulder. The pages were spread out and Heywood was on the phone. "Between you and me," he started, "did Alex tell you what she was going to do?"

Ethel took a moment, then said, "She just told me to let him in first. I swear I didn't know."

"It's okay," he assured her.

"This has been eating me up inside. I…I…just needed to tell someone."

This was the first time Tommy saw her like this. The elder was usually emotionless and unshaken. "Look, everybody's moved on. No one knows your involvement. Let it go, okay?"

She nodded and smiled. "Thank you, Tommy. I'd really appreciate it if you kept this between us."

"You keep being the pitbull you are, Ethel. Your secret is safe with me."

They stayed quiet for the rest of the hour and closed the branch without a hitch.

McDonald's was at 966 3rd Avenue with two stories. The upstairs dining area had a glass wall window looking out on to the street. Gerry walked in around eight fifteen and ordered a number nine, which was a filet of fish meal with fries and a soda. He took his tray upstairs and found a booth in the back of the dining area. With his back to the wall facing the staircase, he ate his meal and waited.

Twenty minutes later, Eugene climbed the steps, making his way to Gerry's booth. "You know I came in here and left twice before you showed up?" he grumbled.

"Now that I've seen you in the uniform, you look so weird out of it, like you a stuntman jumping out of windows and shit."

He was wearing jeans with a leather jacket and a black AC/DC T-shirt. "Very funny…now, whaddya got?"

Gerry wiped his mouth with a napkin, then reached into his jacket and pulled out the copies. "Here you go," he said sliding them across the table.

Eugene examined the pages. "Looks legit. She's reporting everything. I guess S.I.U got it wrong."

"There, see?" Gerry said triumphantly. He was so proud of himself saving Sonyai's ass. He couldn't wait to rub it in her face.

"Okay, I'll pass this along to my contact inside. In fact, they should be arriving any minute now."

A figure caught Gerry's eye climbing the steps at the end of the room. His face fell when the visitor walked up to where they were and sat next to Eugene. Gerry couldn't believe his eyes as Sonyai looked back at him with a cold, piercing stare.

Tanya was finishing up washing the dishes in the kitchen. She walked out to see her mother sitting on the couch and noticed the TV was off.

"Uh, I'm going to bed now," she said and headed to her bedroom.

"Before you go, have a seat next to me please," Cynthia asked.

"Mama I'm really tired—"

"Sit *down*, Tanya," she ordered.

The child walked across the room scared and confused, then took a seat next to her mother.

Cynthia sighed. "I know you're growing up and discovering yourself, I want you to know that you can talk to me about anything, okay?"

"Okay," Tanya answered with a nod.

"If you have questions about what's going on with your body, I'm here to explain things to you."

"I know, mama."

"With that said, look into my eyes, baby," she instructed.

Tanya looked at her, wondering what was going on.

"Are you having sex?"

"No, mama."

"Don't lie to me, Tanya!"

"Mama, I'm telling the truth!"

"Then what the hell are you doing reading books about the joys of sex?" Cynthia asked, holding up the overdue notice.

Lakeshia! Tanya thought. She tried to deflect the situation. "You opened my mail?" she squealed.

"Don't make this about what *I* did. What are you doing reading books like this?"

"I borrowed the book for a friend from work. She has it and hasn't returned it yet! Search my room, that book isn't even here! I can't believe you read my mail!"

"You better not be lying!" Cynthia warned. She didn't want her to see that she felt bad for violating her privacy.

"I'm not. I'll talk to Lakeshia first thing tomorrow to get that book back, but I can't believe you don't trust me! They taught us sex-ed at school, and I know to protect myself if I do anything, but I'm not!" She stormed off to her room and closed the door.

Cynthia sighed and crumpled the letter out of aggravation. "Damn it!" she hissed, throwing the wad in the trashcan.

"I MUST SAY, I am impressed by your resourcefulness," Sonyai began.

Gerry was still grasping the situation as it unfolded. He looked down and chuckled to himself. "There was no S.I.U investigation, was there?" he asked Eugene, not acknowledging her yet.

"No. When Augustus made the call to bring me back, Sonyai contacted me and came up with this plan...to see the lengths you'd go to."

Gerry felt like a fool. He had fallen for it hook, line, and sinker. He finally looked over at the senior clerk. "I did this to clear you."

"That's a possibility. But you're an opportunist...and a constant threat to my leadership. How do I know that you wouldn't betray me?"

"I guess you don't actually." He was at a loss for words. "So what now? You gonna try to get rid of me? Make me disappear?"

"It depends," she said as she looked through the copies and then put them in her purse. "How did you get the ledger from the safe to make these?"

Gerry prepared for this. He reached into his pocket and produced a piece of paper he tore out of his notebook. "Chavez had the combination written down, hidden beneath the blotter on his desk."

She stared at the paper and then back at him, then tried to reach for it. He caught her and pulled back, "Ah, ah, ah," he taunted.

She narrowed her eyes. "He wouldn't be that foolish. I don't know how you did it, and I don't really care. This exercise has taught me more than enough, and I will make the appropriate steps now that we've had this talk." Eugene slid out and walked back toward the stairs. His role in the charade was complete.

She sat up to follow the guard. Gerry called out to her. "You may not trust me, but I did all this to prove you were innocent! I know you're not a thief!" She ignored him and continued walking, her heels echoing in the dining area, leaving Gerry to his thoughts.

FRIDAY WAS PAYDAY, and Robin was excited for the Knicks season closer this weekend. The team made the playoffs as the second seed and would face the New Jersey Nets in the first round. Chicago made the playoffs as well and would likely rest most of their starters Sunday, giving the Knicks an easy victory.

Robin was with Sonyai working the circulation desk, pondering what to do with his extra ticket. He was taking Walter of course, and Jarvis won the coin toss between him and Mouse. Originally, he set aside the last ticket for Franklin, but he told Robin that morning he had a date. Gillian and Kim didn't strike him as basketball fans.

A patron stepped up to the desk wearing a Chicago Bulls jacket. He had a copy of *Rare Air*, the photographic biography of the retired legendary basketball player.

"Hi, I'd like to check this out, please," he said.

Robin held his contempt for the obsessed fan, then opened the book, looking for the date due card pocket. There was a stamp on the first page marking the item as a reference book. He checked the spine and confirmed it by reading the call number Ref 796.323 Jordan.

"Where did you find this book, sir?"

"Um, back there in the right-hand corner," the patron replied.

"Sir, that is the reference section. The items over there are not allowed to be borrowed, only read here. I'm sorry."

The gentleman was devastated. "Aww, I've looked everywhere for a copy, over 10 different libraries. This was the first copy I've seen."

"That's because it's been stolen so many times. This book is so popular many have borrowed it and failed to return it. Hence the decision to mark it for reference."

"Well, I wasn't planning to do that. Isn't there a way you can check it out this one time? I'll even settle for 1 week instead of 3!"

Robin shook his head. "I'm sorry, there's nothing I can do." He slid the book back to him. "Feel free to read it here for as long as you like, until we close."

The fan sighed and picked up the book. "Alright." He walked back to the reference area.

"You know, he's just another basketball player," Robin called back to him.

The patron stopped and walked back. "You're joking, right?"

"I mean, he was a decent player, but not this god-among-men that everyone claimed him to be."

"2-time gold medal Olympian, 3 championship titles, MVP of the Year, All-Star MVP...I can go on."

"Magic Johnson, Julius Irving, Walt Chamberlain..." Robin ticked off with the fingers of his hand.

"All great in their own right. But Michael changed the game. There will never be another player who did what he did and more, not in a million years."

"Well, now he's giving baseball a try. We'll see how he does with that," Robin taunted.

"I don't think it's gonna stick with him. Basketball is in his heart, and despite what happened to his father, he might come back."

"Nah, he ain't coming back. That part of his life is done, he said it himself. His father saw his last game and he wants to keep it that way. Maybe as a coach or a broadcaster, calling games with Marv Albert. I can see that in about 4 or 5 years. But he ain't all that, and he didn't do it all on his own. He had help! We'll see how the Bulls do without him. The Knicks are gonna stomp them Sunday!"

The patron waved his arm and turned away again. "Yeah, whatever. Knicks ain't going nowhere. See ya around, pal!"

Robin chuckled to himself as Sonyai approached him. "What was that about?" she asked.

"Just some trash talk between basketball fans," he dismissed. He noticed Lakeshia walking by pushing a shelving cart and had an idea. "Ma'am, I've been thinking," he began.

She turned to give him her undivided attention. "Yes?"

"Since the day you threatened us, Miss Seabrooke and I haven't said no more than 2 words to each other, have we not?"

"Most of that attributes to the fact you haven't been here for 2 weeks, Walker," she dismissed.

"True, but I like to believe I've earned your trust in obeying your rules."

"Get to the point because I don't like where this is going," Sonyai barked.

"Okay. I have an extra ticket to the Knicks game on Sunday, and I'd like to ask Lakeshia to go with me. It's strictly platonic. We won't be alone. I'll have 2 of my other friends with us. We would be going in the capacity of *friends and co-workers.*"

The senior clerk pondered the request for a moment. "In the spirit of kindness, congregating at a sporting event among friends is acceptable."

Robin smiled.

"As long as she understands that it will not lead to anything between you 2 and it is not to be considered a date, got it?" she insisted.

"Yes, ma'am," he answered. "May I ask her in person later or would you prefer to approach her with the request?"

"You can ask her yourself, Walker. Like you said, I trust you now. Don't ruin that trust by doing something reckless and foolhardy!"

The clerk nodded, then returned to his duties at the computer terminal.

TANYA GOT off the M31 bus at York Avenue and 76th Street. She caught the crosstown bus at 54th and 10th Avenue, a few blocks north from school. Making her way to the Webster Branch, she had to see it with her own eyes. After everything Andrew and she had in the past, she refused to let him go without a fight.

She walked in and took a seat at a table in an inconspicuous corner with a view of the circulation desk. Placing her book bag in front of her, Tanya took out a textbook and stuck her head down pretending to read while scanning the floor.

At the information desk was a short Indian gentleman with a thick mustache and curly black hair helping someone looking for a book. She noticed two female clerks working the circulation desk and several pages between the shelves, but no sign of Andrew. She thought about going upstairs to the children's room when Andrew and a tall blond white woman emerged from a door near the back of the main floor.

"We on for dinner tonight?" he asked.

"I'm closing with Liz, but I think I can sneak out and meet you at Lusardi's," she replied.

"I'll have the linguine ordered for you when you arrive."

"You're so good to me," she giggled.

They separated. He stopped at the circulation desk to brief the two clerks while she stepped outside. Tanya couldn't believe it. Her knuckles turned chalk white as her fist shook violently. She had half a mind to jump him where he stood, whaling on him until he was a bloody pulp, then run outside and finish his new girlfriend off.

Resisting the urge, she stood up and walked through the bookshelves and around to the exit without being seen. Heading west, it would be a serious hike to 86th Street and Lexington in order to catch the 4-train going home. *Yeah, you get linguine for that bitch!* she thought.

Lakeshia walked into the staff room around four twenty-five. Robin was waiting for her, sitting on the couch. She froze as a light gasp escaped her lips.

"I was wondering when you'd show up," he began, then raised his hand. "Relax, I cleared this with Yi. I just want to ask you something real quick."

She exhaled a relaxed breath, then walked to the table. "Okay."

"You a Knicks fan?" he asked.

"Sure."

"Name their starting 5."

"Patrick Ewing, Charles Oakley, Hubie Davis, Anthony Bonner, and Derek Harper."

"It's *Hubert*, but close enough. I've got an extra ticket to the game Sunday. It starts at 3, so you can still make it to school the next day. Wanna go?"

Her eyes lit up like Christmas lights. "Me?" she squeaked.

"There'll be 2 other friends of mine with us. We won't be alone, and this is not a date, okay?"

She sat at the table with a huge toothy smile on her face, silent and overwhelmed by joy.

"Say it, Leelee."

"It's not a date!" she exclaimed.

"Say it without the crazy big smile," he ordered.

She shook her head. "I don't think I can do that," she said, still smiling.

Robin put his hand to his face. "Leelee, I can't stress this enough. Yi doesn't want this leading to anything. It's an innocent outing as friends—nothing more."

She nodded with such enthusiasm she looked like a Pez dispenser.

"I'll pick you up at your place, we go to the game, and I bring you back. Nothing afterwards. This is not a date, you understand?"

"I understand," she replied.

He nodded and stood up to leave. "Okay, give me your address before you leave today. I'll pick you up Sunday at 2 pm, and remember, not a date."

"Right," she said and pointed at him.

Robin headed to the door. He took one last look at her, she nodded again, then he left. She waited five minutes, then leaped from the chair to the table, jumping up and down with her arms stretched out. "Yes!"

Alex pushed the shelving cart full of books into the fiction section. A voice from somewhere made her snap at attention. "Well, well, well. Isn't it a small world?"

She turned to see a familiar face approach her. It was the guy from the nightclub, Mr. Karl Kani. He was still wearing a Kani polo shirt with blue slacks and dress shoes.

"Figured you'd work in a library. You got the exotic yet smart nerd thing working," he said.

"Hey, I am not a nerd. And what are you doing here? You stalking me now?"

"Easy, kitten, it was totally an accident bumping into you again, but I do believe in serendipity."

"Serendipity?" she asked.

"The fates have plans for you and me. You may not want to do the modeling thing now, but I'm promoting a party coming up, and I believe you can make the right connections if you come through."

"If it's a party you're planning, it'll be just as wack as those lines from your tired ass game."

"Why you gotta hate? I'm trying to make you a star, girl." She gave him a questionable look. "It's a fraternity orientation gathering for the freshmen at Hunter College. June 23rd."

"Have you forgotten I'm only 16? I can't go to no college party!"

"I know a guy who does fake IDs, charges $65. You tell him I sent you, he'll do it for free. These frats are all about the connections. They can get you in with the sororities so by the time you turn 18, you're already well known."

He fished out a card from his slacks and held it up to her.

"I still have your card," Alex snapped.

"This is the card for my ID guy. Give it to him and he'll hook you up."

Alex looked at the card, then at him, that devilish grin on his face. She snatched the card from his hand and slipped it into her blouse.

"June 23rd, see you there!" he said with a wink and turned around, leaving the page to her duties.

JANELLE AND SONYAI were back at the Upper East Side Woman's Center after six o'clock,

"It's week 15, second trimester. We should be able to determine sex of child now," the gynecologist announced. She had an assistant with her this time to conduct the ultrasound. Janelle was lying back on a hospital bed with her stomach exposed. The technician administered a gel on the bare midriff.

Janelle giggled. "That tickles," she said.

Sonyai cracked a rare smile on the corner of her mouth.

The doctor tapped a few keys on a keyboard in front of a small computer with a green and black display monitor. The assistant then produced a small ultrasound transducer and pressed it on the gelled stomach, starting the scan. A cone shape appeared on the monitor after a few minutes a shape came to form within the cone.

"Heartbeat is normal."

"I don't see anything," Janelle said while squinting.

"It's hard to see if you don't know what to look for," the assistant replied.

The gynecologist pulled out a pen from her lab coat, then using it as a pointer, circled a part of the monitor. "That's the head," she explained. "There are the arms and legs. Would you like to know the sex?"

Janelle and Sonyai looked at each other, the elder blinked and gave a small shrug.

"No," Janelle answered. "I want to be surprised."

"Fair enough, but baby is looking healthy. Pretty soon, will be kicking like crazy."

"Wow," the teen sighed.

"You want picture to take with you? We can print a copy with imager."

"Sure! I'll show it to Avery!"

The doctor typed a few keys and a machine whirled to life, then spit out a 4x6 photograph. Janelle reached out and held the picture in front of her. Sonyai stared at it for a long time. She held her fist up, covering her mouth, quietly moved by an old memory.

Janelle turned and saw her. "You okay, Miss Yi?"

She put the thought out of her head and resumed her stoic glance. "I'm fine. Um, I'll be waiting outside while you get your things. Excuse me." She quickly turned and left the room. A puzzled look came across the young girl's face. Sonyai stepped outside of the building, took a napkin out from her purse, and wiped away some premature tears. She regained her composure and lit up a much-needed cigarette.

Heywood arrived at his place to find Storming Jackie Daze sitting on the floor in the hallway leaning on a guitar case. She appeared to be taking a nap, indicating she had been waiting for a long time. Her white mohawk danced in the sunlight coming in from the hallway windows.

"Hey," she greeted, stirring out of her sleep.

"Hey," he replied, then pointed to his cheek. "You got a little drool there."

She wiped her mouth, looking down, embarrassed. "Excuse me."

"I didn't know you played," he said pointing to the case.

"Actually, I don't." She opened it to reveal assorted clothes. "It just holds all my belongings."

"Wow, travel light, huh?"

"The life of a musician." She smiled and nodded. There was a moment of awkward silence. "Look, I really don't want to cramp your style," she began.

"You can stay with me for as long as you want," he said with certainty.

"I'm gonna find another club to perform at. It may take some time."

"Not a problem," he said quickly.

"You…you don't even know my name or anything about me. How can you be so trusting?"

"I'm from Wisconsin." He smiled.

"You are?" she asked, tilting her head.

"No. But people from there are known for their gullibility."

She laughed, then he laughed too. She looked at him. "Has anyone ever told you that you look like Jesus Christ?"

"If you want to stay with me, you'll never make that comparison again," he said sternly.

"Ooh, struck a nerve?"

"You have no idea. Now, c'mon. I got leftover Chinese food in the fridge." He held out his hand and pulled her up. She leaned in and kissed him passionately, feeling his beard.

"My name is Jacqueline Daisy. My friends call me 'Jack' or 'Jackie'. And whatever you do, *never* call me Miss Daisy. Ever."

He opened the door. "My name is Heywood, and I wouldn't dream of it."

CHAPTER EIGHTEEN

"Granddaddy! Can I borrow your tie and dress shirt?" Robin called out. He was already in Jon's bedroom closet with the shirt in question on his arm, looking for the tie. Obviously, Jon couldn't hear him, but Robin told his conscience that if he asked, it wouldn't be considered stealing. He found the tie and slipped it over his shoulder. "Thank you," he mumbled.

At a quarter after twelve, he stepped out of the hallway to the living room. Jon put down the Sunday paper and pointed as Robin went to the kitchen for some orange juice.

"Those are my clothes!" he barked out loud.

Robin came out, placing the cup on the bookcase, then looked at him on the couch.

"I asked if I could borrow them and you said okay," he signed.

"When the hell was that?"

"Last night before you went to sleep."

"I may be old but I ain't senile!" He then leaned forward and smelled the air. "Is that my cologne, too, dammit?"

"I think there's a trace on the shirt."

"Bullshit! Who are you trying to impress?" Jon signed, squinting at Robin.

"Nobody! Just going to the game with some friends."

"You ain't fooling me. You did this before with that Anderson girl."

Robin took a long chug from the cup as a distraction tactic, then hightailed it to the door. He turned one last time to face him and signed, "I'll be home around 8!" Then he opened the door and left.

"I DON'T LIKE THIS, Jen. Don't like this one bit!" Rudy Seabrooke said.

He was standing in the middle of his living room, arms folded, looking like a drill sergeant on the first day of basic training. After raising three children and working as a New York City firefighter for fifteen years, the six-foot-five patriarch was not used to situations that were beyond his control.

When Lakeshia first told them about some co-worker from the library taking her to a Knicks game, he immediately refused to allow it. After hours of begging, pleading, even crying, her mother reasoned with him to cave in. Now, with the hour approaching, he realized it was a mistake.

Behind him in front of the television, Lakeshia's two brothers, Quinton and Derrick, were playing on their Sega Genesis. "I didn't go on a date till I was 17. Why does Leelee get a pass, pop?" the elder brother Derrick asked.

Rudy glared at the boy but held his tongue. He had a valid point.

"This is not a date, guys. I don't know how many times I have to say it," Jennifer Seabrooke said walking in from the hallway. "Now, I want none of you scaring the living daylights out this young man when he gets here. Rudy, do not take out your ax! That goes for you 2 boys as well."

"Yes, mom," the boys said in unison.

Standing six-foot-one herself, Jennifer's lightly tanned skin appeared to shimmer when she walked. Her brown hair was neatly tied in a ponytail and she had eyes as blue as the sky. She gave her husband a playful nudge to the ribs, then called for their daughter. "Lakeshia!

Come on out here. Your date will be here any minute. Oops!" she caught herself. "I mean your platonic co-worker friend!"

"Okay, okay!" Lakeshia yelled from her room. A few moments later, her door opened and she stepped out, walking down the hallway.

Rudy's jaw fell as the boys turned from the TV for a moment to look. They all yelled at once. "Oh, hell no!"

Lakeshia was wearing a short metallic skirt and a long-sleeved turtleneck sweater exposing her midriff. Her face was darker than usual due to a heavy application of foundation, blush, eye-shadow and other assorted makeup. "What?" she simply asked.

Jennifer grabbed the child by her shoulders and turned her around, pushing her back in the bedroom. "Oh, no you don't, young lady! You take all that makeup off and put on some clothes! Were you in my closet?" Lakeshia tried to protest, and at that exact moment, there was a knock on the door.

Jennifer called out, "Stall him...and don't take out that ax!"

Rudy and the boys grabbed four of the chairs around the dining room table and arranged them in the living room, then Rudy walked to the door and unlocked it.

Robin stood at the entrance to the apartment as the door opened. He greeted Mr. Seabrooke with a smile. "Good afternoon, sir. I'm Robin Walker. It's nice to meet you. Is Lakeshia ready?" Rudy waved his arm, inviting the visitor inside. "She'll be just a moment. Please come in and have a seat."

Robin took a quick glance inside the apartment and let out a nervous chuckle. "I would love to sir, but I'm afraid we don't have much—"

The giant reached out and pulled Robin in by the forearm. "*I'm afraid* I must insist," he interrupted.

Rudy ushered Robin into the living room where Derrick and Quinton were sitting. He sat Robin on a chair, then took a seat of his own. Robin noticed that he was in the middle of a triangle made up of the Seabrooke men of the family.

"So," Rudy began, "you and Lakeshia work together at the library?"

"Yes," he replied while attempting to keep his cool.

"How long you've been there?" Derrick asked.

Robin turned to look at the older brother. "Since February. A little over 2 months."

"Where'd you get the tickets for today's game?" Quinton asked.

"A friend from school. His mother works for MSG."

There was a pause in the line of questioning as he looked at each of them. "Would you like to know where I was on the night of the 12th, 7 years ago?" Robin asked with a grin.

The trio exchanged glances, not amused by the joke.

"Did Lakeshia tell you what I do for a living?" Rudy asked.

"Uh, no, sir," Robin replied.

"Engine 59, Ladder 30, Battalion 16," both brothers announced.

"Oh! A fireman, huh? Nice! Hey, you ever read *The Fire Cat* by Esther Averill?"

Rudy stared back at him, his eyes piercing his soul like a hot knife through butter.

Robin cleared his throat. "Um, is Lakeshia going to be much longer? Because we really got to go if—"

"Let me show you my ax," Rudy said standing up, walking to his closet.

Robin stammered, "A-a-ax?"

Rudy came back with a twenty-inch long, ten-pound fireman's ax in his hand. Robin tensed up, nearly jumping out of his skin at the sight of the blade.

"When you only have 30 seconds to save someone's life and there's a three-and-a-half inch thick mahogany door in your way, this bad boy will reduce it to splinters with two good whacks!"

The father demonstrated by swinging it in front of himself a few times. The swoosh echoed in Robin's ear as he sat completely still. He knew this was just a typical authority figure intimidation trick, like greeting a potential suitor with a double-barrel shotgun at the door. Still, it was difficult not to flinch.

When Robin didn't say anything at the display of finesse, Rudy took a seat again, leaning on the base of the ax in front of him like a cane. "What kind of man wears a dress shirt and tie and no jacket?" he asked.

Robin blinked hard at the surprise question. "Um, Detective Sipowitz, sir?"

"Who?"

"He's a TV detective on that new police show, *NYPD Blue*?"

Behind him, Derrick elbowed Quinton whispering, "That's that show where you can see all the naked women." and smiled.

"Huh, I don't watch cop shows," Rudy replied.

"Oh, yeah, I'd guess you're more of an *Emergency!* fan then," he said with an awkward chuckle.

Rudy tapped the blade on the tile floor of their apartment with a jarring thud, which finally made the youngster jump in his seat and snap back to attention.

"Alright, pleasantries are over, boy. You keep your hands to yourself tonight and bring my daughter home no later than 7:30 pm sharp, got it?"

"Yes, sir," Robin quickly said.

"Good."

The three guys stood, picked up their chairs, and placed them back at the kitchen table just as the bedroom door opened again. Lakeshia came out followed by her mother wearing a more reserved outfit of jeans and an oversized sweatshirt. Jennifer looked puzzled as she saw Robin sitting in his chair in the middle of the living room with a startled look on his face.

"Why is he sitting? Didn't you offer him a seat on the couch? What happened?" she asked as Robin stood up to greet her.

"It's okay, ma'am. Your husband was just telling me about his everyday heroics. Robin Walker, a pleasure to meet you," he said, shaking her hand.

"The pleasure is all mine. Sorry to have kept you. I know you must be going," she said while Lakeshia grabbed her jacket.

The pair started to leave. "We'll be back by 7," he called back, opening the door.

"Have a good time," Jennifer Seabrooke said with a wave.

"But not too good of a time!" Rudy barked behind her.

The door closed and they walked down the three floors of steps to the lobby.

"Daddy didn't scare you, did he?" Lakeshia asked.

"Naw, not at all," he replied. "You should have told me he was the twin brother of the black guy from all those *American Ninja* movies."

Lakeshia was giving him a weird look over the joke while leaving the building. They walked to the nearest corner when she called out, "Where are you going?"

"The train station, we can catch the 1-train at—"

"I'm not taking the train! Let's call a cab."

He shook his head. "There's no time. We got 45 minutes till tip-off! Let's go."

"I don't take the train or a bus *anywhere!*" she protested.

Robin turned to look at her. "If you were ready when I showed up, we might have been able to catch a cab and make it, but there isn't time, Leelee. One train ride won't kill you!"

She clenched her jaw at the thought of riding in a disgusting, dirty subway car. "Fine! But I'm not sitting anywhere in the car and I'm not touching anything, not even the pole! You'll have to stand behind me being a buffer so I don't fall when the train stops and starts."

He grinned. "You're just using that as an excuse to get me to hold you."

"No, I'm not, that thought never even occurred to me." *But it's a nice bonus!* she thought.

"Alright, let's go! We got to get to 145th Street."

They hurried down the sidewalk heading south.

THE JEFFERSON HOUSES was a project complex in the heart of Spanish Harlem. Lorenzo and Acindina Gonzales lived at 2070 3rd Avenue between 113th and 114th Street in apartment 1509. For twenty years, Lorenzo worked his way up from busboy to sous chef at one of the finest Spanish restaurants on the Upper East Side. But at home, his wife prepared the meals.

"Enzo! Sarah and Tommy will be here any minute! Turn off that damn television and set the table."

"It's the pregame warmups, Cindi! Goddamn Anthony Mason is still suspended! He may not even play in the playoffs now!" He turned off the set. "What I wouldn't give to see the Knicks make it all the way this year. I'd invite the entire team to the restaurant and give them the best meal they've ever eaten! Better than their own mothers!"

"Aye, *cochino*, those bums are going nowhere! Couldn't even get 1st place in the conference. Had it slip away to Atlanta. They'll be lucky they make it past the 1st round—"

The table was set and it was almost three o'clock. Acindina put out a plate of *chicharrones de pollo* as an appetizer, then checked the oven. Lorenzo made himself a *conquito* with the blender. He took a sip, then handed the glass to her and she took a long swig. While holding the glass and pointing, she said, "Don't start anything with Tommy today, okay? He's a good man, treats Sarah like a queen."

"What a waste, that one? Playing football only not to make it to the NFL. Now, working in a library? What kind of job is that for a career, huh?"

"What kind of career was a busboy back in '74, gringo? But I stood by you. Look at you now!"

He smiled. "I told you back then I would give you the world, and you believed me. You gave me a princess—who deserves a prince! Not an *indigente*!"

She caressed his face and looked into his eyes. "She has made her choice, Enzo. You may not have to like it, but you have to *respect* it."

His eyes were hard as stone, molded after years and years of hard labor and determination. "*Elijo no a mi amada*," he whispered.

A knock on the door broke their gaze. He grabbed the glass from her and walked to take a seat at the head of the table. She checked the food again in the kitchen, then answered the door.

Robin and Lakeshia found Jarvis and Mouse waiting for them at the 7th Avenue entrance of Madison Square Garden.

"Where the hell have you been?" Jarvis asked.

"Who's this?" Mouse asked, nodding to Lakeshia.

Robin looked between them and countered with his own question. "Where's Walt?"

"He gave me his ticket," Mouse explained. "Hi, name's Carlos, but everyone calls me 'Mouse'. What's your name?" he asked Lakeshia with a smile.

"It damn sure ain't Cheese!" she replied with a repulsed look on her face.

Robin and Jarvis laughed at the rejection, then Robin introduced her. "Guys, this is Lakeshia, my...cousin. She also works at the library." The pair had gone over their story on the train ride down. She objected at first—the idea of Robin being embarrassed in front of his friends for bringing her along hurt her feelings. He assured her it was the way to go and promised they would walk around the block for a while before taking her home.

"I can't believe Walt. His mother gave us the tickets. How will it look if I show up without him?" They walked toward the entrance as he handed each one a ticket.

"Maybe she won't check on us," Jarvis said. He looked down and read where his seat was. "Wow! Section 107, Row 3. These are killer seats!"

Mouse looked at his. "Whoa, someone might see us on TV! We'll be so close, we'll probably get hit with a ball going out of bounds!"

Robin smiled as he turned to Lakeshia. "Okay, you're on my left while these 2 are on the end of the row to the right."

She beamed a bright smile and nodded.

"And don't get any ideas about putting your hand on my leg. I saw *Coming to America*, I know that trick," he said with a wink.

She grinned at the suggestion. It was like he was reading her mind. "Wouldn't think of it," she lied.

Tommy and Sarah sat and ate Sunday dinner with Lorenzo and Acindina in their apartment dining room. The conversation was minimal with only sounds of silverware clinking and affirmations of the food being well received.

Acindina decided to finally break the ice. "How was your last check-up, honey?" Sarah began, but Lorenzo quickly said, "We're eating. Don't ruin it with nauseating female-doctor-talk," waving his hand.

The curt dismissal offended the daughter. She looked across to Tommy, and they exchanged looks for a second before he looked back down at his plate.

"I've been noticing my nipples are super sensitive now," Sarah blurted out.

Tommy coughed and Lorenzo sighed, slamming down his fork "*Coño!*"

"That's because your breast are filling up and getting bigger. Have you started lactating yet?" Acindina asked.

"Cindi!" Lorenzo yelled.

"Stop it, Enzo! We are talking about this whether you like it or not, and don't you even think of stepping into the living room to watch the game!"

He rolled his eyes and sat contently. The ladies' conversation went on until dinner was finished. The women gathered all the dishes and went to the kitchen, leaving the men alone facing each other at the table.

"So uh, how's the job at the library?" Lorenzo asked.

"Good. Everything's going well," Tommy replied.

The two fidgeted their fingers, thinking of what else to talk about.

"Have you two discussed names yet?"

"We were thinking Tony or Anthony if it's a boy, and Caridad if it's a girl."

Lorenzo nodded. "After her grandmother? Hmm, good choice. Good names both of them."

"Yeah," Tommy agreed.

"While we're on the subject, I wanna ask you something that's been bothering me, *Tomas*."

Tommy winced. He hated it when Lorenzo called him by the Hispanic equivalent of his given name.

"You've been married for 5 years, correct?"

"Yes, sir."

"And Sarah decided, rather than take your last name, to hyphenate and go by Gonzales-Carmichael."

"That is correct, sir."

"Granted if she was a professional who built a reputation, hyphenating would be the logical step, for the purposes of keeping said reputation, correct?"

"Uhh…"

"But she is not working and has not worked a single job since starting college. I made sure she would have the money to keep at her studies with no distractions. I worked 55 hours a week for 6 years to accomplish this. And how does she repay me?"

Tommy kept silent.

"By getting married, becoming a housewife, with a bachelor's in liberal arts."

Lorenzo looked at Tommy, expecting him to say something.

Tommy's thoughts raced through his head. He didn't want to sound confrontational, but he had to defend his wife.

"Sarah doesn't plan on being a housewife forever. Once the baby's walking and talking, we'll have a babysitter and she will find something she's comfortable working at."

"Oh really? What about this hyphenating thing?" Lorenzo challenged.

"A lot of women in the 90's are doing it now as a sign of independence. It's not disrespectful."

"It's wrong! You have to put your foot down and let her know who's boss!"

"How do you expect me to respect your daughter if you want me to treat her like a child?" Tommy replied cooly, struggling to hold in his temper.

"A king knows how to treat a woman with respect yet put her in her place. She is my princess, and she deserves a king!"

"I am her *husband,* not her father!" Tommy barked back. Lorenzo blinked in shock at the outburst. "When a princess is married she becomes a queen. Your problem is you see her as that little girl you raised when she's not! She's a woman now. I'm not her king, she is my queen."

Lorenzo stood up from the table as the ladies stepped back into the dining room. "As long as she's still carrying her family name like a crutch, she will never be yours. And neither will her child!"

He stormed off to the living room as Tommy turned to see a concerned look on Sarah's face.

THE KNICKS WERE MAKING quick work of the Bulls, extending their lead to nine points at the beginning of the fourth quarter. The score was tied at halftime, but a surge at the end of the third quarter solidified the lead with the win just twelve minutes away. Robin checked the clock. It was ten minutes to six. The final quarter of the game would probably last another half-hour.

"Excuse me," a voice snapped him out of his thoughts. The four of them looked up to see a tall white man in a suit in the aisle. He didn't look like an usher.

"I knew it!" Mouse yelled. "This was too good to be true! Damn it, Robin, you gave us bogus tickets and now we're about to get kicked outta here!"

"Be cool, Mouse! Uh, yes?" he asked the visitor.

The man lifted up a tote bag that was on the floor next to him and handed it to Robin, "Compliments of Ms. Shaw. Have a nice day." He stepped up the stairs on the row and disappeared into the tunnel leading to the outer floor. Robin opened the bag. Inside were T-shirts and programs for each of them. He showed everyone and handed them out.

"Wow!" Jarvis said.

"Neat!" Mouse added with a sigh of relief.

He gave the items to Lakeshia and included the tote after pulling out his items. "Keep the bag, kiddo."

She smiled and noticed the new personal nickname he had just given her. "Thank you!" she exclaimed.

He smiled back and then nodded his head. "C'mon! We're heading out!"

"Huh?" she gasped as he took her arm.

They sidestepped past Jarvis and Mouse. Patrick Ewing received a pass from Charles Oakley and took it to the rim with a thunderous slam dunk over Luc Longley. The crowd went wild, standing on their feet and cheering.

"I'm taking my cousin home. Enjoy the rest of the game, guys!" Robin yelled over the noise.

Mouse and Jarvis each gave Robin a thumbs-up. Lakeshia waved at them and the two made their way up the aisle. They waved back and after a few minutes went by Jarvis leaned over to Mouse. "If that's his cousin then I'm Danny Tartabull! Robin on some R. Kelly shit messing around with little Aaliyah over there."

Mouse shrugged. "Hey, age ain't nothin' but a number. Is R. Kelly's first name Robin?"

"I don't fucking know!"

At six fifteen, Cervantes dropped off Robin and Lakeshia back at her place. She was wearing the oversized T-shirt and couldn't stop smiling. He nodded to the taxi driver, who winked back at him in return and then pulled off. As promised, they walked for a while and talked.

"I had a wonderful time!" she exclaimed.

"Ah, ah, ah. That's something you say at the end of a date, and this is not a date, okay? Just say you had fun."

"Okay. I had fun."

"There you go. That's better."

They sat on the hood of a car for a moment. She was looking down at her shoes wondering what to say.

Robin came up with an idea. "Wanna play 20 Questions?" he asked.

She chuckled and nodded.

"Okay, you go first."

"Can we do this again sometime?" she asked.

"Geez, what happened with some easy ones like 'what's your favorite color?'"

She looked on, waiting for him to answer.

He rolled his eyes. "I don't know. Depends. Next question!"

At least he didn't say no, she thought.

"Okay, I've heard it's a sensitive subject, but why do you wear that glove on your hand?"

"My 5 other brothers from Gary, Indiana thought it looked cool." he replied with a grin.

Lakeshia frowned for a second before getting the joke, then giggled, "Very funny, Michael Jackson! Fine, stay mysterious, how about…what's your favorite movie? That should be a fair one."

Robin rubbed his chin. "*The Empire Strikes Back.*"

She grimaced, which he noticed and asked, "No good? What's yours?"

"*Imitation of Life*," she replied. "I watch it every Mother's Day."

"That movie's over 30 years old. Don't you like anything recent? *Batman, Ghostbusters, Gremlins*?"

She laughed. "Okay, your turn."

"Alright. Favorite book?" he asked.

"*Oliver Twist*, read it when I was nine. You?"

"*Garfield at Large*. Just kidding!"

They both laughed this time, then she looked at him. Robin knew what that gaze meant. He darted his eyes while thinking of something to say.

"Lakeshia," he started in a solemn tone, "in order for us to work together at the library, we have to remain just friends."

He regretted it the moment he said it. Her heart was breaking before his eyes. She looked like she was about to cry.

"Robin, I…"

"Look, you are a beautiful girl, and if I were a sophomore at your high school, we'd be necking under the bleachers between 6th and 7th period every day."

She blushed bright red, looking down. He heard a giggle as he continued. "But I'm just a little older now, so..." He let the thought hang, not knowing what else to say.

"But I'm only 4 years younger," she whispered.

"Kiddo, everyone moves on from their first crush. The boys at your school don't look like much now, but one day, a special guy's going to ask you to prom. You'll spend the summer with him after graduation, maybe follow him to college, and stay good friends.

"He'll ask you to marry him and you'll think back to this moment and we'll both share a laugh. Then, you'll thank me for allowing that guy to get his chance. Maybe name your first kid after me." He smiled.

She squinted at him. "You have it all figured out, don't you? Predicting my feelings for me? You really think you know me like that? What I feel in my heart?" She scoffed.

He sighed. "Tell you what, I'll make a deal with you. You listening?"

"Yeah."

"3 years from now, when you graduate and you're 18. The night of your graduation, I'll take you out on an official date, deal?"

She perked up, a smile back on her face. "Deal!"

They shook on it.

"Wanna keep playing?" he asked.

"I really should go up. My daddy...is expecting me."

"Okay."

Upstairs, Rudy, Derrick, and Quinton looked down from their apartment windows to see the pair making their way back in front of the building. It was ten minutes to seven. The trio tried to look inconspicuous, ducking down and hiding behind the curtains, spying from four flights up.

"Now, you're not going to tell the rest of the pages about this are you?" Robin asked. "Only Yi knows, and let's keep it that way."

"You have my word," she promised.

He nodded and they looked at each other, both with weird, goofy smiles on their faces.

"You think they're watching us from upstairs?" he whispered through his teeth.

"Oh, definitely," she replied quietly.

"Uhh," he muttered.

"Umm," she stammered.

"Kiss her already!" Quinton yelled out the window.

Lakeshia's face blushed crimson red as she planted it in her hands. She dared not to look up at Robin, who couldn't resist a chuckle.

"Oh, no you don't!" Rudy's booming voice thundered in the night sky.

She pulled the shirt over her head, extremely embarrassed and humiliated. "Oh my God, Oh my God, Oh my God!" she yelled.

Robin put his hands up at eye-level, pretending to surrender. "I think it's time we say good night,"

"Okay," she said through the shirt. "Can I least have a hug?"

"What was that? You're a little muffled in there," he asked.

She pulled her head out of the shirt, her eyes watering a little as she looked up at him, "C-c-can I at least have a hug?" she asked.

Jennifer walked up and grabbed both Quinton and Derrick by their ears, then nudged Rudy slightly on his calf with her foot.

"Ouch!" the boys winced.

"Hey!" Rudy cried out.

"You give her some damn privacy, you snoops. What is wrong with you? Git!" she said, shooing them from the window. A moment later, she returned to the window and peeked from behind the curtain.

"Leelee, you'll never have to ask," he said, then put his arms around her and pulled her close to his chest. The embrace melted her away as she inhaled a huge gasp of air. She smelled his cologne, she heard and felt his heart beating. She felt the electricity shoot up and down her spine and goosebumps tickle her neck and arms. He held her for what felt to both of them like an eternity. She was enthralled, bewitched, enchanted, and delighted.

He let go and her legs felt like rubber. She couldn't feel her feet on the ground.

"You okay?" he asked.

She couldn't put sound into words, so she just nodded and smiled. Still embarrassed, she started backing away. He gave her a puzzled look and a friendly wave, wondering about her weird behavior. She waved back, then turned and walked inside.

"Goodnight to you, too," he said to no one in particular. He started walking to the nearest corner for the M5 bus heading uptown.

Lakeshia walked inside the apartment floating on air. She actually performed a perfect pirouette in the hallway and curtsied in the living room. "I am never washing this T-shirt and I will track down the scent of this cologne," she said, tittering her way to her bedroom.

Jennifer smelled the air slightly. "Smells like Varon Dandy."

SONYAI EMERGED from the Bowling Green subway station and took a few steps, entering Battery Park. She met Angie at the Netherland Monument, the Flagstaff that greets those entering the northeast entrance near the intersection of State Street and Battery Place. For eight o'clock, the area was still well lit, but there were very few people in sight.

"Alright, I'm here," Sonyai said, a clear grudge in her voice. "Why did you suggest this isolated place?"

"This monument was built in 1926 as a present from the Dutch, marking the historic moment nearly 370 years ago when the Lenape sold this island for 60 guilders. Though the Dutch had been living on the island years earlier, they made the deal in order for them to establish trade operations through the West India Company. Most believe the Lenape agreed to such a minimal payment due to their noncombative nature." Angie turned to Sonyai after the speech. "These people were peaceful, indifferent, disinterested in trade, commerce, or business of any kind. They wanted to be left alone. And I feel the same way."

"But here you are, standing before me," Sonyai said.

"Yes," she agreed. The actions that followed next truly conflicted her. "I have reason to believe Chavez is falsifying memorandums. While retrieving more reserve postcards, I knocked over a box that had special paper, stickers of the seal, and a stamp with President Dalton's signature."

Sonyai was stunned. She would never have imagined that her suspicions were correct after all these years.

"So, what do we do now?" Angie asked.

"We? For someone being noncommittal, you sure are determined to help confront him."

"I'm only helping you because I believe he is doing wrong. You're on your own if I'm mistaken."

"You're not, you'll see. Once we have that box."

The two women said nothing else, then walked past each other heading to different exits. As the sounds of the city filled the air, the night covered their departures in a blanket of darkness.

ROBIN TOOK the bus to Tony's Pizza on Broadway for two slices and walked back home. He felt confident he got his point across and let Lakeshia down gently. When they see each other tomorrow afternoon at work, things would be better between them and Sonyai would be off his back.

Despite Ethel's taunt and that horrible business with Alex, he believed his hardships were finally behind him and the 58th Street Branch would be a good fit. Robin unlocked the door to his apartment and walked in. The lights were still on in the kitchen and living room which took him by surprise. He took two steps inside and froze. The metal apartment door slammed shut behind him as he saw Jon Walker in his bathrobe collapsed in the middle of the living room.

THE END

Call Numbers continues in Book 2

Call Numbers: Loss, Pain and Revelations

ABOUT THE AUTHOR

Syntell Smith was born and raised in Washington Heights, Upper Manhattan New York City. He graduated from Samuel Gompers High School and began writing while blogging his hectic everyday life experiences in 2004. He loves comic books, video games, and watching reruns of Law and Order. He currently lives in Detroit. "Call Numbers" is his first novel.

Syntell is active on Facebook, Twitter and other social media platforms.

CPSIA information can be obtained
at www.ICGtesting.com
Printed in the USA
LVHW080017070619
620404LV00036BA/616/P